ULTIMATE
LOVE
&
BETRAYAL

Toy Easley Keller

YKTA Enterprises, Inc., LLC Books are available for order
through Ingram Press Catalogues

This book is a work of fiction. Names, characters, places,
and incidents either are products of the author's imagination
or are used fictitiously. Any resemblance to actual persons,
living or dead, events, or locales is entirely coincidental.

Visit my website at toyeasleykeller.com

Printed in the United States of America

First Printing: June 2014
By
Sojourn Publishing, LLC

ISBN: 978-1-62747-062-9
Ebook ISBN: 978-1-62747-063-6
LCN: Pending

This book is dedicated to everyone who has helped me accomplish number 1 on my "bucket list."

TABLE OF CONTENTS

PROLOGUE

Madison thought Ryan's graduation day would never come. She was so proud of him—she always had been. But today was special. Maddie was wearing the same lovely, ethereal looking dress and whimsical floppy straw hat that she'd worn as maid of honor to her best friend Terri's wedding a year before. The only addition to her ensemble was a pair of sunglasses because the sun shined so brightly overhead. She sat in the stands with Ryan's family, because in two days, she and Ryan would be married at the West Point Chapel. Everything was ready. However, today, June 5, 1968, belonged entirely to Ryan. Today, he would finally graduate from West Point. After all the cadets had proudly marched onto the field in their uniforms, it didn't take Maddie long to spot Ryan. He looked so serious and stoic as he listened to the proceedings. But Maddie knew him. Inside his heart was breaking. He'd always expected his father to be here to see him graduate. They had even talked about it after dinner last night. It was so hard for her to see the hurt, sadness, and despair in his eyes, but all she could do was hold him in her arms and listen. He had needed to talk it through before he faced today.

Maddie didn't think the speeches would ever end. She wanted to hear his name, watch him walk across the stage, and then watch as all the cadets threw their hats into the air! She wanted to run onto the field and throw her arms around his neck, kiss him, and tell him how much she loved him—had since they were sixteen.

After graduation, the couple spent time with family and friends and putting the finishing touches on their wedding the rest of the afternoon. They visited the floral and bakery shops one last time to make sure that everything was ready for their wedding at high noon—June 7, 1968.

That evening, the couple attended the graduation "hop." Maddie wore a magnificent teal ball gown that exactly matched the color of her eyes. With Ryan in his white uniform, they looked like a picture of a couple that a photography studio would hang in its window to display its work. The two of them shared a table with Ryan's friends and dates, had their photos taken, and danced for a few hours. However, they left early so they could spend some quality time alone together before he had to return to his own hotel room. But first, they took a stroll down to the "kissing rock" one final time.

After the graduation "hop," this historic day was finally over, and Maddie and Ryan were able to escape to her room for a while. He couldn't spend the night; that wouldn't be cool with all the family members around. When they finally returned to Maddie's room, they lay on the bed, holding each other quietly. Then they started laughing and crying at the same time. They both started talking at once, just as they always did whenever they had been waiting desperately to be alone. Maddie told Ryan once more how proud she was of him and how she couldn't wait to be his wife. Ryan ran his fingers through her long, curly, beautiful auburn hair and whispered in her ear that he wouldn't have made it without her total support and told her again he loved her more than she'd ever know.

However, at the time, what he didn't say was far more important than what he did say. He knew he should've told her what he'd been thinking about constantly ever since he'd chosen the Infantry; but he just couldn't do it because he knew it would break her heart. He'd been thinking that they should wait to get married until after he returned from Vietnam. He knew there was a distinct chance he wouldn't make it home, and he didn't want Maddie to have to go through what his step-mother had. He'd finally convinced himself that they should wait. Now, he would have to try to convince Maddie, but he wasn't ready to approach the subject with her yet, so he kept his mouth shut and turned his attention back to her.

They talked about the excitement of the day for a while longer, then turned on the radio, lay together, and started kissing. Every time they made love, it seemed to Maddie that it was even better than the last time. Ryan was always so tender and gentle that it surprised her. He was such a strong man that she always marveled at his gentleness with her. Tonight, he very slowly unzipped her ball gown and immediately tossed it on the floor. Since she wasn't wearing a bra, he slowly caressed her breasts, and whenever he touched her like this, an animal magnetism always seemed to explode inside her. Then, as he always did, he began tenderly to suck at her now firm nipples. He nibbled at her ear lobes and kissed her soft neck tenderly, until her breathing became deep and she began getting wet. Now hot, she had an urgency to remove his clothes and explore his body parts with her lips. She helped him undress quickly, and they lay together, slowly fondling and exploring one another.

They never tried to make love quickly. A quickie had never been their style nor had it been important to them. Maddie slowly rolled on top of him and began to kiss him gently all over. She started at his face, kissing his ears, nose, mouth, and then continued very slowly down his chest. She continued until she reached his manhood, already hard and erect, and then very gently started to suck. Ryan moaned in pleasure, called out her name, and told her he wanted her. Then she came up to kiss his mouth deeply. As he rolled over on top of her, she spread her long legs open wide and wrapped them around him to let him in. As always, when they were in this position, they always looked directly into each other's eyes. On this particular night, something seemed different to Madison. They moved in unison as one, but right before the moment they came, Ryan took her hand and put it at the base of his hard shaft where his seed would flow from him and deposit into her, so she could feel the pulses and thrusts of sperm there. This time she actually thought she felt as his warm seed flowed into her. Afterwards, it seemed they stayed connected for hours, not wanting to separate. Ryan wasn't the type to just disengage after making love or to roll over and go to sleep. He craved closeness as much as Maddie did. Finally, they separated but still held each other close. Making love to Ryan always made Maddie feel complete.

While they were lying there together after making love, Ryan started talking, saying words that Maddie would never ever be able to understand—even many years later.

"Maddie, I've agonized over this decision for months, and I'm afraid you won't understand what I'm about to say. In any other place and time, I wouldn't even have to say it. Madison," he said stoically. "I love you too much to marry you now. I know that's what you want, what you expect, what we've planned, and what you deserve, but I can't. I'll be heading to Vietnam in a few months—we both know that—and it's entirely possible I won't come back. I don't want to make you a widow before you've been a wife. If you'd be willing to wait until I get back, we'll have the biggest wedding you've ever seen—here at the chapel at West Point like we've planned."

Maddie just sat up in stunned silence.

"Say something, please," begged Ryan.

Maddie was quiet for a long time before she spoke. The shock of what she had just heard overwhelmed her with nausea and tears, and she ran into the bathroom and threw up. When she returned, she sat on the side of the bed and finally spoke.

"Ryan, I don't know what to say. I've loved you since we were sixteen; I've waited four years for you to finish West Point. We both decided a long time ago that we'd get married after we finished college. Was I wrong? Now you want me to wait another two years? How can you do this to us? I gave myself to you. You're the only man I've ever wanted and loved, and I know you feel the same way. I can see it in your eyes right now. If you love me, how can you ask me to wait even one minute longer?"

"Oh God!" Ryan pleaded. "I knew you wouldn't understand. I'm trying to do what I think is right. It has nothing to do with not loving you, Maddie; I love you more than anything else on earth."

Her anger now showing, she slowly said, "If that's true, then it seems to me that you'd want to make an 'honest' woman out of me. You'd want to give me your last name. Just how long have you been thinking about this? All the flowers, the cake—everything is ready, and now you have suddenly decided that we aren't going to get married? Ryan, how could you even think of doing this to me and to us?"

"Maddie, I'm doing what I think is best for both of us. I can't go to Nam and not concentrate on my objective. If we're married, I won't be able to give my full attention to keeping my men and myself alive. I don't want to come home to you in a body bag."

"Ryan, I would think that if we were married, it would give you even more of an incentive to come back alive. I love you, for God's sake. You're not thinking of us. You're thinking only of yourself." Her eyes now aflame, her heart pounding with anguish, Maddie screamed, "No! Either you marry me as we've planned for the last six years, or you won't marry me at all."

Ryan was too stunned to reply. All of his years with Maddie, all of his preparation for a career to support her, all of his planning for a perfect life together was ripped out of his heart.

"I guess your silence is my answer," Maddie said quietly.

Maddie rose from the bed, got dressed, and started throwing her clothes into her suitcases, waiting to see if Ryan would change his mind and try to stop her. But Ryan just sat at the end of the bed with a glazed look in his eyes.

After she finished loading everything back into her car (including the box containing her wedding dress), she picked up her purse and her last suitcase and turned to go.

Ryan grabbed her hand and cried softly. "Maddie, please, please, don't leave me. Please say you'll wait for me."

Now hurt and furious, Maddie glared into Ryan's eyes and screamed, "Ryan, you son of a bitch! You'll always be the love of my life, but this is just too much. I deserve a say in what happens in my life, our life! You're not giving me one."

Then—she was gone.

BOOK I:
HIGH SCHOOL

1

The year was 1962. Madison Conrad had just returned from the always crowded swimming pool on the air base with Carol and Brittany. The day had been hot, humid, and windy as usual. Summer in southwest Oklahoma was a nightmare. Being in water was the only way to keep cool, whether it was at a pool or behind a ski boat at Lake Avalon.

Maddie was a dancer and cheerleader, but her personality was really an enigma. When she was dancing or cheerleading, she appeared to be the typical bubbly girl a cheerleader was supposed to be. However, in reality, she was an introvert. She was very quiet in class and wasn't bold enough to talk·to someone she didn't know. This was nothing new. She'd been very shy as a child and would always hide behind her mother's skirt when she met a stranger. Maddie was really two people: the one everyone saw when she was "onstage," and the quiet, subdued Maddie. So the idea of Maddie going up and introducing herself to someone she didn't know was totally out of the realm of possibility. However, once she knew you, she became more outgoing.

As Maddie drove her car into the driveway of her house at the air base, she noticed a boy about her age, sixteen, across the street mowing the front lawn. It shocked her because she'd only seen three small boys at this house before now. What was he doing there? She sneaked another glance at him as she closed her car door. Geeze, he appeared to be really handsome. Since he had his shirt off, he seemed to be quite tall, had black hair—lots of it, and had a great tan; either that or he had olive skin. She was too far away to see the color of his eyes, but she just assumed that they had to be dark brown. She didn't want to appear to be staring at him while he was working, so she quickly entered the front door to her house.

Once inside, she immediately asked her mom if she'd noticed the new boy across the street. Her mom laughed and said that she'd seen him moving clothes and other small items into the house while she was at the pool. But, no, she didn't know who he was.

For some reason, though, Maddie was really interested in finding out who he was. This was strange for Maddie since she'd never really noticed cute guys much. She enjoyed being with her special group of friends. School would be starting in a couple of weeks, and she'd probably meet him then, if not before. It was, after all, a small town, and eventually everyone knew everyone else.

Maddie saw him several times in the days to come, but of course she never had the nerve to go over and introduce herself. She decided that she would bide her time until school began. She was sure she would meet him then.

However, Maddie did call her best friends, Shelly and Kelly, who were identical twins, and told them about this boy who had moved in across the street and that she had seen him first. Her friends were totally shocked that she had admitted she was interested in this new boy, because Maddie didn't date all that much. She was pretty particular when it came to boys, and she never dated more than one guy at a time. Naturally, they were really curious to meet the guy who would have this kind of effect on their friend.

School started in late August that year. Today was registration day for her junior year. Maddie had driven her car, a light aqua 1956 Ford, from the base to her girlfriends to pick them up, even though they lived only a few houses from the school. Maddie was a member of a group of five girls and five boys who were best friends and did almost everything together. They didn't date each other. It wasn't like that. They simply all went to dances and parties together as a group. But if one of the girls did date, it was usually an upperclassman. The guys, on the other hand, did just the opposite—the younger, the better. They were good kids, but they did do their fair share of pranks.

When they entered the cafeteria to select their classes for their junior year, they had already decided to try to get the same classes, teachers, and hours as last year—it was a fairly easy process. You just went to pick up a card from the teacher and class you wanted for a certain hour. The teacher handed you a card and wrote down your name. Once the cards were gone, the class was full.

Maddie saw the newcomer at the English table. He was standing in line to get Mrs. Seymore for English. Since English III fourth hour was her assignment, Maddie came up behind him and finally got up the nerve to speak to him.

"Hi. I'm Madison. Are you new here?" she asked in her pronounced Southern drawl. As soon as she had blurted this out, she couldn't believe she had been so forward and could immediately feel her face start to turn red from embarrassment.

The newcomer turned around as soon as she had addressed him, and Maddie saw that he was even more handsome than she had thought. He was tall, had beautiful dark brown eyes, black hair, and a swimmer's body.

"Hi. I'm Ryan Richardson. I moved here about a month ago," he said in an extremely low, sexy voice.

"Do you live at the base?" asked Maddie, already knowing the answer.

"Yes. I'm thinking I might live across the street from you. I came here to live with my dad and get to know him, since my parents divorced when I was young."

"Are those younger kids your step-brothers?" asked Maddie.

Laughingly, he said, "Yes, I call them the 'rugrats,' because they're three, five, and seven."

"What classes are you signing up for this year? Here's my list." She smiled at him as she handed it to him.

"Our entire group met last night to map out our courses so we'd get the same classes, just like last year. The system seems to work, because each of us takes a stack of forms to the teachers we want. I've been assigned to get us all into fourth-hour English with Mrs. Seymore. The others in our group are headed for chemistry, math, etc."

Ryan and Maddie looked at both of their schedules and saw that they were probably going to have several classes together. Meanwhile, Ryan, trying not to seem too obvious, looked at Maddie and thought that she was the prettiest thing he'd ever seen.

Maddie Conrad was tall, with long dark auburn naturally curly hair and a dancer's body. Since she was wearing her cheerleading outfit, Ryan saw that her long legs never seemed to end. Her skin was bronze, and her eyes were an amazing teal color like those of the warm waters of the Caribbean. Ryan couldn't believe she lived so close to him. How could he be so lucky? His stepmother had told him a cute girl lived across the street, but he didn't believe her until he saw Maddie up close. What did Mom know about "cute"? But his stepmother had been right. In fact, Maddie was so pretty that he was sure she probably already had a steady boyfriend or dated a great deal. He wondered if he'd have a chance with her. Probably not. Besides, he'd never asked a girl for a date yet—he was too shy and insecure. His greatest fear had always been being turned down, so he never asked.

After registration, when Maddie joined her group of friends, she made Ryan tag along with her. Since Ryan was on the football team, he'd already met a couple of the guys and felt a little more comfortable being introduced to her friends. Shelly and Kelly could tell immediately that Maddie was interested in him. This surprised them, because Maddie was always too busy teaching dance and cheerleading to go out much. Besides, she would always rather go out with only their group. Occasionally, she would go out on a date, but she never had a steady boyfriend. Maybe this would be the one, thought her best friends.

Ryan was not only just as shy as Maddie, but he was also a Type A personality like her when it came to work or school. He was extremely bright, especially in math. He was happy that Madison had immediately included him in her group of friends. It made him feel like he already belonged, and that was really important to him since he was the new kid on the block, so to speak. He felt lucky to have met Maddie and be accepted by her friends so quickly. He'd been terrified that he would not make friends at his new school and be a loner the entire year.

After their initial meeting, Maddie and Ryan would speak to each other at their lockers, or, if he was really brave enough, he would walk her to her next class. Sometimes in the evenings, they would even sit on the curb outside their houses and talk for a while.

When, or even if, is he ever going to get the nerve to ask me out? thought Maddie to herself.

What amazed Ryan was that their personalities were so much alike. She wasn't anything like he'd expected, since she was a cheerleader. Like him, she was very quiet until she got to know someone.

It took Ryan two weeks to get up the nerve to ask her out. Since he'd never dated anyone before, he was scared to death that she would say no. But he finally asked her if she wanted to go to the dance that the Rotary Club always sponsored after the home football games on Friday nights. Since he was on the team and she was a cheerleader, it seemed like a good way to get to know each other.

In a small town, football was the only game that mattered in the fall. The students would have a pep assembly every Friday morning and sometimes even a parade with the marching band. The cheerleaders and pep squad officers would also be in charge of decorating the football boys' lockers each week. The entire stadium would always be filled to capacity at each home game. Football reigned supreme on Friday nights in Oklahoma.

After Ryan finally asked her out, Maddie replied, "Sure, that'd be great!" He couldn't believe that she'd actually said yes!

"What took you so long?" teased Maddie, and they both laughed.

Maddie couldn't believe she was so nervous and excited about her first date with Ryan. She'd really never been excited before—nervous, yes, excited, no. It was like her stomach was doing flip-flops. But then she'd never wanted to date someone special before.

After winning the football game, Ryan showered and changed before meeting Maddie at the Rotary

Center. He was even more nervous and excited than she was, if that were possible. In fact, he was so nervous that he was sick to his stomach. He'd never had a date before, let alone with someone like Madison Conrad.

Neither of them had any reason to worry. They discovered very quickly that they had a great deal in common, and, for some reason, they both felt immediately comfortable with each other. Years later, they would both laugh when they looked back on their first date.

Maddie had her car, so at the end of the evening, she drove them back to the base. Ryan didn't even try to kiss her good night. He just hugged her and whispered in her ear that he'd had a wonderful evening.

When Maddie went to bed that night, sleep wouldn't come. She kept playing their first date over and over again in her head. She'd never had such a good time on a date before. After her initial nervousness wore off, they had danced and never stopped talking. She realized quickly that Ryan was someone special, and she wanted to see him again. He was intelligent, funny, and a total gentleman. When they were together, he devoted all of his attention to her. He wasn't the least bit conceited like some of the older guys she'd dated. Before finally falling asleep, Maddie wondered if Ryan felt the same way. He did.

Ryan was on cloud nine after his first date with Maddie. He couldn't believe he'd been so lucky. Not only was she beautiful, but she wasn't an airhead cheerleader either. She had both good looks and brains, too. The fact she was gorgeous was great, but her intelligence was what really impressed him. He wondered why she'd agreed to go out with him, when she could have any guy she wanted. He knew he wanted to see her again and prayed she'd agree. She did wholeheartedly.

Ryan and Maddie started dating each other exclusively almost immediately. Even though everyone knew that they were a couple, they still stayed in the group—now a group of eleven. The two of them did everything together—study, talk, the movies, dances, the drive-in—simply everything.

However, it was the time when they were alone at the reservoir that they cherished the most—merely sitting and talking. They never ran out of things to say to each other. But it took a while for that first kiss to come. When it did, it was more than worth the wait. To Maddie, it seemed as if they'd been kissing each other for years. It seemed so natural and yet sensual. It gave her goose bumps, made her stomach flutter, and made her shiver like magic when his lips touched hers. The shortness of breath, the strange stirring between her legs was all so new to her. For Ryan, it was the first time he'd even kissed a girl, and he loved the sweet soft smell of Maddie's soft lips on his. No, it wasn't a French kiss. That would come later, after they knew each other better. It was a moment that neither of them would ever forget.

Unfortunately, Saturday nights—date night in a small town—were not in the cards for Ryan and Maddie very often, and this frustrated Maddie. Every two or three Saturday nights each month, Ryan had to babysit his three younger stepbrothers. Only after his parents decided that Maddie was a "good" girl, did they allow her to come over and watch TV or do homework together when they weren't there. On many Saturday nights, Ryan also had chores to do while his parents were gone, like doing the dishes, waxing the hardwood floors in the house by hand, or doing the laundry. Maddie would help so he could get it done faster and they'd have some time alone, but she really never understood why Ryan was required to do so much of the housework. Sometimes she felt that his parents were just using him as a babysitter and housekeeper. But of course, she never said that to him.

Most of the time, after the boys were asleep and any chores were finished, the two of them just ate popcorn and watched TV. Every once in a while, though, Maddie would lay her head on Ryan's lap, or if Ryan was really brave, he'd lie beside her on the couch so they could make out a little. At this point in their relationship that only meant kissing, but it never lasted very long either, because both of them were scared to death his parents would return early and there would be hell to pay.

It was interesting to watch the interaction between the two of them when they were at school. When they were around their friends or in classes together, they were very reserved. In fact, they didn't even act like they knew each other in class, even though they sat side by side. They were always friendly, but it was hard to tell they were a couple.

Both Maddie and Ryan were very bright, but Maddie was the language arts and artistic type, while Ryan was the mathematics and science whiz kid. Maddie hated math, especially geometry and trigonometry. She could just never fathom a plane bisecting another plane. So, whenever Maddie had a problem with her geometry or trig, which was often, Ryan would try to explain it to her. Sometimes it worked. Sometimes it didn't. But he was always very patient with her.

2

Anyone who has ever lived in a small town knows that kids have to learn how to make their own fun, and since Avalon was a small town—around 25,000 including the air base—this was also the case. Sometimes on Friday or Saturday nights, the drive-in would have a special—$1.00 a carload. So, all eleven of them would always climb into the back of Garrett's truck. Sometimes they would even take firecrackers with them and they'd sneak and place them under the "date" cars. When the firecrackers exploded and the couple rushed out of the backseat, quickly trying to make themselves presentable, the group would die laughing. It was a foregone conclusion that the group would get you eventually.

Other times, they would go to the river bottom and light a bonfire. Sometimes, one of the members of the group was brave enough to sneak some booze out of his house. The favorite drink at present was called Purple Passion, a mixture of grape juice and grain alcohol, and, of course, the ever favorite beer. Maddie and Ryan would always take a sip of the drink of the night but generally didn't get drunk, because after the first time, they didn't like the headaches and nausea that followed the next day. And, besides, if their parents ever found out, they'd be grounded forever.

And, of course, everyone had their favorite parking spots where they would listen on the radio to Wolfman Jack from Del Rio, Texas, while they made out. The "bad" girls—those who smoked and drank—were always spotted at the reservoir or parked on the side of a farm road; however, "going all the way" wasn't even in the realm of possibility for Ryan and Maddie.

Don't for one minute think that the two of them never had any fights. They did. Mostly they fought over stupid things. Ryan would get a little jealous if he saw Maddie talking to a popular senior boy. It took him a while to learn that Maddie was Maddie and would speak to you if she knew you. It didn't mean a thing to her. That was a bit hard for him to get used to because he was so reserved and basically the quiet type, and yes, he became jealous.

She would get upset with him at times, too. Sometimes she became angry when he had to babysit so much, especially if her high school sorority was having a special dance and they couldn't attend. It would infuriate her that he wouldn't stand up to his dad on those special occasions. It would also upset her when he sometimes became so anal retentive that everything had to be perfect, like his stupid math problems. But all in all, their relationship was on very solid ground. They were a good match. They kept each other on an even keel, so to speak, and they were both falling in love for the first time.

One Friday night at the end of football season, there was a highly anticipated football game. If the Bulldogs won this game, they'd go to the state championships. There was only one obstacle—the other team had an outstanding quarterback. In fact, scouts from several colleges came to watch him play. He was flawless in both his passes and hand-offs. Maddie figured he was about six feet two inches tall, and when he took his helmet off, she could tell he had blonde hair. Even though Avalon lost the close game, it was a game no one would ever forget. And, unknowingly, one that Maddie would someday soon vividly recall.

The school year seemed to whiz by. Suddenly, fall turned into winter. Thanksgiving had passed, and Christmas was rapidly approaching. Their junior year seemed to be flying by.

Maddie decided that she wanted to do something special for her Christmas presents for 1962, especially since she had just found out that her father would be gone to Formosa, Nationalist China, for her entire senior year. She had plenty of money in her savings account to buy gifts for everyone, but she decided that she wanted to give those she cared about the most a gift that only she could give. She decided that she was going to dance for them.

In the evenings after her teaching was over, Maddie choreographed a special dance that she knew her mother and father would love to watch. She practiced endlessly so it would be perfect. Besides, this was what she'd always loved to do more than anything else in the world. Ever since she was five and started dancing in

England, she'd always dreamed of becoming a prima ballerina one day. It was her way of expressing herself. Some people sang; she danced.

Maddie was determined to make every detail of her performance as much as going to the ballet at Covent Garden in England as possible. Maddie paid a seamstress to make a special pink costume for the occasion because she knew this would be the last time she would ever dance like this. The dance and the dress had to be perfect! Maddie mailed four calligraphied invitations: one for her parents, one for Ryan, one for Ryan's parents, and one for Mrs. Bicknell, the woman who owned the dance studio. She invited them to an evening of dancing and dessert on December 23rd at 7:00 PM at the dance studio where she taught.

When the day came, and everyone invited had arrived and was seated, Maddie explained to them what was about to happen. This was going to be her Christmas present to each of them.

"For Christmas this year, I want to give the people I love and care about most in the world a present that, even though it has no monetary value, is one where I can give a part of myself to each of you.

"Mom and Dad," continued Maddie, "I want you to know that I realize all of the hardships you endured in order to let me succeed with my talent. I really don't know how you ever afforded it, especially since I would break the backs of my pointe shoes during every performance. Mom, to you I am especially grateful for all the years of morning practices with me before school. Dad, thank you for driving us across the country during the summers to Carnegie Hall all those years for my free dance lessons. I will be forever grateful."

Next, Maddie turned to Ryan. "Ryan, you've never seen me dance even though you and I have talked about it a great deal. You've only seen me in my teaching mode, but I wanted you to see me actually dance just once, so this will be my special Christmas gift to you as well. I hope you like it.

"To Lonnie, Sharon, and Mrs. Bicknell, welcome. I'm so happy that you accepted my invitation." With that she said, "Here goes. Mom, I know you will remember these steps by heart."

Since it was Christmas and Maddie had danced the part many times before, she turned on the LP record to "The Dance of the Sugar Plum Fairy" from *The Nutcracker* and began. She felt as if she were back on stage again for the very first time. This was Maddie's way of self-expression. The feeling that went into her dance was paramount—the steps were as perfect as they'd always been. Maddie was so graceful with her long legs and expressive arm movements that her mom started to sob. Ryan just stared. He couldn't believe what he was seeing. This was a very private side of Maddie, and he felt honored to be watching her. She moved so beautifully and effortlessly; so light on her feet. How could she jump so high and do such perfect turns? Her footwork amazed him. She seemed to be lost in a different world; one that he'd never known existed or could be a part of. His eyes swelled up with tears— he was so proud of her. Ryan's parents and Mrs. Bicknell also watched in awe at the talented young lady performing for them. Maddie's father watched his daughter the way he had so many years ago. He recalled always telling her at any contests she entered in England that if she made it to the finals, he would come and watch. Ironically, during the preliminaries, she'd always forget her dance and have to make up the steps as she went along. But somehow she always made it into the finals. And, when the finals came, and Maddie knew her dad was present, she always danced perfectly; she always won.

As Maddie's mother watched her daughter twirl and do a grand jeté, she recalled the time when nine-year-old Maddie had been selected to attend Sadler's Wells Ballet and Boarding school in London on a full scholarship. It was the equivalent of America's Julliard. Maddie had been so excited. She had endured the endless physical, intellectual, and actual dance tryouts with a confidence unheard of in someone so young. Her mom also remembered the tremendous anguish, despair, and anger both of them suffered when her father decided he wouldn't leave her behind when the rest of the family returned to the U.S. Maddie and her mom had never really forgiven him. This had been Maddie's chance to explore her dream of becoming a prima ballerina with the Royal Ballet Company of England, and he was not going to give her that chance. As the music came to a close, Maddie performed one last series of spectacular jumps, ending her performance with a double pirouette and a striking final pose.

When she curtsied, everyone stood and clapped loudly, still shocked by the talent and poise this young woman possessed.

Maddie's mom was the first to speak. "Maddie, I can't think of a better present I ever could've received from you. I didn't think I'd ever get to see you dance again. You were just as beautiful today as you were four years ago when we watched you practice onstage at Carnegie Hall. I can truly never thank you enough for letting me see you dance from your heart one more time." Her mom then kissed and hugged her daughter tightly.

It took a few minutes before Ryan was able to speak about what he had just seen.

"Maddie, I can't believe it. I never realized how really talented you are. How did you manage to do all those movements so gracefully, let alone on your toes? This is the best Christmas present I could've received! Thank you from the bottom of my heart." He then stepped over to hug her and kiss her lightly on the cheek.

Ryan's parents and Mrs. Bicknell were equally amazed by what they had seen. They congratulated her profusely and thanked her for allowing them to witness this special gift.

All the praise she received was great, but Maddie was still waiting to hear from her father, a man of few words and even fewer emotions. When he did finally speak to Maddie, it was in the form of an apology.

"Madison, you're the most beautiful dancer I've ever seen. Even when you were very little, I could tell that God had given you a special gift. If I could go back and do things over, I would've let you stay in England. You deserved the opportunity to pursue your dream, but I was selfish and didn't want to let you go. I felt you were too young to be so far away from your family. That's why I tried to make up for it by driving you back to Carnegie Hall each summer for lessons. I remember vividly the year you started your pas de deux training. Remember all those bruises from being dropped on your butt by your partner? I do. I wish I could take it back and had let you stay and study at the best ballet school in the world. Most of all, though, I hope you'll be able to forgive me someday," said her father with tears in his eyes.

Maddie hugged her dad and whispered in his ear, "I love you, Dad. I forgive you."

After Maddie's performance was over, she led her audience to a table she'd set up at the end of the studio. She had decorated the table with a ballet format and had even made snacks like the ones served at Covent Gardens during performances. There was hot tea, tiny butter and tomato sandwich triangles, as well as watercress sandwiches. Maddie also supplied sweets equal to a high tea in England. She had to order them from the town's only bakery, explaining in detail—with pictures of exactly what she wanted—to the pastry chef.

After everyone was finished and had thanked Maddie one last time, Maddie changed her clothes, and she and Ryan stayed behind to clean up. When Maddie turned off the lights before locking the door to the studio, she thought to herself that this really was her final performance, and she started to cry.

As they were walking to her car, Ryan said sadly in a soft voice, "Maddie, I'm so sorry you weren't allowed to pursue your dream, but hey, I would've never met you. I think I saw your soul tonight. You really are an exceptional young woman, and I feel like the luckiest guy alive to have you. Let's go to the reservoir and talk, okay?"

While they were parked at the reservoir, Ryan gave Maddie her Christmas present. He handed her a tiny box wrapped in Christmas wrapping paper. Of course, Maddie tore it open immediately. When she opened the box, she was staring at diamond stud earrings.

"Oh my God, Ryan!" screamed Maddie. "They're just beautiful, but they must have cost you a fortune. You didn't need to spend so much money on me."

"Maddie, I wanted you to have something very special, too. Something I could watch you wear every day, knowing that I was the one who'd given them to you. Compared to what you gave me tonight, this is nothing," said Ryan solemnly. "Merry Christmas, honey. Now, we'd better get home before our folks send out a search party to find us." They laughed.

3

Spring of their junior year also led to the junior-senior prom. Of course, Ryan and Maddie would go together—that was a no-brainer. It was a school tradition that the juniors, decorated, served the seniors their dinners in the school cafeteria, and provided the entertainment. Maddie had been coerced by one of the junior class sponsors to perform a Parisian cancan dance as part of the entertainment. She really didn't want to but finally gave in. At the end of her dance, she turned her back to the seniors and flipped up her cancan dress, so that the seniors could see what was written on her bloomers: "CONGRATULATIONS, SENIORS!" Of course, everyone hooted and hollered. Ryan and Maddie and their group helped with decorating, too. The junior class parents even helped with all of it. The juniors worked very hard to make the prom memorable for the seniors. Both Maddie and Ryan loved the entire experience.

Maddie wore a short plum-colored chiffon dress with spaghetti straps and a full skirt. She even had shoes and a purse dyed to match her dress for the dance that year. Ryan thought the color of Maddie's dress was exquisite with her hair and eyes. She wore her hair up in a French twist with curly tendrils falling haphazardly around her face. Of course, Ryan thought she was the most beautiful girl there.

Ryan wore a black tuxedo. The tuxedo made him look even taller than he was. And Maddie was so proud to be the one to share this moment with him. The entire group sat at the same table and danced all of the fast dances together, but they slow danced with their dates. They all danced for several hours and had their pictures taken as a group, as well as couples, before Ryan and Maddie decided they wanted to be alone.

After the prom, they went to their favorite spot but started laughing, because it was hard to neck in the backseat of a car when they were all dressed up. Ryan did get brave enough to unzip Maddie's dress and pull it down to her waist to expose her breasts to him. Maddie never said a word. She even let him caress them with his fingertips for the first time ever, and Ryan watched her nipples become hard when he touched them. She became so excited by his gentle touch that she arched her back in delight. Ryan thought they were the most magnificent things he'd ever seen. He decided that they were the perfect size—34B. It was also the first time he'd ever touched real breasts. They were so soft yet firm—perky nipples looking up as though asking to be touched. Before this, he'd only seen them in his father's *Playboy* magazines which he looked at when he was sure his dad was flying. For Ryan, to touch real breasts was more than exhilarating! He felt he had won the trifecta! But he felt himself getting hard and knew he had to stop before he couldn't. He lay his head on her chest, and all of a sudden, Maddie started laughing and said that she was picturing what a sight they must be while lying in the backseat together all dressed up, with the top of her prom dress pulled down to her waist. That made them both laugh and helped to keep Ryan from going any further.

After they had been quiet for a few minutes, they had one of the most serious talks of their lives that night. Suddenly, he blurted out, "I love you, Maddie. I can't imagine not having you in my life."

Maddie knew he was telling her the truth. She could see it in his eyes. She really believed that the eyes were windows to the soul. She just lay there quietly, listening to Ryan's breathing for a few minutes before she answered.

"I love you, too. You know, I think I've loved you since the first day we met. I know that sounds corny, but it's true. I also know that what you've just said to me is a huge step for someone like you. But…it also means that our relationship will take on an entirely new dimension. Are you ready for that?"

"Absolutely," replied Ryan.

After that night, Ryan and Maddie knew exactly where their relationship was headed. They would both attend college and then marry. No, they wouldn't be impetuous and get married before that. They were too driven to do that. And besides, their parents would have a fit.

On the way home that night, Ryan also came up with an acronym that would forever be their special secret. Whenever he would write her a note or whisper in her ear "YKTA," it would mean, "You know the answer." That meant "I love you." They promised each other that no matter what, no one else in the world would know what "YKTA" meant—ever. This was one promise that both of them would end up keeping for a lifetime.

In early May of 1963, the class rings they'd ordered in late January finally arrived. Ryan immediately gave his to Maddie—after his parents saw it, of course. Maddie would painstakingly wrap adhesive tape around it, and then paint it with fingernail polish to match her outfits. She wore Ryan's ring their entire senior year.

4

The summer before her senior year was the best summer of Maddie's life. She and Ryan were together every day. Of course, each of them had jobs: he was still a lifeguard at the pool on base, and Maddie continued to teach ballet for Mrs. Bicknell. She still remembered the first time she had gone to the school for a lesson. The teacher instantly realized that Maddie knew much more about dance than she, so she hired Maddie to work for her on the spot. That had been four years ago.

In the evenings, Ryan and Maddie would be content to sit on the swings in the park and talk, and then go to the drive-in or the reservoir.

Whenever they would park at their favorite spot at the reservoir, they wouldn't always just make out, but oftentimes they would talk about their future. He dreamed of going to college at West Point. Would he be accepted? That loomed large over them. If so, how often would they be able to see each other? West Point was a long way from southwest Oklahoma. What kind of teacher would Maddie be? She was leaning towards teaching English—high school, of course. She had two sisters, Michelle and Meredith, but they were eight and nine years older than she, and each of them had married and had several children early, so she had really grown up as an only child. She'd never even babysat except when she helped Ryan. Consequently, she could never picture herself teaching grade school. No, she would teach high school.

Every once in a while, not often, they would talk about sex a little. She told him that she'd never had a sex ed class in school. After all, they lived in the middle of the Bible Belt, for God's sake. Her mom never talked to her about it either. Ryan said he'd had one class in PE in junior high—that's all. He told her that he hadn't learned a lot, but it did explain to him a phenomenon that started happening when he was around twelve. He would wake up in the morning, and his penis would be erect. He had no idea why. He just figured that he needed to go the bathroom. Then, at around fourteen, he would wake up in the morning, and his briefs would be wet. He'd learned in the class that this, too, was normal—weird but normal. They were called wet dreams and were completely natural for boys his age. He would never have asked his mother about it. Thank God for that class.

"When did you start, Maddie?" asked Ryan.

"Start what?"

"You know," said Ryan cautiously.

Embarrassed when it dawned on her what he was talking about, she replied, "Oh that. I guess you would say I was a late bloomer. It happened the summer of my fifteenth birthday."

She told him that she had no idea what was happening to her. Her mom helped her but didn't say much about it or why it was happening. Her mom did tell her that she had called and talked to their doctor about it, because she was late starting, but he said it was probably due to the tremendous amount of exercise she had done for so many years. He told her it happened to gymnasts a lot, too.

"We're quite a pair, aren't we?" laughed Ryan.

"Well, at least we'll be learning together, right? That'll be fun."

"Right," said Ryan as he leaned over and kissed her.

On this particular evening, while they were at the reservoir, Ryan went a little further than he'd ever gone before as they were making out, and Maddie made no effort to stop him. He took off Maddie's blouse and bra, as he usually did, but this time he very tentatively took off her short shorts. He was scared to death and didn't know how Maddie would react. He was in awe as he stared at Maddie lying before him in only her lacy polka dot panties. He took off his tee shirt and lay down on top of her. He also kissed her more passionately and earnestly than he ever had before. Then he very softly took her breasts in each of his huge hands and proceeded to suck her nipples. He didn't know why, but this just seemed to come naturally to him. He could feel immediately that Maddie was getting aroused by the way she started moving against him. This also started making Ryan rise and get hard, but for some reason this time, he didn't want to stop.

Next, he used his tongue to trail all the way down to her panties. He stopped there and very gently placed his hand on her love mound and began rubbing her back and forth very softly. Maddie reacted instantly. Her panties became all wet and she started moaning.

"Ryan, please don't stop," whispered Maddie breathlessly.

He didn't. All of a sudden, Maddie experienced enormous explosions coming from very deep inside her that made her shudder uncontrollably for what seemed to last for several minutes.

"Oh my God!" said Maddie breathlessly. "What just happened?"

Ryan whispered very softly in her ear, "Honey, I think you just had your first climax."

"What about you, Ryan? Did you?"

"Not yet. But I know it's going to happen."

Ryan quickly unzipped his shorts and placed Maddie's hands on his shaft. Maddie started to rub him and discovered for the first time how truly large he was. She kept rubbing his shaft, albeit through his briefs, and they automatically started to move up and down in unison. It only took a few seconds for her to feel his briefs getting wet as he, too, shuddered, moaned, and cried out her name.

"Madison, I just had my first real ejaculation," said Ryan, sounding as formal as a teacher giving a gym class health lecture. Panting, he collapsed on top of her. "My God, I had no idea it would feel this intense! God, I'm so glad you're the one who did this to me for the first time. I know it would've never felt the same if it had happened with anyone else."

"Likewise," whispered Maddie, as she gave him a French kiss, which seemed to last forever.

"I don't want you to worry, Maddie. We didn't make love or have sex. We're both still virgins, but I think we both know there's no going back to necking after this. But I promise you, we won't really make love until our wedding night," said Ryan very seriously.

"I understand," was all Madison could say.

Then he told her that they'd better put themselves back together and get home, or else their parents would start to worry.

Maddie agreed and within fifteen minutes, Ryan was kissing Maddie good night at her front door.

"YKTA," whispered Ryan.

"YKTA," answered Maddie softly.

5

In August of 1963, Ryan and Maddie began their senior year. It would be the last football season, basketball season, school and sorority dances, fall and spring plays. It would all end much too soon.

One Friday on an October afternoon, disaster struck. Their high school principal couldn't find a janitor to mark the chalk lines on the football field for the upcoming football game that night. So, unbeknownst to anyone, Mr. Seward took it upon himself to do the job. In the middle of it, he had a massive heart attack and died on the field with absolutely no warning. When the intercom came on around 2:30 PM that day, right before school was out, the vice principal had to make the announcement to the students. Everyone was in shock. The vice principal and football coach grappled with the decision whether or not to go ahead and play the game or cancel it. In the end, they decided to play it, since the opposing team was already on its way. Everyone—including the people in the stands that night—wore black armbands in honor their fallen principal. It was difficult for the students to comprehend what had happened. It had happened so suddenly, and, in an instant, the students learned that life could be short.

Later that same evening, when Ryan and Maddie were parked, they tried to make some sense of it. Until now, they thought they would live forever. Now, they had come face-to-face with their own mortality. What about all the plans they'd made? Were they stupid to wait? What if something happened to one of them? After much debate back and forth, they decided to try to stay the course they'd set for themselves. Besides, they were young and had their entire lives ahead of them.

However, in late November, the unthinkable happened again. It had been lunch break and everyone was off-campus. When the students returned from lunch, the school intercom was on and a radio was playing over the loud speaker. Maddie had just walked into her journalism class and saw her teacher crying. What was going on? Then they heard Walter Cronkite on the radio say that President Kennedy had been assassinated in Dallas. What was this world coming to? All the students were in shock, and school was dismissed for the next few days.

Ryan and Maddie watched the funeral of President Kennedy and the murder of Lee Harvey Oswald live on national TV together. It seemed so surreal to them. Watching the funeral with the rider-less horse and "little John-John" salute his father's casket was so sad that Maddie fell apart and cried.

Ryan just held her tightly. Time was the only thing that would help everyone in the nation overcome this tragedy...a lot of time.

6

One night, right before Christmas of their senior year, while Maddie and Ryan were parked at the reservoir, Ryan turned to face Maddie and looked directly into her eyes.

"Maddie, I know what I'm going to ask you is probably going to catch you off guard, and it will be asking a lot of you, so I won't expect you to answer right away. Just think about it, okay? You know how much I love you, and that we both still have four years of college to finish, but would you marry me in June 1968 when we've both graduated? I want to spend the rest of my life with you. I've known that for a long time.

"I also know that four years is a long time to wait," he continued, "especially if I get my appointment to West Point. I know there will be lots of other guys at your college who'll ask you out while you're in school, and I don't expect you to sit at home. I want you to have a wonderful college experience—date, have fun. All I ask is for you to wait for me. What do you think?"

Maddie sat frozen in time. She was so shocked by what Ryan had just asked her. This was one moment she never wanted to forget, as if that were possible.

"Ryan, I'd be proud to be your wife. Of course, I'll marry you. Of course, I'll wait for you. But I ask that you promise to do the same. And, of course, I'll save myself for you, but I want you to promise me that you will, too. I know it will be difficult being so far apart, but I also know that it'll be worth the wait. So it's a date. We'll get married in June 1968.

"I love you so much, Maddie," he said quietly and kissed her passionately. As usual, Maddie was aching to be one with him, but that must wait; they could only go so far, and this had now become a habit with them.

That night, however, since Ryan knew their future was assured, he felt the need and had the courage to try to take their physical relationship a little further while still keeping their virginity. Ryan told Maddie that he'd heard the guys talking about it and knew of a way. Maddie agreed to the idea without thinking twice. She trusted Ryan, always had.

Ryan took the blanket out of the trunk that they kept there for the cold Oklahoma winters, and the two of them climbed into the backseat. They undressed each other down to their panties and briefs as usual. However, this time, when Ryan reached Maddie's panties, he took them off. Maddie lay naked before him for the very first time. He could tell how embarrassed she was, but he told her that she was the most beautiful girl he'd ever seen. He kissed her and told her not to be afraid. Everything would be all right. He kissed her while he very slowly slid his hand lightly down to her breasts first. He sucked on each of her breasts greedily, like he always did, as if he could never get enough of them, while at the same time lightly touching her where she had never been touched before.

Ryan, very slowly began rubbing his hand over her mound, his long fingers pressing between her legs. Maddie's entire abdomen began tingling, as though filled with millions of tiny electric shocks. Her thighs began quivering, and her legs spread without her permission. Maddie's hips gyrated involuntarily against his hand, and her passion juices drenched his fingers. Ryan's fingers gently opened her lips and slid his middle finger inside her. Maddie's body exploded with a climax that caused her to arch her back, pushing herself against Ryan's hand. Instead of stopping, however, Ryan started moving his finger gently in and out of her. Maddie couldn't stop climaxing. She had never felt…never even imagined feeling such absolute pleasure. For the first time in her life, her body was totally out of her control—totally in the hands of her lover. And she loved it. She came again and again until, completely exhausted, she begged Ryan to stop.

"Ryan, I can't stand it. I want you NOW!"

Ryan's answer to this was to take his already hard member out of his briefs. Maddie had never seen a real man before, except in pictures of statues. This was different—very different. Suddenly, she was looking at her lover's hard, throbbing sex organ—and it was immense.

Ryan could tell how surprised she was and told her she was the first woman—besides his mother, of course—ever to see him as well. He also told her that he, too, was embarrassed but glad she was the first to see him. Next, he put her hands on him. His shaft seemed so large that she could wrap both of her hands around it, like holding a baseball bat, and the tip was velvety soft, fully visible and glistening with a clear slippery liquid. He showed her how to move her hands up and down his tool and explained that the tip was especially sensitive to the touch. Next, he took her hands and showed her how to rub his cock up and down. Maddie took one hand and rubbed it up and down the full length of his shaft, and, with the other, she very lightly rubbed the tip. Ryan had no choice. He exploded immediately, arching his back as huge amount of milky white liquid spewed from his tip. He groaned, crying out Maddie's name as he came. Then he said in a very low, throaty voice, "God, I love you, Madison Conrad."

Madison was still in shock watching the milky substance spill from him and run down her hand. It was sticky, but she enjoyed feeling the stuff run through her fingers, because this was Ryan—the very essence of Ryan—she was feeling.

When Ryan recovered, he gently took Maddie's hand and tried to wipe it off, but Maddie stopped him.

"Are you sure, Maddie?" questioned Ryan.

"I'm sure." With that she raised her left hand to her mouth and very softly licked Ryan's semen from each of her fingers. It tasted salty to her. It wasn't a bad taste, just one she'd never tasted before. Then, without thinking, she put her lips on the tip of his member and licked it dry.

Ryan marveled watching what Maddie was doing. The fact that she wasn't repulsed by what had just happened made him love her even more.

However, watching Maddie made Ryan want to taste her, too. Without asking her, he quickly raised her legs and spread them apart. He then took his hands and opened her again and inserted his tongue into her, flicking it in and out quickly, lapping her juices from her love lips. It astonished him that this act appeared to come so natural to him. Fascinated with the sweet, musky taste and Maddie's obvious pleasure, he began thrusting his tongue deeper into her. His tongue was inside her when she again exploded in a thrashing orgasm. He didn't stop what he was doing to her until he had made her come three times in quick succession. He loved feeling the very core of her shudder uncontrollably. Now, she truly belonged to him.

Afterwards, as they were lying side by side, Ryan said, "Maddie, we belong only to each other now, and I'm not one bit sorry for what I just did. Are you?"

"Ryan, I'm yours forever, and yes—I know before you say it—we're technically still virgins, and yes, I want it to stay that way. What we just experienced is enough for me until we get married. I only hope you feel the same way."

"Of course I do," replied Ryan softly. "And I know this is as far as we can ever go."

"So do I," said Maddie, still reeling from what had taken place just a few minutes ago.

After holding each other for a long time, it was time for them to get dressed and go home. But before they left the reservoir, Maddie and Ryan exchanged Christmas presents. Maddie made Ryan open his first. She was really excited to see whether or not he would like it.

Ryan opened a very small box, and inside it was a pair of cufflinks; however, it was what was written on the cufflinks that brought him to tears. Maddie had had each one engraved with "YKTA." He couldn't believe he was such a lucky young man to have found someone as wonderful as Madison.

Next, it was Maddie's turn to open her present. Hers, too, came in a small black box. When she opened it, she gasped when she saw a heart-shaped diamond necklace staring at her. She couldn't believe it was actually hers, until Ryan took it from the box and put it on her neck. Then it was Maddie's turn to cry.

They held each other, kissed, and simultaneously said, "Merry Christmas," to each other.

"Maddie, do you know how badly I want you? I mean, really want to make love to you? I know lots of people call it 'screwing,' but I could never perceive of us just 'screwing.' That's never entered my mind. And, yes, I do know, especially after tonight, that you would let me if I wanted to, but we just can't take the chance."

"I know. You're right," replied Maddie. "And, yes, you're right about my letting you if you tried. I guess I don't have the same willpower as you. But I'll wait. What we did tonight will satisfy me until we get married.

On the way home that evening, Ryan and Maddie decided that they wouldn't tell anyone of their plans. They knew their parents would be skeptical and their friends would urge them not to wait. Neither reaction was one they wanted to hear, so they'd keep their decision only between themselves. That would be harder for Maddie than Ryan to do, because she already wanted to blurt it out to everyone she knew. In fact, she wanted to scream it out loud. Ryan, on the other hand, was more reserved. He would tell everyone when he thought the time was right. So, for the time being, only two people in the world knew they were going to get married—Ryan and Maddie.

7

In April of 1964, while everyone, including Maddie and Ryan, was practicing for the play *Bye Bye Birdie*, Ryan received the letter he had been anxiously awaiting. He wasn't aware of it yet, but he was going to be invited to become a West Point cadet. The letter was waiting for him when he came home from play practice. His father and stepmother couldn't wait for him to get home and open that letter.

When Ryan saw the letter, the first thing he noticed was the letterhead. This was it. He took a deep breath and then tore the letter open as quickly as possible.

"I got in!" screamed Ryan, and he hugged his parents. "I got in! I can't believe it! I've got to go tell Maddie." And he raced for the car.

Since Maddie's father was in China, they had to move off the base for her senior year. Her father had found a cute little house for them not far from school and her friends while he was gone.

Ryan knocked on Maddie's door. He knew she was still up, because the light was on in her bedroom. As soon as Maddie opened the door and saw the huge smile on Ryan's face, she knew he'd been accepted. He was headed for West Point.

"Oh my God!" screamed Maddie as she jumped into his arms and he twirled her around.

"I can't believe it. What am I saying? Of course I can. I knew you'd get in. When do you have to leave, honey?"

"I report June twenty-eight," said Ryan.

"That means only three more months together," Maddie said with a trace of sadness in her voice. "Well, were going to make the most of them—that's for damn sure!"

He kissed her deeply and said, "We'll talk it over Friday night. Gotta get to bed." Maddie watched as Ryan appeared to float back to his car and head for home.

The next day at school, Ryan told everyone about his appointment, friends and teachers alike. The principal even announced it on the intercom, much to Ryan's surprise and embarrassment. He'd never been one to boast, but this was the second biggest news of his life—the first being that Maddie and he were going to get married.

As promised, while Ryan and Maddie were parked at the reservoir that Friday night, they talked about his going to West Point and its ramifications. Maddie was the first to address the topic.

"Ryan, do you know anything about what's going to happen once you get there?"

Ryan told her that he knew little. Basic (or "Beast") would be terrible. There would be plenty of hazing his first year, and every minute of his time would be accounted for. He knew he'd have only high-level math classes six days a week (even on Saturdays), along with basic college courses his entire first year. All West Point graduates received the same degree—civil engineering.

"Will you be able to write or call me?" asked Maddie, being a little nervous about facing what was ahead of them.

"Well, I'll do my best, honey. But, truthfully, I don't know what to expect. The only stuff I know is what I've read about West Point in general."

Ryan immediately noticed her discomfort and tried to dispel any of her worries.

"Hey, look at it this way. We'll get married in June 1968 as planned in the chapel at West Point with an honor guard to greet us as we leave as Lieutenant and Mrs. Ryan Richardson." That announcement seemed to pick up her spirits a little.

Four years can't be that long, she thought. *If they both keep busy, the time would go by fast.*

"Ryan, do you remember the talk we had when you asked me to marry you?"

"Of course," replied Ryan, "nothing's changed. We'll both enjoy our college experience. And even though we may date other people, nothing will change our promise to each other. I'm actually more worried about you forgetting about me. You're so smart and cute, Maddie; I know that the guys will be falling all over themselves to ask you out. Besides, I know you'll be a cheerleader, too, and that will make everyone notice you even more."

"Oh, don't be silly," answered Maddie. "There will be lots of pretty, attractive, and available girls at my college looking for husbands. Besides, right now, I can't even fathom going out with anyone except you. And even if I do, nothing or no one could ever take your place. I'm worried that you'll meet some rich girl from a good family back East and forget all about me."

"Won't ever happen," replied Ryan emphatically.

After the discussion about their future, the two of them climbed into the backseat, but now it seemed even harder than ever for them to make themselves stop. What could be the harm if they did? Besides, there were ways to make it safe, weren't there? They'd never really "done it" yet—they were both still virgins.

"Ryan, I know we shouldn't, but why should we stop? After all, we're going to get married," Maddie said quietly.

"Honey, don't you realize it's so much harder for me to say no?" said Ryan. "I want you so much I just ache inside. I want to make love to you more than anything in this world. But I don't want it to be in the backseat of my parents' car. I want it to be in a bridal bed when we're man and wife. I love you too much to subject you to a 'backseat quickie,' as everyone calls it. Please try to understand, Maddie. You can tell how hard this is for me. Stopping isn't a guy's natural instinct, but I do, and I will, because when it happens, I want it to be perfect for us."

Maddie answered by simply starting to cry.

The rest of the school year seemed to whiz by, and *Bye Bye Birdie* was a huge success. Ryan even played

Conrad. It was so out of character for him to swivel his hips while all the girls vied for his attention. A few of the youngsters in the audience even came up to Ryan after the performance and asked for his autograph.

However, the highlight of their senior year was the junior-senior prom. Maddie, Ryan, and their group of friends really looked forward to it this time. It was their turn to be entertained and served dinner.

Maddie told her mother that she wanted a really special dress for the occasion—one she'd never forget. So, since her dad was gone, Maddie drove the two of them to Livingston one weekend to pick out her prom dress. They spent all day looking until Maddie tried "the" dress on. As soon as she tried it on, her mother started to cry, and Maddie knew this was the one. It happened to be long, white, and strapless, with graceful tiers down the back starting at her waist that seemed to flutter as she walked. Maddie was part Cherokee, so the white chiffon dress showed off her perpetual tan. The dress had a huge red satin sash that tied into a huge bow in the back. The dress had an underskirt, which made the gown extremely full. The bodice of the dress was even encrusted with tiny pearls. Since it had such a striking red bow, Maddie and her mom decided that she would need red accessories to go with the dress, so they picked them up while they were in Livingston as well.

On prom night, Ryan showed up at Maddie's door in the white tuxedo with red cummerbund that Maddie had insisted he rent. He had absolutely no idea why he couldn't wear black, but he would soon. Maddie had also asked him to buy her a red and white rose wrist corsage for the occasion, which he did, and she reminded him to be sure to bring along a change of clothes for the after-party.

Ryan knocked on Maddie's door promptly at 6:00 PM, and when Maddie opened it, Ryan couldn't believe his eyes. Maddie looked like an angel, a vision, dressed in white, save for the bright red sash at her waist. Now, he understood the big deal about white and red. This year, Maddie was wearing her hair down, a mass of beautiful curls flowing down her back. On top of her head, she wore a circle of real red roses attached to white satin streamers that her mother and she had made themselves. She actually took Ryan's breath away, and he thought he might begin to hyperventilate! He just stared at her in disbelief, until she started to laugh, took his hand, and pulled him into the house.

"You look so gorgeous, honey! I'm speechless," whispered Ryan as he kissed her on the cheek and handed her the corsage that she had requested.

Maddie's mom promptly started taking pictures, lots of them, to send to her dad. She was so proud of the way her daughter and Ryan looked together. They honestly looked like they were made for each other. She had tears in her eyes as she kissed Maddie good-bye, gave Ryan a big hug, and told them to have a wonderful time.

The prom was spectacular that year. The juniors, with whom their class was very close, had gone overboard to make everything just perfect. The food, the decorations, the flowers—everything was magnificent. Maddie and Ryan had a wonderful time.

Their entire group of eleven sat together at the banquet, and then shared a table at the dance in one corner of the country club where the actual dance took place. The group danced with each other all evening, and they each took loads of pictures of the entire event.

After the prom, Maddie and Ryan went back to her house to change clothes. The group had decided to rent a cabin and go up to Lake Avalon for their own after-party. Maddie's mom just told them to be careful and to look out for each another. She was no fool. Even though she wasn't happy about it, she knew they'd probably have some beer or something a little stronger.

The group had a great time together. They had even invited a few of their favorite juniors to join them. Nothing "bad" happened that night. They danced, drank a little, played hide-and-seek, made out with their dates a little, and stayed to watch the sun rise. Even though Maddie and Ryan weren't able to do what they really wanted to do, that was fine with them just this once. They wanted to be with their friends, the friends they had grown up with and would never forget. All too soon, the group would scatter to different colleges, and who knew when they'd all be together again, if ever.

As Maddie and Ryan drove home from the lake after watching the sun rise, Maddie quietly stated, "This has been our last prom, Ryan."

Ryan sighed and said, "It won't be the last time you'll wear a long white dress, though, Maddie. So smile for me, okay?"

She did.

"Ryan, you haven't ever told anyone what we do when we're alone, have you?"

"What? Of course not. Why would you even ask that?"

"I don't know. Everyone talks about what everyone else is doing, and I was just worried that maybe we're being talked about, too."

"Well, you haven't said anything, have you?" asked Ryan.

"Absolutely not. I'd die if anyone knew about our private affairs. I'd be so humiliated that I don't know what I'd do."

"Maddie, listen to me. No one except the two of us knows what goes on between us. Yes, some guys brag about their exploits, but I certainly don't. Besides, they think I'm too shy to try anything with you. And that's just the way I like it. I listen, and yes, I do learn quite a bit about sex from them, but absolutely no one knows our business except us. Does that make you feel better?"

"Yes. What we do together is just between the two of us. That's the way it should be," answered Maddie.

"Are you sure we're really okay?" asked Ryan once again.

"I'm sure. I guess all the talk that went on at the cabin last night just spooked me a little," answered Maddie.

Not long after the prom, the valedictorian and salutatorian were announced. Ryan was the salutatorian of their class. He'd give one of the graduation speeches.

After taking their finals, the seniors had a week off before graduation. All the seniors were required to do was show up for graduation practice on the required evenings.

It had always been a tradition that the seniors would rent cabins up at the lake (with chaperones, of course). Maddie and Ryan's group of friends rented some of the cabins. They spent the days skiing behind speedboats, swimming in the warm waters of the lake, or sunbathing. At night, the couples would drift off for quiet time together, while others made campfires, sang, and drank beer. They'd only drive into town for graduation practice.

If Maddie and Ryan had ever been enticed into "going all the way," this was the week. But Maddie and Ryan only necked. They didn't want anyone to know about their private business, and since they could never be sure they'd be totally alone, they chose to do nothing. Besides, they would still have several weeks together before Ryan left for West Point.

After four glorious days at the lake with their best friends, it was time for them to go home and make the final preparations for graduation. Relatives would be arriving. Family parties had been planned.

Ryan's mother and sisters would arrive from Ohio for his graduation the next day. She only planned to stay through the weekend, but Ryan was really excited for Maddie to meet his mom. Maddie, on the other hand, was a nervous wreck.

The night before Maddie's graduation, however, disaster struck one last time. Maddie's mom received a call from Oregon that her younger brother Randy had died. He was only forty-six. Her mom was devastated. She would have to leave for Oregon the morning after graduation. Since she was afraid of flying, she decided to take the bus. She told Maddie that she'd have to be gone for two weeks. Because she was the oldest sister, she'd have to take care of some of his affairs after the funeral. Maddie started to cry. She'd always loved Uncle Randy and his crop of wonderful red hair. She told her mother not to worry about her. She could take care of herself. She'd teach her dance classes as usual and take care of the house; everything would be fine. So the night before graduation, instead of getting excited about graduating, Maddie and her mother spent their time getting her packed and ready to go.

Even though she wanted to, Maddie decided not to call Ryan and tell him what had happened. She knew he was enjoying spending time with his mom. Besides, he didn't need to hear any bad news right now, especially before he had to give his speech. No, she'd wait and tell him after graduation.

Maddie took her mother to the bus station the next morning to purchase her tickets and helped her mom all day. Graduation wasn't until that evening, so her mom was ready to go to Oregon well before they had to leave for the commencement exercises. Her mom also insisted that she attend the graduation after-party that the parents had planned. Maddie just needed to be home by 7:30 AM to get her to the bus. She told her mom not to worry. She promised her she'd be home in plenty of time to get her to the station.

Graduation was a very solemn occasion. After the graduates filed into the school auditorium to the sounds of "Pomp and Circumstance," and once the introductions, invocation, and pledge of allegiance were completed, the speeches finally began.

The superintendent of schools, Doctor Patrick, gave the first speech. Maddie wasn't really interested in listening to it; neither was anyone else for that matter. She was anxiously waiting for Ryan's speech. She'd memorized the speech herself, since she'd helped him practice it so many times.

The next speaker was the valedictorian. Her speech focused on the future. Maddie thought that she did a good job, but she knew that Ryan's was going to be much better. Finally, it was Ryan's turn.

Ryan had decided to divide his speech into two parts. The high school years—the funny, sad, heartbreaking experiences they'd lived through—came first. Ryan was able to get all of his classmates to laugh at themselves. The second part of his speech was much more serious. He talked about all the opportunities that lay before them—how it was their responsibility to make the world a better place. He also told them they all needed to do something special with their lives, no matter what they became. If they decided to become teachers, then they needed to be the best teachers they could be. On the other hand, if they decided to be stay-at-home moms, they needed to be the best hands-on moms they could be. Whatever path they chose, they needed to make themselves accountable to others. He ended his speech on a high note by acknowledging all the hard work it had taken for all of them to reach this day.

After Ryan's speech, an Army colonel surprised Ryan by coming onto the stage. After a few formal remarks, he gave Ryan his induction papers for West Point and shook his hand. The entire audience stood and clapped for him. Maddie could tell he was embarrassed, proud but embarrassed.

After graduation, once the graduates had changed clothes, they all met at the town bowling alley for the all-night party that their parents were giving them. Their parents had an ulterior motive for giving them such a huge party. They wanted to keep their children safe for at least one more night.

All kinds of food and sodas imaginable were available to them throughout the night, and all sorts of entertainment was provided for them, too. Some students bowled while others watched movies in a separate room. Others played ping pong. Still others just sat around and talked about the past and the future. Breakfast would be served by the parents at dawn.

Maddie and Ryan went off into a corner by themselves, so that she could tell him the news about her Uncle Randy and her mother's absence for two weeks. They talked for quite a while, and Maddie told him of her proposed plans, but she had no an idea how Ryan would react. But, he readily agreed to her idea. She was really a little surprised when he did, but she felt he probably agreed only because he knew it would make her happy. Besides, they'd have more time to talk about it later. They could always change their minds.

When graduation night was over, and the entire group of eleven was walking together towards the parking lot and their cars, Shelly yelled at them all to gather by her car.

"Okay," Shelly said, "we're all going to make a pact here and now to meet again. Kelly and I have already written the pact. All you have to do is get together in a small circle and repeat it after us. The entire group of eleven put their hands together, one on top of the other, and did as they were told.

"All of us friends standing in this circle tonight with our hands one on top of the other, do hereby promise that for our twentieth class reunion, no matter where we are in this world, we will meet here again. Only death will keep us from meeting this obligation," declared Shelly solemnly.

"We promise!" shouted the group. With that, graduation 1964 was complete.

8

While Ryan and Maddie were driving home from the graduation after-party, for the first time in Maddie's memory, there seemed to be an awkward silence between them. When they reached Maddie's house, he walked her to her door. After he kissed her, Maddie asked him what was wrong. He told her nothing, but she didn't believe him.

"Are we going to see each other tonight, or are you breaking up with me?" Maddie asked suddenly.

Ryan, astonished by the question, answered her quickly.

"Of course, we're going to see each other tonight, Maddie. And, no, we're not breaking up. What are you thinking? That's never going to happen, unless that's what you want. Do you?"

"Absolutely not, but you've seemed a little distant lately," was Maddie's reply.

"Maddie, get some sleep, and yes, we have a date tonight. Don't you remember? My mom is taking us out to dinner."

"Oh my God, yes, I almost forgot. I've just had a lot on my mind. Okay, I'll see you tonight," replied a totally relieved Maddie."

As soon as Maddie walked into her house, she kissed her mother hello, grabbed her mom's suitcase for her, and took her to the bus station for her long, sad journey to Oregon and her brother's funeral.

Maddie spent an extra amount of time getting ready for dinner that night. She wanted to look her best and make a good impression when she was with Ryan's mother and sisters. She agonized over what to wear. She didn't want to appear either too sexy or too prudish. She finally settled on an aqua sheath with a matching short sleeve sweater and stylish white sandals. She couldn't believe she was as nervous as she was. Maddie didn't have any reason to be nervous, and even though she was, she didn't show it. She shouldn't have worried. The five of them had a wonderful dinner. Maddie was outgoing, instead of being shy, around someone she didn't know, and Ryan's mother could see immediately what Ryan saw in her. Maddie was not only beautiful, but she was also very smart. Add to that charming and engaging, and Ryan's mom approved of her wholeheartedly. She could also see that Maddie and Ryan were very much in love with each other. She thought they'd make a good pair—if Maddie could withstand Ryan's being gone to West Point for the next four years, and the awful, but very real possibility, that he would be headed for Vietnam after that. Her son knew that she didn't approve of his going to West Point. She'd told him precisely that several times, because she knew that he would probably be sent to Vietnam eventually, and she didn't want her only son returned to her in a body bag. That's why she hadn't wanted her son to live with his father. As a psychologist, she knew he was at a very impressionable and vulnerable stage in his life, and his father would have a great deal of influence on him. He had. She finally forced herself to think happier thoughts. Besides, this was supposed to be a happy evening.

After dinner, Ryan dropped Maddie off at her house, walked her to the door, and kissed her good night. Since his mother was leaving the next day, Maddie knew that she wouldn't see him tomorrow. But that was all right, because they already had a date set for Monday night.

Maddie slept in late on Sunday morning, but when she finally did wake up, it was time for her to get busy. Her first item of business was to clean the house. She wanted everything to be spotless for Monday night, and, since she would be teaching dance classes most of the day on Monday, today was her only day to do it. It took her several hours to clean and arrange the house just the way she wanted it, but in the end, she was pleased with the results.

Next, she went to the grocery store. She was going to make dinner for Ryan tomorrow night and had decided upon salad, spaghetti, and garlic French bread. Since, they planned on going to the Sonic for dessert, she didn't have to worry about that. She finished at the store as quickly as possible, because she needed to get her sauce prepared and left to simmer for as long as possible. Her sister Michelle was married to a full-blooded Italian whose mother-in-law had taught her to cook the Italian way, and Michelle had showed Maddie once how to prepare spaghetti.

Once Maddie had the sauce simmering, she set the table, using candles to set a romantic mood. She really wanted this dinner to be special for the two of them. After she was finished getting everything ready for the next evening, she decided to go to bed early.

Maddie and Ryan worked most of the day on Monday, but as soon as Maddie finished teaching her classes, she hurried home to get ready for her dinner date with Ryan. She bathed, put on her makeup, did her hair, and then started to put the finishing touches on their dinner. She still had the salad to put together and garlic toast to get ready for the oven. After that, all she had to do was to wait for Ryan.

Ryan arrived at Maddie's for dinner, holding a bouquet of flowers for her. He handed them to her as he entered, kissed her on the cheek, and closed the door behind him.

"God, something smells delicious," said Ryan as soon as he entered the house.

Maddie took the lovely flowers into the kitchen, and, as she was cutting the stems of the flowers and carefully placing them into a vase, Ryan came up behind, put his arms around her tiny waist, and said, "I love you, Madison Conrad."

"I love you, too, Ryan Richardson. Perhaps too much, if that's possible," answered Maddie as she lighted the candles for their first romantic dinner together—just the two of them, totally alone.

Dinner was a total success. Maddie marveled at just how much Ryan could eat. She was glad she had made enough, because he had seconds of everything.

After dinner, the two of them went to the Sonic for dessert as planned. They both ordered chocolate milkshakes and sat there talking and waving to other kids who drove by. Since school was over, the Sonic was more crowded than usual. After making sure everyone saw them, they finished, and then returned to Maddie's house.

Once inside the house, however, they locked the doors, turned on the lamp in the living room, and shut all the blinds. Then they turned on the TV even though they had no intention of watching it.

Finally, when they were completely and totally alone and didn't have to worry about someone seeing them, Maddie took Ryan's hand and led him to her bedroom. For the first time in their lives, Maddie and Ryan lay down on a bed together, just the two of them.

Ryan started laughing suddenly as he looked up. "Well, I can honestly say I've never lain under a canopy bed before."

"What can I say, Ryan? I'm a girlie girl," replied Maddie, also laughing.

His response to this was merely to enfold her into his arms, kiss her, and whisper, "I love girlie girls, Madison. Not all girlie girls, mind you, just one—you."

It seemed like forever since they'd been together, really been together. So, they pulled back the covers on her bed and proceeded to very slowly undress each other down to their usual panties and briefs before climbing under the covers. They had never been in a bed together before now.

Ryan and Maddie were built like they were made for each other. Because they were both tall and slim, their bodies fit together like a glove.

Ryan very gently pulled the sheet back to expose Maddie's body to him. Her body never ceased to amaze him. He very quietly lay on top of her and became hard immediately. He didn't want to embarrass himself and come too quickly, so he started using his tongue and flicked it very lightly over her breasts and then all the way down to Maddie's lower body. Then he went back up to her breasts and sucked and caressed them both very tenderly.

Ryan then proceeded to go back down to Maddie's panties where he softly slipped them off her and dropped them onto the floor. Next, he spread Maddie's legs open as widely as he could. Maddie had never felt so totally exposed in her life, and Ryan could tell.

"Maddie, I love you so much. Please don't be embarrassed when I look at you. I've never seen such a wonderful body. But I think I know what might make you relax a little more."

Ryan then rolled over onto his back beside Maddie and took off his own briefs. Ryan lay next to her, his legs spread open wide, his shaft standing straight up. Then he turned Maddie to face him. He wanted her to see what she did to him.

"Touch me, Maddie," begged Ryan. "Look at what you do to me."

Maddie did as she was told. She gazed at the young man she loved so desperately in amazement. *He must be at least 8 inches long*, she thought. Ryan placed her hands onto his shaft, and she began to move them up and down gently. But then, for some reason, maybe just natural instinct, she stopped. Instead, she rolled over on top of Ryan and took his member and put it into her mouth. Ryan was so shocked that he exploded immediately. He watched her swallow his seed while he shook and shuddered uncontrollably in the throes of his climax.

"Oh my God, Maddie. I'm sorry, but I've never felt such an intense feeling before. Why'd you do that?" asked Ryan.

"Because I wanted to, my love," Maddie said hesitantly. "Ever since I first tasted you, I've dreamed about making you come in my mouth. You have no idea how powerful and sexy doing this made me feel. I'm so sorry if I embarrassed you. It just seemed like a natural thing for me to do."

"Maddie, what you just did, you did because you love me. There's absolutely nothing to be sorry for. I'm not. Actually, by doing that, you proved how much you really do love me. I loved it. In fact, if I had my way, I'd want you to do it all the time. Do you understand what I'm saying to you?"

"Yes," said Maddie quietly, still terrified that she'd been too forward.

Ryan could tell that Maddie was still unsure that what she had done was all right, so he tried to explain to her that it was.

Ryan turned to face Maddie once again and automatically spread her legs open wide again. He then went straight to her core and started kissing it and licking it with his tongue. This was the first time Ryan had ever really examined her. He looked at her intently. He allowed his tongue to wander until he found her clit. As soon as he found it, he began sucking her inner lips. Then he used his tongue on her clit to bring her to an explosive climax. Maddie came immediately, but he didn't stop. He wanted her to feel the same way that she had just made him feel. Maddie kept coming over and over again until she begged Ryan to stop.

"Now, do you understand how wonderful you make me feel?" Ryan finally asked Maddie.

"Yes," she replied hoarsely.

Even though oral sex was considered taboo at the time, Ryan lied and told her that it was just a natural act between two people who love each other, and that there was nothing to be ashamed of. Neither of them had done anything abnormal. They loved each other, and this was how they showed it. He tried his best, but he didn't know if he was getting through to her. He then held her in his arms for a long time and tried to reassure her that everything was okay, but eventually Ryan had to leave.

"Honey, I have to go home. If I don't make my curfew, there will be hell to pay. But we have a date tomorrow night. I'll come over after dinner, okay? We can talk about it some more then. Will you be all right tonight?" questioned Ryan.

"I'll be fine, Ryan," lied Maddie. "I'll see you tomorrow night."

Ryan arrived home just minutes before his midnight curfew. He saw that the light was still on in his parents' bedroom, so he told them good night.

"Glad you made it home on time, son," was all his father replied.

When Ryan finally climbed into bed that night, he couldn't sleep. He kept replaying the night with Maddie over and over in his head. His brain would not shut off. He'd never experienced such a wonderful evening but knew that unless it was with Maddie, it wouldn't happen again for four years. But what really bothered him was Maddie. She seemed so lost and forlorn when he left. He was worried about her. He decided that as soon as he had his first break from his lifeguard duty the next day, he'd call and check up on her.

The next morning, he did just that. He called Maddie at home, but there was no answer. He figured she was probably on her way to teach her ballet classes for the day. He'd call her there while on his lunch break.

When he called back during his lunch break, Mrs. Bicknell picked up the phone. When Ryan asked to speak to Maddie, she told him that Maddie had called in sick. She also told him that she was a little worried since she'd never done this in all the years she had worked for her, so she was teaching Maddie's classes for her. Ryan thanked her, hung up the phone, and dialed Maddie's number again. Still no answer. Now, he was really getting worried.

At his last break before leaving work for the day, he tried her number one last time. Still no answer. He decided that he'd tell his folks he wasn't hungry for dinner so he could get to Maddie's as quickly as possible. He couldn't imagine what had happened to her, but he knew he'd never forgive himself if she were hurt.

Finally, at about 6:30 PM, he knocked on Maddie's door. No one answered, and there were no lights on, so he knocked again and yelled for Maddie to open the door. It took a while, but she eventually did.

Ryan couldn't believe what he saw. He'd never seen Maddie so disheveled. She was still dressed in her adorable pink baby doll pajamas, but her eyes were red and swollen from crying, and she appeared to be in a daze.

Ryan walked into the house and immediately locked the door behind him. He then took Maddie in his arms and just held her quietly. Tears started to spill from her eyes once again, and Ryan could feel her shudder softly as she cried.

"My God, Madison, what's wrong?" asked Ryan quietly.

"Nothing," was all Maddie would say.

"Don't tell me 'nothing.' I've been worried sick about you since last night. I knew I shouldn't have left you, but if I hadn't, I would have been grounded, and that's all we'd need since I leave in three weeks as it is. So, I'm going to ask you once again. What's wrong?" asked Ryan.

He very gently took Maddie's hand and led her to her bedroom where they just lay down together. It took Maddie several minutes to finally speak.

Since Maddie was really sexually naïve, she felt as if her being so forward last night might have made Ryan think she was a slut, and she couldn't stand it if he did. She told Ryan that she was embarrassed about what she'd done to him the night before. She had no explanation for it; she was sick about it. She also told him that all night long, all she could think of was that he now probably thought she was just a whore even though she knew she wasn't. She just couldn't bear the thought that he'd think of her that way—not now, not ever. She also told him that after last night, she was frightened that he'd never want to see her again, and the mere thought of that made her want to die. She didn't know what she'd do if she lost him, especially now. Then she just started to sob again uncontrollably.

Ryan knew that he had to talk Maddie through this; otherwise, he'd never forgive himself. He couldn't imagine life without Maddie, and if anything happened to her, it would be his fault. He also knew Maddie well enough to know that he needed to treat this matter with special care. If he didn't, he'd lose her. It took him a while to get his thoughts together before he started to explain to her what last night had meant to him.

Ryan explained that he couldn't sleep last night either. He knew he shouldn't have left her after what had happened. It was his fault, not hers. He told her the truth. He kept replaying last night over and over in his mind, thinking how wonderful it had been for them. He explained that he'd been surprised that she had been so forward, but it was a good kind of surprise. He also knew that he'd been the driving force in the sexual part of their relationship. She loved him enough to go along with whatever he wanted to try. Yes, he'd heard the guys talk about a way to "do it" but not really "do it."

He'd never approached the subject with her, though, because he didn't know how she would react, and he was afraid that he'd drive her away. When she took it upon herself to do it, it had amazed him. Never in a million years would he have thought she'd have the courage to try it on her own. But for him, that's what made it all the more special. She loved him enough to be bold and to try to show him how much she really did love him. What they did, they did out of love, not out of lust. That was the big difference. Neither of them had ever done that before, but they were both equally responsible for what had happened between them. This was not a blame game they were playing. They hadn't dated anyone else for years, so it was just a matter of time before this would've happened. It was natural. He told her that he'd never allow anyone else even to touch him, much less have oral sex with him. He was not and never would be interested in one-night stands. He went on to explain to her that even when he went to West Point, he wouldn't ever allow anyone to get close to him like this. He belonged to her and hoped and prayed that she felt the same way. It worried him that he was going to be so far away from her for so long. In fact, it worried him enough that if she didn't want him to go to

West Point, he'd turn it down and go to an in-state university to be closer to her.

Maddie's reply was swift and immediate. "Don't say that. You've always wanted to go the West Point, and you're going. I know you've meant everything you just said, but I won't allow it. If I did, I'd never forgive myself, and, in the end, you'd end up blaming me for not having your chance. So it's final. You're going, and I'm going to wait for you, because you're the love of my life and my soul mate."

After that, Maddie and Ryan just held each other for some time. Maddie's guilty moment had passed.

"Honey, get up. Get your shower, get dressed, and then we're going out to dinner."

"Do you need to shower, too? If so, we could save some money and do it together," she said teasingly.

"Madison Conrad, that's an absolutely perfect idea!" yelled Ryan as they both ran towards the bathroom together, quickly throwing off their clothes as they went.

Showering together was a way for Maddie and Ryan to play together and lighten the seriousness of what had happened to them the night before. Of course, one of them was always "accidentally" dropping the soap. They took turns lathering each other's bodies, and Ryan even washed Maddie's gorgeous, long, curly auburn hair. Afterwards, they dried each other off, dressed, and went out. The crisis had passed.

However, instead of going to dinner that night, the two of them decided to go to the drive-in. After they purchased their Cokes and popcorn, and since it was so hot out, they decided to use their blanket and lie on the hood of the car to watch the movie. They had no idea what was playing; neither of them had looked at the sign as they'd entered. However, when the movie began, they knew they were in trouble. They had both seen the movie before and loved it, but it was one that probably wasn't a good idea to watch again, especially after last night. *Splendor in the Grass*, with Natalie Wood and Warren Beatty, was playing.

Ryan asked Maddie if she wanted to leave, but Maddie said no because it was one of her favorite movies. They stayed and Maddie cried at the end as usual.

"Promise me that won't ever happen to us, Ryan. Promise me that no one will ever come between us, not even West Point."

"I promise, honey. Come on. Let's go to your place," whispered Ryan in her ear.

Maddie and Ryan were together every night while her mother was gone, and every night ended with the two of them in her bed together. What had seemed so horrendous to Maddie just a few short days ago now seemed like the most natural act in the world. They were never in a hurry. They always took their time exploring each other's bodies. Maddie marveled that the mere touch of Ryan's hand moving lightly over her body made her shiver with pleasure and desire. For Ryan, the hard part was holding himself back. He never wanted to frighten Maddie again like he had the first time. Afterwards, they'd always shower together before he went home. Tonight was the last time they'd be able to be in bed together. Maddie's mother was due home in the morning.

Before Ryan left that night, he decided to voice his concerns to her about entering West Point.

"Maddie, do you remember a couple of weeks ago when you wondered why I was so quiet and you thought I might want to break up with you?" asked Ryan.

"Of course I do. I could tell something was wrong. What is it? Talk to me."

"Well, I guess I'm a bit overwhelmed at the prospect of West Point. I don't want to embarrass myself, my dad, or you by flunking out. I'm just wondering if I can really hack it. I hate to admit it, but I'm a little frightened at what the next four years will bring," said Ryan with a sense of desperation in his voice.

Maddie had never seen Ryan unsure of himself. He'd always known where he was headed and why. She thought she knew all sides of him, but this one she didn't recognize. She realized very quickly that he needed some cheering up and motivation.

She explained to Ryan that what he was feeling was very natural. Change can be very difficult. They'd lived the last two years basically in a cocoon-like existence. They were surrounded and kept safe by those who loved them. Now, they would both be heading off to different places, different situations, and different challenges. She explained to him that West Point was going to be a far greater change for him than college would be for her.

"Ryan, your entire existence is going to change. You'll have no control over what you do, what you say, where you go. You'll be told how to act, what to study. You'll have few choices the first year. You know that. You'll be taking math classes six days a week. You can do this. But you must do it for you—not for your father, not for me. This has to be the life you want for yourself. I've been concerned for quite some time that you're doing this to make your father happy, not you. But once you make your choice and realize that this is your choice, you'll be able to handle anything that happens while you're there.

"You know I'll support you all along the way, from beginning to end, through all the hard, doubting yourself moments, as well as the proud moments of accomplishment. You alone must succeed, but I'll be right behind you, pushing you along and giving you a kick in the butt if you ever need it," said Maddie sincerely.

"But what if I can't hack it?"

"You can. Just recognize that your entire life will change."

"Are you sure you'll wait for me? Will you really be the driving force behind me?" asked Ryan, almost desperately.

"I'm sure. As sure as anything in my life—as sure as I am that we'll be married four years from now," declared Maddie.

"That's one promise I plan to keep, Maddie. It's the one thing that'll keep me going," said Ryan, with tears in his eyes.

"Okay, enough of this self-doubt from you. Give me a luscious and long French kiss," said Maddie.

9

The day before Ryan left for West Point was spent making sure he was packed. He didn't have much in the way of physical belongings that he had to take with him. Most everything he'd need would be provided for him. He needed a few days' worth of clothes for the long trip to New York, and then on to West Point, which was on the Hudson River, about fifty miles from New York City. Other than that, he just packed a couple of special items that he felt he needed to keep with him. Of course, he took pictures of Maddie and him—all kinds—from formal prom pictures to snapshots at the lake, on hayrides, etc. He wanted, no, needed these reminders of the girl he would marry, even if he couldn't display them and had to keep them in a drawer or his footlocker. He also chose a couple of books to take with him, the most important one being *101 of the World's Best Poetry*. His favorite had always been "Crossing the Bar," but that had seemed too morbid to Maddie. She always preferred Shelly, Frost, and Wordsworth.

Their last night together, Ryan and Maddie went to their spot at the reservoir one last time. Instead of talking first, they both immediately climbed into the backseat. Who knew when the next time would be that they'd see each other and in what kind of setting?

"This is really going to happen, isn't it?" said Maddie softly, with tears starting to spill down her cheeks. "I can't believe it. When will I get to hold you and kiss you like this again?"

Now, it was Ryan's turn to be understanding and appreciate what Maddie was going through.

"It's going to be over in the blink of an eye, honey. We're only going to be separated by distance, not heart. I'll write as often as I can, but I probably won't be able to write much, especially during "Beast." We'll talk on the phone. I'll get to see you. I know we'll see each other at least once this year. I promise you that," Ryan whispered in her ear, having no idea if he could keep such a promise.

Maddie knew what he was saying was right, but she already felt lonely. He was truly her best friend. Who was she going to talk to while he was gone? Ryan was the only person in the world who truly knew her. She wasn't the type to open up to just anybody. She'd always been reserved that way.

"Ryan, I want you to promise me that if your feelings for me change, you'll tell me right away," cried Maddie. "I have a right to know. If you find someone else, you must promise to tell me. Don't lead me on just because you don't want to hurt me. That wouldn't be fair."

"I promise. But that's not going to happen—ever."

71

After that, Ryan and Maddie just lay side by side in the backseat of the car, holding and kissing each other—at times passionately, at times tenderly.

Maddie knew the day he was to leave for West Point would be the worst day of her life. She was right. He had to take a bus to Oklahoma City and then a train to New York. After that, he would once again have to take a bus to West Point. The trip would take several days, several long, boring days.

Maddie, Ryan, his parents, and stepbrothers were all at the bus station in Avalon on that fateful morning to see him off. Maddie thought it should be raining, but instead the sun shined brightly in the cloudless sky. Neither she nor Ryan had had much sleep. They'd been sitting outside in Ryan's backyard, talking well into morning, since they both knew he wouldn't have any free time to write or call during the summer—"Beast" (boot camp) was waiting for him as soon as he arrived.

When the bus arrived, Ryan's dad shook his hand and said, "Make me proud, son." His stepmother and brothers all kissed him and wished him well. Then it was Maddie's turn. Maddie had vowed she wouldn't cry; this was only the first step towards their future life together. She couldn't keep her promise, though, and the tears started rolling silently down her cheek. Ryan was very tenderly wiping them away—but he, too, had tears in his eyes. They had been inseparable for two years. She couldn't even imagine life without him, not talking or seeing him for months at a time. Maddie took Ryan's face in both of her hands, looked him straight in the eyes, and said, "I'll be waiting." Then she put her arms around his neck, kissed him, and almost simultaneously, they both said "YKTA." Ryan turned quickly and boarded the bus. He couldn't stand to see Maddie cry, and he didn't want his father to see him break down.

Maddie watched tearfully and waved to him until the bus was out of sight. Even after she could no longer see the bus, and the others had left, she just stood at the pickup spot, the post office, seemingly bewildered. It was as if she was glued to that very spot. Finally, she was able to start putting one foot in front of the other and eventually reached her car.

Maddie just sat in her car at the bus station for several minutes after Ryan left. Tears were quietly streaming down her face, and she did nothing to stop them. The love of her life and soul mate had just left on a long four-year journey without her.

While Maddie was driving home from the bus station in Avalon, Ryan sat alone in his seat on the Greyhound Bus. He actually had his pick of seats; he chose one by the window in about the center of the bus. He'd put his small suitcase, with a couple of changes of clothes and other toiletry essentials in the small overhead compartment, but he kept his informational packet, his books, and his notebooks on the seat next to him. As he looked out the window and saw the landscape he'd come to know so well start to fade in the distance, he wondered what his future would hold. Would he be able to hack it or wash out at West Point? No, that wasn't an option—he'd make it.

Then his thoughts turned to Maddie. Would she really wait for him? She was so cute and vivacious that he knew all the college guys would be after her. But she had always been brutally honest with him—even when he didn't want to hear it—so he really couldn't fathom her not keeping her promise. He also knew her well enough to know that if she changed her mind, she'd tell him at once. He resolved they had to trust each other—he had no other choice.

They had talked about dating while in college several weeks before he was due to leave. Ryan knew that his options would be very limited, at least the first couple of years, but he wanted Maddie to enjoy her college career, not sit in the dorm every night. Of course, she turned up her nose at the idea of dating anyone besides him, but she promised him that if she met a nice guy, she'd try it at least once. Neither of them mentioned anything about sex, because it really didn't occur to them that it would ever happen with anyone else. They'd both always said that they would be virgins until the two of them decided together to make love to each other for the first time.

Ryan also told Maddie that he wanted her to keep busy—try out for cheerleader, join clubs—anything to make the time go by faster. He'd warned her again that he'd probably not be able to write or call much, but he'd do his best. He also had no idea when they'd get to see each other again. He'd heard that plebes (freshmen) didn't even get to come home for Christmas, but he didn't tell Maddie about that, not yet anyway. He promised her that the minute he found out when he could see her, he'd call so they could try to figure out a way to get her to the East Coast—but it was so far away.

Even though Maddie tried to act strong during these talks, huge tears would well up in her gorgeous teal eyes. Ryan knew he'd have an easier time adjusting than Maddie, because his life wouldn't be his own. He would have no control over it for at least two, maybe even three, years. His every minute would be controlled by someone else—when to sleep, when to eat, when to study, when to march, blah blah blah.

Ryan willed himself back to the present. He watched as the bus passed through farms and stopped at every small town on its way to Oklahoma City. He pulled the window down, and a hot wind hit him in the face like a blast furnace from hell. The bus slowly started filling up with people, all of them going somewhere other than where they'd been, and it was almost full by the time it reached Oklahoma City. He knew that the next part of his trip would be a very long train ride to New York City. He was right.

It took Ryan three days to reach New York City. He passed the time looking at the ever-changing scenery, reading, sleeping, and, of course, thinking of Maddie. He'd even called her while he was in Oklahoma City, waiting for the train to leave. God, just the sound of her voice make him feel both stronger and weaker at the same time. For some reason, he wasn't hungry. In fact, he was a little sick to his stomach most of the time, but he forced himself to eat a few grilled cheese sandwiches and Seven Up. However, the closer he came to New York City, the more excited and nervous he became. He also knew he had another bus ride ahead of him, so he wouldn't be able to enjoy any of the sights of New York. West Point was sort of out in the middle of nowhere. He knew he wouldn't be staying at the famous Thayer Hotel with the rest of the new recruits; there wasn't room. No, he'd be staying in some flea bag motel in Newburgh by himself the night before he was to report for duty.

That night in the cramped motel room was the loneliest night he could ever remember. He talked to Maddie for a long time, and she tried her best to cheer him up, but even she was in tears. He knew he needed to get a good night's sleep, but sleep eluded him. He was too caught up in what the next few days would be like. He tossed and turned, thought of Madison, and even cried quietly to himself off and on. Why was he doing this? He could've gone to Princeton, for God's sake. Was he doing it for himself or for his father—to make him proud? The real answer to that question eluded him. The one thing he did know was that no matter what, he had to make it through.

The next morning, he awoke to a beautiful summer day, surrounded by breathtakingly beautiful scenery. He showered, ate some breakfast, called Maddie one last time, and waited for the bus to take him to the end of this journey and to his home for the next four years.

10

Maddie was inconsolable for several days after Ryan left. He did manage to make a couple of calls to her on his way to the East coast. Those were the moments that Maddie lived for. But she also knew that as soon as he entered Thayer Gate, things would never be the same. The closer he came to West Point, the more depressed she became.

Maddie's mom tried to cheer her up by taking her on a shopping spree to get her ready for her own new college experience. They bought linens, clothes, shampoo, notebooks—things that she would need to take with her. This seemed to help some.

Spending time with her girlfriends helped, too. However, her best friends, Kelly and Shelly, had moved to Arizona right after graduation, and she missed them more than they could imagine. She and her other friends would talk about the past a little, but mostly about the future. All of them were getting excited for college to begin in the fall.

But it was when Maddie was alone at night and having to face the truth that Ryan truly was gone, as well as the helplessness of being left behind, that really upset her. She couldn't eat; she didn't even want to look at food. She lost some weight, but it wasn't really too noticeable, because she'd always been tall and thin.

The only good thing that happened during this time was when her mom received a surprise phone call from her dad telling her he was home and in Vernon, Texas, and to come and get him. In fact, he was home earlier than they had anticipated. Since her mom didn't know how to drive a car, Maddie got the job.

Maddie's father had been gone since last June. He was supposed to be gone for fifteen months on a top security mission that he'd tried to turn down. He had missed her graduation, among everything else. Neither she nor her mother knew what he was doing in Formosa, Nationalist China. He couldn't say. In fact, they had been informed before he left that the letters to and from him would be intercepted and read. Once, a typhoon hit Formosa, and they hadn't heard from him for two weeks, so her mom had contacted the Red Cross—as she'd been instructed to do—to find out if he was okay. Maddie noticed that during his absence, her mother had started to become ill. She lost a great deal of weight in a very short period of time, and Maddie had to take her to the doctor quite often. No one could ever really find out what was wrong with her. No one knew then, when she was only forty-seven, that her mom would be dead by fifty. Maddie could tell how really excited her mother was to see her husband. This particular deployment had been very difficult for her. However, since Vernon, Texas, was only thirty minutes away, it didn't take long for them to reach their destination.

As soon as Maddie saw her father, she was in total disbelief. When he left Avalon, his hair had been brown; now it was snow white. What had happened to him? What had caused it? She'd find out later. Now was not the time to ask those kinds of questions.

If Mom was shocked by Dad's appearance, she didn't show it. She was glad he was home again, safe and sound.

It took some getting used to having Dad back home. It had been only the two of them for a year. Now, whenever Maddie asked to go somewhere, she had to ask both her mother and father's permission, which seemed odd to her since she was leaving for college soon.

The night finally came—after her dad had been home for two weeks—for her to ask him about his overseas assignment. Her father had always been in supply and had checked out TVs, refrigerators, etc., to newcomers to the base. *What could be so top secret about that?* thought Maddie. When she finally became brave enough to ask her father about his time in China, she could not have been more surprised by his answer.

"Maddie," he said in his gruff, supposed-to-scare-the-airmen-to-death voice, "I'm only going to say this once. I wasn't checking out TVs. All of the arms shipments for Vietnam came to me. Then I sent them on to their designated destinations. To put it bluntly, I knew where all the arms were in Vietnam. If this information had gotten into the wrong hands, the buildup would've been lost, and we would have lost this war before it really started.

"This leads me to another bit of info I need to share with you," continued her father. "We're being reassigned to another air base—one in New Mexico. Don't worry, you'll still be going to college here in Oklahoma, but we'll be moving within the next ten days."

"But why can't we stay here?" exclaimed Maddie.

"You'll find out tomorrow. We have a meeting to attend," was all he said.

The next morning, Maddie found out why they were moving so quickly. They were informed that they were being moved for their own safety. Her father's information was just too sensitive and valuable. Other people would be looking for him. None of the family, her sisters and their families included, was allowed to leave the country for twelve months. They were told to expect that they were being monitored. It was determined that her father's information would become useless after the twelve months had passed. Maddie was shocked and scared. She could tell no one what her father had been doing, not even Ryan. They were also informed that the reason they couldn't go to Mexico, Canada, or any other place on earth was because if they were kidnapped, the government couldn't guarantee their safe return. No discussion was allowed.

BOOK II:
COLLEGE

11

Maddie and her father arrived at college a couple of days before school was set to begin. She had visited this college, as well as several others, a few times with friends during her senior year. It was a beautiful campus, just like the ones seen in magazines. The buildings were old but stood proudly, reaching for the sky. The main campus had beautiful large old oak trees and lots of grass where students would sit or lie and study on sunny days. She had chosen this college mainly because it was small in comparison to the larger universities, so it would have smaller classes.

This was also the first time Maddie was going to meet her new roommate. They had talked on the phone several times and had decided how they were going to decorate their dorm room. Beth and Maddie hit it off right away. Maddie's father liked her, too, so that eased his fears somewhat about letting his little girl go. She and her father also met her other roommates. There would be four of them in a two-room apartment on campus. Her dad helped her unpack and would spend one night in town before leaving for home the next day.

At the last minute, Maddie's dad decided to let her have her car on campus, but only if she kept her grades up. Since her dad was letting her have her car, which totally surprised Maddie, that meant he would be taking the bus home. They went to the Greyhound Bus station in Wilmington and purchased his ticket as soon as he'd told her. Maddie spent the final night with her dad in the motel that had been their home for the last two days.

The next morning, the two of them had breakfast together before his bus arrived. Even though she had promised herself she wouldn't cry, when he stepped onto the bus to leave, she did. She'd always been his little girl. She always would be.

Maddie totally embraced college life. She loved it— her classes, her teachers, and her new-found friends. She had been apprehensive about having to make new friends because she was such an introvert, but everyone she met seemed so outgoing that she discovered right away that her fears had been unfounded. She was enrolled in Honors English, American History, Philosophy, Art, and French. She adored her English professor, Doctor Gladys Bellamy. At the time, she was the world's foremost living authority on Mark Twain. She was also the department chair, as well as Maddie's advisor.

Maddie had also seen the announcement for cheerleading tryouts, and since she'd been one for four years already, she signed up, just like Ryan had suggested. She and one other freshman, Terri, made the squad that year. They practiced every day on the grass by the boys' dorm. Since Maddie and Terri could do front and back flips, cartwheels, and other tumbling stunts, they became the designated tumblers for the squad. Their first home football game was only a couple of weeks away, so the routines and their outfits had to be ready shortly. They would spend hours every day learning the routines and getting in sync. But they were fast learners, so they'd be ready to go when the time came.

In the evenings, after her classes and on weekends, she would either study or write Ryan a letter. He had written as promised. It was easy to see that his life was much more regulated and difficult than hers. She always tried to make her letters to him upbeat to keep him going. She told Ryan everything, from funny stories about her classes to how terrible the food was. She also told him that she hadn't dated anyone yet even though several young men had asked. She just wasn't ready.

Ryan would write and tell her that he was scared to death he'd flunk out every day. He explained to her that he was so frustrated and tense whenever his math instructor said, "Take to the boards," that he memorized all the math problems every night, so he wouldn't look like an idiot and screw up in front of everyone. He was doing this while being hauled out of bed in the middle of the night to do some stupid traditional ritual conducted by the upperclassmen. He'd expected some hazing, but he felt that they were taking it to the extreme. The physical and intellectual demands were far greater than he'd ever expected. The food was good, if they got to eat, but that was a story he would actually have to show her later. He really hated being a plebe. Plebes were treated as less than human, and he had expected more from such a grand institution.

One Friday evening in September, while Maddie was writing a letter to Ryan, Terri called and asked if she could come over to talk to her about something. Terri approached her on the idea of going on a blind date. Her immediate response was her usual, "No thanks; I'm spoken for." However, Terri insisted that it would be a double date with her and her boyfriend Matt after the football game Saturday night. "What can happen on a double date?" Terri asked her. When Maddie asked who it was, Terri replied that a blind date was just that—a blind date. But he was cute and she'd enjoy his company. After thirty minutes of constant badgering, Maddie finally agreed—but only to one date.

All day Saturday, Maddie felt like backing out of the blind date. She felt as if she'd be deceiving Ryan if she went. Of course, he knew she'd been asked out before, but until now, she'd never agreed. She even wondered if she could pretend to be sick, but if she did that, she wouldn't be able to cheer. Oh, what the hell, it would only be for a couple of hours, and it was going to be a double date. What could go wrong?

Her first date was that Saturday night after the football game. To Maddie, the game seemed to last forever, and it was hard for her to concentrate on it. However, it was exciting, and it did come down to the last couple of minutes. Their quarterback threw a long

Hail Mary touchdown pass, with only thirty seconds left, which clinched the win for Wilmington.

After the game, while Terri and Maddie were waiting for Matt and his friend to shower and change, the two friends began to talk a little about themselves—their likes and dislikes. They both loved cheerleading and dance. Terri had no formal training but loved jazz. Maddie had an immediate sense that Terri and she would eventually become lifelong friends. She was right.

After waiting in Matt's car for what seemed like an eternity, the locker room door finally opened, and Terri was the first to see Matt and another guy walking towards the car.

"Here they come," said Terri excitedly. "Let's get out of the car and go meet them."

Maddie couldn't believe she was so nervous. The only other time she'd ever been nervous on a first date was the one she had with Ryan all those years ago. She actually felt like sprinting back to her dorm, but instead she did as Terri had asked and climbed out of the car. However, instead of running to meet them like Terri, she stayed by the car, seemingly unable to put one foot in front of the other.

"You guys certainly made tonight's last-minute win a nail-biter!" exclaimed Terri happily when she reached the guys.

"Come on, Jake," said Terri as she grabbed his arm. "I want you to meet someone special."

Jake Kelly already knew Maddie was special. He'd seen her in the cafeteria several times eating with Terri and their friends. In fact, he was the one who had asked Matt to set them up. Matt had explained to Jake that Maddie was spoken for. Her boyfriend of two years was a cadet at West Point. Jake didn't care. He still insisted on meeting her. So after constant nagging, Matt finally gave in and agreed to talk to Terri about it.

Maddie noticed immediately that Matt wasn't as tall or big as his friend. To Maddie, his friend appeared to be about six feet two inches, around 190 pounds, with blonde hair. As they arrived to where she was standing, Maddie noticed that this guy's eyes were the bluest robin egg blue she'd ever seen.

Matt kissed Terri first and then turned his attention to Maddie.

"Hi, Maddie," Matt said in his usual upbeat voice.

"Hi, Matt. I saw you were able to play a little tonight."

"Yeah. Here's the guy I play behind. Maddie, I'd like you to meet Jake Kelly. Jake, meet Maddison Conrad," said Matt.

"Hi, Jake. It's nice to meet you," said Maddie. "What did Matt mean by play behind?" Immediately, Terri, Matt, and Jake all started to laugh at once.

"Well, I can tell you don't know the members of the team very well yet," declared Matt.

"What's that supposed to mean?" asked Maddie.

"Maddie," Terri said, still laughing, "this is Jake Kelly. He's the quarterback of our team."

"Oh my God"—Maddie laughed—"I'm so embarrassed! I feel like a total idiot."

"That's okay, Maddie. You're forgiven." Jake grinned.

"Let's go get something to eat. I'm starving as usual," said Matt.

Jake opened the car door for Maddie, and she slid into the backseat. When he got in on his side, he stayed there. *Thank God,* thought Maddie to herself, *he didn't make any advances.*

The foursome decided to go The Library, a restaurant and bar on the outskirts of Wilmington where all the college kids hung out. Whoever came up with the name The Library was pretty smart. When parents asked their kids where they were going in the evenings, they merely said, "The Library." When their parents received their credit card bills and asked their kids what they'd charged at "The Library," their answers would be that they had to make copies of articles, etc., or pay overdue fines. Their parents didn't realize until much later what "The Library" really was. In fact, some of them never did.

When Maddie finally became brave enough to turn toward Jake and really look at him, she realized that she had seen him on campus several times, mostly at the cafeteria with the other athletes. She was right. Jake was tall and had a great build, and Maddie had to admit to herself that he was really very cute.

While Matt and Terri were talking in the front seat, Jake was able to get their conversation started by telling Maddie that he'd heard she was from Avalon.

"Do you know where that is?" asked Maddie.

"Sure," replied Jake. He went on to explain that he was from Englewood, and that Englewood and Avalon played football against each other every year. This startled Maddie because she remembered a game two years before when the two teams played each other to see who would go to the state championship game that year. Avalon lost because Englewood had such a great senior quarterback.

"You're the one!" exclaimed Maddie.

"I am?" asked Jake. "The one what?"

She then told him about the game and how upset she'd been that Avalon had lost and Jake started to laugh.

"Well, I guess we sort of already know each other then," said Jake. "But now I'm thinking you probably hate me."

"Oh, don't be silly"—Maddie laughed—"I was just remembering where I'd heard your name before. You knocked us out of the state championship game a couple of years ago. But I heard that you were headed on a scholarship to the University of Oklahoma. What happened?"

"Well, instead of red shirting me my freshman year, I was able to play. That turned out to be the kiss of death. I hurt my knee and after that—since I knew I wasn't going to play there anymore—I decided to transfer to Wilmington. So, I not only still have a full scholarship but also get to play the game I love, too. So it's been a win-win situation for me," said Jake happily.

"So you must be a junior, huh?" asked Maddie.

"Yep. I'm majoring in social studies but eventually plan to get my masters in counseling," replied Jake.

"What's your major, or haven't you declared one yet?" Jake asked Maddie.

"Well, I'm leaning towards becoming a high school English teacher," replied Maddie. "I don't think I'm cut out to teach elementary school. That wouldn't fit my personality."

Maddie and Jake continued to talk and get to know each other all the way to The Library. It surprised Maddie that Jake was so easy to talk to. She even chided herself for having been so nervous.

However, when the two couples entered The Library for burgers and fries, it seemed to Maddie that everyone stopped to stare at them. Maddie became very self-conscious, but Jake held her hand firmly and took it in stride. He was used to being the center of attention. Everyone came up to shake Jake's and Matt's hands or gave them high fives for the last minute victory that night.

The four of them found a booth, ordered their meals and enjoyed talking about everything and anything. Maddie discovered that she was having a great time. It had been particularly amazing to watch Jake and Matt eat. One minute, the food was there; the next minute, it wasn't. Maddie found Jake to be a perfect gentleman the entire evening, which actually seemed to fly by.

After driving back to campus, Matt parked the car in the parking lot. Before the guys walked them to their dorms, the four of them talked about going out together again.

"Maddie, I can't remember the last time I've had such a relaxing evening. I'm so glad you agreed to come with us. May I call you again?" asked Jake.

Surprising herself, Maddie answered, "Sure," immediately. "I had a great time, too. I admit I was really nervous and almost backed out at the last minute. I'm glad I didn't."

"Great!" Jake replied. "I'll give you a call soon."

He just gave her a peck on the cheek and whispered in her ear, "Don't worry, I know you're spoken for." Then he opened the door for her.

After Maddie returned to her dorm room, she was inundated by friends wanting to know how her date had gone. When they found out that her blind date had been with Jake Kelly, they were all jealous. Maddie laughed because they spoke of him like he was some kind of god. Of course, they wanted to know all the details about their date, but Maddie chose to tell them only that he was a funny and nice guy. But this didn't satisfy their curiosity. Maddie refused, however, to go into any other details. It was really none of their business. She hoped Jake would also respect their privacy and not say much. He did.

Maddie was the first to date, but she didn't write to Ryan about her date with Jake Kelly for a week. She wanted to think through very carefully just how to tell him and what she did and didn't want to say. She didn't want to hurt Ryan's feelings or make him think anything had changed between them. It hadn't.

As soon as Ryan received the letter from Maddie, he knew immediately that something was wrong. He'd never gone this long without receiving mail from her. At first, he was afraid to open it. In fact, he decided to wait until that evening before lights out to read it.

Once Ryan read Maddie's letter, he knew why she'd waited so long to write to him. She had gone on her first date.

Maddie told him it had been a double date with Matt and Terri and how embarrassed she was that she hadn't recognized who Jake Kelly was at first. She was a cheerleader, for God's sake. She should at least have known who the team quarterback was. Anyway, she told Ryan she had been very anxious and almost backed out at the last minute. She hadn't been out with anyone except him for two years and didn't know how to act.

She also told Ryan that Jake had been a perfect gentleman, and no, he didn't have anything to worry about. Jake was well aware that she was spoken for even before they went out. The four of them just went out for burgers and fries—that's all.

Ryan was worried, though. In fact, he was heartbroken. He knew they'd both discussed this subject before he left and that she would be the first to date because he was too busy being a plebe. He just didn't think it would be this soon. She had told him in letters before that several guys had asked her out, but she had always politely declined. What had made her say "yes" this time? Ryan hoped it was the fact that she would be double dating with her friends Matt and Terri and figured she'd be safe with them along.

Instead of writing her back immediately, he too, decided to wait. He needed time to think before he replied. Ryan was like that. He always thought things through carefully—sometimes too carefully.

When Ryan did reply, he decided it would be better not to act angry or chide her for being the first to date. He knew Maddie well enough to know that this would definitely be a mistake. She would think he didn't trust her judgment. Instead, he asked what kind of a person this Jake guy was. Did he work? What kind of car did he drive? Guy questions. He also reminded her that he'd told her he wanted her to have fun and enjoy college. He said he'd be lying if he said it didn't bother him some; it did, but four years was going to be a long time. They both knew that. However, it didn't have to change all the plans they'd made for their future. He also said he was glad she'd told him and had not decided to keep it a secret. That would have hurt more. He promised he would do the same when the time came. As always, he ended his letter with YKTA. To this, however, he added a P.S. "If you see him again, please keep reminding him that you're 'spoken for'."

Ryan felt better after he dropped the letter into the mailbox. It had been hard for him to concentrate on much else until he'd replied to Maddie. In fact, a couple of nights, he was so distracted that he didn't bother to memorize his homework problems. Sure enough, one time he was called to the board and had forgotten what he was doing. Even now, he could still feel himself turning red when it happened and how embarrassed he'd been.

After that embarrassment, he decided he needed to get his act back together and his life, the daily grind, back into focus. For Ryan, though, that was easier said than done. He decided that he would stand in the endless pay phone lines the next time he had free time and call Maddie. He just needed to hear her voice.

12

About two days after their first date, Jake called and asked Maddie out on a real date. She hesitated for a moment before agreeing, once again feeling guilty because of Ryan.

They went out to dinner on Friday night and again enjoyed just talking about school and life in general.

Jake said he'd like to teach American history and coach football while getting his MA in counseling. He planned to go immediately into the master's program after graduation. He also kept her engaged with clever stories about some of the silly things he and Matt had done in high school. She realized that she was really enjoying his company, especially laughing. She hadn't laughed in a long time and really appreciated his non-threatening attitude.

After dinner, Jake asked Maddie if she would like to see a surprise on his father's farm just outside of town. Before she could object, he made it clear he knew what she was thinking and not to worry. He knew all about her boyfriend.

The farm was not far from town, and he stopped the car once they reached the gate, unlocked it, and then drove to the barn. He climbed out once again and opened the barn door. He picked up a flashlight, opened the car door for Maddie, and led her inside the barn. Once inside, he turned on the overhead light and led Maddie to a tiny stall.

Maddie couldn't believe her eyes. There, lying beside its mother, was a baby colt. Maddie could tell it had been born that day. His mother was still cleaning him off. He was gorgeous, though, Maddie thought to herself.

"When was he born?" asked Maddie.

"I helped birth her this afternoon," answered Jake.

"Her?" asked Maddie.

"Yep. She's a filly."

"You did this all by yourself?"

"Actually, Mom did most of the work. I just helped a little."

"She is this perfect, tiny specimen," marveled Maddie. "Look at those eyes!"

Jake laughed. "Maddie, they all have great eyes. Go ahead, you can touch her but be careful. Mom's very protective right now."

Maddie couldn't believe she was actually able to touch the baby filly. Better yet, she was really grateful to Jake for showing the filly to her.

"What are you going to name her?" asked Maddie, still totally enthralled with the young horse.

"I don't know. What do you think we should call her?"

"Well, let's see. Don't most horses have two names? Why don't we call her 'Jake's Joy'?" said Maddie. "She's going to be a happy filly; I can just tell."

"Okay, 'Jake's Joy' she is. But to us, she'll just be Joy, all right?"

"That sounds perfect. Jake, thank you so much for bringing me here. I've never seen anything like this before. You're right. It was a special surprise."

"Anytime, my lady," declared Jake as he bowed gallantly.

All the way back to town, Jake told her about the farm. His family had owned it for about sixty years. He offered to bring her back some afternoon for a picnic, if she'd like. No strings attached.

"That'd be great. I'd really enjoy that."

"Good. I'll call next week and we'll set a time," replied Jake.

At the door to her dorm, Maddie told Jake what a marvelous time she'd had, and once again he kissed her ever so lightly on the cheek. He knew better than to try anything else, even though he'd be lying if he had said he didn't want to.

Maddie didn't write a letter immediately that night to Ryan about going out with Jake again. She always told him everything and never kept any secrets from him. But she decided to wait until she could really think things through once again and decide how best to explain to him that she enjoyed Jake's company, and that Jake already knew better than to think anything serious could come of this. Terri and Matt had made that clear to him in the beginning. However, she was fully prepared to tell Jake herself if she ever needed to. To her, he was just someone to hang out with, go to dinner with, etc. She just needed time to get her thoughts regarding Jake down on paper correctly so that Ryan didn't get the wrong idea.

The school year seemed to be flying by, and before she knew it, it was October and time to study for her midterm exams. As soon as Maddie found out her grades on her midterms, she was able to send Ryan a short note telling him that all of her studying had paid off and that she had received a 4.0 on her midterms. He already knew how much she enjoyed the small classes and the relationship the professors had with their students. She had made a wise choice not to go to OU.

She also asked Ryan when he'd be able to call. She missed not hearing the sound of his voice. She hadn't talked to him for several months. Of course, she enjoyed the letters, but she really wanted to talk to him. If he could just give her an evening when he might call, it would be something for her to look forward to. She knew he was very busy, but she really needed to talk to him even if it was only to hear his voice again.

Maddie received a call out of the blue from Ryan about a week later. He must have received her message.

"Hi, Maddie. YKTA!" shouted Ryan into the phone.

"YKTA, Ryan," replied Maddie softly. "I didn't expect to hear from you so soon."

"Well, you sounded like you really needed to talk, and I know I did. Sometimes I think I hate it here," said Ryan angrily. "I wonder why I'm putting myself through this. Am I being a masochist or just an idiot? What do I have to prove to myself? I'm sick of all the stupid rules. The ones that make sense to me are no problem, but the others seem like lessons in futility. But enough about me. How are you doing, Maddie, really?"

"Well, from the sound of things, I'm having a much easier and more pleasant college experience so far than you. I don't feel the pressure to succeed that you do at West Point. Things here are probably a lot quieter, and I'm sure much more laid back."

"Have you been dating anyone besides Jake?"

"No, but I don't even consider it dating with Jake. We're just friends."

"Does Jake feel that way, too?" asked Ryan.

"What? I don't know. Hey, Ryan, believe me, Jake can have any girl he wants here, anytime he wants. I imagine he dates lots of girls. I've never asked. It's not any of my business. He doesn't expect anything from me, except good conversation and fun. Are you worried about something you shouldn't be?"

Ryan replied immediately, "I guess I'm afraid that you'll forget about me. I'm so far away, and when I read your letter, I immediately felt someone could be taking my place."

"Nonsense," replied Maddie indignantly. "You know I love you, plan a life with you and no one else. If you are unsure of me, perhaps you're unsure of yourself, too."

"Don't be an idiot. I'm sure of only one thing—I love you and want to marry you," answered Ryan seriously.

Then Ryan started to loosen up and asked, "Hey, you've never told me. Do your panties match your cheerleading skirt like they did in high school? I know, I know, I'm awful."

"As a matter of fact, they do, you dirty old man. The funny thing is, like I told you in my letters, we have the same school colors as high school—blue and white—and the mascot is Brandy the Bulldog. Quite a coincidence, huh?"

"Hey, I thought I was your officer and gentleman— now I'm a dirty old man?" Ryan whined happily. This was the old Maddie—the one who could make him to lighten up and laugh when his Type A personality started getting manic.

"Do you have any idea when I'll get to see you, Ryan? It seems like forever since you've held me. I always feel safe in your arms. Will you be home for Christmas, at least for a few days?"

Ryan waited before he replied. "I honestly don't know. I've heard rumblings that plebes don't get to go home for Thanksgiving or Christmas."

"What? You can't be serious!" cried Maddie. "What in the hell are you going to be doing? I can't believe it."

"Calm down, Maddie. I'll think of something. Maybe you could come here for a football game or a dance. I think there's one in the spring. We may go to New York to meet 'suitable girls' and practice our dancing skills. You could sneak in. I'm sure I'll get some demerits and have to walk the area for hours, but it would be worth it just to see you. Do you think you could afford to come?" asked Ryan.

"What do you mean 'suitable girls'? I'm not 'suitable' enough?"

"You are the only suitable girl in the world for me, Maddie. You know that," said Ryan seriously.

"Okay then. If you don't get to come home for Christmas this year, I'll tell my parents that I want a ticket to come see you for my present. I know I can stay at my sister Michelle's house in New Jersey. Since I have a 4.0, I think my parents will be able to come up with the money. That should be worth something," said Maddie.

Ryan and Maddie talked a few minutes longer. She told him she was considering a business venture with Terri and would write and explain it to him. She wanted his input. He had a smart, practical business sense. After a few more "I love yous," it was time to hang up.

"YKTA," they both said in unison.

After Maddie hung up the phone, she felt much better about the two of them. They were still on the same page even though Ryan seemed to be a little jealous of Jake. Because of that, she decided that the next time she and Jake went out, they needed to have a talk.

That talk occurred the next week.

She and Jake had gone to the movies, ate too much popcorn, and squirmed in their seats from too much Coke. Besides, the film was long—*Doctor Zhivago*. It was beautifully done, though, and she and Jake talked about it, especially the incredible scenery, while parked at the farm.

Maddie found that she was a little nervous about approaching the subject of Ryan with Jake. They had never really talked about it before. She started by asking him why he was dating her when he could have anyone he wanted. His frank reply surprised her.

"Maddie, I don't want to sound conceited because I'm really not, but I know I can have any girl I want and get what I want from them. Sometimes, I do. For me, it's just sex. It's just a sexual tension release. But with you, even though I'd be lying if I said I didn't want to, it's okay. Who wouldn't want to have you? You're probably the most gorgeous girl I've ever seen. I know I've never said that to you before, but you are. I also know that you're spoken for. He's a very lucky man. However, I'm content to enjoy your company and friendship. I feel comfortable talking to you—have since our first date. With the other girls, there is only one thing on my mind. Afterwards, of course, I feel guilty because basically I've just used them. I also have to make it a point to let them know not to expect anything more from me.

"You, on the other hand," continued Jake, "I'd be proud to have as an escort to any meaningful function. You have class. You're smart, witty, and gracious."

"Jake, I think you're giving me more credit than I deserve," replied Maddie.

"No, it's true. You know, we've never really spoken about Ryan. Why don't you tell me about him?"

Maddie thought carefully about his request. What did she want to disclose about Ryan and their relationship? She decided just to start talking and see where it led. She did know that she would say absolutely nothing to Jake, or anyone else for that matter, about their physical relationship. She never had and she never would. She did tell Jake that Ryan was very intellectual, pragmatic, reserved, and a perfect Type A personality. He felt honored to be at West Point but didn't enjoy being a plebe. As long as he could see the point of an exercise, he was fine with it, but he didn't enjoy or really approve of all the hazing. He thought it was stupid, just as stupid as always being called "crothead" when they really meant "dumbass or asshole."

She went on to tell take Jake that she and Ryan had met their junior year of high school. He had moved in across the street from her. They were both air force brats. His father and mother were divorced, and he'd lived with his mother until he was sixteen. Then he decided he wanted to get to know his father better, so he moved to Avalon to live with him and his stepmother. She knew it sounded crazy, but it was love at first sight. Well, at least love after first date. The minute they met, they knew that this was not going to be some fly-by-night romance. They went steady both their junior and senior years. They both knew that everything would change when he went to West Point, but they decided they could handle it. They were supposed to get married in June 1968.

Jake sat very still and thought for a few minutes before he replied, "He's a very lucky man, but I don't want you to think that just because you're spoken for, I don't want to keep seeing you. I know where I stand." With that he turned to Maddie and kissed her deeply on the lips for the very first time. Maddie was shocked, not only by the spur of the moment kiss, but she was also even more surprised by the fact that she had responded to it.

"Friends?" Jake said afterward and hugged her. "Don't worry, Maddie. I won't ever try anything even though I'd want to; I promise."

Maddie was so shaken about the kiss from Jake that when she returned to her dorm, she wrote immediately to her parents to request a ticket to New York for her Christmas present if Ryan didn't get to come home. She knew it would be expensive, but she also knew they'd try their best to grant her wish.

When Jake went to bed that night, all he could think of was Maddie, and the fact that for a brief moment, she had kissed him back before she realized what she'd done.

God, he wanted her. He'd never wanted anyone in his life like this before. This was an entirely new position for Jake. He was not in control; Maddie was. And he knew that she always would be. He never could be—nor would he be—the one to initiate anything more than a kiss. He knew Maddie well enough to know that if he did, she'd stop seeing him immediately, and he wouldn't ever take that chance. He knew Maddie was different. He also knew he was falling in love with her. He didn't want to—he couldn't have her—but he couldn't help himself. He was falling in love for the first time in his life.

Maddie already knew that Jake saw other girls for one particular reason. She was really surprised he'd been so frank about it last night. However, what Jake didn't tell her was that he wouldn't be doing this at all if they were together.

Jake couldn't believe that she couldn't tell that he was crazy about her. But that was Maddie, wonderful naïve Maddie. He also didn't know what kind of hold Ryan had on her, or what their physical relationship had been, except that Maddie had mentioned once, while drinking some wine, that she was still a virgin.

Jake was only human, though, and after being with Maddie for several weeks, he'd become sexually frustrated. Whenever this occurred, he knew he could have his pick of almost any girl on campus. He also knew he was the most popular guy on campus. It had been that way in high school, too. He really didn't know why. Yes, he was decent-looking; yes, he had an adequate personality; yes, he had a nice car; yes, his parents were wealthy, and he was an only child. He guessed the girls all thought of him as a good "catch." And, no, he really wasn't conceited just like he'd told Maddie. The truth was no girl had ever turned him down—no one except Maddie.

On this particular night, he had chosen a cute sophomore. She had a great body, and Jake knew she liked to show it off. Her name was Marilyn, but if someone asked Jake her name a couple of days from now, he wouldn't remember it.

They went to the drive-in and took a small ice chest of beer that a senior football player had bought for him. What he didn't do when he went out like this was take his own car. He always borrowed one of his buddies' cars. He didn't want anyone to see him in public with anyone, except Maddie. He knew there would be talk, but that had never bothered him.

Jake and Marilyn drank beer, ate popcorn, and watched the movie for about an hour before they got down to business. They climbed into the backseat. She was more than ready to give Jake what he wanted. In fact, she took the lead by taking off her cute plaid shirt by herself. She wasn't wearing a bra. Then she unbuttoned Jake's jeans, unzipped them, and grabbed him. Jake was used to forward girls, so he pulled his jeans down himself as she was pulling down his briefs to expose him. Then she unbuttoned her own cutoff jeans and pulled them down. She wasn't wearing any panties either. She'd never planned to. She knew what Jake wanted, and she wanted to be the one to give it to him.

Jake started kissing Marilyn's full breasts as she held them up to him. For some reason, a woman's breasts had always fascinated him. He enjoyed sucking on them one at a time. Marilyn had been ready for Jake for quite some time, so she lifted her legs and opened them wide for him and then took his hard cock into her hands and put it inside her. Jake and Marilyn started driving up and down in unison, and she whispered in his ear, "Fuck me, Jake. I want you."

Jake continued moving in and out of Marilyn faster and faster, until he finally slipped out of her at the last minute and came on her stomach. He wasn't about to take the chance of getting anyone pregnant, and he hadn't had time to put on the rubber he always brought with him on these occasions. Afterwards, he apologized to Marilyn for the mess he'd made, but she wasn't bothered by it in the least. In fact, she dipped her fingers into Jake's semen and put them into her mouth. That didn't surprise him either. It had happened to him a lot, ever since he lost his virginity at sixteen. Jake did take off his shirt and used his tee shirt to clean off Marilyn's tummy. Afterwards, they dressed themselves, climbed back into the front seat, and watched the rest of the movie as if nothing had happened. Jake did tell Marilyn to make sure that she took a good shower when he dropped her off back at her dorm.

"Call me," said Marilyn excitedly as she exited the car.

"Sure will," answered Jake, which was, of course, a lie. He never went out with the same girl like this twice.

Jake always felt guilty when he used a girl in this way. But for Jake sex was just that—sex. He never became emotionally involved with any of the girls he had sex with. In fact, he'd never even had a steady girlfriend until he met Maddie. Before Maddie came into his life, he dated lots of different girls, and they always willingly obliged his sexual needs.

When Jake returned to his own dorm that night, he took a long shower before he went to bed. Sleep should have come easily to him since his pent up sexual tension had been satisfied, but it didn't. He thought of Maddie. He would never have sex with Maddie in the backseat of a car—never. She was special. In fact, he would never have had just sex with Maddie at all. He'd make love to Maddie, and it would never be just a "quickie."

Whenever he thought of Madison before he went to sleep, especially after he had been on a date with someone else, his mind would automatically stir emotions in him that he'd never felt before. He had to admit to himself that he was in love with Madison Conrad. He would do anything for her, absolutely anything. However, before he'd fall asleep, his last thought would always be the same—she's spoken for.

13

In November, rumors were flying around West Point that Ryan's plebe class would be the first one in the history of the academy to be allowed to go home for Christmas.

When Ryan heard the rumor, he couldn't believe it. His first thought was to get into the nightly long phone lines to use the pay phones stashed in the basement and call Maddie. But, after thinking it over, he decided to wait. He didn't want to get her hopes up and then have them dashed when it didn't come true.

The rumor was confirmed on a Sunday evening while all the cadets were eating dinner. As soon as the announcement was made, all the plebes started cheering and clapping—something plebes would never have dared to do under any other circumstances.

As soon as dinner was over, Ryan ran to the phone lines and stood patiently for two hours to speak to Maddie.

Thank God she was home when the call came. She'd been working on a research paper that was due in a couple of weeks.

When the phone rang, Maddie answered it immediately.

"Maddie," yelled Ryan happily, "I get to come home for Christmas!"

"What? I can't believe it!" replied Maddie. "Are you sure?"

"Yes, it was announced at dinner tonight," answered an ecstatic Ryan.

"Oh my God, I'm really finally going to get to see you! I just can't believe it!" screamed Maddie.

"Can you stay with someone in Avalon over Christmas? Will your parents let you? Will they be upset if you don't go to New Mexico to be with them?" he asked, suddenly concerned that it might be a problem.

"I know they'll be disappointed, but they also know how much I want to see you. They know how lonely I've been without you, so I don't think they'll mind," said Maddie confidently.

"I can stay with Debbie in Avalon," continued Maddie. "She always wants me to come and visit her. I'll call her right after I call my parents and tell them the news," she said happily.

The two of them went on to discuss that Maddie would pick Ryan up in Oklahoma City and they would drive to Avalon together. But they also planned to spend one night together in Oklahoma City before leaving for Avalon. It had been six long months since they'd seen each other. Both of them were over the moon with excitement at the thought of being together again.

Maddie called her parents right after talking to Ryan. Yes, they were disappointed that she wouldn't be home for Christmas, but they were excited for her, too. They knew how much she wanted to see Ryan, and six months was a long time for two young people in love to be apart. They approved of her plan to stay with Debbie and said they would send her some money for Christmas this year instead of buying her presents.

After she talked to her parents and received their approval, Maddie called Debbie. Debbie was ecstatic that she would be spending Christmas with her. Debbie and her boyfriend had eloped right after high school. They owned a cute three-bedroom house in Avalon, so there was plenty of room for Maddie.

Maddie didn't get any sleep that night. She was just too excited. She told Betty, her roommate, about her plans, and Betty hugged her tightly and told her how happy she was for her. She didn't know if she would tell Jake, Matt, or Terri about her Christmas plans, though.

In the end, Maddie didn't tell her best friends of her plans for Christmas vacation. She let them believe she was going home to New Mexico. She'd always kept her relationship with Ryan mostly to herself. This was going to be their private time together. No one else needed to know about it.

Maddie didn't think Christmas vacation would ever come. Although she tried to keep busy, the days seemed to last forever to her.

Finally, the day came for her to drive to Oklahoma City. She had packed her car a day earlier. She also planned to arrive in Oklahoma City a day before Ryan, so she could do a little shopping before picking him up. She wanted to buy herself a couple of new outfits before seeing him. She hadn't seen him in what had seemed like a lifetime, so she wanted to look especially cute for him. She found wool slacks, cashmere turtlenecks, and a new blazer—simple but elegant. She also bought Ryan his Christmas present. She wanted to give him something he could actually use while at West Point. She ended up buying him a burgundy Montblanc pen. She hoped he'd think of her whenever he used it. He always would.

Maddie had already reserved two nights at the Hilton, so after her shopping spree, she checked in and ordered room service for dinner. She went to bed early that night, so she could be rested for the week ahead. This night she finally slept—she really was going to see Ryan tomorrow.

The next morning, she awakened early, had room service again for breakfast, and took extra care getting ready. She was going to pick Ryan up at the airport. His parents had paid for his ticket for his Christmas present, so he wouldn't have to waste time spending days on a train and bus. His real mom wasn't too happy he wouldn't be coming to Ohio at all during Christmas, but like Maddie's parents, she understood her son's need to see the girl he loved.

Maddie arrived at the airport early. This was one time that she didn't want to be late. She wanted to be there as he got off the plane. When he finally deplaned, dressed in his West Point uniform (it was cheaper to fly if he was in uniform), she ran up to him and put her arms around his neck, and they kissed for the first time in six months. Neither of them wanted to stop. It had been so long since Maddie had felt safe in his arms.

Ryan couldn't risk checking into a hotel in uniform, so as soon as they located his luggage, he went into the men's restroom and quickly changed into civilian clothes. He put on a pair of grey slacks, black loafers, a burgundy turtleneck sweater, and a black wool blazer. Of course, he very carefully repacked his uniform before he left the bathroom to rejoin the love of his life who was anxiously waiting for him outside.

As soon as they were in Maddie's car in the parking lot, they just grabbed one another again and started hugging and kissing. It had been too long for them to be apart. Finally, after a few minutes, they decided to get some lunch before going back to the Hilton.

The two young people talked nonstop over lunch. Maddie noticed immediately that Ryan had changed. He seemed more reserved to her. *Damn it,* thought Maddie, *West Point had already started to change him.* Thank God it didn't last.

Once they arrived at their room at the Hilton, the "real" Ryan, the one she'd always remembered, came back. The minute the door was locked behind them, Ryan dropped his suitcase and grabbed Maddie into his arms.

"God, it's so good to see you. It's been so long— too long, for me," said Ryan seriously.

"Ryan, I'm the happiest I've been since you left last summer. I was so afraid you wouldn't get to come home this Christmas," answered Maddie.

"Can you believe that the powers that be at West Point finally decided to let us plebes see our loved ones for Christmas for the first time ever?" remarked a still incredulous Ryan.

"Well, I won't get my hopes up, but maybe West Point will finally start adapting to the twentieth century like they should," replied Maddie seriously.

With that, they took off their blazers, and Ryan, holding Maddie's hand, led her to the bed that took up most of their room.

They lay together quietly next to each other for quite a while. Maddie just gazed at the man she loved with all of her heart and soul. She noticed through his clothes that he had changed some physically. He had lost weight, so his cheekbones were more pronounced. But he had the same soft brown eyes she'd always loved.

Ryan also gazed at Maddie. She was even more beautiful than he'd remembered. Her hair was longer, and her curls rolled automatically into perfect ringlets down her back. Her teal eyes seemed even more vibrant, too. He couldn't believe she still belonged to him. Although he kept it to himself, he'd been worried sick every day that he would lose her. After looking at her now, though, he realized she was still his.

Both Ryan and Maddie were nervous about being together physically. It had been six months since they'd even kissed each other. They both felt awkward, and neither of them wanted to take the next step for fear of appearing too forward.

Finally, though, Ryan rolled over on top of Maddie, put her face into his huge hands, and French kissed her passionately on the lips.

"God, I love you, Madison Conrad," declared Ryan desperately. "Are we still on for June 1968?"

"I love you, too, Ryan Richardson, and yes, 1968 can't come fast enough. I want to be your wife more than anything else in this world," replied Maddie seriously.

Once Ryan realized that Maddie still belonged to him, he finally relaxed. He very gently helped Maddie remove her sweater from over her head. Next, he undid her lacy bra and placed it beside her on the floor by her sweater. After that, he unzipped her slacks and slid them off her. Ryan stared down at her beautiful body lying underneath him, wearing just her lacy panties. He thought of all the lonely nights he'd spent at West Point imagining this very moment.

Maddie then somewhat timidly helped Ryan undress. She noticed immediately that he was in perfect physical condition. His arms and upper torso had expanded. She even teased him about becoming "Mr. Atlas." Ryan laughed and told her he didn't have much say in the way his body had changed—it was West Point's fault. So much marching, PT, and "Beast" couldn't help but change him.

"Speaking of 'Beast,'" said Maddie, "what was it like?"

"Like I wrote you in my letters, Maddie, it was eight weeks of hell on earth," replied Ryan immediately.

Ryan then explained a little more about Beast to Maddie. It was hot, humid, and buggy out in the field. They were shouted at constantly, as if they were all deaf, which annoyed Ryan. They learned the basics of being an infantry soldier. They learned how to make and break down camps, how to shoot, and eat the ever wonderful C-rations while in the field. They would only have about two hours once a week to memorize what they called their "Plebe Poop," shine their brass, polish their boots, or, if they were really lucky, write a short letter home. Beast was the basic training that any inductee into the Army had to go through; however, it was more difficult at West Point since they were supposed to be the "chosen ones." Therefore, they were expected to do everything much better than the average soldier.

"Do I even want to ask what 'Plebe Poop' is?" asked Maddie.

"Nope," answered Ryan, "unless you want to laugh all day and not fool around."

"I'll pass then." And Maddie rolled over on top of Ryan.

One night, during Christmas break, after having the only type of sex they could until they were married, Maddie told Ryan about her idea for making money while in college. She was going to ask Terri if she would be interested in opening a dance and cheerleading school. The town didn't have one, and maybe they needed one. She asked him what he thought of her idea.

She was impressed by all of the pertinent questions Ryan asked about it. He wanted to know what kind of partnership they would have. He told her to make sure it was an LLC. He asked her who would teach what classes and if she knew what the overhead would be, etc. Ultimately, though, he thought it would be a good idea. Maddie was excited that he encouraged her project.

Maddie and Ryan had one glorious week together over Christmas, even though Ryan had to return to his house each night by midnight. Both of them had needed this quality time together to cement their relationship. It was difficult being so far apart. But by the time the week was over, there was no question that Maddie and Ryan were going to be married as planned.

After Maddie took Ryan back to Oklahoma City to catch his plane for New York, she cried all the way back to school. She didn't know when she'd get to see him again, and that upset her more than anything else. But once she arrived at her dorm, she relaxed a little and started making plans to start her new business venture. If nothing else, this would help keep her mind off Ryan.

14

After being with Maddie over Christmas, Ryan found it almost impossible to concentrate once he returned to school. He kept remembering the days and nights they were together. Sometimes, he just wanted to pack up his things and leave, but he knew he couldn't. He would embarrass not only himself, but also, more importantly, his father. It took several weeks for Ryan to get his thoughts under control. He wondered if Maddie was having this same problem.

The second semester of his plebe year, he took eight classes. In addition to the ones he took the first semester, he was assigned Intro to Solid Analytic Geometry, Integral Calculus, Foundations in PE, and Map Reading. Great, now he had two math classes—six days a week. He only hoped he could survive the math classes again.

When Ryan heard that Maddie wouldn't be coming to visit him during spring break, he was devastated. She chose not to come because plebes couldn't leave the post, so Maddie couldn't see the point. It was a lot of money for her just to have Ryan walk her around West Point daily and go on "flirtation walk" with him. Other than kissing, there wasn't much privacy for anything else. After such a glorious Christmas vacation, Maddie thought it would be a downer.

While Ryan was worrying about surviving two math classes, Maddie decided to seriously consider starting her idea for a new business venture. Maddie's first step now was to talk to Terri about her idea for a dance and cheerleading studio in Wilmington. She made a lunch date with her immediately. Maddie approached the subject with Terri, who'd become her best friend, over a Caesar salad at the local diner. She asked what Terri thought about opening a dance and cheerleading school. At first, Terri was shocked, but after Maddie explained the details, she became much more interested, even excited.

After lunch, Maddie took Terri to a vacant building that she'd found and thought would be suitable for their needs. All they'd really need to add were walls of mirrors, a bar, mats, and tumbling equipment.

Maddie, Terri, and Matt met for dinner that night and discussed the financing for the proposed venture. Maddie suggested that she put in fifty-two percent of the cash needed and Terri and Matt each put in twenty-four percent. That way, Maddie, who had the knowledge needed for the venture, would have the overriding control of the operation. Maddie had saved much of the money she'd earned teaching dance in Avalon for four years, and she had a full scholarship, so money was not an issue for her. Her father had even offered to help with the financing and would sign the lease for the building himself. Terri and Matt said that they'd talk it over and let her know in the morning, but it sounded like a good business idea to them.

"It's a go!" shouted Terri the next morning.

That afternoon, after their last class, Maddie and Terri had an appointment with the owner of the building that Maddie had found to explore the possibility of leasing it. Of course, their ultimate goal was to get the property as cheaply as possible, and, after much haggling, they came to an agreement.

The next step was to go to the small glass and mirror shop in town. Maddie had already taken the measurements needed for the mirrors. Mike, the owner, said he could have them ready and installed in two and a half weeks. They were on their way! They were giddy with excitement as they left the small shop.

Next, they went to a woodworking establishment. Maddie explained what kind of bars she needed made. They made an appointment to meet the carpenter at the building, so he could measure and decide how many brackets he would need to make the bars sturdy.

In the following weeks, whenever Maddie and Terri weren't in class, they were together ordering mats, harnesses for flips, and a sign for the building. They decided to name their company MTM (Maddie, Terri, Matt) Dance and Cheerleading School. Maddie even found a place in Oklahoma City, where dancing attire, ballet shoes, and pointe shoes could be ordered and shipped overnight.

Maddie and Terri started to advertise the school's opening in the *Wilmington Star* newspaper and other small-town papers close to Wilmington, and spent the rest of their free time at the studio overseeing the progress of the renovations.

The school opened at the end of February in 1965. Maddie and Terri had been amazed at the interest generated for the school. In fact, they were able to form classes and begin the lessons immediately. The ballet and tap classes were divided into age groups. Maddie would only allow fifteen students in each of the classes. This was true for the cheerleading classes as well. Maddie and Terri decided the tumbling classes needed to be smaller. Classes would be taught after school, in the evenings, and on Saturdays in order to keep up with the demand. Maddie would teach the ballet and tap, and Terri would teach the jazz, but they would both teach the tumbling and cheerleading classes.

To Maddie, Terri, and Matt's amazement, the school became an overnight success! The town and its surrounding areas had needed this sort of school. The money just seemed to start pouring in. However, for Maddie, even though the money was great, she'd needed this outlet for her own well-being; she always had. She loved teaching the art form she loved so much. By the end of their freshman year, the company was going strong.

Since Maddie now had a responsibility to her business which required her to stay in town during the upcoming summer, she decided she needed to move out of her dorm and try to find a small place of her own off-campus. However, Maddie had to talk to the administration to get permission to do this. Because she was on a full scholarship and had perfect grades, they agreed to pay the rent on the house that she found if it wasn't too expensive, but everything else would be Maddie's responsibility. This seemed more than fair to Maddie. In fact, she was surprised, and very grateful, that they agreed to pay her rent. She certainly hadn't expected them to be so generous.

After looking at several houses, she found the perfect little one-bedroom house on Seventh Street. It reminded her of a small English cottage, and she planned to make it one. It was on a quiet, tree-lined side street not too far from school or the studio. Besides, the rent was cheap, because most people wanted two-bedroom houses.

She took her best friends to see it, and, of course, they thought the house would suit her perfectly. In fact, Jake and Matt did lots of painting for Maddie that summer, while she and Terri taught classes and went treasure hunting on the weekends.

Maddie moved into her new home in July. She'd already purchased a comfy floral slipcovered sofa and chair and ottoman, and had been able to pick up the rest of stuff at yard sales. She found a great old weathered kitchen table and found four ladder back chairs, all different colors, to go with it. She found an iron double bed and bought a new mattress for it. She also purchased other necessities, such as silverware, plates, glasses, etc., at the local TG&Y store in town. Maddie loved decorating her place and picking up treasures she and Terri had found at garage sales and flea markets.

What she ended up with was the English cottage that she had pictured in her mind for many years. She loved this house. She felt comfortable, free, and at home in it. Maddie even started a small English garden in her backyard—just a bunch of varied flowers in all shapes, sizes, and colors. She found a great deal of pleasure "watching her flower garden grow." She put a small iron table and two chairs on the used brick patio that Jake and Matt had built for her in the back, and in the evenings, she would enjoy sitting and sipping her iced tea, even in the dark. Sitting outside, looking at the moon and stars always had a calming effect on Maddie. For her, summer that year went by entirely too fast.

Of course, Ryan was always on her mind. She continued to write at least every other day and tell him about the progress she was making at school and with the business. He was excited that her venture was so successful. He also said he wanted to see her English cottage, so she took pictures and sent them to him while he was busy studying and doing whatever the hell it was he was doing at West Point.

He had told her that he would visit her in August when he had a month off. But this never happened, and Maddie would never forget it.

The summer after his plebe year, Ryan spent eight weeks at Camp Buckner. It was around seven miles from West Point. This was the summer when Ryan really learned what being an infantryman in the Army was all about. It was West Point's version of Advanced Infantry Training.

During those mosquito-infested, hot, humid weeks, he learned all about warfare and survival skills. He learned rock climbing and rappelling, hand-to-hand combat and hand grenades. He survived the gas mask exercise and especially enjoyed the Special Forces orientation and demonstrations. The cadets learned how to shoot machine guns, lob mortars, determine azimuths, and calculate adjustments as well.

The squads and platoons would learn camouflage, ambush, as well as attack and defensive techniques. But what they were really doing was having their first lessons on how to survive in Vietnam.

One of the exercises that Ryan enjoyed the most was the one with helicopters. He'd always been fascinated with them even when he was a kid. He didn't know it then, but one day, one of those helicopters would save not only his life, but also those of his men.

At the end of Camp Buckner, the cadets participated in the Buckner Stakes right before "Illumination Weekend." It was four days of competition designed to "illuminate" their accomplishments after summer training. Ryan was really disappointed that Maddie chose not to attend. He'd wanted to show her off to his friends, but she felt that she needed to go home and see her parents before school started once again. She hadn't seen them at Christmas, so she felt she had no choice but to go. However, this was a very special weekend for Ryan, and if he'd told her how much it meant to him, she'd have gone—but he didn't. There was competition in all kinds of sporting events, such as canoe races, swimming, military events, and the one he was most proud of all—sailing. In a field of eight, Ryan had won! At the end of the four days, there was a formal dinner and dance where Ryan had wanted to show off "his Maddie" to everyone. He tried to enjoy himself even though he was alone, but it didn't work. He saw lots of cadets with their girlfriends, but Maddie had not visited West Point once yet. His friends were beginning to wonder if she even really existed.

When Ryan's yearling year started—*What a stupid name for sophomore*, thought Maddie—he became an assistant squad leader responsible for a new set of plebes. It was his job to indoctrinate the new clan of would-be young warriors into the ways of West Point. He didn't enjoy all the harassment he'd endured, so when he was no longer a plebe, he decided that he would be better than that. If one of his plebes did something incorrectly, he corrected them and made them do it right. This sometimes took time, but at least he was not demeaning to his men. His cadets, though green, were happy that he didn't act the way some of the other squad leaders and yearlings did. They appreciated the fact that their squad leader had standards, and those standards didn't include hazing.

As a yearling, Ryan's class schedule was once again eight classes. At least, he had a little more flexibility in his schedule. He took History of Europe and America, Fundamentals of Military Science, General Chemistry, and Physics I, along with his other dreaded six-days a week math classes. It was these other classes, though, that kept him sane. He was really wondering why this much math was so important in the grand scheme of things. He would never find out. Even though he didn't know it yet, all the math in the world would be of no use to him when he was in Vietnam.

Yearlings were also allowed off post one weekend each semester. However, West Point's idea of a weekend was from 12:30 PM on Saturday (after classes) until 6:00 PM on Sunday evening. They were also allowed to go to the movies, on post, on Friday nights.

Maddie did come to visit in the fall for one of the dances or "hops," as they were called at West Point. Finally, Ryan was proud to introduce her to his classmates who, of course, had heard so much about her. She definitely didn't disappoint them. In fact, they wondered how Ryan could have caught such a gorgeous and intelligent young woman. But even more than that, they wondered if he'd be able to keep her since he didn't see her very often. She was the kind of girl that all the boys would be after. Maddie enjoyed having Ryan show her around the famous institution, but she was not nearly as enthralled with it as Ryan. To her, it was just a bunch of beautiful grey buildings with a great deal of history. Even though she never said it to Ryan, she felt it was the last place on earth she'd want to go to school. In fact, it seemed to her that the longer Ryan was there, the longer it took to get the "real" Ryan to reemerge. She wondered if by the time it was over, the "real" Ryan would be lost to her forever. And that depressed her.

At least Maddie and Ryan would be together for Christmas again this year. That's what really kept Ryan going—the thought of being with Maddie again.

During Ryan's yearling year, he finally had his first date. Her name was Clara, and she was a nice-looking young woman from Highland Falls attending Vassar College. They went out to dinner on his off weekend. Clara was nice and intelligent, but she was definitely not in Maddie's league.

One Friday night, Ryan invited Clara to come to the West Point Library to study with him. While they were sitting across from one another studying, a cadet guard asked him if he was "escorting." For that infraction, he received a "slug" or eight demerits. This meant eight hours of walking the area. He didn't see Clara again. It wasn't worth it. Maddie would have been.

He also had a date with a cheerleader after a football game and received a demerit for walking with a young woman whose skirt was too short. Of course, Maddie laughed at that one when she read about Ryan's ill-fated dates. What did they think cheerleaders should wear, skirts down to their ankles? It'd be pretty hard to do flips or Herkies wearing a long skirt. She could just picture Ryan trying to explain the logic to the "Brass."

Her answer to him was, "See, it's not worth it to go out on me, huh?" But she didn't seem to mind or be upset that he'd had a couple of dates. He wished she had.

Unlike Ryan's regimented schedule, Maddie's sophomore year really began with a huge bang. She was still a cheerleader, still seeing Jake, still studying and still teaching at the studio. In fact, when Terri told her that she and Maddie had just been nominated for homecoming queen, she was in shock. She was so busy that she hadn't even been keeping up with student life like she always had before. She guessed it had to have been Jake who nominated her, because the football team did the nominations. She was excited that Terri had been nominated, too. Maddie and Terri discussed their nominations during a break in classes at their school. They even toasted each other over a glass of iced tea.

"Can you believe it?" Terri asked excitedly. "This means we have to get outfits and have our pictures made. Maybe we could go to Oklahoma City and find our outfits together," she suggested. "We deserve a break, Maddie. It'd be good for us to get away," she added.

"We'd have a great time!" exclaimed Maddie. "Of course we can go. You're right; we need it and deserve a short break. We've been working our butts off to make this place profitable. Besides, we should feel honored just to be nominated."

Maddie told Terri that she'd call her mom and dad immediately and let them know. She knew they'd want to drive up even though it was a long trip. She also picked up the phone right then and made motel arrangements for them for the long weekend.

"When shall we go to OKC?" asked Terri.

"Well, let's see. How about this coming weekend? We can cancel our Friday and Saturday classes, go Thursday night, and be back in time for the game on Saturday night. What do you think?"

"It's a date," said Terri.

That Thursday, around 8:00 PM, Maddie and Terri drove to Oklahoma City. Jake had insisted that Maddie take his car for the trip. He thought it would be more reliable than hers. He had a great-looking 1965 red Mustang. The two best friends chattered nonstop all the way to OKC. They checked into the Hilton, ate at Johnnie's, and spent the rest of the night talking.

Terri told Maddie how much she was in love with Matt. Maddie agreed that he was a good catch, and she especially liked the way he treated her. She thought they made a great pair. The subject of Ryan and Jake came up, too. Terri already knew a great deal about Ryan from their previous talks, but she wanted to know what he was like when he didn't have to be the perfect cadet. Maddie told her about when he was in high school—kind of shy, hadn't dated until they met, was really smart, and definitely a Type A personality. Everything had to be perfect. And since attending West Point, this had only increased, and she wasn't sure she liked it. It always took him a while to come back to the real world whenever they first saw each other after being apart. She just worried that someday the "real" Ryan wouldn't come back. That was the first time Terri had ever heard her best friend say anything remotely negative about Ryan, and it startled her.

They also talked about Jake. Terri knew how fond Maddie was of him, but she also knew that Maddie didn't recognize that Jake was in love with her. To Maddie, they were just best friends. Matt had told Terri that he knew Jake had never tried anything with Maddie besides a kiss on the cheek or a big bear hug. Terri also knew why. Maddie would have stopped seeing him immediately. She'd never been close to anyone except

Ryan. Terri didn't ask her, but she did wonder what level of intimacy she and Ryan had. Maddie would never speak about it. She did ask Maddie if it bothered her that Jake saw other girls sometimes. Maddie's answer was an immediate "no." She knew why Jake saw those girls—he'd told her. Terri was surprised that Jake had been so open with Maddie about it. Maddie didn't like his going out with other girls just for sex, but there was nothing she could do about it. It seemed to Maddie that everyone wanted to be sure to make it a point to tell her whenever he did. But Terri knew that Jake and Maddie had a special relationship, and the longer it went on, the closer they'd become. Of course, Terri had never met Ryan, but she felt Jake was the best catch in the entire world for Maddie. They seemed so at ease with each other—so together. She wondered if Maddie and Ryan had the same kind of togetherness. In her heart of hearts, she wished that Maddie would choose Jake over Ryan, even though she'd never say that to Maddie in a million years. After talking for a couple of hours, they both fell into a deep sleep.

The next morning, the girls ordered room service and then readied themselves to spend the next two days doing nothing but shopping, eating, talking, and having a good time. They visited Shepherd Mall, Brown's, Rothschild's, and Street's—all popular shopping stores in Oklahoma City.

The two friends found outfits for the parade, pictures, and the homecoming dance. Maddie chose a dark purple suit with an off-white ruffled silk blouse, while Terri found a beautiful blue sheath dress and jacket that matched the exact color of her eyes. For the dance, Maddie chose a teal chiffon dress, while Terri chose a sexy little cherry red number. They also were able to buy accessories for their outfits and even found time to catch a movie while they were there.

They arrived back in Wilmington with plenty of time to get ready for Saturday night's football game.

Their team won again; they were having a great season. Afterwards, the four friends double dated as usual. Both Terri and Maddie were curious to know who had nominated them for homecoming queen.

"That's a no-brainer." Matt laughed while Jake just smiled.

15

T he weeks leading up to homecoming were filled with classes, midterms, and the dance school, just to mention a few. Terri and Maddie had even found a little time to help work on the sophomore float. Thank God, Maddie still found enough quiet time at home to study. Once again she made a 4.0.

Maddie's parents arrived in Wilmington on the Friday afternoon before homecoming Saturday. They immediately called Maddie. Maddie answered the phone on the first ring and gave them directions to her house. She was excitedly waiting outside and waving to them as they drove up.

As her parents exited the car, Maddie was shocked to see a very frail woman get out. Was this her mother? It couldn't be. Maddie had never seen such a dramatic change in one person in such a short period of time. What was going on? She decided, however, to put on a huge smile and wait until she could talk to her dad alone to find out the problem.

"Hi, Mom! Hi, Dad! Geeze, it's so good to see you. You have no idea how much I've missed you guys."

She took her parents' hands and walked them up the used brick pathway that Jake had put in for her last summer.

"Welcome to Casa Conrad," beamed Maddie as she opened the front door for them.

"Oh, Maddie, this place is adorable, just lovely," declared her mom immediately. "The perfect English cottage like you've always wanted since we lived in Cambridge all those years ago. Show me around right now!"

After Maddie gave her folks the short tour, they sat down in the living room, drank some coffee, and visited for a while. Maddie needed to explain the weekend's activities to them.

Saturday morning at 9:00 AM, there would be a big parade down Main Street. All the homecoming queen candidates would ride in convertibles. There would be floats, three marching bands, and a slew of club banners. It would probably take around two hours.

Then, that afternoon at 2:00 PM, the football game would begin. She'd already written down directions for them on how to get there. At half time, the festivities would begin again, culminating with the crowning of the queen and king. After that, she would be able to sit in the stands with them and watch the second half of the game.

She went on to tell her parents that after the game, she'd invited Terri, Matt, and Jake over for a spaghetti dinner. She wanted her parents to meet her best friends. Once dinner was over, the foursome planned to go together to the homecoming dance.

"Honey, why don't we all just go out to dinner? You don't need to be cooking with everything else that's going on," said her mom.

"Mom, everything's ready. We're just having salad, spaghetti, and garlic bread. Besides, all the restaurants around here will be full. Really, it's no big deal," declared Maddie.

"Okay, but we'll get everything ready for dinner while you're getting ready for the dance," said her mom.

"That'll be great," said Maddie. She knew better than to protest and really appreciated their offer to help.

Maddie then had her parents follow her to the motel where they would be staying for the weekend. They ordered pizza for dinner and sat and talked until around 10:00 PM when Maddie noticed that both of her parents, especially her mom, looked tired. Before she left, Maddie told her parents, who were early risers, the best place to go for breakfast, the best place to stand to watch the parade, and what time to be there. Then she kissed and hugged them both tightly before saying good night.

Maddie found it difficult to sleep that night. She was not only worried about her mom, but, yes, she was also excited about the next day, too. Since she couldn't sleep, she got up, cleaned her house, set the table for the spaghetti dinner, and made sure her clothes and accessories were ready and set aside for the next day. *Sometimes I can be just as anal as Ryan,* thought Maddie. After that, she finally fell asleep for a couple of hours before her alarm went off.

Maddie could tell, the minute she looked outside that Saturday was going to be a beautiful fall day— sunny, and thank God, not windy. She called Terri and reminded her she'd pick her up at 8:00 AM. Then she proceeded to have her usual coffee and toast and showered. Of course, she took much longer than usual on her long, curly hair and makeup.

After she put on her purple suit and heels, she took a good long look at herself in the full-length mirror mounted on the bathroom door. She was pleased at what stared back at her. But something was missing. She'd forgotten to put on the diamond earrings and the heart necklace that Ryan had given her as Christmas presents long ago. She immediately put them on and then looked once again in the mirror. That was better. Then she hurriedly grabbed her keys and was out the door, headed for Terri's dorm.

Maddie pulled her car up by Terri's first-floor window and honked.

"Just a minute!" yelled Terri. "I'm on my way."

Maddie couldn't believe that Terri was ready on time. She was never ready on time. *She probably couldn't sleep last night either,* thought Maddie. The two friends talked non-stop as they drove to where the parade was set to begin. They hoped to see Matt and Jake before it began. The football team was also in the parade.

After they parked Maddie's car, the girls saw they were in luck. The football team was gathering across the street from the floats. They spotted Matt and Jake standing off to one side.

Maddie and Terri decided they were probably upset because they had to get up so early on a Saturday morning. Both girls walked quietly up behind the young men, covered their eyes, and shouted, "Guess who?" in unison.

"Well, Matt," said Jake, "I don't know about you, but those voices sound familiar to me."

When Matt and Jake turned around, they saw, standing before them, two absolutely gorgeous young women, smiling from ear to ear and dressed like they'd never seen them dressed before.

"Wow!" was all that came out of Matt's and Jake's mouths.

"We just wanted to say hi before all the hullabaloo starts for the day," said Maddie. "If we don't see you again before the game, don't forget dinner is at my place at six o'clock tonight. And don't be late."

"Got it," said Matt and Jake together as they saluted and then bowed to the two girls. They then proceeded to kiss each of the girls on their cheeks and wished each of them good luck.

"Thanks, guys," replied the girls. Hey, win the game for us!"

"We'll try," shouted Matt and Jake as the girls ran to their convertibles and climbed aboard to wait for the parade to begin.

During the parade, Maddie found her parents exactly where she'd told them to stand, and she waved happily at them while her dad was taking pictures with his old box camera. Seeing her mother again, looking so frail and small, really concerned Maddie. She decided that as soon as the half-time festivities were over, and she was sitting with them in the stands, she was going to make it a point to ask her dad what was wrong with her mom.

The homecoming game started precisely at 2:00 PM, and as soon as the whistle blew, signaling the end of the first half of the football game, the homecoming ceremonies started. The home football team went as a group down to the north end zone, while the opposing team headed for the locker room. The band performed its half-time routine first. Then the floats went around the track. Of course, the senior float won—they'd only had four years to get it right! Next came the banners from all of the clubs, fraternities, and sororities on campus. This time, the Sigma Tau fraternity won the contest. Terri was especially excited since Matt was a Sig Tau.

The final phase of the ceremonies was the crowning of the homecoming queen and king. The entire student body had spent the last week voting for their favorite candidate for queen, while the king was always selected by the members of the football team. The queen candidates rode around the track perched on the back of their convertibles and stopped right at the fifty-yard line. At that time, the football players who had been nominated for king escorted the girls to the stand where the announcement would be made.

Maddie was very surprised to see Jake there to help her out of the car and onto the stage. Matt was also escorting Terri. The girls couldn't believe the guys hadn't told them what was going on. Once everyone was on the stage, the announcement was made. This year's homecoming queen and king were Madison Conrad and Jake Kelly. Maddie was so surprised she didn't know what to do, but Jake did.

Jake took Maddie's hand and brought her to the front of the stage. He then proceeded to hand her a dozen long-stemmed red roses before very carefully putting the rhinestone crown on her head. After that, he gave her a kiss. Not a kiss on the cheek—a real honest-to-God kiss. Maddie was stunned, and, for an instant, shock radiated from her face as she looked at Jake. At this precise moment, Maddie's dad was able to capture the best picture of the day. He knew that Maddie wasn't shocked from being crowned queen. She was shocked by the kiss that Jake had just given her.

"Congratulations, Madison," Jake whispered in her ear. "I knew you'd win." Jake then escorted her back to the convertible and got into it with her. The car drove one last time around the track, with Maddie and Jake waving as everyone cheered.

"Gotta go," said Jake. "See you tonight!" he shouted at he ran back to his team.

It didn't take Maddie long to make it back to the stands to be with her mother and father. Of course, everyone was congratulating her along the way, so she shook a lot of hands and said thank you.

Maddie enjoyed sitting in the stands with her parents. She gave her mom her roses and kissed her on the cheek while her dad took yet another picture. Maddie had been a cheerleader for six years, and this was the first time that she could really watch a game.

She was especially happy to get to watch Jake play. He was a senior now, so this would be his last season as the quarterback of the team. He would turn the team over to Matt soon. Instead of asking her father about her mother as she had planned, she decided to wait until she had a better opportunity. Now wasn't the time.

After the team won the game handily, everyone left the stadium in search of food and to get ready for the homecoming dance that evening. That included Maddie and her parents as well. They went directly back to her house so she could get ready for her dinner party.

"Maddie," said her mom, "go take a shower and redo your hair and makeup. Your father and I will get everything ready for dinner. All we have to do right now is make the salad and heat up your sauce. So don't worry about a thing."

Maddie did as she was told. She was so glad her parents were with her on this special occasion. The only one missing was Ryan. Unfortunately, Maddie knew there would probably be lots of special occasions during her college career that Ryan wouldn't be a part of, and that saddened her. She was right.

After Maddie had showered and done her hair and makeup, she came out with just her robe wrapped around her. She didn't want to ruin her dress while getting things ready for the dinner party. She shouldn't have worried. Her parents had everything totally under control. In fact, Maddie noticed that her mom was wearing the apron that Maddie had made for her as a child in England.

"Hey, Mom, how do you like the apron? I sneaked it out of the house with me the last time I was home. I thought it would fit perfectly here."

"I've been looking for this everywhere," replied her mom." "In fact, I tore the house apart looking for it. You know how much it means to me, but you're right. It really fits here; I'm giving it back to you, only for a while. Don't lose it."

Since everything was almost ready for dinner, Maddie and her folks had some time to go sit in her backyard and have some iced tea. Maddie told them how well the dance studio was going and that she'd take them to see it tomorrow morning after breakfast. They knew she loved dancing more than anything in the world and were really proud of her accomplishment. Her dad told her she was becoming quite the businesswoman. They even talked a little about Ryan. They wanted to know how he was doing at West Point. Maddie merely said things were fine between them, but her parents knew better. It wasn't like her not to chatter constantly about him.

About 5:45 PM, Maddie went to get dressed for the evening while her parents put the finishing touches on their dinner. When Maddie emerged about ten minutes later, her parents couldn't believe what a beautiful daughter they had. The teal dress she was wearing matched her eyes perfectly and made them come alive.

Jake thought exactly the same thing a couple of minutes later when he knocked on the door, with Matt and Terri in tow.

Jake kissed her on the cheek, told her she looked beautiful, and handed her a bouquet of multicolored flowers. He had also brought two bottles of wine for dinner to celebrate the occasion.

Maddie proceeded to introduce everyone to her parents, and while she was busy putting the flowers in a vase and setting it on the small old trunk that served as her coffee table, everyone was able to sit around and get acquainted. Before she sat down, she poured wine for everyone so they could celebrate.

Dinner was a complete success. Everything had been perfect—thanks to her mom and dad. They all had a lively conversation throughout the entire dinner, which made Maddie happy. She wanted her parents to like her friends. They did.

"You guys need to get going to the dance," said Maddie's mom. "Don't worry; we'll clean up before we leave."

"Thanks, Mom," said Maddie sincerely.

She picked up her bright yellow and teal shawl and threw it over her shoulders. It was just the right touch to make her look even more amazing, and made her dark auburn hair look spectacular.

Once the four of them were on their way to the dance, Maddie's dad made an observation. He told his wife that he thought Jake was in love with Maddie. He could tell by the way he looked at her. His wife agreed. But they didn't think that Maddie could tell. She was still too involved with Ryan to realize it.

When the four of them finally made it to the homecoming dance, they had a fabulous time. The guys weren't crazy about fast dancing but did it to make their girlfriends happy. After all, their girlfriends were dancers. The slow dances were a much different story. Jake enjoyed holding Maddie in his arms. She always seemed light as a feather to him. Until tonight, they always danced in the "proper" manner. For some reason, tonight was different. Maddie proceeded to put her arms around Jake's neck. He had no idea about the sudden change, but he certainly wasn't going to argue about it, so he put his arms around her tiny waist.

Maddie looked straight into his eyes and said, "Jake, thank you for the most marvelous day of my life. I'm so glad that we were both crowned together. It means a great deal to me. In fact, it only seemed natural to me that we be together. Also, thanks for being so kind to my parents. I can tell that they like you very much." She then put her head on his shoulder.

Jake felt as if he had just won a million dollars. Maddie really had no idea how much he loved her, and that was okay with him. But he did feel the need to respond to what she'd just said.

"Maddie, you never have to thank me for doing anything. You know how much I love your company, and you're the only person I've ever brought to this dance, just like last year. I'm proud to be your escort."

"Jake, you've always been much more than just an escort to me; you know that. You've become my best and dearest friend, and I'm not sorry in the least that all the other girls here at school are jealous of me. I know you'll always protect me, no matter what. But I want you to promise me that next year, even though you've graduated, you'll be my date again."

"You can count on it," whispered Jake in her ear as he kissed her on her cheek. "Let's find Matt and Terri and get out of here. I have a surprise for the four of us."

Jake and Maddie collected Matt and Terri off the dance floor and they headed for Jake's car.

"What's going on?" said Terri.

"Jake has a surprise for us," replied Maddie. "And, no, I don't know what it is."

Jake drove the four of them out to the farm. He then had Matt help him get some items out of the trunk of the Mustang. He'd planned a picnic for the four of them in the moonlight.

"What a wonderful surprise," said Maddie as she helped set the food on the old picnic table they always had on the property.

"Wow, Maddie! He's a keeper," said Terri seriously.

"Yes, I know," replied Maddie softly.

Jake couldn't believe his ears. Had she really just said that, or was he just hoping he'd heard it? Nope, she'd actually said it. Maybe, somewhere deep inside, he did have a chance with her after all.

Matt and Terri decided to go for a walk in the moonlight for a few minutes, but Jake insisted that they take the flashlight with them so they wouldn't step in any doo doo. After all, it was a farm.

While Matt and Terri were off on their walk, Maddie and Jake went into the barn to see Joy. Maddie loved this filly so much, and Jake had taught her how to ride her, cool her down, brush her, and clean out her stall. She'd come out here quite often to ride Joy or just take her for long walks, especially when she needed a calming influence. Tonight, though, they just fed her with her favorite carrots while they talked.

"Guess what?" said Jake excitedly.

"What?"

"I think Matt's going to ask Terri to marry him— maybe even tonight," replied Jake.

"Oh, my God! How do you know?"

Jake told her that Matt had told him he'd been thinking about it for a while now. He'd even bought her a ring. Perhaps he'd give it to her tonight. Even though he would only be a junior next year, his parents would help them out if that's what he wanted. They loved Terri and thought it a good match.

Do you think she'll accept?" asked Jake.

"I know she will," answered Maddie instantly. "She's head over heels in love with Matt."

"Well, we may know soon enough," said Jake. "Here they come."

Maddie could tell immediately by the expression on Terri's face that Matt had popped the question. She ran up to her and gave her a huge hug, while Terri flashed her brilliant solitaire ring for her to see.

"Congratulations, you guys!" screamed Maddie. "I'm so excited for you both."

Jake shook Matt's hand and gave Terri a kiss. Then he proceeded to open the bottle of champagne he'd brought just in case they could toast.

"Of course, Maddie, you must promise to be my maid of honor. And, Jake, you're absolutely going to be our best man!" yelled Terri happily.

"Of course we will," replied Maddie and Jake in unison.

"When's it going to be?" asked Jake.

"Well, we've decided to have a small wedding right here in Wilmington in late August of 1967," replied Matt. "Then, after a short honeymoon, Terri and Maddie can keep the income flowing in from the dance studio."

Maddie beamed as she said, "This has absolutely been the best day of my life, ever!"

The only thing that could have made this day even more perfect, thought Jake, *was if he and Maddie were getting married, too. Be patient.*

The rest of the evening was spent eating their picnic dinner and planning a wedding.

16

T he next morning, Maddie met her parents for an early breakfast before their long trip back to New Mexico. Then they went to see Maddie's studio before heading home. Her parents were quite impressed that their daughter had become quite the business-woman. When Maddie's mom asked to use the restroom one more time before heading home, Maddie asked her dad what was wrong with her. Her father explained that her mother had been losing weight because she had no appetite. And, yes, she'd been to the doctor. At one time, the doctors thought that perhaps she had leukemia, but fortunately they were wrong. At this point, her doctor didn't know what was wrong with her. They had given her too many tests to count, and her mom was just tired of being poked and prodded.

"Your mom will be fine, Maddie," her father reassured her. "We'll find out what's wrong, and as soon as we know, you'll know. I promise."

That Sunday afternoon, after her parents left, Maddie sat down to write Ryan a long letter. She went outside to her backyard to sit with her glass of iced tea and write. She told Ryan everything that had happened over the weekend, with one exception; she didn't tell him that Jake had been named homecoming king. He already knew she'd been nominated for homecoming queen, but now she was able to tell him she'd won. She told him about the entire day from beginning to end. She also told him she was worried about her mother who looked so frail, and that she'd noticed an uncertain look in her eyes. After she was finished, she signed the long letter with the usual YKTA, put a stamp on it, and actually walked to the post office box down the street and put it in.

A week later, Ryan called again to congratulate her.

"Hi, gorgeous. YKTA. I knew you'd win, Maddie. You're just too pretty and nice not to," said Ryan happily. "I'm so proud of you and everything you're doing. I don't know how you handle all the things you've got going on."

"Thanks, honey, and YKTA to you, too," replied Maddie happily. "I guess it's our Type A personalities. I'm like you; have to be organized," continued Maddie.

"How's your mom?" asked Ryan seriously.

Maddie told him she was really worried. Her mom didn't complain at all about not feeling well, but she didn't have the vitality she used to. Her eyes seemed tired to Maddie.

"Honey, try not to worry. There's nothing you can do. If I've learned anything from being here at WP, it's that sometimes you have no control over what happens."

"Speaking of West Point," said Maddie, trying to change the subject, "are things any better this year?"

"A lot," replied Ryan.

"Are you still happy you're there?" asked Maddie.

"For the most part, yes. There is so much history here, and the mystique is palpable. I get tired of all the marching and not having much time to myself, though. I don't think I'll ever get used to being told what to do every minute of the day. I hate room check. It's amazing how everything has to be just so. I think when I graduate, I'm going to rebel and throw my clothes anywhere I want. But the worst part for me is not seeing you. I miss you more than you'll ever know. I find myself thinking about you at the oddest moments. I could be in the library studying, and all of a sudden, I just put my head down. I want to cry, but of course a cadet doesn't do that. He just carries on. Sometimes I get tired of just carrying on, and I have to retreat into my own little world for a while and think about us. Are we still on for June 1968?"

"Of course we are. Nothing will change that. You have no idea how glad I'll be when our college years are over. All I want is to be your wife, Ryan," replied Maddie earnestly. "I just want to be Mrs. Ryan Richardson."

"Lieutenant and Mrs. Ryan Richardson," corrected Ryan. "I like the sound of that, Maddie. Gotta go—others are clamoring to use the phone," he said hurriedly. "YKTA."

"YKTA," replied a contented Maddie.

Just a few more years, thought Maddie to herself after she hung up the phone, but those years always seemed like light-years away. At least she would see him soon. Christmas was coming, and this year he would be home again. Thank God. They had not had much physical contact since last Christmas. *That's putting it mildly,* thought Maddie. Well, they certainly had time to make up for.

She tried to put Ryan out of her mind, but every time they talked, it was harder and harder to do. She turned her attention to her studies instead. She was minoring in French—she had no idea why. Well, actually she did. In her English program, she had to have ten hours of foreign language; ten more and she had her minor. She didn't even like French. *Oh, screw it,* thought Maddie. She slammed the book down on her desk, put on her tennis shoes, and decided to go for a long walk to clear her head.

Maddie seemed to walk forever. She toured campus, walked down the hill to town, and returned to campus. When she did, she found herself at Jake's dorm. Why did she end up here? Instead of leaving immediately, she had the dorm proctor call his room. He was there. He'd be coming down in a minute. When Jake reached the living area of the dorm and saw her standing there looking bewildered, he knew immediately where to take her.

"Hi, Maddie," said Jake cautiously. "Let's go for a ride."

"Okay," was all she said.

Jake took Maddie to the Toot & Tell (all the students called it the Fart and Fetch), ordered food and sodas—stuff for a picnic—and took Maddie to the farm. After he opened the gate, and they were parked, Jake turned to Maddie and handed her the key.

"Here, this is the key to the gate for the farm. I've been meaning to give you one. I know how much you enjoy it out here, so now you can come anytime you want and won't have to climb over the fence anymore."

Maddie was really grateful for his generosity. He was right; she'd always enjoyed coming here. She felt at peace here. But why had Jake always been so kind and tolerant with her? She wanted to find out.

"Jake," said Maddie, "why have you always been so kind to me? I feel I've gotten much more out of this relationship than you. I don't mean to sound callous, but what's in it for you?"

Jake thought for a few minutes before he answered her.

"Okay, Madison, here goes. All my life, I've basically gotten anything I wanted, especially from the opposite sex. But I've never really had a female friend before. Maybe I didn't know I wanted or even needed one until I met you. Of course, to be perfectly honest, the first time I saw you in the cafeteria, I was blown away by your looks. What was even better was the fact that you were so oblivious about them. I could tell immediately that you don't primp for hours in front of a mirror or spend hours doing your hair. You are who you are, take it or leave it. You really don't have any idea just how pretty you are. I also noticed at that time how animated you were when you talked to your friends. You were full of life and loving every minute of it. That was when I first decided I wanted to get to know you. I knew absolutely nothing about you, not even your name. I'd never even talked to you. Then I received the info from Matt. The first thing he said to me when I asked about you was that you were spoken for. Even though I was really disappointed, I still wanted to meet you. That's why I asked Terri and Matt to try and set up a blind date for us with the two of them.

"After that first date," added Jake, "I realized immediately that I was right about you, and I wanted to see you again. I knew sex was strictly off limits, and that the worst thing I could do was to press the issue. That was okay with me. There were other girls. You know, I feel like you are the first real 'girl' friend I've ever had. I think I could say anything to you. It's very difficult for someone like me to describe how I feel about anything personal. I guess I was brought up to be the strong, silent type when it comes to feelings. But when I'm with you, Maddie, I feel that all is right in the world. I know that sounds like a cliché, but it's true. I forget whatever's bothering me for a while, or sometimes I feel I can just let it out. You're not judgmental. You listen, make suggestions; some of which I may not want to hear but need to. I enjoy your company, your companionship. You should've noticed by now that whenever there is a special occasion, you're the one I ask to go with me—not any of those other girls. I'm proud to be seen with you. It's like whenever I receive an award, I want you there by my side. I need you there. Is anything I'm saying making sense to you?"

Madison didn't answer for a while. In many ways, she felt the same way. He was her go-to guy for anything and everything. She knew that if she needed anything, Jake would be the one she would turn to. She, too, enjoyed his company and the fact that she didn't have to worry about fighting him off. It boiled down to the fact that he, Terri, and Matt were her best friends here at Wilmington. She really did count on Jake—perhaps too much.

When Maddie finally spoke, she spoke so softly that Jake had a hard time hearing her.

"You know, Jake, sitting here at the farm, having this picnic lunch, and talking to you is one of the easiest things I'm able to do. I don't feel threatened by you. You've probably noticed by now that you're the only guy I go out with. Why? I love your company. I don't want to go through the dating ritual with others. I'm content to have only you in my life in this moment in time. I do know how you feel being with me. I feel the same way. But what happens when you graduate in June?"

"Well, I've accepted a teaching and coaching position in Claymont and plan to attend graduate school here. So I guess the only thing that will change will be I'll be living a few miles away and the fact that I'll be making some money," replied Jake.

"I don't believe it! Why didn't you tell me, Jake? How long have you known? Congratulations! I'm so happy for you!" exclaimed Maddie.

"Madison, I haven't known for long, and you're the first person I'm telling. I was hoping that you'd be happy about it. It means we can still be best friends—if you want to, that is."

"What do you mean, if I want to? Of course I do! I was dreading the day you graduated and moved away to who knows where," replied Maddie.

"Good," said Jake. "Now you don't have to worry anymore; at least for another couple of years." Jake leaned over and kissed her gently on the cheek. "Things will work out the way they are supposed to."

"So we are good, right?" asked Maddie.

"Yes, we're good, Madison." After Jake dropped her off at her house, Madison lay on the couch, thinking about the serious conversation they had just had. Ryan was not even mentioned once during the conversation even though his presence was as real as if he were sitting right beside them.

17

Maddie and Ryan made the same arrangements for Christmas his yearling year. They met once again in Oklahoma City and spent a couple of days there before heading to Avalon.

To Maddie, it seemed like Ryan was more of a stranger to her than last year. It took longer for the "real" Ryan to come back to her this time. She was patient, though, because she loved him so much.

Maddie was more embarrassed being naked in front of Ryan than he was. He was used to living around naked men—she wasn't used to being naked in front of anyone other than Ryan.

Ryan could tell this immediately when she came to bed the first night wearing a cute baby doll nightie. He didn't say anything, because he wasn't sure how she would react. Instead, he just held his naked body next to her. He kissed her gently at first on the lips so she'd relax. After she became comfortable around him again, she kissed him passionately and put her hand on his manhood, which was already erect. Just being next to Maddie always made him want her.

Ryan very carefully and deftly removed her nightie and matching panties. Then he started touching her lightly all over. Once his hand, fingers, and head arrived at her being, he knew Maddie was still his. She longed for his touch; she longed for him to make her climax over and over again. He did.

When Ryan's turn came, Maddie was in charge. He let her explore him at will. However, when she finally took him in her mouth, he came immediately. He apologized to Maddie, but she said it was okay. The good thing about being young was that Ryan's recovery time didn't take long.

While they were lying in bed together, they talked about how their school year was going. Of course, he knew Maddie had been crowned homecoming queen this year. But when he asked her who the king was, he was shocked by her answer.

"Jake was voted king by the members of the football team. I guess it was only natural since he's a senior and has been the quarterback for three years," answered Maddie very matter-of-factly.

"Why didn't you tell me before now, Maddie?" asked Ryan, obviously upset.

"Probably because of the way you're acting. I knew it would upset you, and it has. I didn't want you to make a mountain out of a mole hill. I didn't vote for him—his team did. I was just as shocked as you are when it happened. But I was glad. If it had to be someone, at least it was someone I knew."

"Well, that's just great!" said Ryan sarcastically. "Not only do you date him, but you are both the king and queen of homecoming. What's going on, Maddie?"

"What do you mean, what's going on? Nothing's going on. I only date him because he knows about you, and I don't have to worry about his making any advances towards me. With other guys, I'd probably spend the evening fighting them off. I don't have to do that with Jake. He's never tried anything other than a kiss, usually on the cheek. Gee, maybe I should go out with other guys. Would that make you happier, Ryan?"

"Of course not," answered Ryan. "I'm just jealous. I'm jealous that Jake is with you and I'm not."

"Ryan, you've had a few dates, too, haven't you? Anyone steady?" asked Maddie.

"Of course not. I maybe date once a semester," answered Ryan testily.

"Well, that's certainly not my fault. Is it, Ryan? You're the one who is so gung ho army. In fact, every time I see you, you seem worse. West Point has done a very good job indoctrinating you to live, think, and breathe like a soldier. But where is the man I fell in love with?"

"What do you want me to do, Maddie? Quit? I will if that's what it'll take to keep you."

"Of course, I don't want you to quit. This is the life you've chosen for yourself, for us. However, I don't want the 'real' Ryan, the one I know and love, to disappear. You have to be able to find some kind of balance is all I'm saying. I'm not a plebe, not a cadet, and never will be. What I will be is your wife. And, as your wife, I'll expect to be treated to the 'real' Ryan, the passionate, loving man I know, the one who is hidden from view from everyone except me. That's what I want, that's what I need, and that's what I expect," said Maddie confidently.

"And that's what you'll get. I promise. I'm sorry; you're right. I do get indoctrinated to act a certain way all the time, but I have to. Try to understand that. It just takes me a while to get out of that frame of mind. Let's don't argue. I can never win an argument with you, you know that."

"I don't want to argue either," replied Maddie. "Let's just enjoy each other again, okay?" said Maddie as she slipped her hand under the covers once again.

However, at the beginning of the second semester of their sophomore year, Maddie wrote Ryan a long and serious letter. And, as soon as he read it, he knew something was really wrong. Maddie had never been demanding before. He had to figure out a way to see her and set things right. He could almost feel her drifting away from him. He decided to call her immediately and tell her to come back East for spring break this year. His grades would be good enough for him to get leave for the week. But even if they weren't, he'd figure out how to get away. If staying at West Point meant losing Maddie, he'd leave the Point. Nothing was more important to him than Maddie. He'd been so busy, having his every minute accounted for that he couldn't relate to what Maddie was doing or feeling. He'd been so self-absorbed in achieving his own success that he'd forgotten the reason behind his wanting to succeed. If he didn't have Maddie waiting at the end of this road, what was the point of it all? When the phone rang late that night, Maddie was surprised to hear Ryan's voice on the other end.

"Hi, Maddie!" "YKTA."

"Ryan, my God, why are you calling so late? What's going on? Has anything happened?"

"No, I'm okay. It's you I'm worried about."

"What do you mean? I'm fine."

"No, Maddie, we're not fine. I could tell that from your last letter. What's going on? I know I've not been able to be there for you since I've been here, but up until a few days ago, when I received your letter, I didn't realize how much I've neglected you, taken you for granted, and knew something was wrong. Madison, talk to me," said Ryan. "Talk to me the way we used to."

"Ryan, that's pretty hard to do, isn't it? I wish to God I could. But we haven't spoken much like that in two years now, have we? I've always needed that connection to you, Ryan. I've felt it slipping slowly away bit by bit, and I hate it. Yes, I know you love me, and yes, I love you. But I honestly think that you have come to love 'the Corps' more than I, and I can't compete with that. I don't want to compete with that. There are still two years to endure before you finally graduate. Will it get any better? Will you ever get more privileges, or will it always be this way? Yes, there is something wrong. I don't have you to talk to when I need to talk. I don't have you to hold me when I need it, and I'm having my own self-doubts. Hell, the only time

159

we've had alone were the times during the holidays!" cried Maddie.

"What about Jake? Doesn't he comfort you and hold you when you need it?" said Ryan jealously.

"How dare you speak to me like that!" screamed Maddie. "I've done nothing wrong! No, Jake doesn't hold me. We're just friends. But, yes, come to think of it, I do talk to him when I need to talk."

"Do you talk about me, about us?"

"Are you kidding? Hell no! Besides, what difference would it make if I did?"

"Maddie, I don't want to fight with you. I'm jealous. I'm jealous of the time you spend with Jake, and it worries me that he's taking my place. It's not fair, Maddie. I love you. I need you. I want you." Ryan started to cry out of desperation.

Maddie felt awful. She'd never heard Ryan like this before. He was willing to leave the Point for her, if that's what it took to keep her. At least she had someone to talk to; he didn't. Well, at least she didn't think he did.

"Ryan, are you dating anyone?" questioned Maddie.

"What? Of course not. Even if I wanted to, I'd be too damn tired to date. Yes, we've all met some girls, but trust me, none of them comes close to you. I simply won't jeopardize what we have together," declared Ryan.

Ryan told Maddie that yearlings didn't have to stay at the Point during spring break. He could meet her anywhere.

"Why don't we stay with my sister in New Jersey? It wouldn't cost us anything, and she has room."

"That sounds great."

They decided that during Ryan's spring break, she'd cancel her lessons, or Terri could take care of them for her. She'd fly out on Thursday after her college classes and arrive in Newark that evening. Ryan said he'd rent a car and drive down to pick her up. She'd make the reservations ASAP, and he'd call and get the flight times tomorrow night.

Maddie couldn't believe that she and Ryan were going to spend some much-needed quality time together. She was too excited to sleep, so she called and told Terri her plans. *Thank God for Terri*, Maddie thought. She could always count on her to take up the slack when she needed it. But she made Terri promise not to tell Matt where she was going. She didn't want Jake to know.

18

Meanwhile, the thought of another entire week with Maddie was almost more than Ryan could stand. He went through the motions at school, but his mind was elsewhere. Sometimes he'd have to go for a run to expel his pent up energy. Other times, he just closed his eyes. And when the absolute worst times came, late at night, he would masturbate. He didn't like to do that, but sometimes that was the only way he could relieve the pressure. He didn't tell Maddie about those times at first. He didn't want her to think he was getting weird. In all honesty, he didn't know how she would really feel about it.

His classes for the second semester of his yearling year were basically a repeat of the first. There were eight courses, as usual. Joy of all joys, this semester he had two math classes again (and, of course, they were six days a week)—yuk! At least he had a psychology class that he looked forward to.

Finally, the "gloom period" was over again, and his grades were sufficient for him to get to go on spring break.

Ryan rented a car in Highland Falls and made the trip to Newark's airport in record time. He arrived several hours before Maddie, and that gave him time to do a little shopping. He bought another set of civvies, because he only had a couple of pair with him. He had no use for them at West Point, but he wanted to look especially good for the love of his life when she stepped off the plane. He wanted her to want him as much as he wanted her. He needn't have worried. She did.

He bought Maddie and her sister flowers—roses for Maddie and a spring mix for her sister—and he'd also brought along some tee shirts and sweats from West Point with him for her to wear back at school. He wanted everyone there to know that she was spoken for, especially this Jake guy.

That Thursday night, when Maddie came off the plane, she immediately saw Ryan standing there. He was in tan slacks and blue shirt. God, he looked wonderful! If possible, he was even more handsome than ever. She literally ran and jumped into his arms. The two of them, normally so reserved, smothered each other with kisses.

"God, I love you, Maddie," whispered Ryan in her ear.

"YKTA," replied Maddie.

They retrieved Maddie's suitcase and went to Ryan's rental car. They headed immediately for Michelle's house. It only took about forty minutes to get there, and Michelle was ready for them. She had prepared an Italian feast. Neither of them was hungry but ate her delicious meal quickly before going into the basement to talk.

For the longest time, all they did was hold each other. It had been so long since she felt safe in his arms and she never wanted that feeling to end. When he did finally place her gently on the couch and lay on top of her, it was as if they were back in high school when her mother had been gone after graduation.

Maddie and Ryan necked and made out for a long time. He even took off her blouse. She didn't care; in fact, she would have let him do anything he wanted right then and there. He very gently undid her bra and laid his head on her chest, circling her nipples lightly with his tender touch. Maddie became so excited she thought she would explode any minute, but she said nothing. Ryan gradually began to softly kiss her breasts and hold them in his hands. Maddie was still the perfect cup size, and her breasts were high and perky as always. Ryan's large hands with long fingers could span her breasts easily. He started kissing her neck and then went lower and began sucking on her breasts lightly, tenderly, but not in a hard passionate desire. He eventually used his tongue to lightly tickle her nipples, which became instantly hard as usual, and continued down to her stomach. She moaned softly as he made a winding trail of kisses from one side to the other, down to her love mound. Maddie didn't want him to stop, but he did.

Maddie decided it was her turn. She very quickly unbuttoned his shirt and removed it for him. She then undid his belt, threw it off, and unzipped his pants. Her hands went straight for his manhood. It was already erect and seemed huge in Maddie's tiny hand. She massaged him as he groaned in pleasure.

"Madison, I can't stand this," Ryan gasped, "Oh God, I'm coming!"

"It's all right, Ryan. We haven't done anything wrong. I'm glad I can still make you relieve all your pent up tension so easily. It makes me feel like a woman to be able to please you."

"But I want to please you too, Maddie," whispered Ryan He kissed Maddie fully on the mouth as he unzipped her slacks and proceeded to fully undress her. Maddie was already wet in anticipation, as he slowly inserted his middle finger inside her. With his palm lying on her mound, he gently moved his hand in an oval motion. It didn't take long before she felt tiny electric shocks pulsing through her body, taunting every nerve and muscle. Her breathing became deep and panting. Suddenly, Maddie's eyes opened wide and her hips thrust against Ryan's hand. Her entire body was on fire, exploding with indescribable pleasure. She shuddered and then collapsed with a satisfied moan.

"Oh my God, Ryan. I love you so much," said Maddie, breathlessly.

Ryan was too amazed by her orgasm to say anything. He just held Maddie in his arms for a long time before speaking. He told Maddie that even though saltpeter was put into their food to keep their sexual urges at bay, some of the guys masturbated at the Point to relieve the stress.

"Masturbate? What's that? It sounds awful," said Maddie.

Ryan laughed. Maddie knew even less about sex than he did. He explained to her that it meant you relieved yourself. Some people called it self-pleasure.

"Have you ever masturbated?" asked Maddie.

"Yes, but only a couple of times," Ryan lied. "At night, when I would think about being with you, the urge to see you, hold you and to lie beside you sometimes becomes too much for me."

"Well, I've never even heard about it, let alone tried it. I wouldn't ever try it, because it wouldn't be you touching me," said Maddie.

"Just so long as you don't feel the need to have another man help you, okay?"

"That'll never happen."

After that, Maddie and Ryan made up the bed downstairs and climbed into bed together.

Maddie was still a little embarrassed. She hadn't been with Ryan like this since Christmas.

Ryan, on the other hand, was much more comfortable with the situation. He turned over to face her, held her in his arms, kissed her passionately, and said, "I love you, Madison Conrad. I'll see you in the morning."

Maddie whispered softly in his ear, "YKTA."

Maddie couldn't seem to fall asleep. She lay there with Ryan's arm across her, wondering when they'd be able to do this every night. She realized that she longed for the comfort of being in his arms more than anything else in the world. This is where she was meant to be. Finally, after what seemed like forever, sleep came.

In the morning, Maddie was embarrassed as usual. She always thought that she looked like a train wreck. Ryan was sleeping so peacefully that she climbed quietly out of bed and went to the bathroom. She brushed her teeth, washed her face, looked at her hair, and decided there was nothing she could do about it. Then she climbed back into bed and enjoyed watching Ryan sleep so soundly.

Ryan awakened about half an hour later. When he rolled over and saw her lying beside him, he realized that he really hadn't been dreaming. Maddie was really next to him.

"Good morning, love," he said softly before he went to the bathroom. He was gone only a few minutes, but it seemed like an hour to Maddie.

Ryan climbed back into bed and kissed her gently. They held each other and discussed what they were going to do that day. Maddie didn't want to go or be anywhere except with Ryan. In fact, if she had her way, she'd spend the entire day in bed with him. However, before they got up, showered together, and dressed, they had a wonderful session of oral sex like they had grown accustomed to.

After breakfast, the two of them packed a picnic lunch and headed for the shore—to Toms' River. They were going to spend the day at the beach.

The drive took about an hour and a half, and along the way, Ryan and Maddie discussed their future. June 1968 was still the date. Ryan would reserve the chapel and make hotel arrangements. They decided that the ceremony would be—small only their parents and very close friends. Afterwards, they'd do the popular Niagara Falls or Poconos honeymoon for a few days. Ryan knew he'd be going to Ranger School and Jump School, so they decided that she'd drive back to Wilmington and continue to teach while he was at school. Maddie wasn't happy about this idea at all. She wanted to be with her husband, for God's sake! Eventually, Ryan convinced her to agree that they needed all the money they could save in order to start a decent life together. After he received his first set of orders, if it wasn't Vietnam, she'd pack her things and move to their new residence. Ryan would make arrangements for officer's housing for them. Maddie couldn't believe that her dream for the last several years would finally come true.

Maddie and Ryan loved Toms' River. They walked for what seemed like miles along the beach, holding hands while letting the water lap at their feet. They collected shells, kissed, and talked more about their future. When they finally returned to their car, they took out their picnic basket and blanket and found a spot to lie down.

As Ryan spread out the blanket on the hard sand, Maddie unpacked their sandwiches and the bottle of wine her sister Michelle had insisted they take with them. Maddie could think of no other place in the world she'd rather be at this moment than here with Ryan.

"Maddie," Ryan said quietly to her while sipping his wine, "you do know, don't you, that when I tell you I love you, it's my soul speaking?"

"Yes. Me, too. I can't imagine my life without you in it."

"You won't ever have to, Maddie. I'll always be with you. We're going to have a wonderful life together. I know it."

During the ride back to New Jersey, Ryan told Maddie more about West Point. She couldn't understand all the rules and regulations he had to follow and how hard his classes were. At least now he was able to take a few classes that interested him more than last year. He was sick to death of all the math. He was enjoying his English and science classes, though. He shocked Maddie when he told her that he found out early on that he wasn't the smartest kid in school. That was a new feeling for him, and he'd had a hard time accepting it. That's why he tried so hard to keep up. At least he still didn't have to eat the stupid way he did as a plebe, but their marching, parading, and the physical program had progressed from just the basics. They were learning climbing techniques, more advanced evasive tactics in the woods, etc. Ryan was enjoying these exercises. He didn't realize it yet, but he was being groomed to be a professional killer.

He also told Maddie that he hadn't decided what branch of the Army he was leaning towards. He was considering Mechanized (Armor), but Infantry was still an option. Maddie wasn't at all happy to hear that he was even remotely considering Infantry. She knew what that meant—the field, the jungle, Vietnam. But she kept her mouth shut, at least for the moment. She had already heard horror stories about Vietnam, and she couldn't believe Ryan was even considering the Infantry as an alternative. She didn't want him to choose it. *At least with Armor he'd have some protection*, thought Maddie.

After another one of Michelle's fabulous dinners, Ryan and Maddie made their way back downstairs to the rumpus room to watch a little television. Of course, TV was the last thing on their minds. They lay down on the bed immediately, and she melted into his arms. They used this quality time to play with each other again and ended up not getting much sleep that night.

The next morning they decided to take the train from Newark into New York City. The only other time Maddie had been here was when she was a young girl. She'd been invited each summer to come and take private and pas de deux lessons at Carnegie Hall. Her father and mother would drive from California and stay at Michelle's for at least a month so that Maddie could learn to dance with a male partner—lifts, turns, etc. Maddie told Ryan that all she really remembered about those summers was that she always seemed to be black and blue from being dropped on her butt by her partner.

This trip would be so different for her than that last one. She and Ryan decided, as soon as they arrived in the city, that it would take at least another day to see even half of what they wanted. On this trip they visited the grand old lady holding the torch and Ellis Island. It was a very moving experience for both of them, especially Ryan. This was the reason he was enduring West Point—freedom. "Freedom isn't free," both of their parents had told them many times. Sometimes, men had to fight to keep it. Maddie knew that Ryan would end up being one of those fighters before long, and her heart ached about it and the uncertainty of it all. Ryan and Maddie couldn't go up into the crown of the Statue of Liberty since it was under renovation, but they took speaking tours at each place.

On Ellis Island, Maddie and Ryan could not imagine what their ancestors had had to endure just to get into the United States. The weeks at sea, the tests they had to take once they arrived, the long lines of those waiting to be admitted to go into New York City, the long lines of those waiting to go to the mainland and parts West, and even the lines of those waiting to be deported because they were considered undesirables.

After they had had such a somber morning, the two of them decided they needed to have some fun. They took a carriage ride through Central Park, and then went to the Carnegie Deli and shared a sandwich, which neither of them could finish, before heading back to Newark.

Their second day in New York City, Ryan and Maddie visited Times Square, the Empire State Building, and Greenwich Village, which at the time was inhabited mostly by hippies. Ryan and Maddie couldn't believe how the "flower children" were dressed, let alone what they were doing in public—smoking pot, doing drugs, etc. After that enlightening experience, they went back to Times Square and were able to get half price tickets to see a late matinee of *West Side Story* on Broadway. Naturally, Maddie loved the musical version of *Romeo and Juliet*. Next, Maddie, of course, had to visit Macy's. She'd never seen such a large store in her life, except Harrods in London. This Macy's had thirty-five acres of merchandise, and Maddie was overwhelmed by it all. Ryan bought Maddie a navy cashmere sweater and matching slacks on sale, because all of the winter merchandise was half off. Since this was going to be their last night in the city, the two of them took a night-time dinner cruise around Manhattan. It was spectacular to see the city all lighted up at night! They had a very romantic dinner on the ship and were able to drink a glass of champagne, since it came with the dinner, even though neither of them was twenty-one yet.

After the train ride back to Newark and the drive back to Michelle's home, Ryan and Maddie turned off the light that Michelle had kept on for them and immediately crept downstairs to be alone for the last time.

"What am I going to do without you?" declared Maddie. "It's going to kill me to go back to Oklahoma and realize the years we still have ahead of us."

"I know," said Ryan. "Imagine how I'm going to be feeling not having you beside me at night. But, Madison, you'll go back, work hard, keep your 4.0, teach your classes, go to games, and go out with your friends. If you keep busy, the time will fly by. But if you go back and dwell on the years still ahead of us, it will drag by and drag you down with it."

"I know. You're right. What about you? How will you cope?"

Ryan explained to her that he had no choice. He had no decisions to make; they were made for him. "My schedule is not flexible. I will be told what to do, how to do it, when to do it, and sometimes, but not always, why I have to do it. Besides classwork, I'll have artillery training, week-long sessions in the woods learning tracking and all that good stuff. I might even go visit other posts with my group to see how the Army really operates. I know that's what will happen right before my firstie (senior) year.

"West Point is really a place unto itself. It doesn't seem like part of the real world to me. Don't get me wrong—I enjoy being there. I want to succeed, but I'm smart enough to know that I'm being forced to live a very sheltered life. The real world is not going to be like this. They are preparing us to be leaders—'the best of the best,' they like to say. I'm just hoping it works."

"It sounds to me like they're building you guys to be a bunch of warriors, and I don't like that idea one bit," replied Maddie.

Ryan and Maddie decided that they'd do what they had become accustomed to when they were able to spend the night together. This time, however, Ryan took much more time making Maddie feel comfortable nude in front of him. He knew that her body embarrassed her. It shouldn't have. As far as Ryan was concerned, seeing her long, lithe legs, boyish hips, tiny, tiny waist, and perfect breasts made his heart beat faster. She had no idea just how wonderful she looked lying on the bed, with her long auburn curls surrounding her face. He never wanted to stop gazing at that face for as long as he lived.

Ryan, too, was a little embarrassed. Maddie was the only woman who had ever seen him nude. But Maddie marveled at his physique. He, too, had long legs, a small waist, and a very strong upper body. Of course, it was his manhood that had always surprised her the most. She was very inexperienced, but it was obvious that he was quite long and thick. She had always loved watching him rise and enlarge as she fondled him. But sometimes she worried that when they were finally married, perhaps her body wouldn't fit his.

Ryan reassured her that they wouldn't make love until their wedding night. That had always been the promise. He told her not to worry. Then Ryan proceeded to start kissing her from the top of her head to the tips of her toes. It was impossible for Maddie not to move. When he came to her womanhood and started to kiss her there, she automatically spread her legs open to him. When he used his fingers to gently open her, she thought she had died and gone to heaven. She hadn't, not yet. That would happen soon, though. Ryan always used his tongue and lightly licked the opening to her love canal. She started to squirm, but Ryan stopped and quieted her down. When she had relaxed, he once again used his tongue to arouse her, but this time he also put his finger inside of her. The combination of the two always made Maddie explode in ecstasy. There was no other way for Maddie to explain it. Ryan would slow down and then bring her back again. He did it five times before Maddie begged him to stop.

"Ryan, my God, how can you do this to me? I'll never get enough of this." With that she opened her legs wide for him again, took his head, and placed his lips exactly where they needed to be.

After that, Maddie rolled on top of him and said, "My turn."

She started at the top of his head, softly kissing his beautiful brown eyes and his full lips that had tasted her only minutes before. It seemed strange to taste herself, but it was thrilling to be licking Ryan's lips and tasting her own juices. She slowly made her way to each nipple, lightly nipping and sucking them. She used her fingertips to trail down his body lightly. Once she came to the dark hair that covered his already erect rod, she began to softly and lightly fondle him. She moved her hands slowly up and down his shaft. Then, as she'd become used to doing, she put his manhood in her mouth. She heard Ryan moan as he opened his legs.

"Oh my God, Maddie. You have no idea how fabulous this feels," moaned Ryan. "Please don't stop. Promise me you'll do this to me forever."

"I promise, forever and ever," said Maddie softly.

With that Maddie began to lick him from the top of his shaft to his testicles. Ryan always enjoyed having her hold his sack in her hand, so she held them gently as she licked his shaft. She wanted to suck his seed out of him. It took only a few seconds for that to happen. Her mouth filled with his semen as he groaned and moved his hips to meet her mouth. Maddie filled her mouth, and she just automatically swallowed it and then licked up any drops that she could find. She wasn't going to waste even one drop of his love juice.

"Maddie," Ryan said breathlessly, "if I die tomorrow, it'll be all right because of what you gave me today. God, I love you," he said as he buried his head into her neck.

"Honey, there will be many, many days and nights for us in the years to come. We have our entire lifetime before us. Our future is going to be glorious," replied Maddie happily. "I just wish I could give myself to you fully, but I guess this is as close as we can until June sixty-eight."

Their last night was spent talking. They talked about anything and everything the way they used to. Maddie broached the subject of Vietnam quietly. She wanted to know what the chances of his going there would be.

Ryan's reply was immediate. He told her that probably 75 percent of his class would spend their first tour of duty there, especially if they decided to go Infantry. However, he reminded her that before that, there would be another year of advanced training in order to make sure they were ready. As he'd told her before, those West Point officers going to Vietnam went to several schools first. Maddie voiced her concerns—she was scared to death. But Ryan reassured her that even if he did have to go, nothing would keep him from coming home to her. Besides, that was a long way off. Perhaps the war would be over by then. The last thing Maddie whispered in his ear before going to sleep that night was, "Please go Armor."

The next morning, Maddie and Ryan played in the shower together as they had all those years ago in high school, laughing as usual. After that, Michelle had fixed them a magnificent breakfast, and then they packed for their trip back to the airport in Newark.

The drive to the airport was torture for both of them. They felt as if they'd been living in a perfect cocoon, and now the real world loomed in front of them once again. Ryan took her to her gate and waited with her until her flight started to board. Tears welled up in Maddie's eyes and started flowing silently down her cheeks. She cupped his face in her hands, looked into his brown eyes filled with tears, and kissed him passionately directly on his lips.

"YKTA, Ryan," was all she said; then she turned and started for the runway.

"YKTA, Madison Conrad!" yelled Ryan in return.

Maddie thought she would cry all the way home even though she knew she'd see him again in a couple of months. This summer, Ryan planned to spend a week or two with Maddie at her place in Wilmington.

However, that week was never destined to happen. Ryan was selected to go to Sandhurst in England on an exchange program. He tried to make Maddie understand what an honor this was, but he also knew that she would never forgive him. He was right. This would be one of the biggest mistakes he would ever make. But the biggest one, the one both of them would never recover from, was still a couple of years away.

Although Maddie had a rough time on her plane ride home, she tried to be positive about their future. As soon as the plane landed in Oklahoma City, Maddie retrieved her luggage, headed for her car which she had left in the long-term parking lot, and began the one-and-a-half-hour trip home.

For some reason, as soon as she walked into her small house and set her luggage on the floor, a calming peace finally came over her. She sat down on her comfy chair and put her feet up on the ottoman, trying to digest what had occurred over the last week. She belonged to Ryan, and Ryan belonged to her; she knew that. They really belonged to each other—nothing could change that. Any doubts she had about his commitment to her had vanished.

19

The next day, classes and teaching began anew for Maddie. She would keep her 4.0. She'd also save as much money as she could from the dance school so that she and Ryan would have a small nest egg to begin their married life together. She decided that Ryan, as usual, was right. She needed to focus on getting through the next two years as painlessly as possible. When Terri and Maddie had a little time to talk that evening, between tumbling and cheerleading classes, Maddie told her about her glorious week. She did not, however, share any of the intimate details with her. That was just between her and Ryan. No one else needed or, for that matter, had a right to know those moments. Terri wondered how she could wait another two years. It seemed like such a long time.

"I can be very patient when I have to be," said Maddie.

Terri told Maddie that Jake had asked where she was, and she'd told him that Maddie just needed some alone time—to clear her head. She asked if Friday night would be a good night for them to celebrate their engagement to which Maddie immediately answered, "Of course."

That Friday night was the first time Maddie had seen Jake in about ten days. She was surprised to find herself so happy to see him and his smile. The four of them celebrated with a steak dinner at the Main Street Restaurant. Afterwards, Jake and Maddie went to the farm as usual.

So much had happened to her in the last couple of weeks. She and Jake lay on top of the picnic table, looking at the stars like they usually did. It was a beautiful night with a shining moon and not a cloud in the sky. Maddie found herself smiling contentedly. They both spoke in generalities. She wondered if Jake knew that she'd seen Ryan. Probably. Every time they saw each other after she'd been with Ryan, things seemed awkward for a while.

Jake was the first to mention Ryan. "How's Ryan?" asked Jake.

"He's okay. School is tough for him. His every minute is managed by the powers that be. He gets tired of the things he feels are foolish. But they are now doing field exercises, and he enjoys being on the sailing team. He gets to go on sailing competitions, so that gets him out of the Point a little more. He still doesn't like taking so many math or science classes."

Jake always found it difficult to hear Maddie talk about Ryan. Her voice even changed; it became wistful. He never pressed her for more information than she was willing to divulge. He knew she'd clam up. He decided to change the subject.

They talked about Terri and Matt and their upcoming wedding for a while. It really wasn't that far away now.

He then asked Maddie a question he'd been afraid to approach her about until now.

"Maddie, you know I'll be graduating in May. My parents are having a small party afterwards at the Steak House Grill in Claymont. I'm only asking a few class friends to come and wondered if you'd be my date. It would mean you'd have to meet my crazy family, but Terri and Matt will be there for moral support if you need it. I really hope you'll come. It'd mean a great deal to me."

"Of course I'll come!" exclaimed Maddie. "I'd love to share this special moment with you. It's a wonderful accomplishment. I can't believe you'd hesitate to ask me."

"Good. Great! I'll arrange for you to have a ticket to graduation. I'll introduce you to my parents before then, of course, since you'll be sitting with them. I've told them about you, and they're very curious to meet you."

"Oh my God, what did you tell them? That I'm some kind of four-eyed monster?" "Not quite," Jake laughed. *If she only knew,* he thought to himself".

May seemed to appear in the blink of an eye. Finals were finished. Maddie's grade point was still 4.0, although she didn't know how with all the turmoil in her life.

Jake's graduation was next week, so Maddie decided to buy a new outfit. She made the time to go with Terri to OKC in search of a new outfit, as well as Terri's wedding dress. They decide to make it a two-day trip like before and enjoy the freedom from classes.

Maddie chose a beautiful pink floral dress for the occasion. The sundress had a full skirt and halter straps. She also chose a beautifully simple white floppy hat, because she knew it would be warm in the football stands. She picked white small-heeled sandals and a small white bag. Her only other accessories were going to be the small diamond studs that Ryan had given her. Terri chose her dress for graduation quickly—she wanted to try on wedding dresses.

Terri and Maddie spent an entire day at bridal shops. It seemed to Maddie that every dress Terri tried on looked more beautiful on her than the next. However, when she tried on "the dress," she started to cry.

"That's the one!" Maddie shrieked. "You look absolutely like a princess!"

"Do you really think so?"

"Oh yes—that's the one."

The saleslady took down the style number for Terri and tore a picture of the dress from the bridal magazine for her. She reminded Terri to be sure to order the dress at least twelve weeks before the wedding to allow time for fittings.

Then suddenly, the saleslady turned to Maddie and said, "I've been watching you all day, young lady, and I want you to indulge me for a minute. I have a dress I'd like you to try on. It just came in and is one of a kind."

"Oh no," said Maddie. "I'm not getting married."

"Oh, yes, you are," declared Terri. "Just a year later. Maddie, do it for me. Try it on, please."

Maddie hesitated before saying, "Oh, all right. Only for you, though."

The shop owner ran to the back room to get the dress before Maddie could change her mind. When she brought it out, Maddie gasped.

"Oh my God! It's exquisite; simple yet exquisite."

"Here, my dear, go try it on. I'll zip it up for you when you're ready."

Maddie entered the dressing room and put on the dress. She had never seen a dress like this one before. It certainly wasn't the current style of short sleeves. This dress had an illusion bodice that had hand-sewn lace and seed pearls applied to it in all the strategic places. It came down to V at the waist, and then a huge skirt of satin and embroidered lace cascaded from it. It had a high neckline and long illusion sleeves done in the same manner as the bodice. The dress was the whitest white, and the hem of the gown was also scalloped with hand-sewn lace and seed pearls. The matching train was attached at the waist but was unlike any trains she'd ever seen before. It wasn't long and flat. It was full, long, and bubbly. It was gathered in different places, and each gather, which reminded Maddie of a big bubble, was held together with a huge pearl. The train was attached to the dress with a huge bow, also covered with lace and seed pearls.

When Maddie emerged from the dressing room wearing this one-of-a-kind dress, Terri was totally overcome. Tears started streaming down her face.

"You're an absolute vision, Maddie," declared Terri. "You take my breath away. If it does it to me, imagine what Ryan will think."

The shop owner came up behind Maddie with a veil that would end just before her waist. It was attached to a circle of flowers. When she placed it on Maddie's head, with her curls falling down her back, Maddie reminded Terri of an angel in a garden.

"Maddie, I can honestly say I've never seen such a beautiful bride-to-be. You're the only person I know who could wear this dress. You could try on a million dresses, and I'd always say this is the one."

"But I'm not getting married until 1968," proclaimed Maddie.

"I don't care. Get the dress and veil now. It is one-of-a-kind and you must have it," insisted Terri.

"Is it terribly expensive?" Maddie asked the owner.

"Not as bad as you might think."

"How much?"

"Five hundred for the gown, veil, and slip," said the owner.

"Maddie, you can afford it. All you do is save your money for your nest egg," said Terri.

"Do you really think Ryan will like it?"

"Are you kidding? He'll be blown away. Imagine him looking at you while walking down the aisle at the chapel at West Point!" exclaimed Terri.

"But Terri, it's supposed to be a small wedding."

"That doesn't mean you can't have a gorgeous dress. Besides, you deserve it for having to wait so long to wear it," declared Terri. "Buy it."

"All right, if you really think I should."

"I do."

The saleslady advised Maddie to take her dress to the cleaners as soon as she got home and have them preserve the dress for her. That way, the dress would be as perfect in 1968 as it was today. The color wouldn't change, etc. The dress would be put into a large box once it was preserved, and Maddie wouldn't have to worry about a thing. She was going to make the most beautiful bride in the world. Maddie thanked her for the advice and said that she'd do it as soon as she arrived home.

Maddie certainly had never intended to return to Wilmington with a wedding dress. She wondered if she had made a stupid decision all the way home, but Terri kept insisting that she hadn't.

Maddie made Terri promise on her life not to tell anyone, especially Matt, about the dress. Maddie knew that if Terri told Matt, he would tell Jake, and she wasn't ready for that yet. She told Terri that she'd tell Jake herself in her own way and in her own time. Terri promised and vowed this would be one promise she'd keep no matter what.

As soon as she walked into her house, Maddie put the wedding dress and veil immediately into her closet. The next day, she took it to the cleaners to have it preserved as she'd been told.

The next few days were spent getting ready for Jake's graduation. She wanted to get him something special—something to remind him of her. She finally chose a pocket watch, and she decided to have it engraved with "The birth of a Jake's Joy—September 25, 1964. Love Always, Maddie." After choosing his gift, she finally relaxed. She enjoyed working in her English garden. In fact, she decided to make a bouquet of wild flowers from it to give to Jake's mother.

As promised, Jake drove Maddie to Englewood to meet his parents a few days before graduation. His father owned several car dealerships throughout the area, and his mother had been a teacher. They were both very pleasant and easy to talk to, just like Jake. She enjoyed their dinner and was glad to have met them before graduation.

On the drive home, Jake asked Maddie if she'd like to go to the farm. Instead of saying yes, Maddie invited him to her house for a glass of wine. She wanted to give him his present before all the graduation activities began.

Once in the house, Jake took off his coat jacket, undid his tie, slipped off his loafers, and plopped down on the comfy floral sofa while Maddie poured them some wine.

"I'm glad at least one of us is twenty-one!" yelled Maddie from her small kitchen.

"Me, too," replied Jake. "I feel like I could use a glass of wine right about now!" exclaimed Jake.

"Were you afraid your parents wouldn't like me?" asked Maddie as she returned with the two glasses of wine.

"Absolutely not!" said Jake emphatically. "I just don't like getting dressed up."

"Jake, I want to give you your graduation present tonight, because I don't want you to have to explain the inscription to everyone. If I waited, you would."

"Maddie, I wasn't expecting you to get me a present. I don't need one. I'm just glad you're going to be there."

"I know," said Maddie. "But I wanted to get you something. It's a special occasion, and I'm happy you'll still be living close by and be here for night classes for the next two years, so I can unload when I get frustrated. She got up, went to her bedroom, and picked up the gift she had wrapped for him.

"Go ahead. Open it. I don't think it'll bite you," Maddie said, teasing him. Jake carefully unwrapped the package. When he saw that it was a pocket watch, he was speechless. However, when he opened it and read the inscription, his eyes filled with tears.

"The birth of a Jake's Joy—September 25, 1964. Love always, Maddie," he read out loud. "Maddie, I don't know what to say. It's absolutely perfect. It's a day I'll never forget, too." *If only she knew what he really meant*, thought Jake.

"Do you really like it?"

"Absolutely! I'll wear it and treasure it always." And he would.

"Great," exclaimed Maddie. "Now, let's drink this wine, perhaps even the entire bottle!"

"You got it, kid."

They drank wine and talked into the wee hours of the morning. She explained that she was going to take a week off in August and go home to visit her folks. Even though nothing was ever said, she felt her mother needed her. She was concerned about her health.

"Well, try to come back a couple of weeks early, so you can help me decorate my new place," Jake said. "If I do it, it'll be a mess."

Maddie promised she would, and even vowed not to make it froufrou like hers. Well, maybe just a little frou, so it didn't look like a typical bachelor pad. She suggested they go to garage sales and yard sales to find stuff, and that sounded great to him. (Any time he spent with Maddie sounded great to him.)

By the wee hours of the morning, they were both slurring their words. They had finished the bottle of wine, and Maddie was lying on the sofa with her head in his lap. After so much wine, both of them had loosened up even more than usual. Jake even became brave enough to talk to her seriously.

"Maddie, I want you to know something. I know I've said it before, but if you ever need anything, anything at all, just let me know. I'd do anything for you. You know that, don't you?"

"Yes, I know, Jake, and I honestly believe you would. I'll never be able to thank you enough for your friendship. No matter where I am in the world, I know that if I need you, you'll come."

"Always and forever," said Jake softly.

How could she not know how he felt about her? Simple. She was Maddie: trusting, lovable Maddie. He knew in his heart he'd never find anyone like her again, but he also knew that she was still spoken for. Jake left around 4:00 AM., and Maddie staggered to bed. She knew she loved Jake in her own way—not like Ryan, but like Jake.

Finally, the day all four of the friends had been waiting for came—Jake's graduation. It was a beautiful spring-like day with not a cloud in the sky. Maddie was really pleased that Jake's mom appreciated the flowers from her garden. They sat quietly as all the speeches were delivered, and they stood up and clapped when Jake's name was finally called. She could see the tears in their eyes. They were so proud of their son. And they had good reason to be. They had reared a wonderful man: a kind, dependable, well-spoken, strong man.

Maddie's eyes glistened with tears. How in the world had she been so fortunate to find him? Why had he never violated her trust in him? Yes, she was a very lucky woman. He'd taught her so many things—offered advice when she needed it—even said he'd helped her study for some of the classes she'd been putting off and had yet to take. What had she given him in return? She didn't have the answer to that question. She decided to make it a point to ask him, maybe even tonight after the party.

After their caps were thrown into the air, Maddie and his parents went onto the field to congratulate him. When his parents had finished, Maddie hugged him, put her hands on his face, kissed him on the lips, and said, "I'm so proud of you!" The kiss took Jake by surprise. Even his parents, knowing how Jake really felt about Maddie, were surprised by the kiss, happily surprised.

Dinner was wonderful. Terri and Matt and a few of their other friends carried on like kids. They kept making toasts. Finally, they cajoled Maddie into making one. Maddie stood up, held up her glass, and began, hoping she wouldn't make a fool of herself or slur her words in front of his parents.

"We are here tonight to celebrate Jake and his accomplishments. Who would've 'thunk' that the guy who has become my very best friend in the whole world, I met on a blind date—thanks, Terri and Matt— would be the first of the four of us to graduate? I still remember feeling like a fool when I discovered Jake was the quarterback. I was a cheerleader, for God's sake, and didn't even know who he was. Jake, I don't know what you've seen in me all these years, but your friendship, guidance, and support will always be the most important memories of my college career for me. Thank you for taking me under your wing and teaching me how to fly. Thank God, you'll still be here for me for a couple of more years. I don't know what I'd do without you, except lose my wings, crash and burn."

"Here, here!" they all said and drank their champagne.

Terri leaned over to Matt and whispered, "That's the closest she's ever come to saying 'I love you' to Jake."

"I know," said Matt. "Look at Jake. He knows it, too." Matt was right.

The party ended around midnight, and Jake took Maddie to the farm without even asking.

"You looked absolutely stunning today, Maddie," said Jake. "I can't believe you were actually with me."

"What are you talking about? Of course, I'd be with you. And thanks for the compliment. The one good thing about curly hair is that you don't get 'hat hair,'" declared Maddie, shaking her head and laughing.

They left the car and went into the barn to see Joy, the filly they'd named together. Maddie just knew in her heart that Joy knew her. *This was how it had all started—the birth of Jake's Joy*, thought Maddie.

"Promise me you won't ever sell Joy," Maddie said to Jake for the hundredth time.

"I promise, Maddie. Joy will live here in the lap of luxury all of her days because of you."

"Good—just keep promising me that."

"I will."

Once they were back in his car, Maddie asked Jake if he was looking forward to his new job and graduate school.

"I'm actually a little nervous," replied Jake.

"What on earth for? You'll make a great teacher, and school will be a breeze for you," answered Maddie immediately.

The two of them talked about his new-found independence for a couple of hours before he drove her back to her English cottage.

"Would you like to come in for a drink?" asked Maddie.

"Of course."

Once Maddie had changed into short shorts, and Jake got out of his suit and tie, they sat in the backyard sipping their wine.

Maddie told Jake that she meant every word she'd said during her toast earlier in the evening. Jake said he knew it and appreciated the kind words. But Maddie insisted they weren't just kind words—they were the heartfelt truth. She really didn't know what she'd do if she didn't have him in her life.

"Let's go inside," said Maddie suddenly. "Even though it's May, the wind is cool."

Once inside, Jake refilled their wine glasses, and both of them plopped down on the couch like the night before. Maddie lay with her head in Jake's lap once again. She asked him again what he ever saw in her that was so special.

"Great legs, great boobs, tiny waist, and a great butt," was his answer.

They both laughed.

He asked her the same question, and she said the same—except no boobs, thank God—and they both laughed again.

This was why she enjoyed Jake. Jake was Jake. What you saw was what you got.

All of a sudden, Jake bent over and kissed Maddie on the lips, just as she had kissed him after he graduated. Maddie surprised herself by kissing him back. Before she knew it, he was holding her in his arms and started gently rubbing her back. She loved the feeling of having a man's touch again, but then thought where it might lead, and it terrified her. Startled, she immediately tensed and ran for her chair. After a few more minutes of talking, Jake said he was sorry if he had frightened her and left.

The rest of the summer, Maddie kept busy with her teaching. She was disappointed that she didn't see much of Jake. Perhaps he'd decided that he needed to move on with his life. She missed their conversations, though.

In August, Maddie went to New Mexico to see her parents for a week. She was aghast when she saw her mom. She was definitely not in good shape. Maddie asked what was wrong and was told again that the doctors didn't know. Her mother had spent two weeks in the hospital again being poked and prodded. She had given so much blood that her veins had collapsed, and they had to use her feet to get what they needed. However, they had discovered that she had blood clots in her legs, so she was taking the experimental drug Coumadin, a blood thinner that they hoped would dissolve the clots. Maddie was very upset that her parents hadn't told her about how really ill her mom was. They both tried to explain to her that there was nothing she could do, and they didn't want to worry her. They were confident that this medicine would work, and she'd be fine. Maddie was not so sure.

As she was leaving to return to school for her junior year, she made her parents promise to keep her informed about her mom's progress. They did. But all the way back to school, Maddie couldn't shake the fear that something might happen to her mother. She needed to talk to Jake.

Maddie arrived in Claymont around noon on her way back to Wilmington. She knew that this was where Jake was living and teaching now, so she called information to get his new number.

The phone rang only twice before he picked up.

"Hi, Jake. It's Maddie. I really need to talk. Would it be all right if I come over?"

"Of course," replied Jake and gave her directions to his new place.

Once Maddie arrived, Jake was standing in the front yard waiting for her. He could tell by the look on her face, as she got out of her car, that something was really wrong. However, he escorted her inside before he asked her.

Maddie explained to him how concerned she was about her mother's illness and how upset she was that they hadn't told her. She felt that she had a right to know. But Jake told her that her parents didn't want to worry her—there was nothing she could do, and they didn't want it to affect her grades. He told her if they found out anything else, they'd call her right away. He then suggested they go to the farm. She agreed immediately.

Maddie loved the farm. Seeing Jake's Joy calmed her down as usual. She was also happy that Jake wasn't angry with her about the last time they were together, but they did need to talk about it.

"Jake, I'm so sorry for the way things ended between us after your graduation. It's just that I've never really been touched by anyone except Ryan, so it terrified me. I hope you understand and forgive me for acting like a jerk," explained Maddie.

"It's fine, Maddie. It was really my fault. I was out of line. I know the rules. It just seemed natural to hold you. Don't worry. It won't happen again. I promise. I've really missed not having your companionship this summer, too. I don't want anything to come between our friendship. It's too important to me. So we're good again, right?" asked Jake.

"We're good," answered Maddie, happily.

They talked for a little while longer before he followed her to her house to help her unload her belongs to begin her junior year.

20

Maddie's junior year seemed to fly by. Her classes were very interesting; she was now the head cheerleader, and business at the dance school was booming.

Ryan was also given more privileges, since he was now a "cow." *What moron came up with that one?* thought Maddie. In fact, Maddie asked him once that if anyone asked what year her boyfriend was in, should she say "cow" or "junior"? Then she laughed hysterically. Maddie was now able to attend some of the "hops" held at West Point, and Ryan would always reserve a room for her at the Thayer Hotel. Maddie knew it was the most expensive place in town and had told Ryan that he didn't need to spend so much money. She could stay at a smaller motel, but Ryan wouldn't hear of it. The Thayer was safe was all he'd ever say about it. Once she arrived in Newark, her sister would pick her up, and she'd spend the night with her before heading for West Point. Her sister would always let her use her car whenever she flew in to see Ryan. *West Point was purposely out of the way,* thought Maddie. *Difficult to get to and difficult to leave.*

Of course, Ryan was only allowed to escort her to the hotel, never her room. After the last time they were able to be alone, merely a short kiss seemed so wrong. Why couldn't they hold each other? Besides, she wanted to feel the way Ryan had made her feel, and she knew he felt the same way. They had discussed it at length, whispering in each other's ear as they danced. How much longer would it be? Nineteen sixty-eight still seemed light-years away to them.

Ryan's cow year also seemed to be flying by for him, too.

Then, one Monday night, in early March of her junior year, Maddie's entire world fell apart. The date was March 6, 1967, to be exact.

Terri, Matt, Jake, and Maddie had just sat down to have an after-dinner drink at Maddie's house when the phone rang. Maddie answered it, listened for a second, and immediately dropped the phone. Jake ran to pick it up. It was Maddie's father. He was calling from the hospital where he'd just had major surgery. Her mother had died suddenly of a massive heart attack. Maddie was frantic and immediately started to cry. Jake told her father not to worry, that he'd take care of everything on this end and see to it that Maddie made it home. Her dad was very grateful that Jake was there for his daughter.

Jake told Terri and Matt, and they began to cry, too. Terri ran over to hug Maddie and took her to her bedroom to lie down.

"She can't be dead," said Maddie. I just got a letter from her today.

"Have you read it yet?" asked Terri.

"No, it's on my desk."

Terri immediately told Jake about the letter. He found it on her desk, scooped it up, took it out, and put it in the glove compartment of his car. He'd give it to her later—when the time was right.

Jake also called Maddie's doctor, and he said he'd be right over. When he arrived, he ordered Maddie to take a couple of pills. He left the rest with Jake so they would keep her calmed down.

Jake decided that he'd drive Maddie to New Mexico himself. He didn't want her driving in her condition, and he absolutely wouldn't put her on a bus all alone. He immediately called into his school and ordered a substitute teacher for a week. He then called the dean of their college and told him what had happened. The dean said he would notify Maddie's teachers about what had happened and told Jake to tell her not to worry about missing any classes. They'd work it out when she returned.

The next morning, Jake and Maddie left for New Mexico. Jake gave Maddie a pill and made her lie down in the backseat of his Mustang. He wanted her to rest as much as possible. He'd stop later and insist that she try to eat. But for now she needed to rest.

Once Jake arrived in Shamrock, Texas, he awakened Maddie.

"Time for breakfast," Jake said brightly.

"I'm not hungry, Jake."

"Well, I am. So up you get. I know that you could use a good cup of coffee, right?"

"Right; coffee sounds good."

Jake was able to get Maddie to eat some dry toast with her coffee. At least she would have something in her stomach. He couldn't give her the next pill unless she did. Right before they were ready to leave, he gave Maddie another pill. Once again, she slept in the backseat.

Jake decided they would stop for the evening in Tucumcari, New Mexico. It wasn't late, but he thought that Maddie would enjoy a good dinner and a nice hot shower before bed. He found a decent hotel, one of the national chains, and checked in, ordering two double beds.

He helped Maddie out of the car and brought in their luggage. As soon as Jake opened the door, he started to laugh.

"What's so funny?" asked Maddie.

"Maddie, look at the beds. They're the new craze. They're vibrating beds!" laughed Jake.

"What's a vibrating bed?" asked his wonderfully naïve Maddie.

"Okay, honey, watch this," said Jake. "I'm going to insert a quarter into this slot above your bed. Lie down and wait and see what happens."

Once the bed started vibrating, Maddie started laughing hysterically. She'd never even heard of such a thing, let alone been on one.

"I'm afraid to ask, but how do you know about these beds?" asked Maddie, still laughing.

"Don't ask. But let's have some fun. I'm going to insert as many quarters as I have so we can laugh until dinner, all right?"

"All right, Jake. Go for it."

Jake and Maddie laughed together for thirty minutes, until he ran out of quarters.

On their way to dinner that night, Jake stopped and purchased more quarters, so they could laugh some more before bedtime. Maddie told Jake at dinner she didn't think her teeth had stopped vibrating yet. They laughed once again.

When they returned to their hotel, Maddie took her shower first. She stayed in there for a long time, too long for Jake. He knocked on the bathroom door, which wasn't locked, but Maddie didn't answer. Finally, he became so worried that he opened the door to find Maddie crouched in the corner of the shower crying her eyes out. He very gently turned off the shower and helped Maddie dry off. He dressed her in her nightie, gave her a pill, and put her into her bed. He felt so sorry for her. There was absolutely nothing he could do for her; he knew that. All he could do was to be there for her.

The next morning, Maddie didn't remember what had happened, and Jake didn't tell her. It would have embarrassed her to know that he had seen her naked body. She just remembered going to sleep. That was fine with him.

Maddie and Jake arrived in Alamogordo, New Mexico, late the next day. Maddie's sister Meredith from Napa, California, was already there, and Michelle was due in any minute. Maddie immediately started to cry again when she saw her sister and her father. She did have the presence of mind, however, to introduce Jake to them. Meredith had never met Jake, but Maddie's father remembered him from homecoming. The two men shook hands, and Maddie's dad thanked Jake for bringing Maddie down. He was glad she didn't have to take the bus alone.

"I'd never have allowed Maddie to take the bus by herself, sir. She had no choice, really. I was bringing her no matter what," said Jake.

"Please don't call me sir. My name is Allen," answered Maddie's father.

"Jake, may I speak to you in private for a minute?" interrupted Meredith.

"Sure. Why don't we go sit outside for a minute?" replied Jake.

Meredith asked Jake how Maddie was coping, really. She wanted to know the truth.

Jake told Meredith that Maddie was an absolute basket case. He was sure that she was still in shock. He explained to her that the doctor had given him some medicine to give her. He was concerned about her mental well-being, so he wouldn't leave her alone for a minute. He also told her not to worry; nothing happened between the two of them. They'd been best friends for three years. He knew all about Ryan. He'd never ever hurt Maddie.

Meredith could tell right away that Jake was in love with her sister. She was also sure that Maddie couldn't see it. Meredith really liked Jake. He was very handsome, but that wasn't important to her. What was important was that she knew she could trust her sister's care to Jake, and she planned to do just that. She could tell that Jake knew how to care for Maddie, especially at this particular time. She planned on telling Michelle about letting Jake take care of her while they were here.

Michelle arrived about an hour after Maddie and Jake. Maddie was happy to see her big sister. She'd been able to see her more often than Meredith since she and Ryan would sometimes visit there. Maddie introduced Jake to Michelle immediately. Michelle's first impression of Jake was that he seemed to genuinely care for her sister. The two talked for a few minutes, and then all of them went to be with Dad.

That night, Jake slept on the couch, while the girls slept in the two extra bedrooms. Meredith and Michelle decided that Maddie needed to have a room to herself and told Jake that he was in charge of her care since she trusted him. After Maddie showered and was ready for bed that evening, Jake went in and sat on the side of the bed and talked to her for a while. Then he gave Maddie her medicine and stayed with her until she was asleep.

When he came out of the room, Meredith and Michelle thanked him for being there. They could tell how much Maddie depended on him. He merely replied that she would be doing the same thing for him if the situation were reversed. He was just glad he could help his best friend.

The next morning, the girls all went to take care of the arrangements for their mother's funeral. Jake stayed behind with their father. The two men talked a little bit about Madison. Jake could tell that she was very special to him. Maddie's dad asked him if Maddie had ever told him that she was very premature and weighed only four pounds when she was born. He told Jake that she had to be in an incubator for six weeks. He and his wife were afraid they were going to lose her, and they had tried for nine years to have her. Jake was surprised to hear this. No, Maddie had never told him that. Even though Maddie's dad never said anything, he could tell that Jake was in love with his daughter. He liked Ryan, always had, but he came to the conclusion that he liked Jake better. Of course, he'd never tell Maddie that.

Once the girls returned from making the arrangements, Jake and Maddie were selected to go pick out the burial plot for their mother. Jake didn't really think he should be the one to help with this, but Meredith and Michelle insisted. So after lunch, and before he gave Maddie her medicine, the two of them went to the cemetery. They chose a spot that they thought Maddie's dad would like. Maddie had wanted her mother to be buried under a tree, but she knew that her father had insisted she be in the sunshine. In the end, they chose the sunshine.

When they returned home, Jake gave Maddie a pill and put her to bed for a while. During this time, Meredith and Michelle had the sad choice of deciding what their mother would wear to her final resting place. They would leave the final decision up to Maddie, though.

Once Maddie awakened, Meredith and Michelle showed Maddie what they had chosen for their mother to wear. It was the dress that her mother had worn to her high school graduation. Maddie started to cry immediately. Then all of a sudden, she became manic. The sisters headed for Jake.

"Jake," said Meredith, "Maddie's having a hard time right now. We chose Mom's outfit, and she was manic about a pin and apron she'd brought with her."

"Let me get them for you, Meredith. I know what she's talking about. She insisted she wouldn't leave without them—they must have a special significance to her. I'll be back in a minute. They're in the car."

Mrs. Conrad's funeral was held on Friday. It was a small service, but everyone who'd been close to her was there—except, of course, her eight grandchildren. Maddie sobbed during the service. She thought about all the things her mother would miss. Her mom would never see her graduate from college, get married, or see her other grandchildren. When she thought of that, she squeezed Jake's hand even more. Jake had helped her father into the church and was sitting with the family. Her dad was there in person, but not really there. He didn't really know what was going on as he was still being sedated from his surgery. He would have to return to the hospital on Monday. Her sisters didn't cry as much during the service a Maddie. They were much more stoic than she.

At the cemetery, Dad remarked that he liked the spot she and Jake had chosen as their mother's final resting place. Maddie and her sisters each placed a red rose on top of their mother's casket before they left.

Back at the house, the neighbors had set up a feast for them. Everyone talked quietly for a while. Jake took it upon himself to be with her father. He brought him a plate of food and sat with him as he ate a little. At about 5:00 PM, everyone who had come to pay their respects left, and it was just the family once again.

Once the neighbors were gone, and Maddie and her father were alone for a moment, her father asked her about her relationship with Jake. She said that Jake had been a godsend to her. They did almost everything together, but he knew from the beginning that she was spoken for. Her father had recognized from the very beginning, while at homecoming, that there was much more to this relationship, even though his daughter wouldn't admit it. He was no fool, but he knew to keep his mouth shut. Maddie would have to learn about life the hard way—she always had.

Then they sat down to join the conversation and look at the pictures Michelle and Meredith had brought with them of her nieces and nephews. Maddie had three nieces and five nephews. She didn't want a large family, perhaps only two—a boy and a girl. She knew her dad would also be very proud of them, if that ever happened.

"Maddie, this is probably not the time to tell you this, but your mom was so excited that you were going to be a college graduate. You'll be the first one in our family to accomplish this, and she was really looking forward to being there and watching you graduate, honey."

Tears started to trickle down Maddie's eyes once again, and Jake hugged her.

Everyone was going to have to leave on Sunday to return to their "normal" lives. But Maddie knew things would never be quite "normal" for her ever again. Her mother's death had changed her. She knew that her grandmother had only lived to be forty-eight, and now her mom, at barely fifty. She didn't feel that the odds were in her favor of living a long life, so she decided then and there that she'd not just save for a rainy day anymore. That didn't mean she was going to buy a new car or anything. It just meant that if she wanted to do something badly enough, she'd do it. Her mother had always said, "When your father retires..." and look at what had happened. She never reached retirement. She was never able to enjoy time with her husband. She'd never had any real possessions. She always just kept saying, "When your father retires...." Maddie promised herself that she would live like there was no tomorrow.

On their last night together, the entire group, including their father, went to a steakhouse for a final meal together. They didn't know it at the time, but it would be many years before they would all be together again. Later that evening, after dinner, Jake and Maddie went for a drive. They ended up at the park in the middle of town. Maddie decided she wanted to go sit on the swings and see how high she could go. Jake pushed her and watched her finally smile in the delight of the moment. This was the Maddie Jake liked the best— carefree and loving life. Afterwards, they sat close together on the park bench to talk. She only had one more year of school now.

On Sunday morning, everyone said their good-byes. They all took Dad back to the hospital together so he could finish his post-op recovery.

Maddie promised her dad she'd be home in August. He told her not to worry; he'd be fine. She was not so sure.

Jake and Maddie rode in silence for about the first thirty minutes of the trip home. Each was lost in his/her own thoughts. Maddie was thinking about her mom. They had stopped one last time at her grave before they left. Jake was despondent, thinking about Maddie and her loss.

Maddie was the first one to break the silence between them.

"Jake, thank you so much for coming with me. I don't know if I could've done it if I'd had to take the bus here all by myself," she said, squeezing his right hand.

"Maddie, I'd never have let you come back alone— never. Don't you know me well enough by now to know that?"

The rest of the trip, Jake and Maddie talked nonstop, except when he gave Maddie a pill in order for her to rest. They talked about her upcoming makeup work, final exams, and her senior year. They talked about Jake's final year for his master's, too. They decided to spend the night at the same motel as before, so they could laugh on the vibrating beds—which, of course, they did. They must have spent twenty quarters on the beds, but it was more than worth it to Jake. It was so good for Jake to hear Maddie's laugh once again. That night, however, after Maddie climbed into bed, she just lay there crying herself to sleep. Finally, she asked Jake if he would hold her until she fell asleep.

"Of course, I will, honey. I'll lie on top of the bedspread." He put his arm around her, and she finally stopped crying and fell into a deep sleep, holding Jake's hand in hers.

Once back in Wilmington, things seemed to return to normal. Maddie's teachers were so kind. Only one of them made her do make up work—her stupid French teacher. She was glad to be home. She was happy to be teaching dance again. It gave her the expressive outlet she'd been needing, but lacking. And even though she had missed a week of classes, she was able to make decent grades on her finals once again. She had made her first B—in French, of course. She couldn't believe her French teacher was the only one who had made her do makeup work after her mother had just died. She hated, really hated that bitch!

21

Maddie's mother died on March 6, 1967, but Ryan didn't hear about it until well after the funeral was over and Maddie had time to write to him.

He'd been worried that something was wrong because he'd received no mail from Maddie for two weeks. He'd never gone that long without a letter. He even stood in the long phone lines several times and tried calling her, but there was never any answer.

After Ryan finally received her letter, he called her immediately.

"YKTA, Maddie, I'm so sorry about your mom. What happened?" asked Ryan.

Maddie explained to him that her mother had a massive heart attack. She was right by the hospital when it happened, but it was so fast that they still couldn't save her.

"Maddie, why didn't you call me? I would've come. You know that," said Ryan quietly.

"Ryan, I don't know how to reach you other than by mail, remember? You have no phone. Besides, I wasn't able to think straight. I was in shock. Jake, Terri, and

Matt took care of everything. The doctor had me on some drugs that made me sleep a lot," said Maddie.

"How did you get to New Mexico? You didn't drive, did you? Did you take the bus?" asked Ryan.

"No, Jake drove me home. I couldn't drive while taking the medicine, and Jake wouldn't allow me to go on the bus by myself, so he took me," replied Maddie nonchalantly.

Ryan was devastated. The one time Maddie had really needed him, he wasn't there for her. Jake was. He couldn't get angry at Maddie or even Jake for that matter. It wasn't her fault. It was his. Damn it, why couldn't anything go right for him?

He and Maddie talked for a while longer. She explained the funeral to Ryan and seeing her father who had been hospitalized when it happened. Her dad really didn't know what was going on. She and her sisters had to make all the arrangements. In fact, they had to take him back to the hospital before they left.

Ryan could tell that Maddie was still devastated and remembered how close she was to her mom. After they hung up, he called a floral shop in Highland Falls and had flowers wired to her in Wilmington. He had the card say, "I'm so sorry. YKTA."

Then Ryan went back to his room and told his roommate what had happened. It was then that he finally broke down crying for the first time since arriving at West Point. When Maddie had needed him the most, he hadn't been there for her. That's all he could think about. He didn't even go to class the next day. He went on sick call instead.

After he saw the doctor and told him what had happened and how helpless he felt, he went back to his room with some pills to calm him down. After resting for a bit, he sat down and wrote Madison a long letter. He apologized over and over for not being there for her. He vowed it would never happen again. He gave her a phone number to call if there was ever another emergency. The doctor had given it to him. Once he put the letter into the mail, he felt better. What was done was done. He couldn't change the past, but at least it would never happen again.

The rest of cow year, Ryan was very busy. He had his classes, his sailing team, and always in the back of his mind, trying to decide what branch of service he wanted to choose. Everyone at West Point, from instructors to commanders, stressed that West Point produced the best Infantry officers in the world. They felt that all the cadets should choose Infantry, and if they didn't, sometimes the cadets were considered unworthy. Ryan had been considering either Infantry (what they called Idiot Sticks) or Mech (Armor). He knew that Maddie didn't want him to choose Infantry, but she told him that he was the one who had to make up his own mind

Also, at the end of cow year, the cadets chose their West Point class rings. This was a very special occasion for them. They had worked three long hard years, including summers, to get to this point. This was a joyous occasion for the cadets. Ryan chose the army color green for his stone. However, he did have something special engraved inside of it. He had "R&M

YKTA" and the date he would graduate—June 5, 1968. He was going to surprise Maddie and show it to her when she came to visit for ring weekend.

Ryan and Maddie didn't know it yet, but both their worlds were about to fall apart once again.

On June 4, 1967, of Ryan's junior year, his world fell apart just like Maddie's had three months earlier. He was called to the guardhouse and told that his father had died. His plane had been shot down over Laos while trying to help some Marines who were taking heavy fire. There was no mistake that he was dead. His wingman saw his father's plane go down and burst into flames. Ryan just stared when he heard the news. He was in shock. Not his dad. The only reason his dad had volunteered to go to Vietnam was so that he would be home in time for his graduation from West Point.

Ryan called Maddie and was frantic.

"Maddie, my father's plane crashed over Laos," he cried into the phone.

Maddie immediately became sick to her stomach.

"What are you saying, Ryan?"

"He's dead, Maddie. My dad is dead. His wingman saw his plane burst into flames."

"Oh my God! I can't believe it!" screamed Maddie. "Hold on just a second, Ryan." Maddie ran over to the kitchen sink and proceeded to vomit.

When she returned to the phone, she immediately asked what she could do.

"I'm headed to Shreveport. Can you meet me there?"

"Of course I can. I'll get on the road tomorrow morning, early," replied Maddie.

"Don't worry about finding a place to stay," said Ryan. "I'll get a motel room. I know the area a little better. Let me give you my stepmother's phone number and address." And he did. "When you get into town, call me," continued Ryan. "A plane is being sent for me in a couple of hours. I'll see you when you get there."

"I love you, Ryan. I'm so sorry. I'll see you the day after tomorrow at the latest."

"Maddie, call the house in Shreveport and let us know where you'll be spending the night. I don't want you to be out of touch. Promise me you'll do that."

"I promise. YKTA."

"YKTA," answered a sobbing Ryan.

As soon as Maddie hung up, she went to the sink and wretched again. Then she called Jake and asked him if he could come over as soon as possible. It was important that she see him at once.

Jake could sense that something was terribly wrong, so he said he'd be right over.

Next, she called Terri and Matt and asked them to come over, too. Disaster had struck again.

All three of Maddie's friends arrived at about the same time to find Maddie sobbing and drinking a glass of wine while sitting in her favorite chair.

"What's wrong?" they all said, almost in unison.

"Ryan's father's plane crashed over Laos. He's dead," mumbled a numb Maddie.

"What?" Jake asked.

"Ryan's father is dead," said Maddie again. "And before you ask, it's for sure. His wingman saw his plane burst into flames."

"Oh my God, Maddie," cried Terri as she grabbed her and put her arms around her. Maddie was shaking uncontrollably.

Jake went into action. He called Maddie's doctor once again and explained to him what had just happened, and he came over to help right away. It seemed like déjà vu to everyone. At least school was out, so Jake didn't have to call the dean again.

Jake sat beside Maddie, who was now on the couch with Terri. He took Maddie's hand and told her not to worry. He would make all the arrangements to get her to Shreveport as quickly as possible. He called and booked her on a flight to Dallas for the next day at noon. He also contracted a rental car for her when she landed at Love Field so that she could drive to Shreveport as quickly as possible. Jake decided that he'd drive Maddie to Oklahoma City himself and also be there to pick her up when she returned. He definitely didn't want her behind the wheel in the state she was in.

Terri helped Maddie pack. Maddie had no idea what to take, nor did she care at this particular moment, so Terri packed for her. She packed slacks, blouses, shoes, a couple of dresses, and all the other essentials she thought she would need. It didn't take long to get her things together into her small suitcase, but it took much longer to get Maddie out of her state of shock.

When she was finally packed, her four friends sat down with her in the living room. Each of them tried to calm her down enough to get her ready for what lay ahead of her once again.

Maddie tried to listen to their words of encouragement, but she just kept thinking that it was all a big mistake. She just knew Ryan would call her back and tell her it hadn't been Lieutenant Colonel Richardson after all; it had been a different plane that had gone down. That call never came.

Maddie finally started to doze off, and Jake picked her up gently, took her to her bedroom, and tenderly placed her on her bed, covered her with a quilt and turned off the light. While Maddie was finally sleeping, Ryan was packing a few items to take with him to the memorial, and then went to catch the plane that had been sent for him.

The entire trip all Ryan could think about was that his father would never see him graduate. There was no body. His body was with his plane in Laos. Ryan felt his father would've wanted it that way, though. He also knew that he would be in charge of making the arrangements once he arrived in Shreveport. He was glad Maddie was going to be there to support and help him through the worst time in his life.

Jake told Terri and Matt that he'd spend the night at Maddie's and then drive her to the airport in the morning for her flight to Dallas. He wanted Maddie to rest as much as she could before having the task of facing Ryan and his great loss.

Terri said she would take over all the dance classes while she was gone, and Matt would look after the house for her.

Terri knew that Jake was in love with Maddie, and had been for a long time, even though it was obvious that she was spoken for. She thought Jake should move on and had told him as much once, but Jake just said he had the best of two worlds—the one with Maddie in it, and a world where he could have his sexual needs met without any commitment.

Jake and Maddie left early the next morning. He gave Maddie a pill and once again put her into the backseat to sleep. A few minutes before they arrived at the airport, he stopped at a diner so they could get some breakfast. He didn't want her to fly on an empty stomach. Maddie tried her best to eat her eggs and toast, but she felt as if she'd throw up if she took another bite.

Jake checked Maddie in and walked her to her gate. He sat with her, quietly holding her hand until it was time for her to board. He told her to tell Ryan how sorry he was for his loss, gave her the bottle of pills, and made her promise not to take them while she was driving. Then he gave her the papers for her Hertz rental car. He also made her promise to call him collect once she was in Shreveport. He said he'd be waiting for her next week when she returned. Finally, he hugged her tenderly, kissed her cheek, and watched as the love of his life boarded the plane.

22

Meanwhile, once Ryan arrived in Shreveport, he went directly to his stepmother's home. His three younger stepbrothers were there, too, of course. Later, when looking back, all Ryan could remember at first was that many tears were shed and lots of food was brought to them from friends and neighbors.

Maddie's flight to Dallas was so short that she decided not to spend the night and drove directly to Shreveport. She called Jake and told him and that she was on her way. She picked up the rental car, and was on the road to Shreveport before she knew it. During the entire drive, she thought about how to help Ryan through his loss.

When Maddie arrived on the outskirts of Shreveport, she stopped to use a pay phone beside a diner and dialed the number that Ryan had given her. She had no idea who would answer the phone or what she'd say if it wasn't Ryan. She didn't need to worry. Ryan answered on the first ring.

"Maddie, are you okay? Where are you?" Ryan asked.

Maddie described the diner and the cross streets where she was located, and Ryan knew immediately where she was.

"Stay where you are. Go get a cup of coffee. I'll be there in a couple of minutes."

Sure enough, about fifteen minutes later, while Maddie was sipping her coffee, she saw Ryan drive up, park, and enter the diner to greet her. She ran up to him, threw her arms around his neck, and started to cry. He kissed her and told her everything would be all right. Maddie felt badly because she was supposed to be the one comforting him, not the other way around.

"Follow me to the hotel, Maddie, so we can drop off your stuff," he said as they were getting into their cars. "Then we'll go to the house, okay?"

"Okay," was all she could manage to say.

When Maddie arrived, everything seemed to get better. Ryan had already reserved a room for her, and once she put her things down, the two of them left to go directly to the house.

Once they were at Ryan's house, everyone seemed happy to see her. She noticed that Ryan's youngest brother was having the worst time, so she put him on her lap, hugged him and told him how sorry she was.

Ryan gave her a glass of wine and sat down on the sofa beside her. He explained to her everything he knew about what had happened. His father and his group were on a secret mission to help embedded Marines who were under attack when his squad was unexpectedly hit by enemy fire. Enemy planes began chasing them, and even though they tried evasive tactics, his dad's plane was hit and went down so quickly that he didn't even have the chance to eject. His plane exploded upon impact. His wingman saw the entire incident. After he told her what had happened, Ryan started to sob.

Maddie held him tightly, not saying a word. Words were useless at a moment like this; she knew that from experience. About an hour later, Ryan took Maddie back to the Hilton.

"I'm sorry we can't stay together while you're here, honey," Ryan said, "but you know how it is. It wouldn't be right, but at least here we can share some time alone."

"Can you stay with me for a while now?" asked Maddie. "I need some time alone with you."

"Of course I can. I want to. I'd spend the entire night with you if I could. You know that."

They went directly to the bed. They held each other for a long time. Afterwards, Ryan very tenderly unbuttoned her blouse and unhooked her bra. All Maddie did was look at him straight in the eyes. Eventually, he took off her slacks so that all she was wearing was her lacy panties. Just looking at Maddie lying there started to arouse Ryan. It always did.

Maddie helped Ryan take off his polo shirt, his belt, and finally his khaki slacks. The two of them lay beside one another almost naked.

Maddie was the first to speak. "Ryan, I want you to make love to me, really make love to me. I don't want to wait anymore. We're getting married next year anyway, so what difference does it make?"

"Maddie, I thought you were the one who wanted to wait. I thought you wanted both of us to be virgins until we married," answered Ryan softly.

"I don't care about that anymore, Ryan. I want you. I want you now."

"Are you sure?

"Ryan, I've never been surer of anything in my life. Take me now, please," replied Maddie breathlessly.

"I've wanted you for so long, Maddie," said Ryan as he very gently took off her panties. Maddie was now lying before him totally naked, and Ryan would never get used to how truly beautiful she was. She still looked the same as the first time he ever saw her.

Ryan quickly took off his briefs and climbed into bed with her, his manhood already standing at attention. But Ryan wasn't in a hurry. He wanted to take his time and explore every part of Maddie's body before they truly made love for the first time in their lives.

Ryan lay beside Maddie and kissed her deeply on her lips. He gently put her face in his hands and held her head still, so he could kiss all the parts of her face— eyes, nose cheeks, ears. When he started caressing her body gently with his fingertips, Maddie's body started to shudder. His touch always had that effect on her.

When Ryan thought she was ready, he opened up Maddie's legs as far apart as he could. She laid spread eagle before him, and he couldn't believe that in a few minutes, the love of his life would truly be his. He used his hands, mouth, and tongue to explore every part of her being. As soon as he pushed his finger gently into her, she came immediately. Waves and waves rolled over her, and she didn't want him to stop. Every time he moved his finger, she came again. She was totally breathless.

"Ryan," Maddie begged, "please make love to me. Make us one. I want this so much. We've waited long enough."

Without answering, he gently opened her already wet pussy and started to insert himself into her as gently as possible. Maddie was ready to accept him, all of him, and started to move her hips up and down. It was an automatic movement for them. They were pressed together as one, and Ryan's shaft began moving faster in and out of her now. Maddie knew that the first time would hurt her, but she wasn't prepared for just how much. She screamed out loud once in pain, and Ryan immediately stopped. He couldn't bear to hurt the woman he loved.

"Ryan, don't stop. It'll be okay. I want this. I want you. I want you—now!"

Ryan finally pushed himself all the way into her. All at once, it seemed as if they both exploded together. They were both shaking, looking into each other's eyes. They were not virgins anymore. But Ryan was concerned about hurting Maddie. He knew it would the first time. He also knew she would bleed some.

"Are you all right, honey? I'm so sorry I hurt you," Ryan said with a look of concern on his face and tears in his eyes. "I know it hurt you."

"Yes, it did, but it was a good kind of hurt, because it was you," replied Maddie quietly.

They stayed together, entwined as one for a long time before separating. Yes, there was blood on the sheet. Ryan ran to the bathroom and got a warm washcloth to gently wipe Maddie.

"Well," said Maddie, smiling happily at the man she loved, "I guess we're not virgins anymore, are we? We took each other's virginity."

Ryan waited a while before replying, which made Maddie anxious and wonder if he was upset or regretted what had just taken place.

"Madison, I'm not one bit sorry about what just happened. I probably wanted it more than you. I have for a very long time—today just seemed the right moment for us. You belong to me now—only me. That's what I want. I'm yours forever, you know that. Please don't think for one minute that I feel this was a mistake; I don't. It's the best thing that's ever happened to me."

Maddie rolled on top of him and put her head close to his heart so she could feel it beat. Ryan and Maddie knew they'd be expected back at his house soon, but Maddie needed a little more reassurance of their commitment to each other before they got up. She asked Ryan if he'd scheduled the chapel yet and what day their wedding was going to be. However, her heart sank the moment she saw the look on his face. He hadn't done it.

"Maddie, I'm so sorry. I've been studying my butt off for final exams, and then this God-awful disaster occurred. I completely forgot. I'll call right now if you want me to."

"Ryan, you promised me you'd set the date for us. You've never ever broken a promise to me before. How could you just forget about it? It was really important to me. Is there some other reason you've not set the date yet?" cried Maddie.

"Of course not, honey. I just forgot. That's all. I'm sorry. Do you want me to do it now? I can."

"No, now's not the time to do it. Do it when you get back, but please let me know as soon as you do," Maddie replied sadly.

Ryan could tell that Maddie was crushed. He'd been such an idiot. Now she probably hated that she'd given up her virginity to him. She probably thought he was an asshole. He held her tightly and told her he'd call as soon as possible.

Ryan and Maddie showered together, but even though they laughed at each other, Ryan couldn't shake the belief that he'd really screwed up. He had. He decided he'd call from his house as soon as they returned, so he could surprise her that night with the news.

Once they returned to his house, they were both engulfed with the plans for his father's memorial. It would be very simple—just the family and close friends at the base chapel. All the older family members would be asked to say a few words, and Ryan, the eldest son, was to be in charge of making the arrangements.

Ryan went directly to the base chaplain. The memorial would be the next day. However, while he was there, he also called back to the Point to ask the chaplain if there were any dates still available for his wedding in June, right after his graduation in 1968.

After the chaplain looked at his booking journal, he told Ryan that June 7th was open, so Ryan booked the date on the spot as he'd promised Madison he'd do. She would become Mrs. Ryan Richardson at the stroke of noon on June 7, 1968, two days after his graduation.

On his return to his stepmother's house, he told the family of the arrangements for tomorrow's memorial. After lunch, he told them that he was going to take Maddie back to the hotel. He wanted to write his tribute to his father in a quiet place.

When they returned to the hotel, he told Maddie he needed some time alone for a few hours. She understood completely, so he left her at the hotel. He told her he wouldn't be gone long.

Ryan went straight downtown. He'd never needed money while at West Point, so any money he'd received from graduation gifts, birthdays, and his small monthly stipend from West Point had simply gone into his checking account. He had remembered to bring his checkbook with him, thank God; he was going to need it now. Ryan found a reputable jewelry store to buy Maddie her engagement ring. He chose a very simple ring for her. It was a one-and-a-half carat round solitaire, with a matching diamond wedding band that would eventually surround it. He was very proud of his choice. He had the jeweler call his bank to make sure the funds could be wired and were available immediately, so he could take the ring with him. He knew they might have to return the next day to get it sized, but he needed to take that ring with him right now.

His next stop was a floral shop, where he bought her one long-stemmed blush rose—Maddie's favorite.

When Ryan returned to the hotel room, he found Maddie crying softly on the bed, her back turned away from the door. He closed the door quietly and lay down behind her on the bed. He slid the rose under her nose. Maddie saw the rose immediately and deeply inhaled its sweet fragrance. She then turned to face Ryan.

"Maddie, I know I'm not worthy of your love, but I love you with all my heart—always have and always will. And you know that whenever I say that, it's always been my soul speaking."

Upon saying that, he produced a small black velvet box, got down on one knee beside her, and said, "Would you do me the honor of being my wife on June 7, 1968?"

Maddie was speechless as she looked at the ring Ryan held out to her. It was perfect—simple and perfect. Maddie put her arms around Ryan's neck, kissed him passionately on the lips, and answered, "Ryan I'd be honored to be your wife." This was another of Maddie's "remember forever" moments.

Ryan gently slipped the ring onto her finger. It actually fit. They both admired the ring together. They lay on the bed and held each other close again until they had to return for the dinner his stepmother's friends had prepared for all of them.

When dinner was almost over that evening, and before dessert was served, Ryan told his family that he had an announcement to make.

"Most of you know," he began, "Madison and I have been together since we were sixteen. She's waited for me patiently for five years, and now I have only one year left. Even though this may not be the right time to make such an announcement, I think Dad would approve. I want all of you to know that I've asked Maddie to be my wife and she's accepted. We'll be getting married on June 7, 1968, at the chapel at West Point. I know that both Dad and Maddie's mom will be there with us in spirit. Dad always loved Madison. So, I want to present the future Mrs. Ryan Richardson to all of you. Show them your ring, Maddie," he said as he kissed her on the cheek.

Totally surprised, Maddie stood up beside Ryan and embarrassingly held up her left hand. The ring looked huge on her long slender fingers.

Everyone hooted and hollered, and Maddie curtsied. This was also another one of those "remember forever moments" for Maddie—two in one day! Everyone came and surrounded them to congratulate and hug them both. They always wondered when this day would finally come, and now it had.

But the next day was very difficult for all concerned. There was no body; it was with his dad's plane in an enemy land far away. Since Ryan was the oldest son, he deemed it his responsibility to take charge. At his father's memorial, Ryan talked about how empty he would now feel not having his father present at his graduation from West Point and his marriage to Maddie. That was the only reason his father had volunteered to go to Vietnam in the first place, so that he would be home in time to witness his graduation. Ryan's speech was so moving. He had always been an eloquent speaker, and this time was no different. He spoke of how proud he was to be his son, and that he was so happy that he'd had the chance to really get to know him when he decided to live with him in Avalon. He spoke of happy times, funny incidents, as well as what kind of father he'd been to him. He managed not to break down until the end. Then his sorrow engulfed him, and he started to sob. Maddie instantly got up, went to the podium, and gently guided him back to his seat.

After his father's funeral, Ryan went to rejoin his class at Fort Benning. When Maddie left Shreveport, she and Ryan were happy that at least they'd meet again at Fort Sutton later that summer. As they kissed each other good-bye, they both said YKTA at the same time. As always, whenever this happened, they always laughed together.

Maddie drove back to Dallas, returned her rental car, and made it to her gate in plenty of time. The flight home was only about thirty minutes. However, while on the plane, Maddie took off her engagement ring and put it into its box. For some reason, she didn't want Jake to know that she was officially engaged. She wasn't ready to tell him yet. In fact, she wasn't ready to tell anyone, not even Terri.

Jake met her at the gate with his usual huge bear hug. Maddie always loved those hugs from him. They gathered her luggage and retrieved Jake's Mustang from the car park.

The drive home was about sixty-five miles. Jake asked Maddie how Ryan was doing. He could only imagine how hard it must have been for him. Maddie had told him about Ryan's father being a pilot in Vietnam now, so that he could be home for his son's graduation. What a terrible disappoint for him. Maddie told him that he'd work through it, but it would take time. She was still trying to cope with the loss of her mother.

"How is Joy?" asked Maddie, wanting to change the subject.

"Well, I honestly think that she misses you and her carrots," replied Jake.

"Would you like to go see her when we get home?" he continued.

"Absolutely. Joy always makes me happy."

They stopped at the grocery store as soon as they arrived in Wilmington and bought stuff for a picnic. They quickly picked up fruit and stuff for sandwiches. Next, they stopped at the liquor store, and Jake bought some wine.

Maddie was glad to be home and was anxious to see Joy. When they arrived at the farm, Maddie fed Joy her beloved carrots and also went for a short ride on her.

While Maddie was riding Joy, Jake made sandwiches, put out some fruit, poured some wine, and put everything on a blanket under the tree, so they would be in the shade and out of the hot June sun.

After Maddie had finished her ride and had brushed Joy down, she went and lay down on the blanket with Jake. She was glad he was still going to be a part of her life. He was really very important to her. They talked a little about Maddie's senior year and the classes she would be taking. Jake laughed when she asked for his help with her math, science, and statistics class.

"Of course, I'll help you. But I can't imagine why you waited until the last minute to take those easy classes. Only stats might give you some trouble," said Jake.

"I always put off doing things I don't want to do or feel that I can't do well," replied Maddie seriously.

"Madison, I never knew that about you. To me, you've always been the one to tackle everything head on," answered a surprised Jake. "What else don't I know about you, young lady?"

Maddie told Jake that her life was an open book, and that he knew her better than anyone else, including Terri. But he didn't know that she wished she could live in a little cottage in England, somewhere in the beautiful Lake District one day. She also told him that she felt she was a Type A-B personality. It depended upon the occasion. She didn't consider herself to be a moody person, nor was she unhappy. In fact, other than the fact that her mother's death still haunted her, and she had nightmares about Ryan's dad's going down in flames, she considered herself a happy person. She also wanted a lap dog to keep her company someday. She just loved little dogs—not Chihuahuas, though. And, of course, he already knew that her favorite color was pink—the shade of pink of her pointe shoes. She loved lilac bushes, gardenia bushes, weeping willow trees, and blush roses. She also told Jake that she only wanted two children—a boy and then a girl, so her daughter would have the big brother that she'd never had. That was about it.

"Wow!" said Jake. "You just said a mouthful. Most of it I already knew, but you threw me when you mentioned a cottage in the Lake District and lap dogs," replied Jake happily.

"Okay, Jake. It's your turn. Tell me some things about you that I may not know yet."

Jake told her that his life was pretty much an open book to her, too. Perhaps she didn't know that he enjoyed reading, especially mystery novels and biographies. He enjoyed gardening. He and his mother had had a garden almost every year. He especially liked growing beefsteak tomatoes. He said that he hadn't thought about children yet, but he knew he wanted more than one. He was an only child and had missed not having any brothers or sisters. Even though she probably wouldn't agree, he told her he was really a quiet person at heart. Money didn't mean that much to him. He'd always had enough and never really abused the fact that his parents were quite wealthy.

What Jake didn't say to Maddie, though, was really much more important than what he did. He didn't tell her he was madly in love with her, wanted to marry her, and wanted her to have his children. He also didn't say that he'd be able to give her anything she ever wanted, including that cottage in the Lake District and a lap dog. Those are the things he'd probably never get to say to her. Merely thinking about it made Jake sad.

Maddie could tell that there was something he wasn't telling her. She knew him that well. She also recognized that he'd become quiet.

"Jake, I know you, really know you. There is something you aren't telling me. What is it?"

"It's nothing important, Maddie. I'd rather not talk about it, if you don't mind."

"Of course, you don't have to tell me anything you don't want to, but you know I'm a good listener if you ever want to talk about something."

After talking and drinking the rest of the bottle of wine, the two of them picked up their things, and Jake drove Maddie home.

"Would you like to go out to dinner and a movie tomorrow night?" asked Jake.

"Sure thing," replied Maddie.

23

Ryan was excited that after his stint at Fort Benning, he'd be going to Fort Sutton and meet Maddie again.

Maddie drove down to Fort Sutton, near Livingston, for a long weekend at the end of July. Ryan had reserved a room for her at a decent hotel near the post. She was supposed to meet him later that evening.

Since she arrived early, she decided to take advantage of the pool and decided to swim and sunbathe a little before Ryan returned from his artillery training. That's where Ryan found her lying face down on a lounge chair wearing a black-and-white polka dot two-piece swimsuit. She'd unhooked the top, so she wouldn't get a tan line. Her long wet hair surrounded her face. When Ryan saw her there, she looked prettier to him than she ever had. Her natural tan was getting darker, while her dark auburn hair was getting sun-streaked. He bent over her very quietly and softly whispered, "YKTA, Madison."

Maddie was so startled that she grabbed her top over her breasts and sat up immediately.

"Oh my God, Ryan, you scared me to death!" exclaimed Maddie. "I wasn't expecting you for hours."

"Here, let me hook your top up for you, young lady. I don't want anyone else to get to see what I see," said Ryan as he fastened her top.

The two went together to their room. No one noticed or, for that matter, cared that the two of them were sharing a room. This was an Army town, after all. They were used to soldiers and young women entering and exiting at all hours.

Once they were in the room, though, Ryan grabbed Maddie to him and kissed her deeply. That kiss contained all his feelings for this woman. He adored her. She had to know that.

"Hello, to my future wife," said Ryan cheerfully.

"Hi, to my future husband. How are you doing, really? Believe me, I know what a difficult time this is for you—actually, for both of us," said Maddie.

They sat in the two club chairs in the room and chatted for a while about things in general. It was decided that Maddie would attend Ring Weekend, and for Christmas this year, they would go to see her father and his mother. Ryan hadn't seen Maddie's father in four years. He wanted to ask him for his daughter's hand in marriage—do it the right way. Then they would go to Ohio and see his mother. Maddie hadn't seen her since high school graduation. They were going to talk about their upcoming wedding.

Ryan and Maddie still planned on a small wedding—only a few family members and friends. She wanted Terri to be her matron of honor, and, of course, Matt had to accompany her. Ryan had chosen an old friend from Michigan as his best man. They'd been friends since grade school. Maddie's father and sister Michelle, as well as Ryan's mother and sisters, would also attend, but Meredith couldn't attend since she was dealing with a deaf son. So that was it—it would be very small, very intimate.

After going out for dinner, the two of them climbed into bed early. Since neither of them were virgins any longer, the tension between them subsided some, and they were able to relax. They both lay nude together in bed and took a great deal of time exploring each other's bodies. Ryan couldn't believe that Maddie's body was so perfect. The only blemishes he could find on her otherwise flawless skin was a small birthmark on the back of her neck and one on her left wrist —but that was it. The rest of her body was perfectly proportioned. She had no hips to speak of, and her long legs—which she'd wrap around his back when they made love— made a perfectly rounded heart. Maddie felt the same way about Ryan's body. He was tall and slim, but his entire body was firm to the point that he looked like an Adonis to her. Of course, neither of them had ever been with anyone else, so they had no one to compare each other to.

Since they had lost their virginity together, neither of them was afraid of hurting each other. The deed was done. Now, they enjoyed lovemaking very slowly. Ryan had asked Maddie if she wanted him to use protection, but Maddie said no. She saw no reason for it since they were getting married. Neither of them was really worried about her getting pregnant. They saw each other so seldom that both of them thought the chances would be slim. But if it did happen, it happened. Maddie wanted two children, a boy and a girl. Two was plenty for Ryan, too. Not always, but many times, Maddie and Ryan were usually able to come at the same time. Perhaps it was because they'd been together for so long and knew each other so well. Or perhaps it was because their bodies fit together so perfectly. That's the way it was this time. When Ryan knew Maddie was ready for him, he entered her gently. Then, as their movement became autonomous, he'd plunge his engorged member deeper inside her and move harder and harder until they finally exploded together. As usual, they never separated quickly after making love. They always stayed together as long as possible, almost as if this time could be the last time.

Maddie and Ryan spent three days together at Fort Sutton. One evening, they went to the movies; another, they walked around the post so Maddie could get a feel for what life as the wife of an officer would be like.

Once again their good-byes were not sad. Maddie would see him soon during Ring Weekend at West Point. Ryan had told Maddie about his ring, and that he had something special engraved in it. But he wanted it to be a surprise, so he wouldn't tell her what it was.

They kissed each other passionately one last time before leaving the motel room. They both knew that their long wait was almost over—only one more year before they'd be married.

After being with Maddie at Fort Sutton, Ryan was headed to work at the New York Military Academy for a month where he taught National Guard OCS and actually received some pay for this stint.

While Maddie was driving from Fort Sutton back to Wilmington, she did what she'd done ever since they'd become engaged. She took her ring off and put it in its tiny box in her purse. Maddie knew that Ryan would've been hurt to his very core if he knew that she wasn't wearing his ring at school, but for some reason, she didn't want anyone to know, especially Jake. She knew Jake well enough to know that if he saw a ring on her finger, he'd probably stop seeing her. She knew it wasn't fair to Jake, but she wasn't ready to let him go. He'd come to mean too much to her.

Maddie spent most of the rest of the summer before her senior year helping Terri with her wedding plans. The two of them picked out the flowers for the church, the cake, and then went over the last minute plans for the reception at the Park restaurant. Even though Maddie had taken three days off toward the end of July to see Ryan at Fort Sutton, by the first week of August, everything was ready.

Since everything was ready for Terri's wedding, Maddie also took a week off the first part of August to go and see her father.

Her dad told her that he was going to retire like he and her mom had decided and move back to Oklahoma. He was going to live in Norman, Oklahoma. That wasn't a surprise to Maddie, but what came next was.

"Maddie, go look in the garage," said her dad.

"Why?"

"Honey, just go and look," said her dad impatiently.

Maddie did as she was told. What she saw sitting there was the most beautiful 1966 Mustang she'd ever seen. It was dark green with a tan parchment top. It was absolutely gorgeous. In fact, she couldn't really believe her eyes.

"Maddie, I was going to wait and give you this for your graduation present, but since you travel so much, I want you to have it now. I'd feel better knowing that you were in a newer model than the one you've been driving all these years. Your mother knew that this was what you wanted, and I agreed with her. I hope you like it, honey."

"Like it? I love it!" Maddie immediately ran over to her father and gave him a big kiss. She only wished that her mother could have been here to enjoy this moment, too.

Maddie drove her new Mustang back to Wilmington a week later. It drove like a dream and didn't miss a beat. Maddie still couldn't believe it was hers. She even stopped in Claymont and showed it to Jake. He, too, was surprised and gave her a big hug, saying that she deserved it, especially with her grades and everything else she'd been through this past year.

Then she headed home to get ready for Terri and Matt's big day next week.

Maddie was the maid of honor, and Jake was the best man at Matt and Terri's wedding. Since the wedding was so small, they were really the only ones involved. Matt had chosen two of his fraternity brothers as ushers, and Terri had asked two of the cheerleaders to be in charge of the reception.

Doctor Sill, the philosophy instructor at their college, was the one who would marry them. Maddie really liked the idea of having someone they knew personally to do the honors. That wouldn't be the case at her wedding. She didn't know the West Point chaplain.

Terri had chosen yellow for the color of her wedding and had helped Maddie pick out her dress. It wasn't a solid yellow, but more of a spring-time summer print dress, much like the one Maddie had worn to Jake's graduation. She wore a round crown of white daisies on her head, with long yellow ribbons trailing down her back. Since Maddie hadn't cut her hair in many years, it was now almost down to her waist. It fell in perfect ringlets. She really didn't have much control over her hair, so she just let it be what it was—beautiful. Maddie also carried a bouquet of soft yellow roses and daisies. Jake wore a black tuxedo with a light yellow cummerbund and a light yellow rose in his lapel.

Terri had insisted on going against tradition. Instead of Maddie walking in front of her, and Jake standing at the altar with Matt, she wanted Maddie and Jake to walk hand in hand down the aisle together before she walked in on her father's arm.

As Maddie and Jake walked slowly down the aisle together, holding hands, he whispered in Maddie's ear, "You look absolutely gorgeous, almost ethereal, to me."

Maddie quietly said, "You look pretty damn handsome yourself, Jake Kelly," and beamed her beautiful smile at him.

When Terri walked in, she looked magnificent. Her white dress fit her like a glove, and her train followed behind her like a kitten's tail. Matt's eyes were filled with tears when he saw his wife-to-be walking proudly toward him. He was ready to be a husband and take care of Terri for the rest of his life.

The wedding itself only took around twenty minutes. While the guests went to the reception, the entire wedding party stayed behind for pictures. Jake had already made up his mind to buy some of the pictures, especially those of Maddie and him together. He had to admit, they made an extremely attractive couple. Of course, he felt Maddie was the one responsible for that.

At the reception, both Jake and Maddie toasted the newlyweds. Jake's toast was a clever synopsis of growing up with Matt as his best friend. He had everyone laughing when he told a few of the antics they had shared throughout the years. Naturally, he knew they would be happy, and he was glad he was now going to have the "sister" he'd never had.

Maddie's toast was a little more subdued, but funny as well. She couldn't imagine not seeing Matt and Terri together. They were two sides of the same coin. Terri was her best friend, and the three of them were running a successful and very profitable business. She ended with the statement that after their honeymoon, Terri had to get back to work.

Once Terri and Matt left, Maddie and Jake helped clean up before heading for Maddie's house. The minute they walked in the door, Jake took off his jacket, tie, and cummerbund, undid the top button of his shirt, and took off his shoes. Maddie proceeded to take off her daisy crown, went into her bedroom, and slipped out of her dress and shoes. When she returned, she was wearing a cute navy-and-white checkered tie top and matching navy short shorts. After that, she poured some wine for both of them.

"Well, I'm glad that's over," said Jake. "I didn't think Matt was going to make it."

"I knew everything would be perfect!" declared Maddie happily.

Both Jake and Maddie were happy that Matt and Terri were married. They made a good couple and hoped they'd share many years of happiness together. The one thing that Jake didn't say was that he'd wished it had been a double ceremony.

24

Both Ryan and Maddie would feel that their final year in college went by like a blur.

Ryan couldn't believe it. He was finally a firstie (or senior in all other circles). It had taken three long hard years and summers to get here. He became a brigade executive officer. He was the senior five-stripe cadet captain. He couldn't believe he was this lucky. But it really wasn't luck—his dedication and effort was finally being rewarded. Ryan was going to be responsible for the brigade staff, acting in the absence of the first captain, coordinating with the regimental XOs, parades, ceremonies, inspections, and corps trips, as well as being the secretary of the Honors Committee this year.

As the secretary of the Honors Committee, Ryan was on the board and wrote the required reports after a decision was reached concerning the disposition of a cadet's case. That year, several cadets were dismissed from West Point for cheating or lying. One was dismissed because he knew what was going on and failed to report it. Around fifteen cadets were expelled during his firstie year.

Ryan was taking some difficult courses this year. He took Structural Analysis, U.S. Army in the Cold War, Military Leadership, International Relations, Twentieth Century Warfare, and other required courses for his civil engineering degree. His favorite course while at West Point was the History of Military Art, which was a study of warfare. Since he was probably going to serve in the Infantry, he found this class fascinating. West Point had done its job. They had made Ryan into a warrior. Advanced training before he went to Vietnam would make him the professional killer that Maddie had feared.

As a firstie, the cadets had enormous privileges. They felt free for the first time in three years. They weren't in prison anymore. They received six weekends off-campus each semester, which included missing Saturday classes and parades. Oh, they still received their fair share of demerits. Ryan even received one for dust on his phone. As a brigade executive officer, there was a phone in his room for official use only.

As a firstie, he could have his own car, so he and his friend John would take long weekends and go to the Jersey Shore, where he and Maddie had once spent time during his spring break. They went to Toms' River. Ryan was very familiar with the town. He would always remember two songs that were popular his senior year, "It's a Beautiful Morning" and "Norwegian Wood." He and John would sing as loudly as they could whenever they came on the radio. Sometimes they would even get a crew together and go sailing. Ryan always loved being on the water.

When Ring Weekend finally came, Ryan picked Maddie up at the Newark Airport. She was so excited to see him again. Their wedding was getting closer and closer. Of course, Maddie had brought gorgeous and classic clothes with her. Ryan was so proud to introduce his fiancée to everyone she hadn't met yet.

When Ryan finally received his ring, Maddie grabbed it immediately and looked for the inscription inside. Ryan had her read the inscription out loud— "R&M YKTA." After she read it, huge tears glistened in her beautiful teal eyes. She was so proud of Ryan.

The Ring Hop was formal. Ryan looked exquisite to Maddie in his white dress uniform. His olive complexion and dark hair and eyes were magnified by the white uniform. Maddie and Terri had gone to Oklahoma City to find Maddie's dress. Maddie had chosen a bright turquoise formal gown for the occasion. The top was strapless and beaded, and the skirt was full like a ball gown. Maddie wore her hair up, with long tendrils trailing her French twist. Together they made the most striking couple at the dance. Of course, their pictures would turn out to be ones that some portrait studios would've loved to use as advertising. They really made an attractive couple.

Ryan and Maddie had a wonderful time during Ring Weekend. They visited the chapel where they would be married and spoke with the chaplain who would perform the ceremony. He also took Maddie on Flirtation Walk again, a half-mile walk through the woods along the bank of the Hudson River. It had been there for over one hundred years. At one point in the walk, there is an overhanging rock that is called "Kissing Rock." According to legend, couples are to kiss there so the rock won't fall. Ryan and Maddie kept the tradition alive and well.

When it was time for Maddie to leave, he drove her back to her sister's house in New Jersey, so she could stay and visit with Michelle about the wedding. Ryan wanted to spend the night with her, but he had to report back to school or lose some of his hard-earned privileges. At least they would be together again this Christmas.

During Christmas break, Maddie and Ryan visited both of their parents together as planned. Maddie's father, who had moved to Norman, Oklahoma, gave Ryan his approval to marry his daughter, but he reminded him that she couldn't cook. Of course, cooking was the last thing on Ryan's mind at this point. Maddie died laughing when he told her what her father had said to him. Maddie's father was proud of Ryan and the fine young man he'd become, but he also liked Jake just as much, perhaps even a little more. But it was Maddie's life.

Maddie was very nervous when it came time to go to Ohio and meet Ryan's mother again. She was worried. She shouldn't have been. Ryan's mother was happy her son was finally going to marry the woman of his dreams. She liked Maddie and thought the two of them would make a good match. Maddie and Ryan discussed their wedding plans with his mother. They explained they wanted it to be very intimate. She agreed with everything they had decided, even down to the color that Maddie had chosen—pink. Naturally, Maddie would choose pink. She'd been a dancer for so many years. Maddie even asked his mother to wear pink, which was not the usual tradition. Since Maddie's mother was dead, she wanted Ryan's mother to wear pink for her. His mother was honored to oblige Maddie's wishes.

When Christmas break was over, Maddie flew back to Oklahoma City and drove her car back to Wilmington. As usual, she put her ring away. Even though her wedding was only six months away, she didn't want Jake to know about it just yet.

During February of their firstie year, the cadets chose their branch of service. All the cadets met in the South Auditorium. They could choose among Infantry, Armor, Artillery, Engineer, or Signal Corps. They selected their branch by their order of merit, their overall ranking in the class. When it was Ryan's turn to make his selection, he chose Infantry, as he'd told Maddie he might. He was just happy that the selection was finally over, and he knew what lay ahead of him. Vietnam was always in the back of his mind. But the uncertainty had been nerve-wracking for Ryan. He knew that Maddie still wanted him to choose Armor, but he'd made his own decision, as she'd told him to do. As soon as he returned to his room after their boisterous party, he wrote to Maddie and told her of his choice. Needless to say, Maddie was not one bit happy with his choice.

Also, during the spring, the firsties would perform their *One Hundred Days* play. It was a spoof of their years at West Point. Ryan was asked to be in it, but he declined. He'd rather watch it in the audience. It really was funny. They spoofed some of their favorite teachers and some of the other officers at the academy. Afterwards, the firsties held a big party off-campus. Ryan attended but Maddie wasn't with him. He'd see her during spring break, though, which was not far away.

Maddie and Ryan met for his final spring break at West Point. They stayed a few days with her sister. The downstairs rumpus room became their home away from home again. They'd become very comfortable with this arrangement. They especially relished their nights alone.

Ryan and Maddie talked about their wedding plans constantly. They were going to go to West Point and order the flowers for the wedding. Ryan had already reserved the rooms at a nice hotel in Highland Falls for the wedding party. He and Maddie decided against the Thayer Hotel since they were on a budget. However, the pre-wedding breakfast and the reception would be held in a small banquet room there. Maddie chose pink roses with white babies' breath and her favorite lilacs as the flowers for their wedding. Ryan chose Maddie's wedding bouquet but wouldn't let her know what it was going to look like. He wanted it to be a surprise. She and Ryan chose everything else together, even the cake and the music. Maddie and Ryan chose Johnny Mathis's "The Twelfth of Never" and "Moon River" (her mother's favorite song) as their wedding songs. The cake had already been ordered. Maddie had visited a good bakery in Highland Falls and ordered it when she had visited during Ring Weekend. It was going to be a three-layer cake: one layer white, one layer chocolate, and one layer marble. The icing would be white, and the cake would be covered with pink roses trailing from the top of the cake down each layer. As was the tradition, the top of their cake would be frozen for one year, and then thawed and eaten by them on their first anniversary. She told the baker not to worry as she would bring the top of the cake with her. She had found two Christmas ornaments that she was going to use for the top of the cake, an Army soldier and a ballet dancer. It would be perfect and different. That was going to be Maddie's surprise for Ryan. He'd love it. She just knew it.

Ryan's last year at West Point was rapidly coming to an end. As a firstie, he finally felt as if—for the first time—he was in a real college, like Madison. He was ambivalent about how he felt about leaving. He'd been here for four years now; this had become his home. But he was happy that it was ending, so that he and Maddie could marry and start their life together.

25

Maddie's final year in college kept her just as busy as Ryan's. She was not only taking her education classes, but she was also taking those three courses she had told Jake about. The math and science classes were a piece of cake for Maddie, but she absolutely hated the educational statistics class. Thank God for Jake. He helped her reason her way through it even though Maddie felt bell curves were stupid. When she did her student teaching during the second semester, and eventually throughout her teaching career, she planned on letting the chips fall where they may. She never believed in that crap anyway. To her, if a student deserved an A, he'd get an A. If he deserved an F, he'd get an F. The only thing she would do, when considering between a D or an F, was if the student had turned in all his homework and participated in class, but for some reason, just couldn't get it, no matter how hard he tried. When those few occasions arrived, she'd opt for the D; otherwise, the F would stand.

This was Maddie's and Terri's last year of being cheerleaders. Matt and Terri would graduate this year, too. A sort of melancholy set in. She didn't want her college years to end, but on the other hand, she was excited and happy because she and Ryan would finally be getting married. It had been a long four years, and she was ready to start her life with him.

However, right now, she and Terri were busy forming new classes at the dance studio. They did make arrangements for the dance classes to be taught Monday through Thursday this year. Maddie and Terri had also decided to keep the studio open the next summer, because even though she and Ryan would be married, he was headed for different schools in Georgia and North Carolina by that time, so Maddie wouldn't see that much of him anyway. Since he'd chosen Infantry, he would be training to stay alive in Vietnam, which they both knew would follow in 1969. Of course, she'd fly back and forth a couple of weekends a month. Their school had been making loads of money since it first opened, so money wouldn't be a problem. Besides, Ryan would also be making some decent money himself when he became a second lieutenant; not as much as Maddie—but enough.

Maddie also continued to see Jake regularly. She always felt so comfortable and at ease with him. They continued their platonic relationship. After that one incident, Jake had never dared to try anything inappropriate other than his bear hug and kisses on the cheek. She was well aware that he was getting sexual gratification elsewhere. She wasn't deaf—she'd heard the rumors. They didn't bother her, though, because she knew why he was doing it. But she was worried about Jake, so she decided to talk to him about it.

True to her word, the next evening after dinner at his place, she did. They were sitting on the comfy herringbone sofa that Maddie had helped him pick out while drinking the last of the wine they had with dinner when Maddie brought it up.

"Jake, I probably shouldn't be bringing this up, but I want to ask you something, and it's personal, okay?" Maddie said quietly between sips of her third glass of wine.

"What's the matter, Maddie? Go ahead and ask. I've never lied to you before and never will."

"Jake, I know it's not my place to pry, but rumors have been flying around about you, and of course, they're aimed to get back to me as usual."

"What rumors?"

"Oh, you know. For the last four years, every time you've gone out with a 'specific' kind of girl for a 'specific' reason, I'm one of the first to hear about it. But that's never bothered me. What does bother me, though, is that you don't get any physical problems. I can't believe I'm saying this to you. I'm so embarrassed," said Maddie nervously.

Jake started to laugh. "Oh, darling, naïve Madison. You're talking about venereal disease or 'the clap,' aren't you? I'm fine, really. I always use protection whenever I'm with one of 'those' girls. You know what protection is, right?"

"A prophylactic?"

"Yes, Maddie; but, most people call it a rubber," answered Jake, still laughing. "Madison, if this is a problem for you, I'll stop seeing other girls for that reason."

"Nonsense," replied Maddie. "It's your life, and you're entitled to see whomever you want for any reason you want.

"Jake, would it be better if you and I stopped seeing each other? That way you could do as you please and not worry about my finding out and worrying about your health?"

"Madison, that is absolutely the last thing I want. Our friendship means more to me than any of the other girls in the world. Besides, I only see girls from college, no one in Claymont. In fact, lately I've been using one of your tricks. Whenever one of them from Claymont comes on to me—and yes, they do—I just tell them, 'I'm spoken for.' It seems to be working, too," replied Jake half laughingly.

"Well," said Maddie, changing the subject abruptly, "you know how the second semester of my senior year, I have to do my student teaching?"

"Sure," replied Jake. "It's about this time of the year when the list comes out. Where are you doing yours? I hope it's not some little one-streetlight town sixty miles away."

"Don't' you dare laugh, Jake Kelly, but I'll be at the high school in Claymont."

"Oh my God, I don't believe it! Everyone wants to do their student teaching in Claymont, because it's so close and is a 2A school. That's great, Madison. How'd you get so lucky?" asked Jake, just before he started laughing hysterically.

"I told you not to laugh, Jake! Beats the hell out of me why I was chosen. If it's going to be a problem for you, I can ask to be reassigned," replied Maddie nervously.

"Are you kidding me? That's the best news I've heard in a long time. Besides, I'll get to see you on a daily basis, and I'll love that."

"Okay. At least you'll be there to show me the ropes."

"I'll be more than happy to, my lady," said Jake as he bowed deeply. "Congratulations, Madison," he added. "It's really the best assignment you could receive."

"Good," replied Maddie in a relieved voice. She hadn't known how Jake would feel to be in the same school with her. She honestly had absolutely no idea how delighted Jake was.

They talked about how things worked at Claymont High. Jake was going to be an invaluable source of help for her during her student teaching. Jake told her lesson numero uno was to get in good with the janitor and then went on to explain how and why.

Once again, which seemed to be becoming a common occurrence, Maddie fell fast asleep in Jake's lap after too much wine. He very tenderly covered her with a blanket and went to bed, wishing more than anything in the world she'd be in the same bed with him.

When Maddie awoke the next morning to the smell of breakfast cooking, she realized where she was. She had spent the night on Jake's couch."Hi sleepyhead," declared Jake. "I thought you could use a decent breakfast." He then handed Maddie her first cup of coffee for the day. He knew it took at least two cups of coffee for Maddie to become a human being every day.

Maddie took the coffee from him eagerly. *He knows me better than Ryan,* was the first thing that popped into Maddie's head. Well, the two of them had been through a lot over the last four years. He'd always been there for her, especially during the worst times of her life. Ryan had not.

As Maddie and Jake were having breakfast, she asked Jake if he would attend her graduation along with her father, as well as Terri and Matt. They were all graduating together, and they were her family.

"Isn't Ryan coming?" asked a surprised Jake.

"Nope. He has finals to study for, so I haven't even bothered to ask him," replied Maddie very matter-of-factly.

"I'll be honored to be there. But I think you've forgotten something, young lady. I'll be getting my masters this year, too, so you'll have to put up with my folks again, if that's all right with you."

"Oh my God, I forgot you're finishing, too!" She proceeded to get up from her chair and sat on Jake's lap. She put her arms around his neck, kissed him on the lips, and said, "Congratulations, Jake Kelly. I'm so proud of you. Of course, your parents are invited. It will be great to see them again. Let's plan the party of all parties for all of us," declared Maddie.

"Sounds good to me. Why don't we have it here? That way it'll be very private for all of us," asked Jake.

"That's a great idea. We'll have it here, and Terri and I will plan everything."

On May 23, 1968, five days before Maddie was to graduate, disaster struck Maddie a third time. Maddie's father called to tell her; he was in Veterans' Hospital in Oklahoma City and wasn't going to be able to make it to her college graduation or go with her to West Point and walk her down the aisle. She couldn't believe it. Not again. Not now!

Maddie talked to Mary, her father's new lady friend, who told her that her dad was having some breathing problems, but not to worry. He was going to be fine, and as soon as he was better, he'd be up and around and as good as new. She knew the timing was awful, and her dad was being very stubborn about waiting until after June 15th. But the doctors told him that if he went, he probably wouldn't live to see June 15th. They even had to sedate him after they told him.

Maddie said she'd drive to OKC the next day, but Mary told her no. He'd be taking tests for the next two days and seeing her would upset him even more.

"Just give him some time, Maddie," Mary told her. "He really needs to rest as much as possible in case he eventually has to have surgery. I'll keep in touch and will call you every day with updates."

When Maddie hung up the phone, she was stunned. Absolutely no one from her family was going to be there for her graduation. She sat down and sobbed. *What else could go wrong?* she thought.

As usual, the first person Maddie called was Jake in Claymont. Once she told him what had just happened, he told her to stay put; he was on his way. Then he called Terri and Matt and told them to meet him at Maddie's. Unfortunately, this kind of déjà vu was becoming a habit.

Jake found Maddie sitting on the patio in her backyard, still sobbing. *God, why did such a beautiful and kind woman have to go through this again? She didn't deserve it. She'd been through enough in the last two years to last a lifetime,* thought Jake. He very quietly opened her screen door and came out and kissed her on the top of her head.

"Oh, honey, I just don't know what to say. I'm so sorry. It's not fair. What can I do to help?"

"Nothing," said Maddie, trying to brush her tears away. "I can't believe it, Jake. I don't know what I've ever done to deserve so much heartache."

"Maddie, they always say that God doesn't ever give us more than we can handle."

"Well, He better know that I can't handle any more after this!" declared Maddie angrily.

"Honey, I know this is a huge blow, but sometimes things happen that we have no control over. You know that better than anyone. Your dad would give anything to be here. It's not his fault he's ill. You know that," said Jake lovingly.

He took Maddie by the hand, led her inside, and poured them some wine. The two of them sat on her sofa, and he put his arm around her and hugged her close. She laid her head on his shoulder. Maddie honestly didn't know what she was going to do without Jake. He'd been her rock ever since they'd become friends four years ago. He'd never let her down. Not once. Not ever. She didn't even want to think about it. Ryan would never allow her to keep in touch with him after they were married. No, that was not even in the realm of possibility.

Once Terri and Matt arrived, Jake brought them up to speed. Terri started to cry and Matt was trying to keep his act together for Jake's sake.

After a while, Maddie stopped crying and told them she had to stop feeling sorry for herself. Her three best friends would be with her, and the party they had planned was still on. She said she knew her dad would be with her in spirit, and she'd show him all the pictures when she went to see him at the hospital.

Once Maddie started being optimistic and rational, Jake was once again amazed at the strong woman he'd come to know and love. He knew he'd never get over Maddie, no matter how hard he tried. In fact, he'd decided he probably wouldn't get married, because he knew he wouldn't find anyone any better than she. He'd already told his parents exactly how he felt. They didn't want to believe it, but they knew their son and he meant every word of it.

Jake slept on Maddie's couch that night. In the middle of the night, Maddie came in and awakened him to talk. She made him scoot over so she could lie beside him on the couch.

"I can't sleep, Jake. I need to talk. I don't know what I'm going to do without you. I don't want our friendship to end. I honestly think that you know me better than Ryan. Whenever I've needed someone, you've always been here for me. I don't know what I'll do, knowing that I won't have you in my life anymore. You know that Ryan and I are getting married on June 7th. I know Matt has told you. I haven't said anything about it to you, because, once I do, I know our days together will be over. I love you, Jake. Not in the same way as Ryan, but maybe the different way I love you is better than the way I love Ryan. I just don't know what to do," said Maddie tearfully.

"Maddie, you love Ryan. You've loved him for six years. You don't know how much I wish things were different, but they aren't. But I'll always be here for you if you ever need me. You can count on that, I promise," said Jake gently. Thank God it was dark, so Maddie couldn't see the tears in his eyes.

But Maddie did notice them when she kissed him like she'd never kissed him before. He held her closely to him as they cried together. After that, Maddie silently returned to her bed, but neither of them could sleep the rest of the night.

26

G raduation day for the four best friends turned out to be a beautiful day all around. The weather was even compliant—sunny, not windy, and actually cool for the end of May.

Jake's parents and Matt's and Terri's parents had made it a point to treat Maddie as one of their own. They knew her father was in the hospital.

Jake graduated first since he was receiving his masters. Matt, Terri, and Maddie blew kazoos when his name was called. They had sneaked them in under their robes.

Maddie graduated next because her grade point was so high. All of her friends and their parents cheered wildly. Maddie was so glad she wasn't alone on this special occasion.

Matt and Terri were able to graduate together, which only seemed fitting. After all, they both had the same last name now.

After graduation, everyone changed clothes and met at Jake's house in Claymont as planned. Maddie and Terri had had a great time decorating his place. They planted funny secret things throughout his house, things that reminded them of the last four years together. Their parents had ordered the cake and brought champagne to the celebration. Matt and Jake were in charge of cooking steaks, and Maddie and Terri had prepared the potato salad and baked beans in advance.

The party lasted well into the night, and everyone made funny toasts and told funny stories. Finally, around 11:00 PM, the "old folks" headed for home, and that included Matt and Terri.

However, before they left, Maddie had a chance to talk to them alone for a few minutes. Maddie asked Matt to walk her down the aisle at her wedding since her dad wouldn't be able to, and, of course, he'd agreed instantly. He said he'd be proud to do it. They knew that Maddie would now be driving back to West Point by herself since her father wasn't going to be able to go. They made her promise she'd call them each night along the way so they knew she was all right. She agreed. They were going to fly out and then get a rental car. They'd arrive the evening of the 5th and would meet her and Ryan the next morning at breakfast with everyone else. Just knowing they were coming made Maddie feel better.

After Matt and Terri left, Jake and Maddie were alone for the last time before she became a married woman. They both knew it. They both felt awkward. But Jake hadn't given Maddie her graduation gift yet. He had thought long and hard about what to get Maddie. He couldn't buy her any jewelry, because he knew that Ryan would go ballistic, so he'd come up with another idea. He went into his bedroom and returned with her gift.

"Go ahead, open it, Maddie. I want you to know how proud I am of you," said Jake.

Under the circumstances, she hadn't expected a gift from Jake. Maddie had absolutely no idea what it could be. But when Maddie opened it, she immediately started to cry. She was looking at a leather-bound book inscribed in gold with "Maddie's College Years: 1964–1968".

"Madison, I didn't expect you to cry. If I'd known that you would, I would've given you something else," said Jake quietly.

"Oh, Jake, I love it. It will always be priceless to me! Maddie was looking at a book of photos—photos of the two of them and Matt and Terri over the last four years. Pictures of them with Joy, at homecoming, at the lake, at her house, painting each other instead of the walls—an entire memory book of the last four years. Jake had left nothing out—not even her mother and father, her mother's funeral, or even the two of them together at the faculty party in Claymont. He'd even written funny or emotional statements under the pictures. She couldn't believe that he was such a sensitive man. This was something she would always cherish. However, she decided to wait until she got home to read the note that Jake had written to her at the end of the book.

"Jake, you really have no idea how much this means to me. I will treasure it and keep it with me always, no matter where I am." Then she started to cry again.

"What am I going to do without you?" sobbed Maddie unhappily.

"Madison, don't make me cry again. I can't stand it. Do you think I want you to go? Don't you know I've loved you for years? But you must follow your heart, and your heart is with Ryan. I know that. So please, let's just kiss and say we'll see each other again in a few weeks after you return from your honeymoon, okay?"

"Okay," said Madison. "Thank you so much for my precious gift. I'll see you in a couple of weeks." Then she kissed him passionately and was gone.

Jake sat with his head in his hands. God, he loved that woman so damn much, but she belonged to Ryan.

When Maddie arrived home, she couldn't sleep, so she got up and looked at the book that Jake had given her again. This time she took the time to read what Jake had written to her at the end of the book.

My dearest Madison,

I wanted to give you a very special keepsake for your graduation, something that would remind you of your college years. Really, I should say "our" college years—yours, mine, Matt's and Terri's.

I hope whenever you look at these pictures, it will bring back memories only the four of us can really appreciate—the good, and yes, also the bad. We all grew through each of these experiences.

I want you to know that your friendship, and yes, your love, have made me a better person, a better man. That would never have happened without you. Thank you.

As you embark on your new life, I wish you all the love in the world. You deserve it. You are the kindest, sweetest, funniest, prettiest, and yes, smartest woman I've ever known.

In the future, if you need anything, anything at all, just call me and I'll be there. You know that.

Congratulations, Maddie. You deserve the very best that life has to offer. I will miss you more than you will ever be able to imagine.

Much love,
Jake

P.S. Don't worry about Joy. I will <u>always</u> keep my promise to you!

After reading Jake's tribute, Maddie went to her refrigerator and opened a bottle of wine. She poured herself a large glass and went and sat outside. Her tears mixed with the wine as she thought of Jake. She loved Jake. She knew that. But she loved Ryan, too. Even though she knew she probably shouldn't marry Ryan while also loving Jake, she was determined to go through with the wedding. She and Ryan had waited long enough. They'd been together for so long, and that had to count for something. Yes, she decided. She wanted to and needed to marry her first love. With that she went inside to get ready for her trip.

She very methodically started packing for her trip to West Point and her wedding. She had already made a list of the items she needed. *"So much like Ryan,"* she thought to herself.

She packed her clothes in stages. First, she packed what she was going to wear to Ryan's graduation, along with all the accessories. The dress for the graduation "hop" she placed in a large plastic bag to hang in the backseat. In another suitcase, she packed what she thought she'd need for her honeymoon at Niagara Falls. In yet another bag, she placed those things she'd need each day and night along the way. Her final bag held all of her shoes, cosmetics, etc., she'd need for the trip. She had even picked up some fruit, munchies, and soda and put them into a small cooler in the front seat with her. The next to the last item that she placed in the car in the backseat under her ball gown was the box containing her wedding dress. The final item she placed into her car on the floor in the front seat was her graduation gift from Jake. She planned to show it to her dad and sister Michelle, as well as Matt and Terri when they were alone.

Matt had said he'd take care of the house for her until she returned, so after one last look around her beloved cottage, she put on her engagement ring, then locked both of the doors and left.

Maddie was on her way. She should have been deliriously happy, but thoughts of Jake kept creeping into her head. She just didn't want to let him go, but she knew deep down that she had to. It wasn't fair to him. Even though she said she'd see him when she returned, she decided she wouldn't. He needed to get on with his life. Fall in love with someone else, get married, and have children. If she kept seeing him, it would be selfish on her part. No, she wouldn't and couldn't do that to him.

Maddie stopped in OKC and visited her father in the hospital as planned. Her dad didn't look well. He was weak and had IVs and a breathing machine hooked up to him. He apologized over and over again, with tears in his eyes, that he wasn't there to watch her graduate and, more importantly, wouldn't be able to walk her down the aisle. Maddie said everything she could think of to keep him from feeling guilty. She even showed him the book that Jake had given her for graduation.

Maddie's father thoroughly enjoyed looking at the book, knowing all too well that Jake had been in love with his daughter for a long time. He just wished she could see it. He thought she was making a mistake by marrying Ryan but knew better than to open that can of worms. Maddie had to do what she had to do. Before she left, he kissed her and told her he hoped June 7th would be the happiest day of her life.

Maddie had allowed herself plenty of time to get to West Point. She traveled on Route 66 as far as she could and made it a point to stay in reputable hotels. She kept her promise and called Matt and Terri each night. She also planned to spend a couple of days with Michelle before heading north to West Point.

Michelle and Maddie were nine years apart in age. Michelle had married while they were still living in Cambridge, England. She was the oldest of the three girls.

Michelle was always happy to see her baby sister now that Maddie was older. When they were young, however, it was a different story. She and Meredith always remembered their mother saying, "Take your baby sister with you," almost everywhere they went. What a "downer" that had been having to drag their baby sister along.

Michelle and Maddie stayed up late in the evenings, talking whenever they were alone. This time was no different. Maddie showed her sister her prized possession—the book. They looked at each picture, and Maddie would explain the situation that had set up the picture. They even cried together when they saw the pictures from their mom's funeral.

Maddie explained to Michelle why their dad wasn't with her, but Michelle had already talked to him, as well as Mary. Maddie told Michelle that Matt would now be walking her down the aisle. Michelle thought that was a great idea.

The night before Maddie was to leave for West Point, the two sisters had one last heart-to-heart talk. Michelle started the conversation.

"Madison, are you absolutely sure you want to marry Ryan? I know you love him, and have for many years, but there is more to marriage than just love."

"Of course, I'm sure I want to marry him. I've known that for six years. It's about time, don't you think?" replied Maddie.

"Has he changed any since attending West Point?" asked Michelle gently.

"Naturally, he's changed. It takes a while each time we see each other for the 'real' Ryan to come back to me, but he does. Once he does, he's not only the love of my life, but also my best friend," answered Maddie.

"Are you willing to be an Army wife, honey? Don't you remember all the times when Mom was left alone while Dad was gone? Do you want to live that way, too?"

"Michelle, I know what it's going to be like being an officer's wife. This is the life that Ryan has chosen, and, since I love him, I choose it, too. Yes, there will be separations; I'm ready for that. Yes, I know he'll go to Vietnam, too, and yes, there's a chance he'll never come back, but I've already faced that demon as well. I'm in love with Ryan enough to take that chance," said Maddie earnestly.

"Okay," said Michelle. "All I want is for you to be aware that you aren't sixteen anymore and don't have to marry Ryan unless you really want to."

"I do," replied Maddie wholeheartedly.

"All right, baby sister, let's get to bed. You need to get a good night's sleep before you're off to Ryan's graduation and your wedding day. I'll see you at breakfast on the 6th with everyone else as planned."

With that Maddie went to bed downstairs, the place where she and Ryan had spent so many glorious nights. The last thing she thought about before closing her eyes that night was her upcoming wedding day. She couldn't wait to become Mrs. Ryan Richardson.

27

H *ow could Ryan do this to me?* Maddie asked herself. Even though she, too, had doubts, in the end her heart had won out. She wanted to be Mrs. Ryan Richardson more than anything else in the world—she always had. She'd already waited six long years to get married, and now, two days before their marriage, he'd asked her to wait two more years? Absolutely not! She was done.

As soon as Maddie reached the Mustang, she threw her last suitcase into the backseat, threw her car door open, and was locked inside within about thirty seconds. After she started her car, she backed it out of its motel parking space, shifted into drive, and took off—away from West Point, away from Ryan Richardson—forever.

Since it was only around 3:00 AM, Maddie drove the winding two-laned streets out of the wooded West Point area as quickly as possible. She knew she should slow down; there were deer in the area or she could slide off the edge of a curve, but she didn't care. She didn't care what happened to her at this point. She didn't even know how far she had driven before she saw the lights of a fairly large township. She knew it had been a couple of hours, but she'd been crying ever since leaving the hotel, so she wasn't really sure of much of anything at this point.

She slowed the car down to the legal limit as she entered the outskirts of the town and decided to stop for a cup of coffee. She knew she looked like hell, but she didn't care—she needed the caffeine and the bathroom.

When she entered the all-night diner, a few patrons turned to look at her. It was hard to miss Maddie with her long, dark, wild-looking auburn hair, along with a red face and swollen eyes from all the tears she'd shed. When the waitress came to take her order, she asked Maddie if she was all right. Maddie just nodded and asked for a cup of coffee. A couple of minutes later, the waitress, Lori, returned with the coffee and a piece of warm cherry pie a la mode. Lori told Maddie it looked like she could use a little cheer-me-up and not to worry; it was on the house. Maddie just looked up gratefully at this complete stranger's kindness.

After Maddie finished her coffee and pie, gassed up the Mustang, and used the bathroom, she was on the road again. When she finally saw the signs for Route 66, she turned on her radio to keep her company. But the music just made her start to cry again.

She drove all the next day and stopped for the night at a decent motel. She was exhausted. Maddie ordered some pizza and a soda. She tried to watch a little TV on the small black-and-white one in the room, but she dozed off. A few hours later, she awakened to find that she had been crying in her sleep—her pillow was soaked. She took a long hot shower, washed her long hair, and put on her nightie she'd thrown into her overnight suitcase. Then she went back to bed, pulled the covers over her head, and tried to go back to sleep, but it was pointless. She kept thinking of Ryan, what he had done to her, to them, and to all the plans they'd made over the years. It seemed so easy for him to say those words—wait a little longer. He didn't even get up and try to keep her from leaving him in the middle of the night. The Ryan she knew would never have allowed that. Hell, he didn't even get up off the bed and try to stop her while she packed. What was wrong with him?

Finally, since Maddie couldn't get back to sleep, she got up, dressed, repacked her suitcase, and headed towards home once again. She didn't feel like stopping for an extra early breakfast, it was still dark out, but she did need her large coffee. So she stopped at a large truck stop and forced herself to eat some toast with her coffee.

Once ready for the road again, she climbed back into her trusty car and kept heading west; however, more tears started spilling from her eyes once again. It seemed to Maddie that she'd cry all the way back to Oklahoma. The truth was that she didn't stop crying until she reached the western edge of Missouri. Finally, Oklahoma was only a few hundred miles ahead. She'd be home in a few more hours. She really had no idea how long she had been on the road. She didn't even remember if she'd spent another night at a motel on her way home.

Maddie must have made her way home in record time. She arrived at her lovely, welcoming home in Wilmington around 4:00 AM. She pulled her car into the driveway and just sat in the car. She held tightly to the steering wheel and started to cry again, but she finally forced herself to get out and take the one small suitcase inside with her. The rest could wait until tomorrow, or forever, as far as she was concerned.

She continued sobbing as she closed the door behind her. She'd been in shock the entire trip home. Right now, she wondered if she could find a few of the pills that she had left over from Ryan's father's funeral; she wanted to take one, just to calm her down and help give her some much-needed sleep.

She looked into the cabinet in the bathroom but didn't see them. Then she remembered she'd put them in the drawer in the nightstand by her bed. She hadn't really slept since leaving West Point. She knew she shouldn't, but she took three pills and chased them with a glass of wine.

28

After she had gone, Ryan sat on the end of the bed and sobbed all night. He didn't get any sleep. He didn't deserve any sleep after what he'd just done.

He had no idea how he was going to tell everyone at breakfast that he had called off the wedding and that Maddie had left. Would they understand his reasoning, or would they side with Maddie? *That's a stupid question,* thought Ryan. Of course, they wouldn't understand what he'd done, much less why he'd waited until the last minute to do it. Hell, right now he couldn't even understand it himself. At the time, his logical mind knew it was the right thing to do, but now he knew he had been wrong, so very, very wrong.

He knew that his life had just changed forever and it was his own damn fault. He didn't care what happened to him now. He really didn't. He could die in Vietnam now like his father, since that's what had been on his mind these past few weeks. Maybe he really did have a death wish.

After totally destroying his future with Madison, Ryan tried to explain to the group gathered for breakfast what had happened the previous evening. He tried his best to make them understand his reasoning, but no one agreed with him, not even his mother.

Terri was the first to respond to what had happened, and she went berserk. "How could you possibly allow Maddie to leave in her car in the condition she was in? Where is she? Hell, she could be dead by the side of the road, and we don't know it, you asshole! I can't believe she waited for you when she had so many other chances to meet decent men. You may have graduated from West Point and believe the Honor-Duty-Country crap, but you certainly 'dishonored' Madison, and your 'duty' was to keep her safe. You don't even know where she was going, so we don't know where to start looking for her. Don't ever call us and ask if we've found her. You don't deserve to know. I hope you have to worry about her and what you did to her for the rest of your life. I hope you end up in hell. That's what you deserve after what you've done!" screamed Terri, and then she slapped his face as hard as she could.

Matt agreed with Terri. He told Ryan that if anything happened to Maddie, it would be his fault, no one else's but his. Matt and Terri added that they were going to try to find her. With that they left.

Michelle, Maddie's sister, was sobbing. "How could you do this to my sister? I can't believe you did it. I'm hoping that she goes to my house. I'm out of here, too. I never want to see or speak to you again."

Ryan's mother scolded him next. "Ryan, I don't approve of your decision. Maddie should've had a say in what you were thinking. You didn't give her that, and that wasn't fair to her. It was her life you were talking about, too, not just your own. You've lost the one thing in your life that was a constant support to you. Now you'll be on your own, and every day you'll have to live with the consequences of this decision. If anything happens to Madison, her friends and sister are right—it will be your fault. I can't believe my own son would do this. You've disgraced me and our family. I love you because you're my son, but I'm ashamed of you and your actions." She gave him a shame-on-you look and left with Ryan's sisters.

After that hideous confrontation, Ryan was left alone with his best man. John said he never thought he'd forgive him either. He was terribly worried about Maddie. She'd been gone for hours, and no one had any idea where she was. Then he left, too.

Ryan was alone. He'd made a huge mistake. He realized that now. How could he have thought this would work? They were right. If anything happened to Maddie, it would be his fault. He didn't know what to do. Should he try to look for her? If he found her, what would he say? What would she say? In the end, he just sat on a chair alone and sobbed.

Everyone was right. He'd regret what he'd done for the rest of his life.

Ryan didn't know it yet, but he wouldn't see Madison again for sixteen years and during those years, he would lead the life of a nomad—looking for but never finding happiness. That would be his penance for letting Madison Conrad get away.

29

After Matt and Terri left the breakfast, they headed straight back to the airport in New York. They had to stand in line for what seemed like hours in order to change their departure date and time. They were going to be on the next flight out but had to make two stops to get home as soon as possible.

After they had changed their tickets, Terri called Jake and told him briefly what had happened and asked him to go and see if Maddie could have made it home so quickly since she had such a head start. If the car was there, she'd be there, Terri told him. Jake said he'd go immediately and would wait for her even if she hadn't arrived home yet.

Jake took a quick shower, shaved, and dressed, and was immediately on the road towards Wilmington. Claymont was only twenty minutes away.

When he arrived at Maddie's street, he saw her car. *Thank God,* thought Jake.

He was scared to death she'd had a wreck, had become lost, or had just decided to disappear for a while. He parked his car behind hers, ran up to the front door, knocked, and screamed out her name. The house was dark, with the exception of a small light in her hallway.

Nobody answered the door, but Jake knew Maddie was there. He knocked and screamed her name again. Finally, not knowing what else to do, he kicked the door in with his leg. Once inside the house, Jake turned on the lights in the living room; it was empty. Next, he tried the bedroom. He found Maddie sprawled across the bed with her clothes on. He then saw the bottle of pills and the glass of wine and screamed her name as loudly as he could.

"Madison, can you hear me?" he kept screaming while shaking her at the same time. But she didn't answer him.

He immediately got her onto her feet and started walking her back and forth. She finally started coming around when the phone rang. Jake answered it after the first ring, thinking it was probably Matt and Terri again, but it wasn't.

"Hello?" said Jake.

"Who is this?" replied Ryan.

"This is Jake; who are you?"

"This is Ryan Richardson. Is Maddie there?"

"Stay away from her, you son of a bitch. If I ever see you, I'll kill you myself. Then you won't have to worry about dying in Vietnam. Don't ever call here again!" yelled Jake as he slammed down the phone.

"Who was that?" mumbled Maddie.

"Wrong number," was all Jake said, trying not to show his anger as he yanked the phone cord out of the wall.

"Honey, we have to get you into the shower, okay? You're not waking up fast enough."

Maddie just nodded her head.

Jake took off Maddie's shirt, shorts, and shoes, but kept her bra and panties on, so she wouldn't be embarrassed later on. He turned on the shower to lukewarm and put her in. He kept his arm on her to hold her steady. He didn't want her to fall. After about ten minutes, Maddie seemed like she was coming around enough, so Jake turned off the shower, wrapped a towel around her, and put another one around her wet hair. He dried her off as she sat on the end of the bed and put her chenille robe on her.

Next, he took Maddie into the kitchen with him while he made a pot of strong coffee. Maddie just sat still and stared straight ahead, not saying a word. Finally, once the coffee was made, he handed a mug to Maddie and poured one for himself.

"Madison, listen to me. What did you take? I need to know. If you won't tell me, I'll have no choice but to take you to the hospital and have your stomach pumped. Do you understand me?" asked Jake gently.

"Yes. I just took three pills and one glass of wine. That's all. I swear. I was just so tired. I haven't slept much in the last couple of days," said Maddie sadly. "I guess you know what happened," she continued.

Jake told her that Matt and Terri had called him and asked him to come and see if her car was here, and yes, they'd explained to him what had happened.

"He wanted me to wait another two years—two more years. To put it exactly, he said he didn't want to make me a widow before I had a chance to be a wife. How's that for six years?" said Maddie morosely.

"Honey, sometimes things turn out differently than we've planned for a reason. I know that doesn't make much sense to you now, but someday it will. Here, let's get your wet undies off and nightie on, and I'll help you get to bed," said Jake tenderly.

Maddie nodded once more. Once she removed her bra and panties, he helped her on with her nightie. He tried not to notice what a beautiful body she had, but it was impossible. He put her into bed, pulled the covers up to her chin, and kissed her on the forehead. He could tell she was still in shock.

"I'll just be out on the sofa if you need me. Don't worry; I'm not going anywhere."

Maddie finally answered him. "Jake, would you sleep on top of the covers on the bed with me again like you did in Tucumcari? I just don't want to be alone. Please stay."

"Sure, honey," was all Jake replied. He lay on top of the covers with his arm around her for the rest of the night.

The next morning, Jake awakened early. He saw that Maddie was sleeping soundly. He carefully got out of bed so he wouldn't disturb her, and he went into the kitchen and made another pot of strong coffee. He knew Maddie would say she wasn't hungry after she awakened, so he just made some toast for her after she had her first cup of coffee.

The coffee smell moved Maddie to get up. She wrapped her chenille robe around her and headed for her kitchen, still fuzzy about the night before.

"Hi there, sleepyhead. Want some coffee?" asked Jake pleasantly.

"Duh, are you kidding? When have I ever turned down a cup of coffee?" smiled Maddie.

The two of them sat across the table from each other, sipping their coffee like a young married couple. Only they weren't.

Jake was the first to speak. He told Maddie that he'd fix the front door that morning, but he wanted to suggest some other ideas with her.

"Shoot," said Maddie.

"Do you remember the phone call last night at all?" asked Jake.

"Sort of, not really, though," answered Maddie.

"Well, the call was from Ryan. I told him not to call here again, and then I pulled the phone cord out of the wall. Actually, I said a little more than that, but that's not important. What is important is that I think you need to do two things and do them today, but only if you want to."

"What two things?"

"Well, first of all, I think you should get an unlisted phone number if you don't want to talk to Ryan. I also think you should get a post office box, so that if you get a letter, it will automatically be 'Returned to Sender—No Forwarding Address.' Now, I'm only suggesting this if you don't want to have anything else to do with him." He added, "It's entirely up to you, Maddie."

"You're right. I don't want anything else to do with him ever again. Let's do this stuff this morning, okay?"

"Sure thing," said Jake. "Now, I'm going to make us some toast so you'll have something in your stomach. Will you promise me that you'll at least try to eat it?"

"Jake, I'm sorry if I scared you last night. I was just so tired. I know I shouldn't have done it, but I only wanted to get some sleep. Really, I wasn't trying to hurt myself. I need you to believe me," said Maddie earnestly.

"I know, Madison. But I was so worried about you. I would never have forgiven myself if anything had happened to you," replied Jake sincerely.

About that time, Matt and Terri arrived. Terri ran over to Maddie and just held her close. She told Maddie what had happened at breakfast, but Maddie told her she really wasn't interested. As far as she was concerned, Ryan died to her on June 5th. In fact, Maddie changed the subject, and Jake made it a point not to say anything to their friends about what had occurred the previous evening.

Maddie told Terri that she wanted—no, needed—to get back to work as soon as possible. She and Jake had some errands to run today, but she would be back at the studio tomorrow.

BOOK III:
TWINS

30

E ven after all the humiliation Maddie had suffered from her botched wedding to Ryan, she was at the studio bright and early the next day. She was glad to be back. Keeping busy kept her from thinking about how both furious and depressed she was about what had happened.

The only problem Maddie encountered after her return to Wilmington, which started to become visible to everyone who knew her, was that she was losing weight. She wasn't hungry. Jake made sure she'd have at least one decent meal a day, but he noticed that she really only picked at her food or moved it around on her plate.

"Maddie, you've got to eat," said Jake anxiously to her one night.

"I know, but I'm not hungry. It'll probably take me a little while to get back on track."

The rest of June and July passed without incident. Maddie never spoke of Ryan, not even to Terri. Terri didn't push her. She knew that Maddie would talk only when she was ready.

By late August, however, Maddie noticed that she had started to gain back the weight she had lost, and more. She also noticed that it was all in the same place, her stomach, and she'd always had a very flat one. She hadn't thought anything about it because her periods had always been irregular. But she couldn't ignore the fact any longer that she might be pregnant, so she made an appointment with her doctor.

A few days after seeing Doctor Bennett, his nurse called and asked her to come back in. *Oh God*, thought Maddie, *this can't be happening to me. Haven't I been through enough?* When she sat down in his office, she knew exactly what he was going to say before he said it. She knew her body was changing, and changing rapidly. Her breasts were getting much larger, but until she heard the doctor say it, she had chosen not to consider it. To her, ignorance was bliss. That's the only way she could deal with it.

"Madison," said Doctor Bennett as he sat down in his chair across from her, "we've received the results from your tests."

Madison interrupted him, though. "I know, doctor. I'm pregnant, aren't I?"

"Yes," answered her physician kindly. "But I need to give you a brief exam. Don't worry. I just need to listen for a heartbeat and measure your tummy. There were some irregularities in your blood test."

"Let's do the exam and talk after that, okay?" replied her doctor.

After her exam, Doctor Bennett shocked Maddie when he told her he wasn't positive, but he thought he'd heard two very faint heartbeats instead of one. This would explain the abnormalities in her blood work.

"Twins?" was all that Maddie could get out of her mouth.

"Yes, I think so. Of course, I'll know for sure in another month. But for right now, that's what we have to consider," replied her doctor gently.

After making her next appointment, Maddie left her doctor's office in a daze.

Twins? Oh my God, thought Maddie. She drove straight back to her house. She needed to think.

Once inside her home, Maddie made herself a glass of iced tea and went and sat on the patio out back. As she was slowly sipping her tea, she tried to figure out what her options were. Should she have an abortion? She knew it was illegal, but she knew she could find a doctor who would do it. After all, this was a college town. She also knew that there were pills she could take to abort a pregnancy. Some of her pharmacy student friends talked about it once in the student union. Could she get some? Could she really do it? It would certainly solve her problem. She decided she wouldn't tell anyone yet, but she also knew her days were numbered. If she really was carrying twins, then she'd start to show very quickly. She needed to talk to someone, so she called her sister Meredith in California.

Meredith calmed Maddie down immediately. She already knew about what had happened with Ryan. Michelle had called her. After listening to what Maddie thought her options were, Meredith told her she'd forgotten the most important one—she could have the babies. It wasn't their fault. Besides, no matter what Maddie thought of Ryan now, those babies had been conceived out of love. That had to count for something. Meredith even suggested she move to California. That way she'd be around family, and she and Tom could help her out. She also suggested it would probably not be a wise idea to tell Dad.

Dad, thought Maddie. Oh God, she knew she couldn't tell him what had happened. He thought she was happily married now. If he knew what was really going on, he'd probably either have a heart attack or want to find Ryan and kill him himself!

After talking to Meredith, Maddie called Michelle. The two of them basically had the same conversation. Nothing was decided, except that they all agreed not to tell their father.

Maddie thought a long time about what her sisters had said to her, and they were right. The lives inside her hadn't asked to be born. It wasn't their fault. It was hers—hers and Ryan's. After going back and forth, Maddie made her choice. She would have her children.

Maddie told Doctor Bennett her decision at her next appointment. He'd known that under the circumstances, Maddie would consider abortion. But he also knew her well enough to know that in the end, she'd do what was right.

Maddie talked to her doctor about the possibility of moving to California to be near her sister. He told her that might be a wise decision, but if she did decide to leave Wilmington, she had to do it by the end of November. Since he'd figured her due date to be around March 5th, he felt it would be too dangerous for her to travel after that.

Since Maddie had started to show quite a bit, she made it a point to avoid Jake. This was her problem and hers alone. She did need to talk to Terri, though. Her teaching days were over. She called Terri right then and there and asked her to come over.

Once Terri arrived at Maddie's, Maddie poured her a glass of wine.

"What? You're not having any?" asked Terri.

"Nope, no can do, at least not for a few months," declared Maddie. "I'm pregnant with twins, and yes, before you ask, Ryan is their father."

"What? I can't believe it!" exclaimed her best friend.

"Well, believe it," said Maddie very matter-of-factly.

She told Terri that she'd be moving to California and wondered if she and Matt would buy out her interest in the studio. Maddie also told her that she had one exceptional student who could teach the ballet classes for her.

"The only other thing I want from you and Matt is to promise me that you won't say anything to Jake. I need to be the one to tell him. I also want you to promise me that you'll never tell Jake or anyone else where I'll be living," said Maddie.

"But doesn't Ryan have a right to know?" asked Terri.

"Absolutely, positively not! These are going to be my children, mine alone. I will rear my babies by myself. We both know that if I told him, he'd want to get married immediately. He didn't want to marry me in

June, so I know he'd be marrying me just because I'm pregnant. Nope, that's not going to happen. As far as I'm concerned, all Ryan did was contribute his sperm," declared Maddie adamantly.

"Okay, Maddie. I understand completely where you're coming from after what he did to you. I'm sure Matt and I will be able to come up with the money to buy out your portion of the studio. I'll talk to him as soon as I get home. In fact, I won't even tell him why you're moving until I absolutely have to. You know I'll help you in any way that I can," said Terri as she hugged her best friend.

"Terri, thanks for being such a wonderful friend. I guess I'm still in shock, but there's no denying it now," said Maddie as she hugged her growing belly.

Terri talked to Maddie the next day. She and Matt made a more than generous offer to Maddie, which she accepted immediately. The money would help keep her afloat for a couple of years.

Since the doctor had told Maddie that any traveling she did had to be completed by Thanksgiving, she kept busy deciding what to take with her to her new home and what to leave behind. It took until October 31 to complete the sale of the studio to Matt and Terri. However, she and Terri had held a huge garage sale early in October when the weather was cooler, and she was able to get rid of most of those items she no longer wanted or needed. What was left she donated to the Salvation Army.

Maddie kept her comfy English cottage couch, chair, and ottoman. She also kept her dishes, pots and pans, towels, and sheets. She kept all of her personal belongings, including her clothes, shoes, books, and any other important documents. Terri helped her decide everything else. By October, she already felt as big as a house and still had five months to go. She was all babies. She hadn't gained weight all over—just in her tummy and boobs. She'd really become upset the first time she looked down and couldn't see her feet! She could only imagine what she'd look like in five more months.

Meredith and Tom arrived in Wilmington by the end of October to help her move. They flew in to Oklahoma City, and Matt had picked them up. Once they arrived in Wilmington, everything was already packed and ready to load into the U-Haul truck they had rented. Tom would drive the truck and follow Meredith and Maddie in Maddie's beloved Mustang. Once the papers were signed on October 31 for the sale of the studio, it was time to say good-bye.

For Maddie, the worst part of leaving Wilmington, was saying good-bye to the people she loved and who meant the world to her. Only Terri knew exactly where Maddie was going. She didn't want Ryan to find her— ever—not after what he'd done. Even Matt didn't know exactly where in California Maddie would be living. Maddie explained to Terri that she'd only call her occasionally, because it would be safer for her that way.

Saying good-bye to Jake and not being able to tell him where she was going, was much worse than she had imagined. They met at the farm, so Maddie could say one last good-bye to him and Joy. Even though she hadn't been able to ride her for several months, she had gone out to see her at least three times a week and give Joy her favorite treats, but only when she knew Jake wouldn't be there.

Jake was already at the farm when Maddie arrived. Maddie had made it a point not to see him for a couple of months after she discovered she was pregnant. She was embarrassed. When Jake did see her, he was taken aback when he saw how pregnant she was. He was so surprised that he didn't exactly know what to say. Instead, he came up to her and kissed her on the cheek and told her she looked beautiful.

Maddie's immediate response was, "Yeah, if you don't mind not seeing your feet. Jake, I wanted to see you here because this is one of my favorite places in the world, and I needed to say one final good-bye to both you and Joy. I've always felt so at home here.

"I'm sorry I didn't see you before now," Maddie continued. "The truth is that I was so totally dumbfounded when I found out I was pregnant and about everything that had happened at West Point that I couldn't face you. It's obvious that I'm pregnant—with twins, no less. Yes, Ryan is their father, and before you ask, no, he doesn't know and never will. After what he did to me, I'll make sure of that. As far as I'm concerned, these are going to be my children, and if I have anything to say about it, they'll never know their father. Jake, I can't tell you where I'm going, but please understand that I'll be safe and so will my babies."

Jake was dumbfounded, too. He had no idea what had happened over the last four months. Every time he'd called Maddie, she acted as if everything was fine and busy teaching at the dance studio. Boy had he been wrong! He knew Maddie well enough not to ask her about it. Instead, he tried to keep his composure and asked her how she was feeling and when was she leaving.

"Actually, Jake, I'm leaving tomorrow morning, but I wanted and needed to see you before I leave. I want to thank you for being the best friend I could ever have hoped for. I've been so lucky to have known you. You've made my life so much richer. You're the one person who has never questioned my decisions, and I've always been so grateful for your guidance, and yes, love. I'll never forget you for as long as I live," continued Maddie with tears streaming silently down her face.

"Maddie, why won't you tell me where you're going? I think I deserve to know that much."

"The fewer people who know where I'll be, the better for everyone. I don't want Ryan to be able to find us. Not now, not ever!"

"Have you at least told your dad what's going on?" asked Jake, already knowing the answer.

"Are you kidding? He'd kill me if he knew I was pregnant and not married. I'll let him know after the twins are born…maybe when they're around two."

"Maddie, that's not fair to your dad. He lost your mom; he doesn't deserve to lose you, too," said Jake.

"He hasn't lost me, Jake. I'll tell him where I'm living and working, but not about the children. Believe me, it's better this way. Besides, if he knew, he'd probably go to Vietnam and kill Ryan himself.

"Please believe me when I tell you that I'll miss you terribly," continued Maddie. "I really can't even imagine not having you in my life anymore. It's been agony not being able to see you these last few months. I don't even think I've really accepted this myself yet.

"Jake, just promise me one thing. Please don't ever sell our filly. I couldn't bear it—promise me, Jake," said Maddie with desperation in her voice.

"Maddie, I've promised you a million times that Joy will always be with me, no matter where I end up," said Jake as he hugged her. "She's safe with me—she always will be," he added. Jake sensed some of the tenseness leave Maddie's body once she knew that Joy would be okay.

"Jake, I want you to take care of yourself, find someone you truly love, marry, have children, and be happy," said Maddie softly.

Jake's immediate thought after she said that was he'd already found his soul mate, but of course he didn't say it. Instead, he told her he wished the same for her.

Maddie's reply surprised him. "I don't think that's in the cards for me anymore. My only focus will be on my children, making sure they are loved, happy, and safe. I don't foresee another man in my future."

"Maddie, don't say that. I really think that Ryan deserves to know about his children. Think about it rationally for a minute. He has a right to know."

Maddie immediately became defensive. "Ryan deserves absolutely nothing, Jake. In fact, he died to me on June 5, 1968. And he'll stay that way. You know what he did was inexcusable, so there's no sense talking about it."

Jake knew better than to press the issue. Instead, he asked her to please stay in touch with him.

Maddie very gently cupped his face in her hands and said, "I can't, Jake, but please always remember that you mean the world to me and will be in my heart forever." With that she rubbed Joy's nose, kissed Jake directly on his lips, and then struggled to climb into her Mustang. Then she was gone.

Jake stood next to Joy and watched the only woman he'd ever truly loved leave him. Tears streamed silently down his cheeks as he not only worried what was going to become of Maddie, but also wondered how he was going to go on without her. The prospect was too much for him to fathom right now. Instead, he petted Joy, led her quietly back to the barn, and told her softly that everything would be all right. He promised their filly that he'd find a way for them to see Maddie again, and that was one promise he intended to keep.

31

Maddie was heartbroken after she left Jake and Joy at the farm. Like Jake, she too, had tears streaming down her face. She was a mess by the time she arrived at the motel where Meredith and Tom were waiting for her.

Meredith instinctively knew that she had to calm Maddie down quickly. It wasn't good for the twins if their mother was in such distress. She held Maddie in her arms and just let her cry herself to sleep, which took only a few minutes, because Maddie was exhausted both emotionally and physically.

Early the next morning, after breakfast, the three of them started their long trip to Maddie's new home in Napa, California. They decided not to rush the trip because of Maddie's condition. Since Maddie had to stop at every rest stop along the way to go to the bathroom, frequent rest stops were the norm for this trip. It was as if Maddie had to go every forty-five minutes like clockwork. Perhaps one of the babies was pushing on her bladder.

Of course, Meredith wouldn't let Maddie drive the Mustang. She ordered her to put her seat all the way back and put her feet up on the dashboard to keep them from swelling up like balloons. The two sisters would have some real quality time to talk during the long drive, but Meredith knew that Maddie needed to start thinking out loud about her future, whatever that may be.

Meredith and Tom owned Campbell Realty, so she had already started to look for a suitable house for Maddie. She knew exactly what kind of house her sister wanted. Ever since they had lived in England, Maddie had always wanted an English cottage. Meredith had already found the perfect house for her. In fact, she was so sure that Maddie would love it that she'd put down the deposit for it, so no one else could buy it before Maddie had a chance to see it. Meredith decided that now would probably be a great time to tell her about it. Hopefully, it would cheer her up.

"Maddie," Meredith began, "I think I've found the perfect house for you and the twins. I even put a deposit on it. Let me tell you about it. First of all, it's an English cottage-stucco with a huge fenced backyard. It's already totally landscaped like an English garden, like the ones we always loved so much as kids. There's also a huge weeping willow tree in the front yard and gardenia bushes all around the front door. They'll smell glorious next spring."

"Oh my God, Meredith!" exclaimed Maddie. "Why haven't you told me about it until now? Tell me about the inside, too. So far, it sounds just perfect for me. You know how desperate I've felt about finding a suitable place."

"Well, I wanted to wait until we were alone and had plenty of time to discuss it. Maddie, you're going to love it. I just know it! It has three bedrooms, two baths, all new appliances, leaded glass front door, new paint, a wonderful used brick fireplace, and gorgeous wood floors. It also has a formal dining room, and the kitchen is plenty big enough for you and the twins. There's only a one car garage, but there is a washer and dryer in a small alcove on the way to the garage. I think it's really a perfect house for you and the twins."

"Sis, it sounds amazing, but will I be able to afford it? I'm not going to be able to work full time until the twins are older. I plan to tutor as much as possible, though."

She told Maddie that she'd arranged a lease/purchase plan for the house, and she knew that Maddie had more than enough money for the down payment. With the money Maddie had received from selling the studio, the inheritance their mother had left each of them, and the money she'd saved for her marriage to Ryan, she wouldn't have to worry about money for a while. She'd even have plenty of money left to furnish the house and the two nurseries, buy carpets, curtains, whatever she'd need.

Meredith excitedly told her sister more about the house. The name of the street was Hope—how appropriate was that? It was also within walking distance to Napa High School on Jefferson Street, where she knew she would someday have a job. Tom, who knew everyone in town and wielded a lot of influence, had already talked to the board president and personnel manager of the school district, and they said a position would be waiting for her when she felt the time was right.

Maddie was stunned by all the arrangements that her sister and brother-in-law had already made for her. The house sounded too good to be true, and to know that she'd have a teaching position when she was ready was almost too much for her to fully comprehend. Maddie started to cry softly, because she was so overwhelmed.

"Hey, this news is supposed to make you happy, so why are you crying?" asked Meredith. "Let's talk about how we're going to decorate your new house. No more tears."

"All right," responded Maddie and then changed the subject to happier thoughts. "Meredith, I have absolutely no idea what colors to paint the babies' rooms. I could have two boys, two girls, or one of each. I guess if I had a choice, which of course I don't, I'd like one of each. Wouldn't that be fun? It really doesn't matter, though, as long as they're healthy."

"Well," replied Meredith, "I guess we could paint one room a soft yellow and one room a pale green."

Maddie thought about it for a minute and decided that was a great idea. They'd go shopping for paint and hire a painter once they closed on the house. She also decided they would have to buy two of everything exactly the same. That thought was so exciting to her that she just put her arms around her belly to make sure the twins were still moving—they were.

The trip to Napa, California, took the threesome four days. During that time, Maddie was able to start focusing on the future instead of hating the hideous past. Meredith knew, even though she didn't agree, that her sister would never tell Ryan about his children; however, she knew better than Jake and didn't voice her opinion.

In 1968, Napa was still a small, beautiful, sleepy town right in the middle of the California wine country. The scenery was spectacular—rolling hills of trees and grapes, nothing like the flat country in Oklahoma. The smell of eucalyptus trees as they entered the town filled Maddie's senses with delight just as much as the amazing countryside.

The first night they spent at Meredith's house on one of several hills overlooking the quaint town. The house felt like a place of refuge for her. She loved sitting on the deck overlooking the valley, sipping her iced tea, while Tom and Meredith enjoyed their evening ritual of drinking a glass of wine and watching the sunset.

The next morning, Meredith had scheduled a doctor's appointment for Maddie so she could become acquainted with her new obstetrician. To Maddie's total surprise, she was a woman, which was almost unheard of in 1968. Maddie liked Doctor Walker immediately and knew that she'd feel comfortable having her deliver her twins. After the doctor measured Maddie's tummy, she decided that she needed to take the time to do an x-ray, so she could see which way the twins were lying in the womb. She didn't want to, but she felt it necessary for Maddie's best shot at bringing the twins to full term.

Maddie was amazed when she saw the x-ray. She was looking at two children, both appearing to be perfectly normal but very small. Doctor Walker seemed pleased with what she saw, but she also cautioned Maddie to take it easy the farther along she became. The last few months were going to be very important for the growth of the children, because this was when they'd gain their weight. The doctor also told her that she wanted her to take a nap every afternoon with her feet elevated to help prevent serious edema problems. She said she wanted to see Maddie twice a month until the middle of December; then she wanted to begin seeing her every week. The doctor said she couldn't paint, move furniture, or do anything strenuous, but she and Meredith could pick out paint, furniture, or whatever in the mornings as long as she rested in the afternoon. Doctor Walker told Maddie to have the movers place her belongings where she directed.

After Maddie's doctor's appointment, she and Meredith went out for lunch at a small diner that offered good food, lots of choices, and even better, low prices. While they were eating lunch, Maddie told her sister that she wanted to see the house on Hope Street. Meredith agreed on one condition: they would only stay one hour; then Maddie had to rest. Maddie resisted her sister's idea, but Meredith insisted it would be the only way they would visit the house today. Otherwise, it could wait until tomorrow. Maddie, although unhappy, finally consented to Meredith's plan.

Maddie watched intently out the window as they drove down Hope Street to see which house might become her new home. The tree-lined street was well kept, and all the houses had a pride of ownership appeal. When they finally stopped at 1846 Hope Street, Maddie stared in amazement. Meredith had been right. It was the perfect English cottage—newly painted light beige on the outside, with shutters painted dark burgundy on each side of the huge picture window. The used brick steps leading up to the covered front porch just added to the ambiance of the half—leaded glass front door. Maddie couldn't wait to get inside and look at it, a house she knew she already loved.

Once inside the house, she realized that everything Meredith had told her, right down to the dark wood floors, used brick fireplace, the large rooms, and two tiled baths, was exactly as she'd imagined it. The kitchen, although small, was large enough for two highchairs and a small table. That room was located in the back of the house with a sliding back door that led to a newly stained deck. Once on the deck, Maddie saw her future perfect English garden come to life in her mind, like the one she had remembered from living in England for so many years. In the spring, she'd plant flowers of varying sizes, shapes, and colors like the ones she had planted in Wilmington. This time, though, they would be placed carefully in the already raised beds made of railroad ties, which would make them even more beautiful. The lawn, like in the front, would once again come to life in the spring. The yard was fenced, but bushes hid the fence all around the three sides. There was even an English garden style iron gate on one side of the house. Eucalyptus trees stood proudly in one corner of the yard, holding the wooden swing that Meredith had told her about.

"Meredith, I want this house. Can we sign the papers right now? I have a cashier's check with me that will cover the down payment and any closing costs. I don't want to lose this house. Please, sis, it'll make me feel so much better if I know that this will be my new home," said Maddie excitedly.

"Maddie, the only reason I'm going to say yes is because I already knew you'd love it, so I had the papers prepared before Tom and I left for Oklahoma to come and get you. We'll go together, and it should only take around twenty minutes. Then you must promise me that you will rest every afternoon like Doctor Walker has ordered."

"I promise!" yelled Maddie excitedly.

With that Meredith took Maddie first to her office where the final deal was struck, and they headed back to Meredith's house where it took Maddie only a few minutes to fall into a deep sleep—probably the best sleep she'd had since her nightmare at West Point had begun.

32

Maddie's English cottage sofa, chair, ottoman, and all of the other special pieces that she couldn't part with fit perfectly in her new home. The other items she needed the two sisters found at garage sales, flea markets, or Montgomery Wards, the largest store in Napa. Since she didn't have a dining room set, she found a great old farmhouse plank table at a small used furniture store and used the six different colored ladder-back chairs she'd brought with her to go with it. She bought a small round table and two chairs for her kitchen, leaving plenty of room for two highchairs.

The most important items for Maddie to buy, however, were the furnishings for the babies' rooms. She had the painters paint the rooms a soft yellow and a pale green as planned, and then decided to use the opposite colors for the café-style curtains that she picked out at Wards. This was where she also bought identical cribs, rockers, and dressing tables for the twins. Maddie hadn't decided on a special motif for the rooms until one day when she and Meredith went to Santa Rosa for a craft fair. There she spied two identical sets of large handmade Raggedy Ann and

Andy pictures. Her decision was made. After that, their rooms just seemed to materialize into the perfect rooms for children. Everything else that Maddie needed for the twins, such as clothes, bedding, diaper bags, etc., was provided for her from the baby shower that her sister held for her. The only thing that she requested was that no one bring anything in pink or blue. Maddie couldn't believe the gift that Meredith and Tom had given her— a diaper service. That was a dream come true for her.

After Christmas 1968, Maddie was ordered to bed rest for most of the day. She was starting to have major problems with edema, and her doctor was becoming concerned that Maddie wouldn't be able to carry the twins to term.

Unfortunately, Doctor Walker was right. The twins weren't due until early March, but one afternoon, in the middle of January, Maddie started bleeding profusely and started having labor pains. Terrified, she called Meredith at work.

"Sis, I'm bleeding a lot and I'm scared to death I'm going to lose my babies," she screamed.

Meredith dropped the phone and sped to Maddie's house, picked her up, and took her to Napa's Queen of the Valley Hospital. She drove Maddie directly into the emergency entrance, and Doctor Walker, who was already there doing rounds, came running, ordering her staff to transfer Maddie to the OB ward. After a short exam, the doctor knew that the twins were in distress, and that they wouldn't be able to come into the world naturally. She had no choice but to the deliver them by Caesarian section and ordered an operating room, stat!

Then she told Maddie, who was still bleeding profusely, what was about to take place.

"Maddie, we must take the babies early, and I'll have to take them by a C-section or they won't make it. You're bleeding too much. Do you understand what I'm saying?" asked her doctor.

"Do whatever you need to do, but keep my babies alive," cried Maddie.

Then the anesthesiologist immediately put a mask over Maddie's face, and the surgery began. It took much longer than expected because of the trauma Doctor Walker found after making her initial incision. The baby boy was born first, weighing 3.9 lbs., and about 90 seconds later, a very tiny baby girl weighing 3.2 lbs. was delivered. After being weighed and measured, the twins were immediately placed into incubators and wheeled to the nursery.

Maddie's doctor discovered that the lining of Maddie's uterus was pulling away from its wall, causing uncontrollable bleeding. Without an emergency hysterectomy, she would die.

Meredith was also frightened. It bothered her to see such tiny babies hooked up to monitors and life-assisting machines. Even more frightening was the realization that their mother was still in surgery. *What could have gone wrong?* She was worried.

Meredith was also the first to see the twins. She thought that even though they were very, very tiny, they were spitting images of Maddie and Ryan. The perfect little boy had a shock of black hair like Ryan, while the tiny little girl had dark auburn curls like Maddie. As soon as Maddie's hysterectomy was completed, and she was settled into a private room, Meredith was by her side, holding her sister's hand. It took a few hours for Maddie to become fully conscious and recognize that she was hooked up to all kinds of machines.

"Meredith," a groggy Maddie asked, "what's going on? Are the twins okay?"

"Maddie, the twins are perfect—very tiny but perfect. They're in incubators because they are so premature," said Meredith, trying to sound optimistic. Your sweet little boy has black hair and your darling little girl has dark auburn curls.

"When am I going to get to see them?" asked Maddie anxiously.

"I'm sure that as soon as the doctor talks to you and feels you're strong enough, the nurses will wheel you down to the nursery. I'll go find her for you right now."

Meredith went to the nurses' station, and the head nurse paged Doctor Walker. She came quickly, and Meredith explained to her that Maddie was now awake and wanted to see her twins.

"Let me talk to her first," said Doctor Walker, and she rushed into Maddie's room with a huge smile on her face.

"Hi, mom of twins," said Maddie's doctor happily.

"Are the twins okay? Meredith said they were very tiny and in incubators."

"They're fine, Maddie. They are very, very tiny, though. Your baby boy came out first, weighing 3.9 pounds, and then your little daughter arrived about ninety seconds later, weighing in at 3.2 pounds. That's why they're in incubators. They need help to gain weight and to make sure their lungs are fully developed before we can let them go home. Tomorrow morning, I'll get a wheelchair and take you to the nursery myself."

"Doctor, what's wrong? What aren't you telling me?" asked a terribly concerned Maddie."

Now was the time for Doctor Walker to explain to Maddie about the hysterectomy, and she didn't know how Maddie would react. She began by asking Maddie if she remembered that when she came into the hospital, she had been bleeding profusely. She told Maddie that there was a specific reason for that. She told her that the lining of her uterus had started to pull away from its wall, and there was no way to repair it. There was just too much damage. In order to save all three of them, she had to remove the damaged uterus. She told Maddie how sorry she was but that meant she wouldn't be able to have any more children.

Maddie's answer totally surprised her doctor. Instead of getting upset and starting to cry, Maddie seemed very calm.

"As long as I have the twins and they're all right, then I'm okay. I don't need any other children."

"Maddie, you're a stronger woman than most I've known. You seem very pragmatic. We'll do our best to take good care of your beautiful new babies. However, you've just had major surgery. If you don't have any complications tonight, you'll see your little ones tomorrow morning. I promise."

The next morning, after examining Maddie, the doctor and Meredith helped her into a wheelchair to take her to the nursery.

"Are you ready, Maddie? I need to warn you that it will be very painful for you since you've just had major surgery and are still quite weak," her physician told her seriously.

"You bet, Doc! Let's go see my kids," replied a weak but happy Maddie.

Meredith and Maddie had to dress in gowns and masks before they were allowed into the nursery. As soon as Maddie saw her tiny children hooked up to all kinds of machines and tubes, she started to cry. They were so small, and it seemed to her that the tiny beaded bands on their wrists would have fit on Ryan's finger like a ring.

She saw that the twins looked a great deal alike even though they were fraternal. The most obvious difference was their hair color: her baby boy had black hair and her little girl's was dark auburn, just like Meredith had told her. They both had brown eyes and olive skin—a perfect combination of Ryan and her.

Meredith, seeing a little fear, and maybe even a little resentment in Maddie's eyes as she looked at her children, tried to bring some happy thoughts into the situation.

"Maddie, have you picked out names for your twins yet?"

"Yes, I think so. My handsome son will be named Rob Lee Conrad, and my beautiful daughter will be called Rory Leann Conrad."

"Rob and Rory!" exclaimed Meredith. "Those are perfect names. I knew you'd come up with something unusual, but these are really clever. Rob and Rory it is. But don't you think that perhaps their last name should be Richardson?" asked Meredith quietly.

"Over my dead body!" declared Maddie adamantly. "His name will be on the birth certificate, because I don't want them growing up thinking I didn't know who their father was, but their last name will be Conrad."

Maddie and Meredith were allowed to stay in the nursery for only ten minutes, and then Meredith wheeled Maddie back to her room. She'd be allowed longer visits in the days and weeks to come, but for now Maddie was just too weak. In fact, she almost fainted getting out of her wheelchair.

When Maddie was back in her bed, she fell into a deep sleep from sheer exhaustion. As soon as Meredith felt assured that Maddie and the twins were safe, she left the hospital for home. She, too, was exhausted.

Tom had a glass of wine ready for her. Meredith kissed him and headed straight for the telephone to tell Michelle what had happened. Michelle offered to come out to Napa to help with the twins, but that would have to wait until the preemies were strong enough to come home.

Then she turned to Tom and said, "I don't know how long the twins will be in the hospital. I'm thinking around six weeks. In a way, even though it'll drive Maddie crazy, it might be a good thing. It will give her time to heal physically as well as emotionally. It's so obvious that Ryan's the father of these children. Wait until you see them. I also know that Doctor Walker won't let those gorgeous babies go home until she's sure that they'll make it."

"Meredith, the twins and Maddie will be fine. We all have a great deal of confidence in Doctor Walker and her judgment. I love you, honey. Now let's get you some rest. You look absolutely exhausted, too," said Tom to his wife.

Once Tom and Meredith were in bed, she told Tom that the twins were going to be named Rob and Rory Conrad. Tom thought the names sounded perfect. He wasn't surprised in the least to hear that their last name wouldn't be Richardson. He knew that never in a million years would Maddie give Ryan any inkling that he had children.

33

Maddie was released from the hospital seven days later, but she wasn't able to take her babies home with her. She was heartbroken even though she knew Doctor Walker was right. She absolutely had to give them their best chance of making it. However, she went to the hospital several each times each day to hold them. Merely holding them close to her chest made her feel like a mother, and she could tell that they sensed who she was. But it was agony for her sitting at home alone, waiting for the day she could bring them home with her.

Meredith tried to keep her busy by taking her out for breakfast or dinner or eating meals with her family even though Maddie was never very hungry. By the time the babies were able to come home, Meredith knew her sister would've lost all her baby weight and more.

Night-time was the worst for Maddie. She had trouble sleeping. She'd get to sleep and then suddenly wake up in the middle of the night, worrying that something would be wrong with at least one of the twins, perhaps Rory, since she was the tiniest. Even though she tried to be optimistic, something kept nagging her in the back of her mind. But Maddie was wrong.

Finally, after six weeks in the hospital nursery, the big day came. The babies had gained enough weight, and their lungs had developed enough that Doctor Walker gave the thumbs up sign. On the day that Maddie brought them home, each of the twins weighed a whopping 5.5 pounds. She and Meredith each held one of the twins while Tom drove. Maddie was surprised to see that all her neighbors had staked blue and pink balloons in the yard, as well as a huge sign saying, "It's a boy AND a girl!" They were even standing outside to welcome the newcomers to the neighborhood. Maddie was so overwhelmed that tears started to roll down her cheeks.

Michelle was flying in the next day for a week to help, and the ever-efficient Meredith had already made up a schedule of her close friends to come in and help. The neighbors had also met with Meredith and volunteered to help the young mother. Maddie was grateful for all the help. She knew she'd need it. She did.

Looking back, the first six months were a total blur to Maddie. If she wasn't feeding the twins, bathing the twins, or changing diapers, she was trying to get a little sleep. Thank God for Meredith, Michelle, Meredith's friends, and her neighbors. She didn't know if she would've made it without their help and support. They all worked like an assembly line. The first time both of the twins slept through the night, everyone cheered!

The twins were absolutely adorable and looked almost exactly alike, with the exception of their hair color. They were growing by leaps and bounds and were also very happy and outgoing children. They seldom cried, and once they started crawling, thank God for playpens and naps.

Maddie was with the twins twenty-four hours a day. In the spring and summer she would take them in their stroller for walks around the neighborhood. Sometimes, though, her neighbors would walk the children so that Maddie could have a much-needed break. They all delighted in seeing the twins. Her neighbors would even go grocery shopping for her, do her yard work without her even asking, and offer to babysit so Maddie could have some free time. Of course, the twins were the stars of the block. They were both so darn cute and outgoing that everyone wanted to hold them.

The little ones took their first steps at ten months. Maddie was able to capture the moment with her camera. It was amazing to watch her children imitate each other all the time. If one of them pulled himself up into a chair, the other one would follow. If one of them spoke, so did the other one. Maddie was amazed when her children seemed to start talking in sentences when they first opened their mouths. She knew this definitely wasn't the norm. Maddie had decided early on that she wanted her children to become best friends. She wouldn't even consider the idea that they might become jealous of each other. Maddie was one lucky lady. The twins were about as perfect as they could be, and would be, lifelong best friends.

BOOK IV:
VIETNAM

34

Ryan had absolutely no idea that on June 5, 1968, that Maddie was pregnant. He still didn't understand why Maddie had rejected his idea to postpone their marriage until he was safely back from Vietnam. He lay on his bunk and just stared at the ceiling for what seemed like hours. *My reasoning was so logical,* he thought. *I spent months trying to be considerate of Maddie's needs—future—OUR future. How could Maddie not get it?*

Tears filled his eyes. *Oh my God, what have I done?* he thought. *Why did I think she would wait? She has no idea how dangerous Nam is. She doesn't know that my chances of coming back in one piece are slim to none. Maddie doesn't need a crippled lover or blind husband,* he rationalized. *But she's so damned stubborn; she'd say it wouldn't matter. But I know it would. It would to me.*

Ryan broke into a cold sweat. He had insisted on making a decision that affected both of them, and it had just cost him the important person in his life—in his future. Now, he was going to have to go it alone, and he knew he would think of Madison every day for the rest of his life.

Two weeks later, Ryan boarded a military transport to Fort Benning, Georgia. He would go to Ranger, Paratrooper, Jump, and Airborne schools, as well as Infantry Officers' Basic Course before shipping out for Vietnam. If he was going to survive this war, he would need much more training in warfare tactics than he'd learned at West Point. This was a different kind of conflict, a war where the enemy and friendlies all looked alike. Vietcong didn't fight in the normal fashion either. They used improvised booby traps, pitfalls, and ambushes. Ryan needed to learn their tactics, so he could understand their strategies. At West Point, he had learned how to be a leader—now, he needed to learn how to keep himself and all of the men under his command alive.

During training, Ryan wrote or tried to get in touch with Maddie every day, but all the letters came back "Return to Sender-No longer at this address." Once he even called Terri—that was a huge mistake. Terri said she didn't know where Madison was, and even if she did, she would never tell him in a million years. She told him what she thought of his decision, and that he'd never find anyone else like Madison. She ended the conversation by calling him an asshole. Of course, he'd expected that, and Terri was right. Days became weeks, weeks became months with no response. Eventually, he gave up and focused on learning ways he could stay alive in combat. But that didn't stop him from thinking about her—every night.

Just before he received orders for Vietnam, Ryan was promoted to first lieutenant. He had always imagined that Maddie would pin on his advancements, but now that was never to be, so he asked his mother to pin on his silver bars. Soldiers headed to Vietnam usually received a thirty-day leave. With Maddie out of his life, Ryan only used two weeks. If he had known he was the father of twins, he would not have been so eager to go. But now he wanted to go and get it over with.

Lieutenant Richardson flew to Oakland, California, and then caught a military bus to Travis Air Force Base for his flight to Nam. He was surprised that MATS, the Military Air Transport Service, was using a commercial jetliner. The Army had contracted a funky new company called Braniff, and their brightly colored planes looked very strange on a drab Air Force runway.

The servicemen boarded by rank, so Ryan took a decent window seat in the front of the plane. He watched intently as everyone boarded. It was easy to recognize those men who had been there before: there was a certain look in their eyes, like a shell-shocked stare. Ryan wondered if he would have the same stare after his year was over. The new guys were easy to spot, too. Some looked nervous; others looked scared, and a few tried to hide their fear by joking around.

Once the plane was in the air, many of the younger guys started harassing the cute stewardesses. One guy might drop something in the aisle, so that the stewardess would have to bend over to pick it up. The other guys would try to look up her short skirt. Ryan really felt sorry for these women, but he knew these were probably the last American females they would see. Except for nurses, most of these men would not see an American woman for the next year. Maybe never.

It was impossible for the passengers to realize the gravity of their situation while flying on a fancy airliner that served meals and showed movies. If the guys on the plane weren't watching movies, they were playing cards, writing letters to loved ones, or talking among themselves. Some, like Ryan, tried to get some sleep, but it was difficult with all the distractions.

The plane stopped in Hawaii for about an hour, just enough time for the men to stretch their legs, and buy some junk food, magazines, or paperbacks. The entire flight would take over twenty, long hours; they were going half-way around the world.

Ryan thought about Maddie during the entire flight. If he hadn't screwed up, they would already have been married a year. He wanted her to take him back and marry him; Ryan still had no explanation for why he had done what he did. He'd been a fool—an arrogant fool. He was afraid he would pay for his mistake for the rest of his life. He would never find another woman like Maddie.

The closer the plane got to Tan Son Nhut Air Force Base outside of Saigon, Vietnam, the quieter the plane became. The men began to realize how serious their situation really was. Most of them, including Ryan, wondered how many of them would make it home alive. None of them knew exactly where they were being sent in Vietnam. They would find out where they were headed once they were on the ground.

Ryan was no different than the other first-timers. He looked out the window and saw a lush green mountainous country that looked very peaceful and beautiful from the air. It was only when he saw flashes of light that he realized he was going into a war zone.

Everyone entering Vietnam, for the first time, would remember the eerie feeling when the plane door opened. It was like a scene from a horror movie, when the main character was about to do something that seemed perfectly innocent and safe—but every viewer knew some terrible tragedy was just a breath away.

As he stepped off the plane, the first thing that hit Ryan was an intense humid heat and a stench unlike anything he had ever smelled before. It seemed to him like a combination of raw sewage, rotting vegetables, and something else he couldn't quite recognize. Eventually, he would come to know that smell all too well.

Ryan and the other soldiers deplaned and immediately boarded what looked like a khaki-colored school bus. It had a quarter-inch steel plates welded to the side, and the windows were covered with a heavy wire mesh, apparently to deflect grenades and other objects thrown by the Vietcong infiltrators. Countless dents, scratches, and holes were a sobering testament to this welcoming ritual. Although it had an armed escort, the bus travelled only during the day. Ryan thought, *Welcome to Vietnam, asshole.*

The bus brought all incoming soldiers to the 93rd Replacement Depot to get combat gear and deployment orders. Of course, Ryan already knew he was going into the boonies. He had chosen to be a grunt, and that's where grunts went. He also knew he would be a platoon leader, and he'd have to earn the respect of the men under his command. Just being a first lieutenant wouldn't make his men trust him. Far from it. He would have to prove himself to them, especially the vets. Some of them would already have had experience in the bush, while others like himself would be a FNG (fucking new guy). In the end, all the training in the world would not prepare any of them for what they were about to experience.

The Army had set up a patrol base close to a village north of Da Nang near the South China Sea. Ryan was dropped in via helicopter and greeted by a hand of GIs, low-ranking enlisted men, who were there to off-load C-rations, ammunitions, and, most important of all, mail from home. The same men threw garbage and trash back onto the helicopter before it took off.

Ryan's first impression of his platoon was one of total disarray. He very quickly discovered that the troops assigned to him lacked adequate field training. Some of them had been protecting a bridge in Anh Khe using armored personnel carriers for protection. But they were so "rusty" on dismounted infantry tactics that they were a danger to themselves and their unit.

Ryan ordered his top NCO to assemble the troops. He couldn't believe how awful and un-military they appeared. Everything in Ryan's training had focused on the need for discipline, precision, and spit-shined boots. These troops were sloppy, unshaven, and lethargic.

"This is First Lieutenant Ryan Richardson," said the gunny sergeant.

Ryan stood at attention, looking as sharp as he wanted them to be. He spoke slowly, loudly, and firmly. "My job is to make sure all of you get out of this hell-hole alive."

A doubtful murmur rippled through the troops; they'd heard this crap before. Ryan knew they were thinking, *Who does this FNG think he's kidding? The closest he's been to a live round was at some firing range. This new bastard is going to get us killed!*

Ryan walked among the men, staring sternly into their eyes, and looked disapprovingly at their unkempt uniforms. Then he strutted back to the front, faced them, and barked, "You men look—like shit! I don't see a single shined boot or a polished buckle." He paused for effect then smiled and said, "Excellent. FUCKING EXCELLENT! Shiny buttons may make the reporters and politicians happy, but over here, shiny stuff will get you killed."

Well, that wasn't what the men expected to hear from a new West Point graduate. Collectively, they thought, *Maybe this officer would be different from their last three COs.* Ryan continued, "But that's not all that gets you killed. Some of you guys are pretty salty; you've watched officers and buddies get blown away and somehow—you SOBs are still alive and we're going to learn from you. And believe it or not, the Army has learned a few things about fighting this war, too, and you are going to learn them from me."

Ryan also made sure his men kept up their personal hygiene. Even though it was the squad leaders' responsibility, he personally checked his troop's feet for trench foot, made sure they shaved, checked scrapes and cuts for infections—whatever was needed to keep his platoon safe and free from disease. Most of his men were quite thin—eating the dreaded C-rations for four weeks at a time would do that to anyone. Everyone, including Ryan, hated the supposed eggs and ham C-ration the worst. It was green, and no one would eat it, unless they were running low on everything else or the resupply helicopter was late. The bartering for canned peaches and the ever-popular lime Kool Aid mix was always a sight to behold.

As dangerous as the VC were, Ryan knew that the local wildlife in Vietnam could be even worse. At one of his schools before he left for Vietnam, Ryan learned that the ponds, streams, and rivers were infested with deadly crocodiles and huge, man-eating tigers roamed the jungle. But they glossed over the fact that one hundred and forty varieties of snakes call Nam home; but Ryan had done his homework before he left for Nam. It was during one of Ryan's daily *How do you stay alive?* training sessions, that Ryan talked to his men about different types of snakes they might encounter.

"Corporal Blevins," said Ryan.

"Yezzir," snapped the seasoned non-com, with a pronounced southern accent.

"This is your second tour," said Ryan. "What have you learned here that will help the rest of us stay alive?"

"Snacks, Sir. Fuggin' Pie-zun snacks. Li'l onez, big onez, gynormous onez, all colors. Dayz on duh groun, in duh treez, in yer gear, in yer buy-yed…ever god-dam wheres! Dis fuggin' plaze gots cobras, My-lay-sian pit vi-puhs, bamboovi-puhs, green treez vi-puhs. Oh, dem deadly bastuds is everwhars. Dere ain't no good snacks, but duh worstest is Two Step Char-lee. Y'all gets bited by them fuggers and you iz de-hy-dra-ted in a couple stay-ups."

That part of his explanation wasn't exactly true, but made the point. A surgeon at base camp told Ryan it generally took an agonizing hour for krait poison to kill a man. Even in the relative safety of a fire base, a soldier could wake up with a poisonous snake inside his clothes, coiled against his warm body. If the man moved in his sleep or rolled onto a viper, the snake could bite. Ironically, that's what happened to Blevins two weeks later. His official death certificate read "Killed in action." Ryan's men would be haunted by his death forever.

Ryan also knew that there were several soldiers that he would have to rely on to keep his men safe. The radio operator and point man were two of them.

Mitch was one of the new guys. He was Ryan's new RTO—radio telephone operator. Most guys didn't want to be the RTO, because the radio was heavy and the whip antenna was like waving a red flag at the enemy. *On the plus side,* Mitch thought, *this radio is our only connect with "home," and if we come under fire, I don't want to rely on some other asshole to call for help.*

Mitch quickly learned how to work the radio, but field protocol was a different issue. The Vietcong knew a radio was a dead giveaway for an officer, so Ryan's primary concern was to make sure Mitch was NEVER directly in front or behind him. Not wanting to frighten his RTO, he said, "Private, we need to protect this radio. I'm a target for the VC, so whenever we're on patrol, you are to keep two or three men away from me. Do you understand? That is an order! In the event of an attack, I will come to you, not the other way around." He drilled this instruction into him daily, but Ryan soon learned, in the heat of battle, nothing goes as planned.

The other soldier Ryan had to rely on was his "point man." Rich was the eyes and ears of the platoon. He led the way, listening and looking for any kind of disturbance or potential ambush. If his point man stopped, they all stopped, and nobody moved until he gave the all-clear signal.

After a month in the jungle, the group would spend one week at a designated firebase for a little Rest & Recuperation. "Little" was right! This R & R was no walk in the park. The VC loved to infiltrate firebases to knife sleeping soldiers and slip back into the jungle, so maintaining perimeter defenses was a never-ending job. Each day, Ryan's men patrolled the area, fixed razor-sharp concertina wire, replaced VC booby traps with their own, and set up ambushes to catch the night marauders.

On the bright side, while at the firebase, soldiers were able to listen to music. Some of Ryan's favorite songs at the time were, "We Gotta Get Outa this Place," "Proud Mary," and the one that seemed the most apropos, "Who'll Stop the Rain?" Many Nam vets felt that this should be the national anthem! The week of "luxury" at Firebase Charlie always passed quickly. Then it was back into the jungle for another four weeks of terror.

Ryan had only been in Vietnam about three months when his platoon was ambushed. The morning of August 7, 1969, was hot and humid, like most summer days in Nam. Ryan hated the humidity and almost daily rainstorms. He hated walking through rice paddies and pulling foot long leeches from his body. It seemed to him that he was always soaking wet. *If there really is a hell,* Ryan thought, *this must be it.*

It was mid-afternoon. Ryan and his men were headed back to their patrol base on a trail that ran alongside a "friendly" village nestled close to a large hill mass. This village was one of their "pacification" projects, and local children were playing nearby, so they felt relatively secure. The undergrowth on their left was so thick it was even impossible for wild hogs to move through it, so no one expected an ambush to come from there. But fifty yards ahead, at about two o'clock, the trail wound through a large clearing. It had been bordered by a tree-covered ridgeline that could have hidden a dozen VC before the B-52s carpet-bombed the area and blew all the trees into toothpicks. Now, there was just a gradual slope up that hill. It was strewn with tall grass, moss-covered rocks, and hundreds of small bushes. It was an ideal playground for young children to play hide-and-seek. The bushes were also just big enough to hide the opening of a "spider hole" concealing the tiny body of a VC warrior.

Ryan's platoon had been here before, without incident, and this was exactly where the children were playing. Still, he had instructed his point man to be especially vigilant. G-2 (Army intelligence) had noted enemy movement in the area, and Ryan was ordered to check it out.

The children laughed and waved in recognition of their American friends; subconsciously the platoon relaxed its alert. Some of the guys waved back. Suddenly, dozens of small bushes around the children fell over as the trap doors beneath them revealed their lethal trove. AK-47 fire ripped through the leaves, through the bushes, through the exposed flesh of the young decoys, and into Ryan's second squad. The Vietcong were crafty and vicious, but their lack of fire discipline had focused most of their initial shots on the front of the middle squad. The two men in front of Ryan died instantly, as bullets missed their armored helmets and vests and turned their heads into bloody mush-covered fragments of shattered bone.

The sacrifice of these brave lead men gave squads one and three the time to hit the ground, identify targets, and return fire. Ryan had trained them well. Unscathed by the initial attack, the weapons and fire disciple of those squads were precise and relentless. Now trapped in their own ambush, the VC's shallow spider holes quickly turned into shallow graves. The entire battle lasted less than ten minutes, yet, by the time the attackers were killed, seven US soldiers were dead and nearly half the platoon was badly wounded. Many who escaped wounds had AK-47 "souvenirs" lodged in their protective vests.

When the ambush began, Mitch anticipated Ryan's call for help and started running towards his commander with the radio. It was a huge mistake. An errant bullet crashed through Ryan's arm, sending his rifle to the ground. Moments later, a deafening explosion blasted Ryan, his radioman, and two other soldiers several yards off the trail. (The VC were masters at finding US munitions and making them into booby traps to hurt our troops.) This time they found a deadly Claymore mine, a directional antipersonnel device our troops usually detonate remotely. The VC had rigged a hidden trip wire that the platoon would trigger when they dove for cover, and they repositioned it to spray the trail with searing metal fragments.

Ryan had been blown off his feet by the mine. He tried to get up but fell on his face as leg bones sliced through his right calf muscles. He didn't feel any pain at the moment—that would come later—as shock and adrenaline were strong anesthetics. His ears were ringing so loudly he couldn't understand the voices, but he saw lips moving and knew there was a lot of shouting.

Mitch had been hit by the Claymore, too. He couldn't move his legs but felt so guilty that he'd been out of his assigned position, that he used his hands to pull his body and the precious radio to his commander's side. The air was filled with acrid smoke, as well as screams from wounded men and dying children. They were the VC's sacrificial lambs caught in the crossfire.

Thankfully, for the wounded soldiers, platoons are large enough to rate a medic with them on patrol. "Doc" Barclay, a corpsman, moved up the line, checking the injured. When he got to Ryan, he reported that four of the eleven-man second squad were dead, and three others, including Ryan, were seriously wounded. The other two squads had missed the VC's frontal attack. None of their men were dead, but at least half of them had sustained non-life-threatening wounds. Most important, the first and third squads had wiped out the VC. Ryan instinctively reached for the radio to send a situation report and call for a medevac helicopter, but both of his arms were was so badly hurt he couldn't pick up the phone. Doc grabbed the radio and made the report, and then he directed the medevac chopper where to land.

Several Huey gunships arrived with the medevac choppers and circled the landing zone while squads one and three secured the perimeter. There was no way Ryan could walk. Doc Barclay carried him, and two guys helped get Mitch and other men to the chopper. The medevac corpsman did a quick triage and administered morphine and whatever first aid he had to save lives. The dead soon were piled in the choppers, next to the wounded, like a cord of wood.

It had taken the medevac chopper about thirty minutes to reach them. It seemed much longer. Later, the thing Ryan remembered was being very thirsty and feeling sweaty. It took him awhile to realize that the sweat he felt was really blood; he was covered in it—his and the two men behind him who were killed by the Claymore.

The thirty-minute flight back to the Battalion Aid Station seemed to last forever. Ryan insisted on sitting up, so he could check on his troopers, but he quickly passed out. He slept until the chopper thumped to a landing, and he saw corpsmen waiting with stretchers. As a medic stepped forward to help, Ryan reached towards him and, still groggy, started to fall out of the chopper. The medic grabbed Ryan's right arm, and there was a loud "snap." *Well, shit!* Ryan thought through his haze. *I just broke my arm—and I didn't feel a thing.* At the aid station, the medics stabilized Ryan and put aircasts on this right arm and leg. Then he was airlifted to the 67th Evac Hospital in Qui Nhon for real treatment.

The 67th was like a medical assembly line: orderlies put Ryan and his injured men on stainless steel gurneys, cut off their bloody uniforms and boots, cleaned their wounds, and prepped them for surgery. For most of these men, it would be the first in a long series of painful operations. Many would lose limbs, and the survivors would carry scars for the rest of their lives. Later, Ryan recalled seeing a very bright light, feeling the very cold gurney, and watching blood and whatever else go down a drain in the concrete floor. Then everything went blank.

The morning of August 8, 1969, Ryan woke and discovered he was covered in bandages everywhere— his legs and arms, his back, and his butt. In the heat of combat, and the numbing shock, he had no idea how serious his injuries were. He knew he had a broken arm and leg, and something was seriously wrong with his right calf. But what were all the other bandages for? He carefully tried to move all parts of his body. They seemed to work, which was good, but he couldn't feel some things, especially his right leg and left arm. This scared him to death.

Typically, Ryan was more worried about his men than himself. How were they? Did they make it? One of the nurses told him his two front men were killed in the first VC volley, and the two men directly behind were killed by the Claymore blast. Mitch, his RTO, had also been hit by the mine, but incredibly, because he had just run in front of the two men, he had no injuries aside from his feet and ankles. Of course, nearly all the bones in both of his feet and ankles had been shattered. Doc Barclay said later that Mitch would eventually walk, but all the bones in his feet and ankles would have to be fused together.

Ryan was relieved to hear that at least Mitch would walk again. Rich, his point man wasn't so lucky. Rich had only a minor bullet wound, but it had lodged in his spine, and he was paralyzed from the waist down. The last Ryan heard his point man was being sent into neurosurgery.

Later that same day, the company first sergeant and an officer came by and gave him his West Point ring and wallet from the company safe, minus the money in his wallet. The first sergeant filled him in on the condition of his men and told him that the effort Ryan had spent training his platoon probably saved most of their lives. When he left, he saluted Ryan and said, "Mighty proud to have served with you, sir. We're gonna miss ya."

That was nice, Ryan thought to himself. Then he shook his head in disbelief. *What kind of son of a bitch would steal a wounded soldier's money?* A Vietnamese orderly came by pushing a cart piled with Purple Hearts and tossed one onto Ryan's bed—no ceremony, no speech, not even a "Thanks for getting your ass shot off!" This certainly wasn't the way he'd envisioned his career.

The next day, Ryan was indeed medevac'd from Qui Nhon to the 249th Army General Hospital, Asaka, Japan. This was when he realized his wounds were really serious. He knew that if a soldier had minor injuries, he would be treated in theater. If recovery was going to take at least a month, he would be sent to Japan. If it was going to be at least three months, he'd go to Hawaii. If it was going to be longer than that, he would be sent home. Ryan didn't know it at the time, but eventually, he would end up back in the United States.

Ryan was at the 249th Army General Hospital in Asaka for six weeks. He had a cast put on his arm but not one on his right leg, and he learned to dread the twice daily change of dressings. His wounds had been sutured together with metal staples and then covered with gauze. The idea was to let the wounds try to heal from the inside out. This procedure greatly improved the healing process and reduced infection and gangrene. However, it was also excruciatingly painful, because the gauze would stick to the wound and steel sutures. When the gauze was removed from the wound, so that more Betadine solution could be applied, the pain was almost unbearable.

Because of this, the nurse or orderly who personally changed the bandages was very important. For the first few weeks, it required three people to change Ryan's dressing: one to do the work and two to hold him down. Looking back, Ryan remembered two people who treated him in Asaka—one he called "his angel," a female nurse who was kind, thoughtful, and gentle. She was on duty in the evening and early morning and whispered softly in his ear to see if he needed anything. The other one was a sergeant whom he nicknamed "Attila the Hun." This guy was cruel and seemed to enjoy hurting him. Each time Attila would come to dress his wounds, Ryan would will himself not to show the man that he was in pain. He wasn't about to let this man see him cry. He came to believe Attila hated all officers.

During his first few weeks in Asaka, Ryan's mental attitude wasn't in much better shape than his broken body. However, it didn't take long for him to be thankful that he still had all of his body parts. The man in the bed next to him had lost his leg from the knee down, and he would scream in anguish every time the nurses would change his bandages. But compared to many other soldiers, this man was lucky. And Ryan knew there were many men much worse off than he.

One day Ryan received orders to Valley Forge Military Hospital near Carlisle, Pennsylvania, and he realized his tour in Vietnam was over. He also knew his right leg was in very bad shape. His right calf had been shredded by the booby-trapped Claymore mine and need much more repair work and grafting to prevent amputation from the knee down.

After all his preparation, Ryan had lasted only three months in Vietnam. He had dedicated himself to become a really fine "leader" and went the extra mile to learn all the tricks of his trade. Yet, when put in charge of keeping his men alive, four had died, one was paralyzed from the waist down, and fully half of his forty-man platoon suffered serious injuries. Part of his mind said, *No one could have known the VC would use children as decoys,* but he still felt that he and only he was to blame for what had happened. He needed to make it right.

> "I came home, flying home,
> seeing the coastline of my home,
> my country and my home, was it home?
> It was so strange to be back home,
> An alien stranger back home.
> I left the guys to come home,
> I was lucky to come home,
> Would the guys be coming home?
> I wanted to go back to my home,
> to the guys and my home."
>
> Anonymous

35

Ryan was evacuated to the United States after about a week. He remembered one part of the flight vividly. The plane had stopped in Alaska for refueling at about 2:00 A.M., and a group of women boarded the plane offering everyone hot chocolate, coffee, and homemade cookies. Ryan couldn't believe that these nice ladies would be up that early in the morning to offer them some comfort. He was so thankful that it brought him to tears.

It wasn't until Ryan arrived at Valley Forge, Pennsylvania, that he was able to contact his mother via a mobile phone cart. His mom had heard absolutely nothing from the Army for several weeks, except a telegram stating that Ryan had been "slightly wounded." The lady who helped him with the phone call also gave him a medallion that said, "To a wounded soldier. Thank you for your service." Ryan would always treasure this act of kindness and would keep that medallion forever.

It was at Valley Forge that large casts would eventually be put on Ryan's right leg and arm. It was also here that Ryan had a huge skin graft. A large piece of skin was taken from his left thigh, leaving an exposed area that was like the worst road rash imaginable. A few days later, the skin was grafted onto his right calf. The graft was considered a "dead" skin graft, rather than a "live" one, which would have been done right away. The main problem Ryan encountered during this portion of recovery was not only the excruciating pain from his left thigh, but also the horrendous smell of rotting flesh on his right calf. The stench reminded him of Nam, and it gave him nightmares. But the doctors were hopeful that the skin graft would form scar tissue over Ryan's exposed calf muscle and nerves on his right leg. It took two months, but he was lucky; it worked. He wasn't going to lose his leg.

His rehab started in earnest at this time. He was doing exercises to try to get the damaged ulna nerve in his left arm to strengthen, so that it would work properly again. Since his right arm was in a full cast, as well as his right leg, he wasn't able to eat by himself. He hated that he couldn't even feed himself. Finally, he and the nurses figured out a way in which Ryan could hold a spoon in his left fist. Ryan was also given a wheelchair and then crutches to use, so he could finally have the dreaded catheter removed. He was finally becoming semi-mobile again.

Ryan contacted his old friend Ben, who came to visit him every weekend from Washington, DC. By early October, Ben was finally able to pull some strings and get him transferred to Walter Reed Army Medical Center in DC. He was placed in the officers' orthopedic ward, affectionately called Ward 1. Ryan didn't know it at the time, but this was the "party ward." Once a week, usually on Friday nights, the ward would have a party. Ward 1 had quite a reputation. There were many bachelor officers on the ward, and their parties were legendary.

Ward 1 became a much-needed mental therapy for Ryan. There was always someone there in worse shape than he. It was here that he finally started to focus on what he could do, instead of what he couldn't. Ryan started reconnecting with his world in Ward 1.

Ultimately, the time came when Ryan was allowed to take some convalescent leave, so he went back to Ohio to see his family and friends. Physically, the travel was very difficult for him since he was still in a full arm and leg cast and on crutches. His mother had even arranged a blind date for him while he was home. He didn't want to go, but he also didn't want to disappoint his mother, so he went. What a mess! He felt like an invalid, and even though the girl was nice and pretty cute, she was no Maddie. How much better things would have been if Maddie had been by his side. She was the strong one. She would have pulled him through this much faster than he was managing. He'd asked his mother if she had heard any news about Madison, but she hadn't. At least she didn't tell him what a fool he'd been again. She didn't have to—he knew it.

In December, Ryan was back at Walter Reed, and the doctors felt his leg had healed enough to shorten the leg cast to knee-length. What a relief! He could actually walk short distances without crutches, but more importantly, he found that his knee would still bend. Shortly, he left the crutches behind for good and started using a cane.

Once Ryan was basically mobile again, he only had to go to Walter Reed once a week for "grand rounds." Here he would be evaluated and learn what medical follow-up was needed. Since Ryan was mobile, he moved in with his friend, Colonel Perry, in Alexandria. There were other former West Pointers staying there as well, so Ryan was finally entering the real world again. This was very good for him emotionally.

There had never been any question in Ryan's mind that he would not be going back to Vietnam. He would. He had unfinished business there. However, the possibility that he might not be allowed to go back a second time also entered his mind. He seemed to develop almost an obsession with death, like a death wish. Morbid poems, like "Crossing the Bar" and "I Have a Rendezvous with Death," intrigued him. In fact, he became very fatalistic about life. He believed that whatever would be would be. But he also believed that he'd make it back. The enemy had tried the first time and had missed; therefore, irrationally, he felt himself to be a little immune.

In January 1970, Ryan's last cast finally came off. Now, he had to prove to the powers that be that he could still be an infantry soldier. He had to prove that the muscle and nerve damage in his right calf would not be a hindrance or handicap to himself or others in the field.

Ryan started training daily. His endurance was shot (he needed to stop smoking so much), and at first his calf would swell up the size of a watermelon after just running around the block. But he kept at it and finally felt the time was right for him to make his move. He asked for admittance to Pathfinder School at Fort Benning, Georgia, and then asked to be assigned to the 101st Airborne in Vietnam. During Pathfinder School, the soldiers focused on slinging supplies underneath helicopters and finding landing zones. In order for his negative medical report to be removed from his Army file, Ryan also had to run a mile in under six minutes and ten seconds. About a week before the scheduled run, however, Ryan's toe on his right foot started to give him trouble. In fact, he could hardly walk, let alone run. He made it, but only after digging out a piece of shrapnel that had migrated from his ankle to his toe. But he had reached his goal.

After the five-week Pathfinder School, Ryan spent another two weeks training in Florida to prepare for his return to Vietnam. During that time, he met a girl who helped her father as a bartender. He took her to dinner one evening, and then for the first time since June 5, 1968, Ryan got laid. He was surprised at how different it felt having sex versus making love. The sex part was great—a lot of pent up energy expended, but it was absolutely the antithesis of making love to Madison. With Cheryl, there was no emotional connection. With Maddie, it was the emotional connection that had been just as important to him as the sex.

It occurred to Ryan that he could have sex with anyone, and it would do the job, so to speak, but that was all it would be—sex. Since Ryan had only been with one other woman in his life, the concept of sex just for the sake of sex was an entirely new idea, one he wasn't sure he would ever really understand. Most men didn't seem to have this problem. They enjoyed sex with anyone at any time. However, Ryan was the type of man who had learned through Maddie that what he craved as much as the sexual aspect of the act itself was the closeness, the feeling of oneness with another human being. He'd had that with Maddie; they were one when they made love. Once again, and for the rest of his life, he knew that he had screwed up the most important relationship he would ever have. This bothered him even more than his perceived "failure" in Vietnam—and always would.

With the news that the negative profile in his Army medical file had finally been removed, he was getting set to return to Vietnam. His rehab and retraining had taken about a year, so he was headed back for his second tour at about the same time he'd left for his first tour.

36

Ryan didn't make captain when he returned from his first tour like most of the other officers. In fact, he didn't make captain until right before he was headed back for his second tour. Ryan believed that this was because of his "failure" the first time.

Captain Richardson flew on the commercial airline, the Flying Tigers, on his second trip to Vietnam. It was June 1970. The flight was an exact repeat of his first flight. They landed at Tan Son Nhut Air Force Base, the same as before, and received their orders once again at Bien Hoa.

This time around, there were several differences for Ryan. One, the locations were different; two, he was no longer a platoon leader; and three, this time he would have several different duty assignments.

Ryan's first position during his second tour was as a battalion supply officer for three months. He was in charge of making sure the men in the bush received their full rations of supplies and, more importantly, received them on time. Ryan lived in Phu Bai, just south of Hue during this time. However, even though he didn't have to, he made it a point to go out to several firebases via helicopter to assure that the men's needs were being met.

In October 1970, Ryan's position changed. He was made commander of A Company. Once again, he was humping the bush with his men as often as he could. After all, he was still a grunt, no matter what his rank, and this is what grunts did. However, as a commander, he had to deal with more day-to-day logistics and other distractions, such as personnel issues.

One such personnel issue was a constant headache for Captain Richardson. One young inductee, Daniel Castle, should never have been in the Army in the first place. He was a detriment not only to those around him, but also to himself. He was caught smoking pot on the firebase, but even worse, he was also caught smoking it in the bush, which made him a clear and present danger to his fellow soldiers. Ryan had him sent to the rear immediately, and Daniel was given an Article 15 and busted to an E-1.

Two months later, Daniel was caught using heroin in the bush, which was even worse. This time he was court-martialed and spent some time as a resident in the infamous Long Binh jail. Even this didn't seem to change his reluctance to go back into the bush.

Daniel tried every trick known to mankind to keep from going back into the bush—his excuses varied from having a toothache, the flu, spider bites, you name it. Then, he finally decided he was a conscientious objector. He thought for sure that this would keep him out of the jungle. However, Captain Richardson informed the young man that his information was incorrect. What it did do for him was allow him to turn in his M-16 rifle in favor of carrying a six-foot, ten-pound stretcher. He was still in the boonies, but now he had no weapon for protection. Daniel lasted about a week before giving up his CO status in order to regain his M-16.

Daniel Castle wasn't destined to return to the United States alive. No, he wasn't killed in action. He just happened to be in the wrong place at the wrong time. While he was at a firebase, he went to an NCO club and was drinking a beer when another soldier totally lost control, went berserk, switched his M-16 to automatic, walked into the club, and sprayed the entire room. Daniel was one of the four casualties that night.

In May 1971, Captain Richardson extended his commitment in Vietnam to eighteen months. The final seven months that Ryan was in Vietnam, he served as a ranger company commander as part of the 101st Long Range Patrol Company.

Ryan would organize special teams of six men who were then dropped in by chopper for about four days to investigate enemy activity and report back. Since he was the commander, Ryan was only able to be a member of the six-man group on one mission. The rest of the time, he would spend around four hours a day on choppers, making sure his recon teams were safe.

One young soldier's death had a lasting effect on Ryan. Ranger Sheridan was one of the members of a six-man insertion team. Three days into a four-day mission in the jungle, his group came under fire, and Ryan had to order an extraction. Captain Richardson decided to participate in this extraction himself. The chopper was under heavy fire during the extraction, and Jim Sheridan was the final soldier aboard. Ryan tried to pull him into the chopper when a VC's bullet hit Jim in the back of the neck. The round exited out of Jim's right eye, splattering blood and brain matter all over Ryan. He was dead before Ryan pulled him aboard the chopper. Captain Richardson held Sergeant Sheridan to his chest in the chopper all the way back to Camp Eagle. No one said a word.

Ever since Ryan had survived the ambush and injuries of his first tour, he had felt some kind of immunity to being killed in Nam. But he wasn't prepared to witness the death of one of his men like this. He felt personally responsible for Sergeant Sheridan. Even though he knew there was nothing he could have done differently, Ryan never did completely forgive himself for Jim's death. It would end up haunting him forever. Why didn't that bullet hit him instead of Sergeant Sheridan? He was just as close in the sniper's sight as Jim, and he was an officer. Why wasn't he the target? Was it just dumb luck?

Writing letters home to the parents of his fallen soldiers was one of the most difficult tasks Ryan ever had to perform as a company commander. His letter to Sergeant Sheridan's parents was the worst one he ever had to write. What made it even worse for Ryan was that his parents wrote a thank-you note back to him.

In September, Captain Richardson's ranger company was ordered to move from Camp Eagle to Camp Evans, about twenty miles from Hue. It was at this time that the rangers were also ordered not to go into the jungle on any further missions. By December, the rangers of the 3rd Brigade were told to stand down. They were ordered to turn in all their property and were disbanded.

That same month, Captain Richardson was ordered to take the property book to the U.S. Headquarters in Saigon. He hopped rides on several different choppers to get to Saigon to hand in the book. When Ryan went into the headquarters, he was surprised to find that the building was air-conditioned. As he opened the door, a blast of cold air hit him in the face—the first cold air he'd felt in eighteen months in Vietnam. Captain Richardson turned in the property book and quickly returned to Camp Evans to wait for orders. Ryan was in Saigon all of about fifteen minutes during his two tours in Vietnam.

Some of Ryan's men, the lucky ones, were able to go home early. Ryan and the other soldiers who were left were reassigned to the 1st Brigade of the 1st Cavalry Division. These soldiers remained in Vietnam until April 1972. Ryan was the last commander of L Company (ranger) 75th Infantry Regiment.

Since the war was over, so were Ryan's years as a grunt. He remained in the Army, however, serving in different capacities. With no more wars for Ryan to fight, the Army selected him to attend Harvard to pursue his master's degree in public administration, which he did. He knew that he would then go back to his alma mater and become an instructor.

Being an instructor at West Point was an honor for Ryan at first. He eagerly taught all the classes nobody with more seniority wanted to teach. He worked very hard on his lesson plans to keep the information he was giving to his cadets current and relevant whenever possible. He even saw several of his old classmates who had also become instructors. Ryan taught history, nuclear warfare, and basically any classes that were needed. He even wrote a chapter about nuclear warfare for a book that was ultimately published.

But after four years with absolutely no recognition for all the time and effort he had put into being a good instructor, Ryan decided to leave the institution that he loved more than anything else in the world—except Maddie, of course. It was time for him to move on.

Ryan spent several years at NATO headquarters in Belgium and wrote speeches for the generals. He thought it ironic that after all the math he'd been forced to endure at West Point, he would ultimately use his verbal and writing skills much more than any math classes. Whenever he was granted leave, he traveled through Europe. He still fondly remembered Maddie during his travels. He wished that she'd been with him to experience all that he saw. He just knew that she would have loved it. He would have been right, too.

In 1982, Ryan returned to the United States and contacted his close friend, Colonel Perry, who had helped him so much during his rehab. Perry was now a brigadier general, and he assigned Ryan to serve as his attaché at the Pentagon. Ryan was now a lieutenant colonel and was climbing the ranks at a fast pace.

It was now 1984. Twenty years had passed, and Ryan was reminded of the pact that the "group" had made on graduation night. Everyone had promised to return, unless they were six feet under. Should he keep his promise and go or just let it be? In the end, he decided that he would go. He wanted to see his old high school classmates, especially Garrett, Stan, and the twins, Kelly and Shelly. But most of all, he wondered if Madison would go to the reunion. He hadn't seen or talked to her for the last sixteen years. He had no idea where she was, if she was married—nothing. Maybe she wouldn't come for fear that he might be there. He knew Maddie well enough to know that it would be a very difficult decision for her to make.

What if she did come? What would he say to her? How would he act? More importantly, how would she react to seeing him again after what had happened? Ryan had never stopped loving Maddie. He'd had a very short-lived marriage of eighteen months under his belt, but he knew from the beginning that the marriage was doomed from the start. Lori wasn't Maddie. It was as simple as that. He would always unfairly compare the way Lori did things to the way Maddie would have done them. At least their marriage had ended amicably, and there were no children involved.

Yes, he decided. He would keep his promise and attend the twentieth class reunion. He made arrangements to fly to Oklahoma City, pick up a rental car, and reserved accommodations. He would arrive Friday in Oklahoma City, drive the three hours to Avalon, and attend the meet-and-greet party, albeit a bit late.

BOOK V:
CALIFORNIA

37

It took Jake six months to pry Maddie's whereabouts out of Terri. At least now he knew she was safe and with Meredith. But he also knew that he had to see her. No matter what it took, he would see Maddie again, and soon.

Once he knew that Maddie was living in Napa, California, he immediately bought a map of that area. He was particularly interested in the towns of Vallejo and Santa Rosa. He decided on the spot that he would try to get a teaching position in one of those cities for the next fall. That way, he'd be close enough to keep an eye on Maddie and the children who had probably just arrived.

He called both cities, and he was in luck. Vallejo was going to need a history teacher and assistant football coach for the next school year. He mailed them his transcripts, resumé, and letters of recommendations immediately. He even included a picture of himself, so that they could see he was a clean-cut young man.

As soon as the personnel director read over Jake's qualifications, he knew that he'd found his man. He picked up the phone and offered Jake the position, sight unseen, and Jake said yes without any hesitation.

He was moving to California to be close to Maddie! Since Jake had told his parents the story of what had happened to Maddie and Ryan, they were not the least bit surprised by his decision. They knew he'd loved Maddie for many years now.

Jake's parents were a godsend to him. They told him to find some acreage with a nice house, and hopefully a barn, and they would pay cash for the property for him. He could pay them back in monthly installments with no interest. Jake's eyes filled with tears upon hearing this. They wanted him to follow his dream and be happy. After all, he was their only child.

Jake suddenly remembered that he already knew a realtor in that area. He remembered that Meredith and Tom owned a realty company. He didn't know what would happen, or even if she'd be willing to help him, but he had to give it a try.

He obtained the phone number for Campbell Realty in Napa, California, and dialed it immediately. When the receptionist answered, Jake asked to speak to Meredith Campbell regarding buying some property.

"This is Meredith Campbell. How may I help you, sir?

"Hi, Meredith. I don't know if you remember me or not, but I'm a friend of Maddie's. I'm Jake Kelly."

"Hi, Jake, of course, I remember you," said Meredith. "It's really good to hear from you. Maddie talks about you all the time. What can I do for you?"

Jake told Meredith that he'd accepted a teaching and coaching position at Vallejo High School for the next year. He would be moving out there the first part of June. He said he was looking for about five acres somewhere between Vallejo and Napa, hopefully on a hill, with a nice house and a barn if at all possible.

Meredith asked him what price range he was looking at, and he replied that money was not going to be a problem if he found exactly what he wanted. He also told her it would be a cash deal.

"Would you be able to start looking at properties with me as soon as I arrive?" asked Jake.

"Of course, Jake. There are simply lovely horse properties out here. I'll start researching them for you right away. If I find any that I think you'd be interested in, I'll call and send you pictures. How about that?" asked Meredith.

"That would be perfect, Meredith. Thanks. I have one other request, though, that is very important to me and non-negotiable. I don't want Maddie to know that I'm moving out there. Please promise me you won't tell her. I'll see her myself when I feel the time is right."

"I promise, Jake. But I can already tell you it's going to be really hard for me to keep my mouth shut. But I promise, I won't say anything to her," replied Meredith.

"Thanks. Please call me when you find some properties that might interest me. Talk to you soon."

When Meredith hung up the phone, she went straight to Tom's office, shut the door, and sat down.

"What's wrong?" asked Tom.

"Nothing, absolutely nothing!" exclaimed Meredith, with a huge smile.

She told Tom about her conversation with Jake. Tom had always heard nothing but great things about him from both Maddie and Meredith. The two of them decided they'd work together finding the perfect property for Jake.

It took a few weeks, but the two of them found two properties that they thought might suit Jake. Both properties were situated on hills overlooking either the bay near Vallejo or the vineyards in Napa. She had toured both properties and taken pictures. The houses were both large, stucco, and two-storied. One was California Spanish architecture with a tile roof. The other one, the one that she actually thought Jake would prefer, looked more like a country estate.

Meredith called Jake to tell him what she'd found and described them both to him.

The only question that Jake asked Meredith was, "Which one would Maddie like the most?"

Meredith wasn't really very surprised by the question. She told him that Maddie would absolutely love the large country estate house with the guest house.

"You said it's brand new, is that right?" asked Jake.

Meredith told him it had never been lived in. There were six bedrooms, a huge master suite with a fireplace, six full baths, a study, a formal dining room, a huge country kitchen with all of the best appliances, a breakfast area with a huge bay window overlooking the pool, and, instead of a formal living room and den, it had one huge great room with a built-in bar and another fireplace. There was even a small wine cellar. Meredith also told Jake about the separate guest house, and the entire property was beautifully landscaped. And yes, there was even a small red barn on the property.

Before Jake could ask, Meredith told him that the owners had built the place as their retirement home, but at the last minute, they decided to move to Florida to be closer to their children and grandchildren who lived back East.

"Buy it, Meredith," said Jake. "Please get me the best deal possible. Once you've come to terms on the price, let me know. I'm going to leave it in your hands. Send me some pictures of it and let me know how to pay for it. I'll be in California on June 3rd. I'll call you when I get to the outskirts of Vallejo; we can meet and you can take me to see the house. Does that sound all right to you?"

"That's perfect, Jake. And, no, I haven't said a word to Maddie."

"Good," replied Jake. "Remember your promise. See you soon."

As soon as Meredith hung up the phone, she went directly to Tom's office again and shut the door. She told Tom which house Jake wanted, and that the only question he had asked was if Maddie would like it. That didn't surprise Tom at all.

As soon as Jake received the pictures of his new home, he was delighted. It was just the kind of house he knew Maddie would love.

He took the pictures over to his parents' house in Englewood. They, too, were very pleased with what they saw and realized it was a very good investment. In a few years, it would be worth at least double the price they paid for it.

Jake's dad also had him pick out a new Mustang convertible for his birthday, which was July 7th. Jake tried to convince his father that the one he had was fine, but his father insisted on a new car since he had such a long drive ahead of him and was starting a new life. Jake finally settled on a deep navy metallic one with a tan convertible top.

Jake decided to take only a small U-Haul trailer with him containing his clothes, books, memorabilia, pictures, and sports' equipment. He could buy everything else he needed once he arrived in California.

Jake had also talked Matt into driving his truck with the horse trailer containing Joy. There was no doubt that Joy was going with him. He'd promised Maddie he would never leave her. Jake bought Matt a first-class return plane ticket for him, but most of all, he was happy that Matt was going to be able to spend a few days with him in California before his return.

The two best friends left for California on May 31st. They were allowing themselves four days to get there, mostly because of Joy. The trip would be hard on her. The two men had a great time on the trip West. Neither of them had ever been to California, so watching the different scenery and terrain in each state thoroughly intrigued them. Of course, they traveled almost all the way to their destination on the legendary Route 66.

In the evenings, after they had stopped for the night, they'd find a nice steak house. Afterwards, before they went to bed, they would talk about Jake's new adventure. Matt just didn't want Jake to get hurt. He had no idea how Maddie would react the first time she saw him. Jake said it was a chance he was willing to take. He wanted—no, needed—to be close to Maddie. He wanted to watch over her. Of course, he'd love to marry her, but he knew her well enough to know that it was absolutely the last thing on her mind right now.

They arrived on the outskirts of Napa at a place called American Canyon, about halfway between Napa and Vallejo, on June 3rd, around 11:00 AM. Jake went and used the pay phone outside a small grocery store. Meredith answered on the first ring. She told them to stay put, and she would come to them.

It didn't take Meredith long at all to get to them. She jumped out of her car and ran to give Jake a huge hug. Then, she shook Matt's hand. She had heard a lot about him and Terri from Maddie, too.

"Okay. Follow me to your new home," said Meredith excitedly.

It took a little while to get to Jake's new house, but when he saw it, he was overwhelmed. It was a gorgeous piece of property. Meredith had been right. There was even a small red barn for Joy.

Meredith gave them a tour of Jake's new place, and its beauty amazed him. He was really proud that this would be his new home. Matt went crazy about the pool and even jumped in with his clothes on.

Meredith helped the young men move Jake's few belongings into his new home, and then Jake and Matt very carefully and gently guided Joy out of the trailer. Jake let her walk around her new home, so she would become familiar with her new surroundings. After a while, they took Joy, and the hay they had brought with them, into the new barn and into her new stall. Joy was home.

Meredith insisted that the guys stay with her that night. So after they stopped by the realty office for Jake to sign what seemed like a million papers and provide them with a cashier's check for the property, they followed Meredith to her house.

Jake and Matt spent three wonderful days with Meredith and Tom. They went to San Francisco for two days and did nothing but shop for furniture for Jake's new house. He picked out a large distressed leather sectional with two matching chairs and ottomans, end tables and a coffee table for the living room. However, he was always keeping Maddie's taste in the back of his mind. The accessories they picked he made sure to ask Meredith if Maddie would choose it. The formal dining room had a massive distressed dark wood plank table and high-back chairs that matched it perfectly. It was formal yet informal. He also bought the matching buffet. For his bedroom, he picked out the newest thing on the market— a California king size bed. He'd never seen a bed that large before. He chose a medium distressed fruitwood chest, dresser, mirror, armoire, two tables, night stands and a large four-poster bed that matched the set. It was absolutely one of the most beautiful bedroom sets that Meredith had ever seen. He picked out a round glass top table for the breakfast room and decided to custom order the shelving for his study. In one of the extra bedrooms, he bought a blue denim slip-covered loveseat that could be made into a bed. For the other bedrooms, he also picked out beautiful sets with an old-world feel. In fact, everything that Jake picked out had that old-world feel to it, because he knew Maddie's taste so well.

Jake made Meredith select the accessories for the house. He didn't care about what color she chose, just so long as Maddie would like it. Meredith was like a kid in a candy store. Money was no object, so Meredith chose the best money could buy. Meredith picked out lamps, linens, comforters, towels, pots and pans, a set of Grand Baroque sterling silverware, Lennox china, Waterford crystal, as well as everyday dishes and glasses—just about everything, except clothes for Jake. Jake and Matt went and had some beers and seafood at Pier 39, while Meredith shopped at Nordstrom's, Macy's, Gump's, and Bruno's. Of course, Meredith had a great time. She couldn't believe that cost was not a problem for Jake. His parents had given him a book of checks from their account to be used to decorate the house.

When the house was furnished, and everything was in place, Meredith just knew Maddie would adore every inch of it when the time came for her to see it. Those three days were difficult for Meredith. She called to check on Maddie every day, and it just about killed her not to tell her that Jake was here, but she kept her promise and kept her mouth shut.

On the fourth day, Jake took Matt with him to Vallejo to see his new school. When he went to the personnel office and met Doctor Johnson for the first time, Jake was very impressed. So was Doctor Johnson.

After Jake finished filling out all of his paperwork, he and Matt followed Doctor Johnson to Vallejo High School. At first sight, the two of them were amazed at the size of the school. It was twice as large as Claymont and had all the up-to-date equipment any teacher could ask for. He met the principal, Doctor Jackson, and his department chair. He liked Eddie Robinson immediately. The feeling was mutual. Jake knew right then and there that he'd made the right choice to move here.

Next, Jake and Matt toured the entire facility, and when they arrived at the PE department, they couldn't believe all the new equipment they had. This was when he met the head football coach, Bob Mason.

"I've been waiting for you to get here, young man. We have a summer passing league here that I'd like you to help with."

"That will be great, sir. I'm ready to start tomorrow if you need me," answered Jake.

"Son, don't call me 'Sir.' My name is Bob, or just 'Coach' will do," said his boss. Since your specialty is as a quarterback, I'm going to make you my quarterback coach, if it's okay with you."

"That will be great, Bob."

"We start next Monday night here at the field— 6:00 PM. See you then!" shouted Bob as he was walking away.

Matt and Jake couldn't believe the sports' facilities at this school. They had better facilities than their college in Oklahoma. They looked at a large, new fully equipped weight room, locker rooms twice the size they'd ever seen, and a stadium that was enormous for just a high school. The entrance even looked a little like the one Jake had seen once of the Rose Bowl in a sports' magazine.

The night before Matt was to leave for Oklahoma, he stayed at Jake's new home. The two of them sat outside and drank beer and talked, especially about Maddie and Terri. Jake asked Matt if he thought Terri would ever consider moving to California. But Matt said that Terri was Oklahoma born and bred, so she'd probably never even consider moving. Jake told him to at least bring her out for a vacation sometime. Matt knew he had plenty of room. Matt said he'd try, but told Jake not to get his hopes up. The one reason she might come out for a visit, though, would be to see Maddie.

Jake told Matt that he didn't plan to contact Maddie right away. He knew she was busy with three-month-old twins night and day, but he would drive by her house sometimes on the weekends. He thought he'd wait until the twins were already walking before he reentered her life. Matt thought that would be a good idea.

The next morning, Jake took Matt to the Oakland Airport and hugged his best friend tightly, thanking him again for all the help with his move, and then he watched Matt as he boarded his plane for home.

38

The summer seemed to fly by to Jake. He was coaching the summer passing league, and Bob, his coach, was really impressed at how well he could relate to the players. He also attended the new teacher seminars and departmental meetings when they began in August. After he found out that he would be teaching American History and U.S. Government (two upper-level courses), he took the teacher's editions of the textbooks home with him and started making lesson plans.

A few times (not too many, though), he drove into Napa. His Mustang was the type of car someone might remember if he went too often. His heart stopped when he saw Maddie for the first time in what seemed to him like a lifetime ago. She was still the tall, thin, gorgeous woman he'd fallen in love with at first sight. She was tan and seemed to thoroughly enjoy walking the twins in their stroller. *Motherhood is good for Maddie,* thought Jake. However, the twins seemed older to him than three months.

Jake also continued to decorate his house, with Meredith's help, of course. They had to decide on window coverings as well as outdoor furniture. He decided to have the front door changed. He wanted one that was clear leaded glass. By the end of the summer, his house looked like a model home. And it was easy to keep clean. He hired a maid service once a week, but since he was a neat freak, he kept the place fairly tidy. The house was finished just before the football team started two-a-day practices, which were exhausting for everyone, including Jake.

School started the day after Labor Day in California. Jake was surprised at how excited he was to meet his new students. In fact, the night before school began, he even had trouble sleeping. Would the kids like him? More importantly, would they respect him? He always prided himself in doing his best with anything he tried, and this was no different. Jake didn't need to worry.

Jake's students adored him. He was young, handsome, smart, and knew how to make learning history fun. He wasn't like any of the other teachers they'd had before. He didn't just assign the students to read a chapter and then answer the questions at the end of the chapter. He talked to his students about what they were going to read first in order to get them interested in reading the chapter. He would also try different ways of answering the questions at the end of the chapter. Sometimes he would have a roundtable discussion; other times, he would put the students into groups. He always tried to make learning history more than merely memorizing a bunch of dates. In fact, since he was teaching American history classes, he talked to the junior English teachers and asked if they minded if he had his students read the play *The Crucible*. They were delighted. It made their life easier.

Jake quickly made a name for himself as a good teacher who not only could relate well with his students, but also could infuse fresh ideas and try different ways of teaching. Part of this was probably due to the fact that he wasn't really that much older than his seniors. He was also aware, since he'd been exposed to it in Claymont, that a few of the girls in his classes would develop crushes on him. Since he wasn't wearing a wedding ring, the girls thought he was fair game. Jake, in his naiveté, didn't consider it anything serious or something he needed to worry about. However, he was wrong.

California was nothing like Oklahoma. The girls in California were very different. They were much more forward, and since there was no dress code, during the spring and fall, they would all wear short shorts, halter tops without bras, and flip-flops. After all, California was the epicenter of free love, especially San Francisco, right across the bay. Jake was totally shocked the first day of school. He tried not to show his amazement and remained professional, but to say it was a little distracting would be an understatement. It took him a while to get used to it, but he did.

Jake also earned the respect and admiration of his players and coaches. Bob, his head coach, thought he'd died and gone to heaven when Jake came into his life. He truly knew the game well. He was not only the quarterback coach, but he also suggested some new plays that Bob didn't know. Bob felt that the Apaches had a real shot at the state title this year, not only because he had mostly seniors and juniors on his varsity team, but also because Jake had made David Armstrong into a class-A quarterback over the summer during passing league.

Football season seemed to go by in the blink of an eye for the Vallejo High School Apaches that year. And they actually did what Coach Bob had predicted they might do. The team went undefeated and went on to win their first state championship in eight years. Bob was well aware that Jake had a big hand in this.

Jake's parents flew into town to watch the state championship game and stayed with Jake for a week. Both of his parents could tell immediately that their son was happy and loved living in California. They both also loved the property that Jake had purchased and all the improvements he'd made. Jack told his mom that he didn't do it all by himself. Meredith, Maddie's sister, had helped him with everything. Of course, his parents were not fools. They knew that Jake had bought the property and furnished it, hoping that one day Maddie would live here, too.

Jake told his parents that he wouldn't be home for Christmas this year. Meredith had invited him to spend Christmas at her house, so he wouldn't be alone. He went on to tell them that Meredith had come up with a plan for Maddie and him to meet on Christmas Day. Meredith thought that if Maddie saw Jake, she'd think it the best Christmas present she could ever receive. The twins were walking now, too. Besides, it would be the twins' first Christmas, and Meredith wanted Jake to be a part of it. Jake had reluctantly agreed. His parents said they could certainly understand why being here for Christmas this year was so important to him, but they made him promise that he would come home to Oklahoma next year.

His parents asked him if he'd ever seen the twins. He told them about the one time he saw Maddie walking the twins in their stroller one Sunday afternoon. Obviously, he didn't stop, but from what he could tell, Maddie had a little boy and a little girl. He added that all of them seemed healthy and happy.

Jake thoroughly enjoyed his parents' visit. He took them to see his high school, San Francisco, Stanford, and of course, Napa, to visit the wineries. He even drove them by Maddie's house. She was not outside, but they could tell that she had already put up Christmas lights in preparation for the holiday. Jake's mom thought Maddie's house looked adorable.

Jake was really sorry to see his parents leave. Since it had always been just the three of them, they'd always been very close. He knew they'd come out to check on him, and they were satisfied that he was happy and loving life. He hugged and kissed both of his parents before they boarded the plane for their flight home. He also promised that he'd be home for a visit next summer, and he would remember his promise about next Christmas.

The closer it came to Christmas Day, the more nervous Jake became. He hoped that Maddie would be happy to see him. He was dying to see her again and very curious to meet the twins. He had no idea what to get anyone for Christmas presents. He finally decided on a huge wine, cheese, fruit basket, and a bottle of Dom Perignon for Meredith and Tom and some educational toys for the twins. Knowing Maddie, she was already teaching them colors, shapes, etc., so he bought some teaching puzzles and books for them. He did buy the little boy a big red truck and the little girl a sweet baby doll. However, he had a very difficult time trying to find just the right gift for Maddie. He finally settled on a wide gold bracelet and had it engraved on the inside with: "Joy is here! Merry Christmas, Maddie. Love, Jake." He also included the date 12-25-69.

Meredith had asked him to come over on Christmas Eve and spend the night, so there wouldn't be any mix up in her "plan." Jake agreed and arrived bearing gifts for under the tree. He parked his car in the garage so Maddie wouldn't be curious. Meredith had spent much of the day with her, helping her wrap gifts for the twins. She had stayed until they had gone to bed.

When Meredith finally arrived home, she found Jake and Tom having some eggnog and talking. Meredith ran in to give both of them a kiss before pouring some eggnog for herself.

"My God, what a day! I haven't been this nervous since we got married, Tom," said Meredith as she sipped her drink.

"Honey, you weren't nervous when we got married. We eloped to Lake Tahoe." Tom laughed.

The rest of the evening, the three of them wrapped packages and started preparations for Christmas dinner. Maddie and the twins were scheduled to arrive around

2:00 PM the next day. Jake asked Meredith how she planned to have him meet Maddie.

"Oh, I have it all figured out," Meredith answered happily. "Once Maddie and the twins are in the house and have settled in, I'm going to tell Maddie that Tom and I have a very special Christmas present for her this year. I'm going to make her close her eyes. When I tell her she can open them, you'll be standing there!" declared Meredith triumphantly.

"But what if she doesn't like her surprise?" asked Jake nervously.

This time Tom answered. "Jake, believe me, she's going to love it!"

"Trust us, Jake, she'll be delighted," said Meredith.

Needless to say, Jake found it impossible to sleep that night. It was like when he was little, waiting for Santa to come, only this time, he was waiting for Maddie.

39

On Christmas morning, Maddie got the twins up as usual. She took each of them by their tiny hands and walked them into the living room still dressed in their pajamas, so that they could look at what Santa, that guy in the red suit and long white beard, had left for them under their Christmas tree.

The twins were ecstatic, and, of course, Maddie started snapping pictures right away. The twins opened their gifts together, laughing and giggling, going from one gift to another. Then they started playing with the wrapping paper and sticking bows all over each other. They even put one on mommy's head. Maddie was having the time of her life, probably even more fun than her children.

After all the presents had been opened, and she'd fed the twins their favorite French toast for breakfast, she bathed them and let them play with their new toys until around 11:00 AM. Then she explained to them that they had to take their nap early, because they were going over to Aunt Mimi's and Uncle Tom's for dinner later that day. While the twins were asleep, Maddie took her shower, did her hair and makeup, and put on her new Christmas outfit. She decided to buy herself a new dress for Christmas this year. She hadn't bought herself any clothes since she'd arrived in Napa. She found a beautiful red and black plaid dress at Macmillan's. The top of the dress was solid black velvet, while the full taffeta skirt was red and black plaid. A big red bow tied at the waist. She put on black hose and black patent flats to go with it. She would be happy that she did.

When the twins awakened, she told them that since this was a special day, they had special outfits to wear, too. Maddie had found a black toddler's suit with a plaid vest for Rob and a matching plaid party dress for Rory. She then proceeded to pack the car with presents and all of the necessities it took to take the twins anywhere. They arrived at her sister's house promptly at 2:00 PM.

"Merry Christmas, everyone!" shouted Tom and Meredith as they opened the door. Tom immediately took Rob and Meredith took Rory, while Maddie unpacked the car and put the presents under the tree.

When Maddie finally took off her coat, Tom handed her an eggnog. He knew she was going to need one.

"Thank God. I really need this, Tom," said Maddie as she finally relaxed and sat down on the loveseat by the glowing fireplace.

Maddie told Tom and Mimi about all the pictures she'd taken of the twins opening their presents and what fun it was watching them stick bows all over each other.

"Speaking of presents," said Meredith very calmly, "Tom and I have a surprise Christmas present for you this year, Maddie."

"What? After everything you've done for me this year, I don't want or need a thing," said Maddie.

"Madison, shut up and turn around. Close your eyes and keep them closed until I say you can open them," ordered her sister.

"Okay," said Maddie and did as she was told.

A couple of seconds later, Meredith told her sister to turn around and open her eyes.

When Maddie opened her eyes and saw Jake standing before her, it was a good thing she didn't have the eggnog in her hand. She would have dropped it immediately out of shock.

"Oh my God! Oh my God!" was all that Maddie could say at first. She couldn't believe her eyes.

"Jake, it's you! It's really you, isn't it?" screamed Maddie as she ran up and jumped into his arms, hugged him, and gave him a huge kiss on the lips.

"Yes, Maddie, it's really me. Merry Christmas, Madison," said Jake.

Madison just stared at Jake, utterly speechless. He looked wonderful as usual. He was wearing tan corduroy slacks, a plaid shirt under a burgundy cashmere sweater, and matching burgundy loafers. She was never so happy to see anyone in her life!

"But how did you know where—?"

"Did you honestly think that I couldn't pry it out of Terri eventually? I'll give her that. It took six long months before Matt finally told her to tell me," replied Jake.

"Does Ryan—?" started Maddie.

"Absolutely not!" assured Jake.

"Ryan had called Terri but she had told him to go to hell. In fact, she said that hell would freeze over before she told him if she knew where you lived, which she didn't." Jake saw the instant relief in Maddie's eyes and changed the subject. "But hey," said Jake. "Why don't you introduce me to your two adorable children?"

"I'd be happy to, kind sir," answered Maddie with the look of a mother's pride in her eyes.

She had the twins, who had been looking at the Christmas tree and more presents, come over and meet "Uncle Jake." The gregarious twosome toddled over and very politely introduced themselves to him.

Rob was the first one to speak. "My name Rob," said the handsome little boy who held out his hand to shake Jake's. "Me ninety seconds older!" he declared proudly.

"How do you do?" replied Jake as he shook his tiny hand.

Rory then stood beside her brother and said the same thing, except she said, "Me younger."

Jake had never seen two more beautiful or polite children. Even though they were fraternal twins, they looked very much alike. Just as he had noticed that one time while watching Maddie wheel them in their stroller, the only real difference between the two was their hair color. They were truly adorable children, but Jake would have expected nothing less from Maddie.

After that, the two toddlers headed for the Christmas tree again and gazed with longing at the presents under the tree. This was the clue for the adults to sit down and open the gifts. Maddie was so pleased with the educational gifts that Jake had bought them. He told her he'd found a specialty store in Vallejo that sold only educational toys, and, of course, Maddie wanted to know the name of it immediately.

Meredith and Tom had bought the twins clothes. They were growing so fast that it was hard for Maddie to keep up. They also loved the wine and cheese basket that Jake had managed to hide in his car overnight. They decided that the champagne would be served with dinner.

The last present opened that day was the one from Jake to Maddie. He just hoped she'd like it. He'd never really picked out anything special for Maddie before other than the amazing book he'd made for her graduation. When Maddie opened the box, she gasped when she saw the wide gold bracelet.

"Look at the inscription inside, Maddie," whispered Jake.

Maddie read it out loud. "Joy is here! Merry Christmas. Love Jake 12-25-69." As soon as she read it, her eyes filled with tears. He had kept his promise.

"But where is she?" asked Maddie excitedly.

"I'll show you tomorrow, okay?" replied Jake.

"Oh, I can't wait to see her." Maddie gushed.

Maddie and Jake sat together and talked nonstop all afternoon and throughout dinner. Jake even helped feed one of the twins. They talked mostly about Matt and

Terri and his parents, but when she asked him how long he was going to get to stay, all he answered was, "We'll talk about it later."

Maddie could honestly say that this was the best Christmas she'd ever had. It was the one she would remember until the day she died.

Tom and Meredith were giddy over what they'd been able to pull off. They'd never seen Maddie this excited since the twins were born. They were very proud of themselves, especially Meredith, for being able to keep her mouth shut for so many months.

When it came time to take the twins home and put them to bed, Maddie suggested that Jake follow her to her house.

"Where is your rental car, by the way?" asked Maddie. She hadn't seen an extra one in the driveway.

Jake told her that Tom and Meredith had him park it in the garage last night, so she wouldn't suspect anything.

After joyful and tearful good-byes, Jake followed Maddie to her house, even though he knew exactly how to get there. Each of them carried one of the sleeping babies inside. And while Maddie changed their diapers and put on their pajamas, Jake carried in the Christmas loot from the car.

When the two of them were finally alone, Maddie poured each of them a large glass of wine. She wanted to know everything he'd been doing. Did he still teach in Claymont? How long was he going to get to stay?

This was going to be the moment of truth for Jake, and he didn't know how Maddie was going to react.

"Actually, Maddie, I'm not living or teaching in Claymont anymore."

"You're not? What are you doing?"

Jake explained to Maddie that he had the opportunity to teach history and be an assistant football coach in Vallejo. He'd moved out here last June, and Meredith and Tom had helped him find five acres of horse property in the hills overlooking Napa.

Maddie was stunned! She was absolutely speechless!

"You mean you've been here all this time and never came by?" she finally said.

"Well," answered Jake, "I wasn't quite sure you'd want to see me, much less know that I'd actually moved out here."

Once again Maddie was speechless.

"Do you mean that Meredith and Tom knew you were here the entire time but didn't tell me?" questioned Maddie.

"Don't blame them, Maddie. I made them promise not to tell you. I knew you were a new mother of twins and were very busy nurturing them. I didn't think the time was right to come back into your life until now. You've had more than enough to deal with—what happened with Ryan and then the birth of the twins.

"But where are you living exactly?" asked Maddie.

Jake told her that if she wanted, he'd take her and the twins to see his new home and Joy tomorrow.

"Are you kidding? If I want to? Hell yes, I want to. I'd go right now if I could."

"Good. It's a date. What would be the best time for you? What about 9:00 AM after the twins have had their breakfast? Would that be all right? I'll come and get you, and we'll make a day of it. Besides, I'd like to show you around and let you ride Joy if you want. Would that be good?"

"Absolutely!" replied Maddie happily.

The two of them sat and drank wine and talked into the wee hours of the morning like they used to in college. He told Maddie he loved teaching in Vallejo and that his team had recently won the state championship in football. He also thoroughly enjoyed the weather out here and thought San Francisco was one of the greatest cities he'd ever seen.

In turn, Maddie told him about the twins—how little they were and so premature that they were in incubators for six weeks until they weighed enough and their lungs had fully developed. They had been born on January 20th, but her due date hadn't been until early March. She went on to tell him that she spent those days at the hospital, helping to care for them, because it was too lonely for her to be at home by herself.

To change the subject, Maddie gave Jake a tour of her house. It fit Maddie perfectly, thought Jake. It was a comfy home. He especially liked the backyard. He knew it was the kind that Maddie had always wanted.

As they talked, Jake could tell that Maddie was exhausted and quickly fell asleep in his lap from too much wine. So, like he had done so many times while they were in college, he gently took her shoes off, picked her up, and put her to bed. He made sure he locked the door on his way out. To Jake, there was precious cargo inside that house.

After Jake left Maddie's house, he stopped at a twenty-four-hour supermarket that had started to become popular in California. He filled his entire basket with as much food as it would hold. He bought jars of toddler food that he thought the twins might like, along with steaks, hot dogs, cheese, wine, munchies, beer, and, of course, carrots for Joy. He also bought a couple of cans of SpaghettiO's, which he remembered he'd loved as a child. He filled the basket with milk, bread, and stuff for sandwiches, fruit, and even diapers and few educational toys he found in the toy aisle. He wanted to make sure he had enough of everything for tomorrow. He also bought several bouquets of flowers to decorate the house with.

When he arrived home and had put the groceries away, he made sure the house was spotless. Before finally going to bed, he went to the barn to tell Joy that she would see Maddie the next day.

Jake only slept a few hours that night. He was much too excited to sleep. The minute he'd seen Maddie today, he knew he was still as much in love with her as he'd ever been. He loved this woman more than life itself. He couldn't wait to show her the house that he'd really bought for her, hoping that someday she'd agree to live there with him.

As soon as Maddie awoke that morning, she realized that Jake had to put her to bed—again. For some reason, whenever Jake and Maddie drank wine and talked, she ended up falling asleep in his lap. It must be because she always felt so safe and relaxed with Jake. God, she had missed him! She didn't realize just how much, though, until yesterday's surprise.

Maddie fed the twins their breakfast, gave them their baths, and then proceeded to dress them in matching jean outfits. She then packed all the food, formula, toys, clothes, etc., she thought they might need for the day into their monogrammed diaper bags.

After she put the twins into their playpen so they could play, it was Maddie's turn to get ready. She showered quickly, but took more time with her hair and makeup than usual. She decided that she would wear jeans, boots, and fisherman's knit sweater with a scarf. She packed an extra pair of shoes, slacks, a knit hat, and jeans, in case it was muddy where they were headed.

Jake knocked on the door at 9:05 AM. Maddie immediately greeted him with a big smile and kiss. It took a while, but the two of them finally loaded the car and strapped the children into their seat belts in the backseat of the Mustang.

"How far is it to your house?" asked Maddie as Jake pulled out of her driveway.

"Not too far, probably around fifteen minutes," answered Jake.

"Do you like your new place?"

"Absolutely! I honestly love the house. It's pretty big, but the price was well worth it. The views are what I enjoy the most, though," replied Jake happily.

It took about ten minutes before they started climbing into the hills surrounding Napa. At first, there were several houses on the sides of the road, but the higher they went, the houses seemed to disappear. Finally, Jake turned the Mustang onto a newly paved road that now served as his driveway. The driveway was covered on both sides with huge oak and eucalyptus trees. Maddie absolutely had no idea where she was.

All of a sudden, Jake's house came into view, and Maddie couldn't believe her eyes. What she saw wasn't a house—it was a country estate. The house was an enormous two-story and looked like an English manor house. All it needed was ivy covering the outside walls and Maddie could have been back in England.

"This is your 'house'? This isn't a house. It's huge; it's gorgeous; it's beautiful!" Maddie laughed.

"Madison, yes, it's large, but it's just a house, okay? You're embarrassing me."

She should have known he'd say that. Jake had always been very humble. "I'm sorry. I'm just so surprised; that's all. It really is magnificent."

As soon as they reached the circle cobblestone driveway, and Jake had stopped the car, Maddie jumped out. She unbuckled the twins and helped them out of the car. Jake picked up Rory, and Maddie lifted Rob onto her hip.

Jake asked Maddie if she would like to see the house or Joy first, already knowing the answer.

"Oh, Jake, please let me see Joy first. It's been so long, and I've missed her so much," replied Maddie.

Jake directed the four of them to the new small red barn on the far side of the house. The barn door was already open, and Maddie, still holding Rob, started running toward the barn.

"Maddie, slow down!" yelled Jake. "Joy isn't going anywhere."

Maddie continued running. She couldn't wait a minute longer. When she entered the barn, she finally slowed down, so she wouldn't startle Joy. She came up to her slowly, holding her hand out so Joy could remember her scent.

Joy looked beautiful to Maddie. Jake had taken care of her lovingly as he had promised. Maddie introduced Rob to Joy by saying merely, "Rob, this is a horse. Her name is Joy. Can you say 'horse' and 'Joy' for me?"

Rob replied immediately in his tiny voice, "This is a horse. Her name is Joy."

Jake had been standing at the barn door, holding Rory, watching Maddie interact with Joy and Rob. He saw both the mother and teacher in her at once. When he finally walked over with Rory, Jake said exactly the same words to her as Maddie had to Rob, and Rory answered immediately just like her brother.

The two wide-eyed children very carefully petted Joy's head. They had never seen a real horse before and were delighted. When Joy shook her head, all four of them laughed together.

After visiting Joy for a few minutes, the four of them walked slowly back to the house. It took a while, since the toddlers were interested in stopping along the way and checking out rocks, twigs—anything they could find. But that was okay. Maddie was very patient with them.

When they finally reached the house, Jake went ahead and opened the front door for them. Maddie had the twins carefully wipe their feet on the front door mat before they entered. Once inside, Maddie just stared in disbelief. She seemed stuck to the floor.

Jake took Maddie's hand and said, "Let me give you a tour."

He took her through the house room by room. Each room seemed more perfect than the last to Maddie. She loved every single room of the house. It truly was an exquisite house decorated exactly the way she would've done it. She wouldn't change a thing.

Next, he escorted Maddie and the twins to the backyard. The raised gardens surrounded the covered winterized pool, as well as the covered barbecue and the stucco gazebo with outdoor fireplace. Maddie was speechless. Last of all, he showed her the guest house, which was bigger than her own. It took a while for Maddie to take in the entire estate.

When the four of them reentered the house, Jake started to kindle the wood in the fireplace and made hot chocolate for the four of them in the kitchen, while Maddie unloaded the car with all of the stuff she'd brought with her for the day.

Maddie changed the twins' diapers and gave them some toys to play with. Then she went into the kitchen to help Jake fix lunch for the twins before she put them down for their naps.

"Jake, do you have something I can use to warm Rob and Rory's lunches in?" asked Maddie tentatively.

"Of course," answered Jake, "but can I ask you something first?"

"Anything."

"Maddie, have the twins ever had SpaghettiO's?"

"No, why?"

"Well, I just remember how much I loved them when I was little. I bought some, just in case you'd allow them to try it," said Jake anxiously.

"What a wonderful idea! Let's do it," laughed Maddie.

The twins loved their first taste of SpaghettiO's. Maddie fed Rory while Jake fed Rob. They even allowed the twins to grab them with their hands. Of course, they ended up with more of it on their hands and face than in their mouths. Maddie and Jake just laughed.

As Maddie was cleaning up the twins before putting them down for their naps, Jake made a salad for the two of them and poured two glasses of wine, so they could eat in front of the fireplace when Maddie was finished. He set their lunch on the coffee table in front of the fireplace.

Finally, the two of them were alone at last. Maddie asked lots of questions about the house, and Jake mostly answered all of them the same way. Meredith was responsible. Meredith had found the property; Meredith picked out that piece of furniture. However, Maddie knew Jake well enough to recognize himself in the house, and she also knew that Jake was his own man. If he didn't want to do or buy something, he wouldn't.

Jake had deliberated all last night whether or not to approach the subject of Ryan with Maddie. He finally concluded that he needed to know if Ryan was still in the picture. He had to know how Maddie felt about him and exactly what had happened. The problem was he didn't know how Maddie would react when he asked. Eventually, though, the right time came for him to find out.

"Maddie, I don't want to upset you on such a wonderful day, but I'd like to ask you a couple of questions if you don't mind?" asked Jake quietly.

"Go ahead, shoot," replied Maddie.

Jake took a deep breath before he began. "All right. What happened between you and Ryan? Why didn't you get married as planned?"

Maddie answered him immediately. "I told you before; he decided he loved 'the corps' more than he loved me."

"I don't believe that for one minute," answered Jake.

"Well, you should," said Maddie very matter-of-factly. "Like I said, two days before our wedding, he asked me to wait for him until he returned from Vietnam. His exact words were: 'I don't want to make you a widow before you're a wife.' I couldn't believe it, and I'd waited long enough, so I said no. I got into my car and drove home. Ryan died to me the night of June 5th, 1968."

"But what about the twins? Doesn't he know about them yet?" asked Jake.

"Absolutely not, and he never will. These are my children. I am responsible for them. I will rear them. Their last name is Conrad. I did put his name on their birth certificates only because, in the years to come, I didn't want them to think that I just slept around and didn't know who their father was. And while we're talking about it, Jake, I was a virgin until Ryan's father died. He's the only man I've ever been with. Is there anything else you want to know? I'm an open book with you, always have been and always will be."

"Only a couple more. Are you still in love with Ryan?"

"No," was all she answered.

"Is there someone special in your life now?"

"Nope. I haven't even thought about it to tell you the truth. I've been a little preoccupied as you can tell," laughed Maddie.

Jake didn't speak for a little while after that. He was digesting what he'd just heard and was trying to decide if Maddie had told him the truth about Ryan. In the end, he decided he had to believe her. She had never ever lied to him in all the years they'd known each other. She wouldn't treat something as serious as this lightly.

"Okay, Jake. It's my turn to ask a couple of questions, all right?" asked Maddie.

"Fair enough."

"Why did you move out here? You had a perfect life in Oklahoma."

"I moved out here for one reason and one reason only—you. When Terri finally told me where you were, I wanted to make sure you were all right. My so-called 'perfect' life wasn't perfect anymore because you weren't in it.

"My parents were very supportive of my move. They're the ones who wanted me to have a good start in a new place. They gave me the money to buy this property. They've known for a long time how much I love you. They knew I had to come out here and supported my decision," Jake answered.

This time it was Maddie's turn to wait a while before making a response.

"I'm really glad you're here, Jake. But I don't want you to feel burdened with me and two babies. I resolved after I discovered I was pregnant that they would be my responsibility—mine alone. I'd never ask another man, or anyone else, to take on that burden. You're not responsible for what happened to me, Jake. I alone am responsible. I trusted Ryan because I loved him, and he betrayed that trust. I don't know if I'll ever be able to trust a man with my heart again. Besides, who would want a woman with twins and who couldn't have any more children? I didn't tell you, but when the twins were born, I had so much internal damage that the only way to save the three of us was to do a hysterectomy. My child-bearing days are over," Maddie finished with a hint of sadness in her voice.

"Maddie, do you trust me?"

"Of course. I always have and always will."

"That's all I need to know," answered Jake as he leaned over and gave her a kiss on her cheek.

A few minutes later, Jake and Maddie heard the patter of little feet as Rob and Rory toddled into the room and climbed up onto their laps, now that their naps were finished.

The rest of the day, the four of them spent playing. Maddie rode Joy for the first time in two years. She loved feeling the cold air on her face as she raced across the property on the beautiful filly. Afterwards, Jake took each child separately for a slow walk on Joy. They each squealed in delight.

Jake convinced Maddie to spend the night at his house. The twins were being so good and having such a good time that she felt it would be okay. Besides, she trusted Jake. She knew he wouldn't do anything inappropriate unless she agreed first. He never had and never would.

After dinner, Jake and Maddie gave the twins their baths, and then Jake taught them how to blow bubbles. The twins were so hysterical to watch that she laughed so hard she started to cry. Maddie went and grabbed Jake's camera to capture pictures of this special moment. After their baths, Maddie put them to bed on their makeshift pallets. She and Jake each read them a story as they were going to sleep.

When Maddie and Jake were finally alone once more, Jake said, "Madison, you have the most wonderful children in the world. You're a very lucky woman. I can already tell they're quite bright. You are so patient with them. It really amazes me."

"Thank you. They really are very special. In fact, I don't know what I would have done if both of them hadn't lived. They were only three pounds when they were born, so very tiny. But they had the will to live; I just knew it. And, yes, I agree with you. I can already tell they're quite intelligent. They're such fast learners. I guess you can tell I'm a very proud mom."

After sitting and drinking wine and talking until midnight, Jake suggested that perhaps they should get to bed. He showed Maddie to a guest bedroom that he had especially decorated for her, just in case this day ever came. However, Maddie's next comment caught him totally off guard.

"Jake, what if I don't want to sleep alone tonight?" she asked.

"Maddie, you'll be the one who'll decide when the time is right for you to be with someone else. If it's tonight, and with me, you already know how I feel. But it's up to you. I don't want you to feel pressured into doing something you aren't quite sure about," he said seriously.

"Jake, I want to be with you, just you. But if we're together, I won't go along with your being with other women, too. I am a one-man woman. I won't share you," she replied.

"Madison Conrad, you are the only woman I've ever wanted to be with; you know that. Do you honestly think I'd jeopardize our relationship by being with someone who means absolutely nothing to me? You know me well enough to know that, don't you?" he asked.

"Yes. But I needed to make myself clear."

"Well, then, let's go to bed, Madison," said a delighted Jake.

"I'll race you to the bedroom!" yelled Maddie as she started to run.

40

Maddie arrived at the master suite first. When she opened the door, she stopped immediately. The room seemed much larger than it had during her tour of the house.

Jake stood at the doorway, watching her. She was looking out the big picture window, transfixed by the city lights far below. She didn't hear Jake come up behind her.

"Maddie, are you sure this is something you want to do? You know we don't have to do this tonight. That's certainly not why I invited you to spend the night here. You should know me that well," explained Jake.

Maddie turned to face Jake before she answered. "I know, Jake. That's why I agreed to stay, but I want to. I honestly didn't realize how much you really meant to me until yesterday. I sort of knew how you felt about me in college, and I had feelings for you then, too, but I was too stubborn to admit it to myself. I was so absorbed with Ryan that I wouldn't allow myself to see past my nose and realize you were much more than just my best friend."

Jake just put his arms around her and kissed her deeply for the first time ever in his life, and Maddie kissed him back as though making up for years of lost passion.

One minute they were kissing, and the next they were lying on the bed together. They started talking about sex. Maddie tried to explain to Jake why she felt she was very inexperienced compared to him. She told him she was afraid that he would find her boring and she was embarrassed. Jake started laughing.

"Maddie, I've wanted to make love to you for six years. "Boring? You're the most exciting woman I've ever known. There is no way I'd find you boring. I've wanted to make love with you for six years. Yes, I've had sex with other women, but there's a helluva difference between 'having sex' and 'making love.' I've never made love to a woman before, so I'm little nervous, too. My God, what if I don't please you?"

They both looked at each other seriously for a few seconds before they both started to laugh. Jake lit the fireplace and turned on some soft music, while Maddie went into the bathroom and took a shower. When she came out, she was wrapped in a towel and was also using another one to towel dry her hair.

"Jake, do you have a shirt I can wear tonight? I didn't bring anything with me."

"Sure thing. Check the closet or the drawers while I get my shower," replied Jake.

When Jake got out of the shower, he found Maddie in bed; the shirt she had picked out was laying neatly at the foot of the bed. She was lying on her side, gazing at the flickering fire. Jake got a lump in his throat; she looked even more beautiful in the firelight. He went over to the other side of the bed and climbed in beside her. When he did, Maddie turned over to face him.

Maddie could tell that Jake was just as nervous as she was, if not more, so she made the first move. She very quietly and gently slid on top of him. She kissed him deeply while he very lightly traced her back with his fingertips. She found that she shivered under his touch, and when she did, he very quickly rolled over on top of her.

Jake was a very strong man, always had been, so he kept his arms bent so that his weight wasn't on her. He looked straight into her eyes and said, "Maddie, relax. It's okay if we don't make love tonight. There's always tomorrow night. I don't want you to have any regrets."

"It's not that. Not that at all, Jake. Trust me. I want you to make love to me. I don't want to wait. I'm just nervous. You've been with so many beautiful women that I'm afraid that I won't measure up," Maddie said honestly.

"Maddie, since our first blind date, you've been the only woman I've ever wanted and couldn't have. Do you have any idea how that felt? All I wanted was to be able to touch you, but I knew I couldn't. I knew if I did, I'd lose you forever, and I wasn't willing to take that chance. We've talked many times about the only reason I saw other women. The truth is I haven't been with a woman since I saw you the last time eighteen months ago. I just haven't been interested. So you're not the only one who is out of practice, okay?" Jake replied.

With that he lay beside her and started trailing his fingertips down to her breasts. Even after two children, her breasts were still full and high. He circled her nipples, and they instantly became hard. She moaned softly as he continued down to her stomach, which was as tight as that of a young girl who had never given birth. The only thing he noticed was the long, thin scar from the hysterectomy. He gently explored the scar with his fingertips, and whispered, "That's kinda sexy." Then he kissed her ear and returned his attention to her nipples. He sucked lightly on each one, being careful not to hurt her. He buried his head between them and sucked on them alternately. Maddie squirmed with excitement and that pleased Jake. He was thrilled that she was responding to his touch so well that he became braver.

Jake lightly flicked his tongue on her milky skin, all the way down to her being. Then he nuzzled her inner thighs to get Maddie to spread her legs. As she did, his butterfly licks moved to her love mound.

"Oh God, Jake, don't stop!" she moaned. He didn't. He continued to suck and use his fingers to get her ready, and she moved her hips back and forth under him. He loved the taste of her sex and the way she responded to his wandering tongue. Her breathing was getting rapid and shallow, her moans were getting lower and her juices were flowing. Jake knew she would come soon, perhaps several times. Then it would be his turn.

Unlike Jake, who'd probably been with more women than he could count, Maddie had only been with one man before. When it came to sex, she and Ryan were total novices; clumsily, but lovingly, learning together. With Jake, it was completely different. Jake knew exactly what he was doing—what buttons to push and when. Maddie discovered that Jake and Ryan were about the same size, but there the similarity ended. Jake really knew how to get a woman hot and make her come, over and over again. Somehow, he could keep himself from coming, even when he was inside her trashing orgasms. And when he was ready, he could make them come together.

All of a sudden, Maddie shocked Jake. She rolled over on top of him and said the words she had only said to one other man in her life: "My turn."

Jake allowed Maddie to explore his body at will. She kissed him deeply before she started going slowly down his body, kissing him as she went. Every kiss, every lick made Jake's manhood grow even larger. He'd always been well endowed, at least that's what all the other women had told him, but he still wondered silently what Maddie thought. She took him in her mouth, and he felt as if he were dying and going to heaven. She used her mouth and hands gently but firmly as she slid up and down his shaft. Finally, he knew he would be coming soon, so he rolled over on top of her and eased himself into her.

They began moving in unison; Jake's pulsating and throbbing shaft moving in and out of her. She was very tight, and Jake fit inside her like a glove. Then, for the briefest second, time seemed to stop and they came together in one incredibly, unbelievable orgasm. Totally spent, Jake looked her directly in the eyes and said, "I love you, Madison." He was a quiet lover, too, like Ryan. She was glad—she hadn't known what to expect this first time. It was as if all those years of waiting had boiled down to one perfect moment for both of them. They held each other tightly but quietly in the throes of their release. Maddie and Jake were one, and each of them felt fulfilled as never before.

The two lovers stayed together for a long time, not wanting to separate, afraid it would break the magic spell. Jake finally knew what it felt like to make love to someone he loved more than life itself. It wasn't like anything he had ever experienced before.

Jake was the first to speak. "Sweetheart, I didn't hurt you, did I?"

"What?"

"I said, I didn't hurt you, did I? That's the last thing in the world I'd ever want to do."

"No, Jake, I'm fine. Just stunned is all."

"Why?"

"Well, I'm sure it's obvious I haven't had much practice. I was amazed at what you could do to me, the way you moved when you were inside me, and that you had so much self-control."

"Maddie, remember what I said a few minutes ago? This is the very first time I've ever made love to a woman. In fact, it's the very first time I've ever said 'I love you' to a woman when having sex. Not only that but it's the first time I've ever kept my eyes open when I climaxed."

"Wow! That's a lot of firsts, Jake."

"Yep. But it was well worth the wait," replied Jake. "How do you feel about our first time, Maddie?"

Three descriptive words came out of Maddie's mouth immediately: "I feel loved, satisfied, and complete." Then she kissed him deeply and said the words he'd waited for so long to hear. "I love you, too, Jake Kelly."

"Is there anything about making love that you know you don't like?" asked Jake.

"Well, I don't have too much experience with different positions, but I do know that I don't like 'spooning.' Ryan and I tried that once and I hated it. When a man makes love to me, I want to see him, not have my back to him."

"Good—tried it myself once and didn't like it either. Maddie, I love you. I can honestly tell you I've never experienced a moment like this before. I simply can't describe the feeling to you," Jake said seriously.

"I know. You don't have to say a word. Maybe all the waiting was worth it for us. Maybe we just had to take the long way around to get here. Making love to you tonight was so natural after I overcame my shyness. It was like I'd been making love to you all my life. Does that make any sense?" asked Maddie.

"Of course, I feel exactly the same way, like I've been waiting for you all my life. All the other girls were nothing compared to this," replied Jake.

Jake went into the bathroom and got a warm wash cloth. They took turns wiping each other off before he handed her the shirt she had picked out to wear to bed. They both drifted asleep almost instantly in each other's arms. Maddie hadn't slept this deeply since the twins were born. Right before Jake fell fast asleep, he thanked God for finally giving Maddie to him.

The next morning, Maddie awakened to find Jake gone. She looked at the clock. Oh, God, it was 9:30 AM. The twins!

Maddie raced into their room to discover they were gone, too. She ran down the stairs and headed for the kitchen. There sat Jake, Rob, and Rory on the floor. They were eating Cheerios together. Rob would put one in Jake's mouth; Jake would put one in Rory's mouth; and Rory would give one to Rob. Maddie stared at the three of them dumbfounded. Then she started laughing.

"Can I join the club?" asked Maddie happily.

"Hi, Mommy," said the three of them in unison and made room for her in their circle.

"Thank you," mouthed Maddie to Jake.

"Anytime," replied Jake.

After the twins were fed, Jake cooked Maddie a real breakfast as she dressed the twins for the day. Once they were playing together, Maddie wandered back into the kitchen to the delicious smell of coffee and bacon.

"Jake, you're going to spoil me," declared Maddie as she sipped her coffee.

"Now that's something I'd love to do," replied Jake. "How do you feel about last night?"

"Truthfully?" asked Maddie.

"Truthfully," said Jake, holding his breath.

"Well, I can honestly say, I've never felt so fulfilled in my entire life. Last night was absolutely perfect for me. And I want more nights like that with you, and only you. What about you?"

"Well, at first, I was afraid it might be too soon. But once I got over being nervous, like I said last night, I finally knew what it felt like for the first time in my life to make love to the woman I love desperately. And I want more nights and days like that with you forever, and only you, too," answered Jake, looking Maddie straight in the eyes.

"Oh, you'll probably get tired of me after a few months."

"Not a chance in hell."

The two of them decided that they should probably go back to her house and let the children play for a while as they packed a few things to bring back to Jake's house. Jake told Maddie he didn't want to rush her into anything, but that he'd like for the twins to be comfortable whenever they visited his house. Maddie agreed, so they packed up toys and clothes that could stay at Jake's. Maddie also packed a few things of her own to take back there.

A few days before Jake was due to go back to work, Meredith offered to watch the twins for a couple of nights so that Jake could take Maddie to San Francisco. They stayed at The Mark, the famous hotel on Nob Hill.

Jake thoroughly enjoyed spoiling Madison. They bought outfits for Maddie and toys and clothes for the twins at Macy's. He also took her to the design center that Meredith had used when furnishing his house, so the two of them could design two bedrooms and a playroom for the twins in one of the spare rooms. They sat together and picked cribs that would convert into beds eventually, ordered matching chests, rockers, dressing tables—two of everything. Maddie had already told Jake that window seats would be nice, because they could also serve as toy boxes. Jake's carpenter would start on them and the other built-ins they planned together in a couple of weeks. Maddie and Jake also decided that the playroom should be painted a soft, soothing yellow. They picked a yellow wallpaper border containing frolicking blue and pink bunnies as the theme. They chose a soft blue paint for Rob's room and a soft pink for Rory's, and then used the same border as seen in the playroom. They also had bed linens made to match each room. The last item on the list for Maddie was to have someone paint the twins' names on their bedroom walls.

During their last evening at The Mark, after a romantic dinner, they held hands in the elevator as they waited to get to their room. Their room had a spectacular view of the city, so Maddie and Jake sat on two club chairs, sipped their wine, held hands, and looked silently at the city.

Jake was the first to speak.

"Maddie, you don't mind my becoming a part of the twins' lives, do you? I don't want to appear to insert myself into your life if you're uncomfortable with it."

"Of course, I want you to be a part of their lives. I can tell they're already getting very attached to you. My only concern is that you'd eventually like to have a child of your own someday, and I can't give you one. I just don't want you to be there for the twins one minute and then gone the next. That wouldn't be fair to them or to me. I really wish I could give you a child of our own, but I can't," said Maddie wistfully.

Jake explained to Maddie that it really wasn't important to him. She and the twins were all that he needed to be happy. He did have one concern, though.

"Maddie, what will happen if Ryan ever finds out about the twins? Will he want them? Will he want to be a part of their lives?"

Maddie's response was immediate. "As far as I'm concerned, the only part that Ryan has played in their lives is donating his sperm. I've never considered them to be his children or him to be their father. In fact, I don't want him ever to know about them or to be a part of their lives."

"But is that really fair to the twins or Ryan?"

"Honestly, I don't care about fair, Jake. As I told you before, the twins are my responsibility—mine alone."

Jake decided to leave it at that for now.

When they made love that night, it was as wonderful as it had been the very first time. In fact, each time seemed to get better and better. They relaxed, laughed, and had fun. They experimented with different positions and decided what they did and didn't like— what felt awkward, what felt comfortable. Jake was larger than Ryan physically, which meant he was also very well endowed. Jake was a wonderful lover, and Maddie was secretly thankful to all the girls that he'd been with before.

For Jake, Maddie's naiveté delighted him. She really was a novice but was always willing to experiment. She wanted to please him. She didn't know it, but Jake would have been pleased if they'd only made love in the missionary position. Just having Maddie's body next to him turned him to mush. In fact, one glance from her excited him.

Maddie and Jake completed each other. His Type A-B personality calmed and balanced her Type A.

After school started once again, Maddie and Jake fell into a familiar routine. Most days Maddie stayed at her house until the twins finished their afternoon naps. Then she would take them to Jake's, where she'd go see Joy, brush her, walk her, and let the twins give her carrots. Maddie would always fix dinner for Jake. He'd usually be home around 6:00 PM every night. By then the twins had usually had their supper, but he always delighted in helping with their baths, so Maddie would wait for him. After their baths, Rob and Rory would play in their newly designed playroom, while Maddie and Jake had dinner together. Maddie and the twins always spent the night at Jake's and on the weekends as well. They would work on their landscaping, planting more trees, rose bushes, and, of course, Maddie's favorite, lilac bushes. The twins also enjoyed digging holes in the dirt.

41

O n Valentine's Day 1971, Jake had asked Meredith if she would mind watching the twins. He'd planned a special evening for Maddie. Meredith was pretty sure what he was going to do, so she readily agreed.

Jake had made reservations at a new and exclusive French restaurant in Napa and had requested a quiet, out-of-the-way table for two. He'd also ordered a dozen of Maddie's favorite blush roses. Since he'd told Maddie they were going out to dinner, she took special care that night to look her best. She wore a red turtleneck cashmere dress with black accessories. In her heels, she was almost as tall as Jake. She looked stunning when Jake arrived home that night. Maddie had picked out gold cuff links for Jake and had them engraved with J & M. She hoped he liked them. He would. He'd love anything Maddie ever gave him.

When they were at dinner, he ordered some Dom Perignon. He toasted their second Valentine's Day together. She knew immediately that the roses on the table were from him. He'd remembered the color she liked even after all these years, which really surprised her. Maddie gave Jake his gift while they were waiting for their meal to be served. When Jake saw the cuff links with the initials on them, his eyes became misty. He leaned over the table and kissed her deeply, saying, "I love you, Madison Conrad. These are perfect."

Then it was Jake's turn to give Madison her gift. He didn't think he'd ever been so nervous in his life. This was a very bold move for him. Not that he wasn't ready, he was. He just didn't know what Maddie's reaction would be. Would she think that it was too soon? Before he gave her the gift, he told her how much he loved her, and that he'd never been happier in his life. Maddie fulfilled him. She made him feel complete. He also told her he'd already become so attached to the twins that he couldn't ever imagine not being there to watch them grow up. He loved them like his own. Then he rose from his chair and told her he'd be back in a minute.

When he returned to the restaurant, he was carrying a large package. The moment he reached their table, Jake got down on one knee and asked her softly. "Madison Conrad, would you do me the honor of becoming my wife?" asked Jake softly. He produced a tan Peke-A-Poo puppy with a black velvet box attached to her collar and handed it to Maddie.

A proposal was the last thing Maddie had expected this evening. She stared at him in shock. Then she cuddled the puppy she was holding and stared at the box. She opened it to find the most exquisite ring she'd ever seen in her life. It was a three-carat round solitaire with one-carat triangle-shaped sapphires on each side, representing Maddie's birthday. The ring literally took her breath away.

Maddie waited a few minutes before she replied, and that made Jake even more nervous. Finally, she said, "I love you, too, Jake, with all my heart, and I would be proud to be your wife, but how do you feel about long engagements?"

"Maddie, we could be engaged forever just so long as I know you're mine and only mine. But what do you mean about long engagements?"

Maddie explained to him that she had vowed never to marry until she had reared her children. As she had always said, the twins were her responsibility and hers alone. She didn't want a man to feel burdened with rearing children who weren't his.

Jake replied immediately, "But Madison, I'd adopt the twins tomorrow if you'd allow it. If not, I still want them. Don't you understand? I know I'm getting a package deal. I wouldn't have it any other way."

"Okay, Jake, I accept, under one condition. We aren't in a hurry to get married. After everything that's happened to me, it may take me quite a while to change my way of thinking. Can you deal with that?" asked Maddie with a huge smile on her face.

"Agreed," said Jake as he slipped the huge ring on her left finger.

"Jake, this is the most beautiful ring I've ever seen," commented Maddie as she watched it sparkle in the candlelight, still holding the puppy to her chest.

After dinner, when they went over to pick up the twins, Maddie proudly showed her sister her engagement ring and the new addition to the family.

"I just knew it! I told Tom I thought Jake was going to propose. Congratulations to you both. I'm so happy for you. It's been a long time coming!"

"Only about seven or eight years," laughed Jake excitedly.

"You two go home alone tonight. We'll keep the twins. It's time for you to celebrate," said Meredith as she pushed them out the door.

Maddie and Jake headed home without the twins. It seemed strange to them to be in the huge house without the patter of little feet. Both of them even remarked on it simultaneously. Once they were in their bedroom, Jake lit the raised two-way fireplace, while Maddie filled two glasses with Dom Perignon. It was nice having a morning station with a small refrigerator, glasses, coffee pot, and sink in the bedroom.

Jake already had a small dog bed with an alarm clock in it, so that hopefully their new addition would sleep through the night.

"What shall we name our new addition?" asked Maddie.

"Well, why don't we wait until the twins see her and let them have a say in her name, too?"

"That's a perfect idea," said Maddie.

"Jake, I can't remember the last time I've been this happy since the twins were born."

With that, she started to undress him very slowly one step at a time. First, she unbuttoned his shirt. Next came his belt. Then she slowly unzipped his slacks and very gently started to massage him. She helped him off with his slacks, briefs, and socks. He lay there on the bed perfectly nude in front of her.

Jake truly had a magnificent body. He worked out with the football team in the weight room at school and was a runner. To Maddie, he was a perfect physical specimen. And after the first time they had made love, he didn't feel the least bit embarrassed to be nude in front of her.

Suddenly, Jake pulled Maddie to him and said, "My turn," he grinned. "Sound familiar."

He helped pull her dress over her head, very slowly undid her black lace bra, and watched her full breasts seem to explode from their confinement. He stopped what he was doing for a few minutes to kiss and fondle her breasts, which now truly belonged to him. He took off her sexy black garter belt and black stockings one leg at a time. When he finally arrived at her cute lacy panties, he was already hard. He tenderly removed her panties and kept his hands and head where they were. He kissed and licked Maddie gently until she came. He then used his fingers and could tell that she was already wet and ready for him. It was then that he told her of a new position he'd heard about. Maddie was, as usual, eager to experiment. He told her it was called the sixty-nine position and directed her how to place herself. This way they could have oral sex together. Maddie loved it. She loved having Jake's huge manhood in her mouth, sucking and massaging him with her hands up and down his shaft, while he was busy kissing and using his fingers to make her come. They both came together almost immediately and groaned together. Since neither of them were loud lovers, there was never any loud screaming when they made love. And Maddie had always swallowed Jake's semen. It made her feel close to him.

"Wow!" said Maddie after what they had just tried was finished. "I loved that. What about you?"

"I feel like I've just died and gone to heaven," replied Jake hoarsely.

After that, this became one of their favorite positions. They even quickly arrived at the point where they both knew when each of them would be coming, so that they'd roll over and complete their lovemaking with Jake inside her.

42

When the twins were almost three and a half, Jake decided he needed to approach Maddie on some ideas that he had. He waited until after they had made love and were relaxing and talking like they usually did before going to sleep. Maddie was snuggled close to Jake, with her hand on his chest, while he had his arm wrapped around her. Jake figured that this was as good a time as any to talk to her about his ideas.

"Madison, I want to ask you something, and I don't want you to get upset, okay?" said Jake quietly.

Just the question put Maddie on alert, but she said, "What's up?" as casually as she could.

"Well, Rob and Rory are now going on four, and we both know they are exceptionally bright. How would you feel about having them tested? I talked to our school psychologist who has her PhD, as well as her own small private practice on the side, and she thinks it would be a good idea, just to get some sort of starting point concerning their intelligence. I could take you to meet her and talk to her, and she'd be able to explain to you the process better than I. You could also watch them while they were testing through a one-way window. We could both watch them together, if that would make you feel more comfortable, honey. But it's totally up to you."

Maddie waited for a few minutes before she replied. When he said he wanted to ask her a question, she'd been afraid he wanted to get married. This idea had never entered her mind. Maddie thought about Jake's suggestion for a minute before she answered him.

"I'll agree with certain stipulations. First, you and I will both talk to the doctor together. Second, yes, I want you with me to watch the children during the test. And third, if at any time during the test either of the twins becomes frustrated or agitated, the testing will stop immediately. Do you agree?"

"Absolutely. I want to be with you, and I'd never allow the twins become upset. I'll set up a consultation for the two of us tomorrow."

Jake also wanted to talk to Maddie about a couple of other things. He figured he might as well tell her how he felt and let the chips fall where they may.

"Maddie, what do you think about putting the twins in a preschool? They wouldn't have to stay all day, but I think it would be good for them to learn social interaction skills. They need to learn how to play with others. We could get a nanny/housekeeper. She could take them to school, pick them up, and take care of them until we came home from work. You'll notice I just said 'we.' I think it's time for you to start teaching—to do what you spent four years training to do. I sense that there's something missing in your life. I think you'd love teaching. But if you don't feel comfortable leaving the children just yet, I can understand that, too. I know how devoted you are to them, but I think teaching would fill a void in you."

Maddie was amazed by what she'd just heard. "Jake, I can't believe it. I've been thinking about exactly the same thing. I definitely agree with preschool and my teaching, but only if we can find the perfect nanny," I don't know how I can afford both preschool and a nanny, too," said Maddie.

"Honey," Jake smiled, "money is not a problem and never will be, okay? My parents gift me $25,000 a year to help with their taxes. And now they've told me they're going to take over the house payments and use the property as a rental for tax purposes. In other words, we are not only the owners of the house, but also the renters. You know me, Maddie, I've never bragged about being rich. I've always just figured I've been lucky."

"Okay, but I'll pay for the pre-school—they are my responsibility. I guess we need to start looking for the perfect preschool and perfect nanny, huh?"

"Yes, but both of us must agree on where and whom we choose, okay?"

"Of course, honey," answered Maddie.

Since Jake was on a roll, he decided to ask Maddie the most important question he wanted to ask her since they'd become engaged. All she could say would be "no."

"Madison, if you don't agree with this, it will not upset me. Well, maybe it will just a little. We're engaged and plan to marry someday, but the point is that we're together, a team. We will both be there for our kids as they grow up. What do you think about having them call me Daddy instead of Uncle Jake? I know it will help them in school. Mommy and Daddy will go to their parent-teacher conferences together, etc. What do you think?"

Maddie rolled over on top of Jake and kissed him passionately. Then she said, "My twins will have the best daddy in the world."

"One final thing. Maddie, would you and the twins move in here with me permanently? I know you'll want to keep your house on Hope Street, and I agree that we should. But what about renting it out to a special couple? It would give you added income, but it would still be yours. What do you think?"

"I think I love you more than you'll ever know, Jake Kelly," before she kissed him again.

Jake felt as if a great weight had been lifted off him. He was going to be a daddy to Madison's children, their children—a responsibility he would never take lightly.

The last thing Maddie said that night to Jake was to admit to him that she was afraid he was going to ask her if she was ready to get married yet.

"Maddie, I told you before, you'll be the one to decide when the time is right," answered Jake simply. "I love you enough to wait a lifetime if I have to." With that he gave her a huge hug and kiss good night.

The next morning at breakfast, Maddie tried to explain to Rob and Rory what was going to happen. She told them that she and Uncle Jake were going to be married, so he will be their daddy from now on. She had each one of them say "Daddy," and when Jake saw them and then heard them say it in their tiny voices for the first time, his heart melted and his eyes filled with tears.

It didn't take long for "Uncle Jake" to disappear. The twins would crawl up on his lap and say, "You're our daddy now, huh?"

"I sure am," Jake would always answer proudly. Ryan may have been the sperm donor, but Jake was their daddy.

That same day Jake called Doctor Carter and made an appointment for the two of them to come in for a consultation. She had an opening in two weeks, so Jake took it and told Maddie. She was fine with that. In fact, she was a bit curious herself about their IQs.

Maddie also called some pre-schools to visit. They wouldn't leave the children with just anyone. Jake babysat the twins while Maddie went to visit the schools. She looked at several before narrowing them down to two. Jake would have to go with her, and they'd decide together. After all, they were now really a team.

When Maddie returned home around 1:00 PM and told Jake she had narrowed the list to two, she wanted the four of them to visit them together after the twins' afternoon naps were over. Maddie told Jake that one of them was a regular preschool and one was a new kind of school called Montessori. Jake knew Maddie well enough to know which one she was already leaning towards. But he wanted to see them for himself since he considered them his children, too.

After the foursome toured the two schools, Maddie asked Jake and the twins which one they preferred. Jake told Maddie that the ultimate decision was hers and hers alone, but he was leaning towards the Montessori school. The twins agreed, trying their best to pronounce Montessori, but it came out "Mount Sori." She, too, had wanted the progressive school, so they signed Rob and Rory up immediately, requesting only that they be placed in the same class. They would start the day after Labor Day in September, when the new classes were formed, which would be in only a couple of months.

The next morning, Maddie called Tom and asked him if he could speak to his friend at Napa High School about her starting to teach that fall. He said he'd call him immediately to see if there would be an opening in the English department in September.

The following morning, Tom called Maddie and told her she was in luck. She had an appointment with the personnel director the next day at 11:00 AM. Maddie was ecstatic! She ran outside where Jake was playing in the pool with Rob and Rory. Of course, Tinker, their puppy, just sat at the edge of the pool watching them. No water for her, thank you very much.

"Jake, I need to talk to you now; it can't wait. I have an interview for a job tomorrow morning."

Jake got the twins out of the pool and brought them to Maddie to dry off and she peppered him with questions.

"Whoa, honey; don't worry; you'll do just fine. You are articulate, knowledgeable, and the personnel director will think you're so cute, he'll hire you on the spot." Jake laughed. "You have nothing to worry that pretty little head of yours about."

But Maddie's Type A personality came out in spades. She asked Jake what kinds of questions to expect and took great care deciding what to wear the next day.

But Jake had been right. She needn't have worried. She was offered the job on the spot, just like he'd told her. She would be teaching freshman and sophomore Honors English in the fall. Jake had never seen Maddie this excited since the night they became engaged. Maddie, Jake, and the kids celebrated her success that evening by going to their children's favorite place, McDonald's.

A few days later, Maddie and Jake met with Doctor Carter regarding the twins, Maddie felt comfortable around her immediately. She asked the psychologist several questions regarding the tests she was going to perform on her children. Dr. Carter took them to the room and showed them where the test would take place, and Maddie was pleased to see that her children would think they were playing games. She agreed to the tests with the stipulations that she and Jake could watch, and if one of the twins appeared to become anxious, the testing would stop.

The day of the test, Maddie and Jake told the twins they were going to get to play with some new and very special toys. Rob and Rory were excited about the news and wanted to go immediately. Maddie dressed the twins in matching play clothes as usual, so they wouldn't suspect anything different was going to take place.

Maddie had already known that the twins should be tested. Rob and Rory's pediatrician, Doctor Lois Bennett, had recommended it to her before. The twins had walked at ten months, could tie their shoes, and spoke in complete sentences very early on.

Maddie and Jake told the twins they were going on a fun-filled field trip. Maddie found Doctor Carter to be a very kind and caring woman who immediately made the twins feel comfortable. She talked to each of them and discovered immediately that they were very verbal and their vocabulary was very extensive for their age. She took each of them by the hand and led them down the hall into a playroom with all sorts of activities. The children grew excited when they saw all the "toys."

The doctor talked to each child and led them to opposite ends of the room where each of them had a table filled with activities. While they played, she walked back and forth and took notes on each child. The children had absolutely no trouble putting puzzles together and playing with spatial objects. After they finished playing with the "toys" in record time, each child headed for the books situated at the end of the table. When this happened, Doctor Carter went back and forth and listened as each of the twins read the simple books out loud. She was amazed to discover that even when one of them came upon a word they couldn't pronounce, they would try to sound out the word phonetically, just like Mommy had taught them. After this, she brought the twins back to Maddie and Jake.

"You two have two very, very bright children. I'll write up my report and discuss it with you by next week. Thank you for allowing me to meet your extremely precocious youngsters. It's been delightful. You're very lucky young parents."

"Thank you, doctor," said Maddie. "We know how lucky we are to have them." With that they took their children to McDonald's for some French fries again as a treat.

A week later, as promised, Maddie and Jake met with Doctor Carter. She told them that she felt that both of the youngsters, Rob and Rory, were gifted and exceptional, but she would like to check on them yearly.

"Just what does gifted and exceptional translate to in terms of IQ, doctor?" asked Maddie. Jake already knew the answer. Joyce Carter had already shared the results with him at school, but he'd said nothing to Maddie.

"Well, if the twins keep on the same track that I think they will, I would estimate their IQs to be around 160. Of course, it might go higher as they grow. It will depend, though, on what kind of teachers and stimuli they have," said the doctor.

That night in bed after making love, Maddie and Jake talked about their children. They decided that they would have the best schooling possible, but Maddie insisted on two things. One, they would go to a public school, and two, they were not to be placed in "gifted" classes. She didn't mind "honors" classes, though. She had known too many other kids who were brilliant but who were socially immature because they were in only gifted classes. Other than that, the only thing she wanted was for Jake and her to let them experience as much of life as possible.

"I agree. So let's start taking them to special places as soon as possible, okay? We need to take them to both fun places like Disneyland and the zoo, as well as to museums and art exhibitions. Don't you think so?" asked Jake.

"Of course, I do. Let's start taking them to places on weekends and during our breaks from school, okay?"

"Perfect," said Jake. "I want them to experience all life has to offer. I want them to be in sports if they want to, to be in clubs as they grow up. I want them to have as normal an upbringing as possible even though they are too bright to imagine."

"Jake, what if the teachers want to have them skip a grade or two when they're older? What do you think?" asked Maddie.

"Let's cross that bridge when we come to it. We'll do what we think is best for both of them. However, we'll both have to agree on the decision, okay?" replied Jake.

"Agreed. It will always be a joint decision. I love you with all my heart, Jake Kelly. You know that, don't you?" as she rolled on top of him once more.

"Yes, Madison, and I love you more than life itself," answered Jake. With that Jake put his arm down beside the bed to pick up Tinker and placed her on her pallet at the end of their bed, which long ago had become her new home. He'd been right about Maddie's going back to work, and they had also found the perfect nanny for the children. So she felt comfortable going back to work full time that September.

Maddie loved her students. They were bright and challenging. In fact, they reminded her of her own children. She always had to stay one step ahead of them and anticipate their questions before they asked them, so she'd know the answers.

After teaching Honors Ninth and Tenth English her first year, the department chair gave her Honors Tenth and Eleventh the next year. He wanted to let her follow her students and see how far she could take them and see how well she was able to get her students to perform. Maddie was an excellent teacher, and the principal and department chair could tell she loved her job.

Jake could also see Madison blossom once she started teaching. She was more fulfilled. He even felt her teaching had made her a better mommy, if that were possible. She seemed to have an endless supply of energy and patience. She even kept to her promise never to bring papers home to grade. She would either do them before or after school. When she walked into their home every day, she was just Mommy. He was even amazed that she still found time to take care of and ride her beloved filly.

43

Rob and Rory had a wonderful childhood. Their mother and father had provided all kinds of activities for them while they were growing up. Mom and dad made sure to keep them grounded, but also planned family outings ranging from the fun of Disneyland and zoos to visits to all the museums in California. During the summers, the family took trips to places of interest in the United States. The visit the twins loved the most was their two-week stint in New York City. Two weeks didn't seem enough time to see and do everything they wanted. They loved the Broadway shows and especially all of the museums. Their favorite was the Guggenheim. They could've spent days wandering through it. They also enjoyed the Avant Garde art galleries and experiencing food from all over the world.

Another one of the twins' favorite places to visit was Boston and walking the Freedom Trail. Seeing Paul Revere's house helped to cement what they were learning about the Civil War. Maddie and Jake also took them to Gettysburg, and another year they visited the southern states. Maddie would always remember laughing when Rory kept asking her where Tara's house from *Gone with the Wind* was located.

Maddie and Jake even took the twins to Washington, DC one summer. The twins loved the Smithsonian and could have spent weeks there, but they also visited Mount Vernon and Williamsburg. Both parents were glad they'd decided to take the twins to DC before 1981; Maddie didn't to have to deal with any unanswerable questions when "The Wall" was erected.

At age five, the twins had been placed into first grade. But that didn't last long. They had only been there for one week before their teacher gave them their final checkout test for the first grade, which they had both finished in record time and received perfect scores. After talking to Maddie and Jake, they agreed that the twins could be put into second grade. However, Maddie insisted they be put into the same class.

Meanwhile, Jake was starting his seventh year of teaching, and over the years Jake would have several of his students for both their junior and senior years, since he taught American History and U.S. Government. This particular year, a new student named Tasha Thompson walked into his American History class. Tasha had been a cheerleader throughout all of high school and was the typical bubbly, blonde, tanned, and well-built femme fatale. Jake knew the type well. That was the type he himself had dated in high school. Her junior year, Tasha had sat quietly in the middle of the room, not saying much. She was smart as a whip, and, of course, always made A's. Her junior year, she didn't look at Jake too much, but the truth be told, she was totally enthralled by him and decided she was in love with him.

Tasha made sure that she was in his U.S. Government class her senior year, too, but this time, she sat in the front row. Jake didn't think much about it since he knew that she went with his quarterback. They had gone together for a couple of years. Jake had absolutely no idea that Tasha was in infatuated with him. He did notice that she talked to him more, either before or after class, but it was always about an assignment, so he was totally in the dark. However, if the truth be known, Tasha had thought of nothing or no one else since she first stepped into Jake's classroom when she was sixteen. She'd even come to make herself believe that given the chance, they would get married and she'd have his children. This eventually became Tasha's only goal in life—to marry Jake Kelly. It may take a few years, but she was sure she could accomplish her goal.

One day, at the beginning of Tasha's senior year, after football and cheerleading practice, Tasha decided to follow Jake home to see where he lived. She followed at a safe distance, especially when he started his climb into the hills of Napa. When he turned onto his property, however, she didn't follow. Instead, she went a little farther up the road and parked. Then she double backed and walked down the tree-laden lane, making sure to keep herself hidden by the trees. When she finally reached Jake's house, she couldn't believe what she saw. *How could he possibly afford a mansion like this on a teacher's salary?* she wondered to herself. *He must have rich parents; that could be the only explanation,* thought Tasha. That made him an even better catch.

As she watched from the trees, however, she suddenly saw Jake and another woman hug and kiss each other. Then, to make matters worse, she saw him pick up two children to get a kiss hello. *Who in the hell are these people?* wondered Tasha. She knew for a fact that he wasn't married, but it looked like he had a ready-made family. To make it even worse, Tasha was able to get a good look at the woman when she faced the window. Even from a distance, she could tell this woman was beautiful.

Tasha started to cry the minute she saw the woman. It seemed as if all her dreams and plans over the past year were gone in an instant. She had truly convinced herself that she could have a life with Jake. She had no idea he was seriously involved with a woman and her children. She watched a while longer as they sat down to dinner. Tasha thought that both of the children looked to be around six and looked a great deal alike. *Twins,* thought Tasha. Jake had twins. The only problem was that neither of the children looked anything like Jake.

After watching a while longer, Tasha made her way back to her car. Once inside, she started to sob. Jake was taken.

She couldn't believe it, but she had just seen it with her own two eyes. She finally started her car and cried all the way home to Vallejo. Her parents were wealthy, but evidently not anywhere in the same class as Jake's. Jake worked because he wanted to, not because he had to.

The minute she walked into her house, she headed straight for her bedroom. She undressed and turned on her shower. She sat on the ledge in her shower and cried her heart out. She still couldn't believe what she'd just witnessed. *It isn't fair,* thought Tasha. *I know I can make him happier than that bitch. I wonder what kind of a hold she has on him. If he's with a woman with two children, he must really love her.* That thought made her cry even more. But Tasha was not one to give up easily on something that she wanted, and she wanted Jake.

In bed that night, Tasha started formulating a plan to free Jake from the woman and her children. But in order to do this, she really needed to know more about the woman and her daily habits. So, that night before bed, Tasha told her mother that she wasn't feeling well, so she wouldn't be going to school tomorrow. Her mother, already well into her third vodka tonic, was oblivious to her daughter and merely said, "Okay, honey. I'll call in for you." Since her father was on a business trip in London, at least she didn't have to explain her crying to him.

The next morning, Tasha, knowing her mom would sleep until around noon, got up early, dressed, and headed back to Jake's house. She was really proud of the fact that she didn't get lost; it would have been easy to do. She parked her car in the same place and made her way on foot again up to Jake's house.

Jake and the woman were having breakfast with their kids, but there was another car parked in the driveway. Then she saw another older woman enter the breakfast room to help with the children. *A nanny*, thought Tasha. *She must be a nanny!* She was right.

Tasha watched as Jake pulled his Mustang out of the garage and leave for work. A few minutes later, another garage door opened, and a woman in a 1966 Mustang pulled out. Tasha immediately raced back to her car so she could follow her and see where she worked.

To her complete surprise, Tasha followed Madison directly to Napa High School on Jefferson Street. She was a teacher, too. *What does she teach?* wondered Tasha. She watched as the woman got out of her car, carrying her briefcase into the school with her. Tasha couldn't believe how beautiful she was. Tasha was a cute, petite, blonde cheerleader herself, but she wasn't even in the same league as this woman. This woman was tall, lithe, and had incredible skin and hair. She wasn't close enough to see the color of her eyes, but if she had, she would have been even more upset.

Meanwhile, Jake was oblivious to Tasha's interest in him. He did notice that she wasn't in class today, but he figured she probably had a late-night cheerleading practice. In fact, she was just the kind of girl he'd always dated until he had met Maddie. After meeting Maddie, no other girls stood a chance with Jake even though that certainly didn't stop them from trying. Jake was definitely a one-woman man, and that woman was

Madison. *She always would be,* Jake thought to himself as his students were reading their government chapter.

Tasha was no dummy. Her quick thinking led her to the front doors of Napa High. Once inside, she went directly to the receptionist and very apologetically stated that she thought she might have bumped a Mustang in the parking lot. She wanted to know who owned the car so she could leave her a note with her name, phone number, etc., on the windshield. The smiling receptionist was more than eager to comply. She informed Tasha that the 1966 Mustang belonged to Madison Conrad, the Honors English teacher at the school. Tasha thanked her profusely for the information and then left the school.

Once Tasha was out the front door of the high school, she could hardly keep herself from jumping for joy. Jake wasn't married! Her name was Madison Conrad. Tasha couldn't believe it! She honestly believed that once Jake saw her as a real woman and not a student, she would be able to lure him away from Madison. Unfortunately, Tasha had no idea what an idiotic notion this was. It would never happen.

Tasha knew she'd have to play it cool until graduation. No way in the world would Jake jeopardize his career by dating a student. Besides, she already had a boyfriend—he was a senior, too, and had even played football for Jake. Steve was a nice enough guy—fun, popular—but not in the same league as Jake. Besides, Steve was going to UC Irving in the fall, while she was headed to UC Berkeley, so they'd be going their separate ways soon.

Tasha dedicated the next few weeks to watching what kind of routine Madison and Jake had. She even wrote down in a notebook not only the times of their comings and goings, but also where they went. She eventually had an entire notebook full with who did what when.

Tasha continued to flirt with Jake a little at school, but not in an overt way. She'd ask for help with a question or stop by before or after school a few times to say hello. She always made sure, though, that she had a specific reason for seeing him, so he wouldn't get suspicious. He didn't.

Graduation couldn't come soon enough for Tasha. Once she graduated, she would have all summer to put her plan to seduce Jake away from this "Madison" woman into action. One day, when she was talking to Jake before school, she nonchalantly asked him his plans for the summer. He told her he hadn't made any definite ones. He said he might go back to Oklahoma to visit his parents before football practice started again in August. That and the summer passing league would keep him busy. Since Steve had played on Jake's passing league team every year, she already knew where he'd be every Monday, Wednesday, and Friday evenings.

No one could ever accuse Tasha of not being bold. She always had been, and, up until now, she'd always gotten what she set her sights on. But this was different. She couldn't very well go up to Jake and tell him she wanted to fuck his brains out, even though that's exactly what she wanted to do. Instead, she had to make it a point just to bump into him at different places she knew he frequented. She decided that the best time to make her move on him was in late June. She could be patient until then. Besides, it was only a couple of weeks away.

Tasha became obsessed with Jake. She had convinced herself, that given the chance, she could make him hers. In fact, it was all she thought about. She had even gone so far as to purchase a couple of bridal magazines. She followed Jake and Maddie everywhere, but they never became suspicious because she always used different cars—her family had several. In fact, she was so self-absorbed with Jake she became a stalker.

Jake always gave his students his home phone number at the beginning of each semester in case they were having trouble with an assignment or research paper, just so long as they didn't abuse the privilege. It was his own private line—his and Maddie's main line was unlisted because the ghost of Ryan was always lurking in the background. Until now, Tasha had never called him, but that was about to change.

Tasha called Jake and asked him if he could meet her to talk about college. She was really scared of going to Berkeley. She knew that this was probably the most liberal college in the United States, and she didn't think she'd fit in. Jake being Jake took the bait, and they agreed to meet at a coffee shop in Napa.

Jake was already waiting when Tasha arrived. He was surprised by the way she looked. Instead of looking like the bubbly cheerleader he'd always known, she looked very sophisticated and grown up—just the image Tasha wanted to project. Once they were drinking their coffee, Jake noticed that Tasha was fidgeting; something was definitely wrong. However, he decided to let Tasha open up in her own time. In the beginning, they talked about life in general, and she was able to get Jake to talk about his life a little. No, he wasn't married, but yes, he was engaged and had been for several years. Tasha asked him why he hadn't married yet, but all Jake would say was that the time wasn't right. She asked him about his fiancé, but did it so subtly that Jake didn't think a thing about it. He told her he had met Madison in college and fallen completely head over heels for her immediately, but she had another boyfriend who was at West Point, so he was content to date her with no strings attached.

"But didn't it bother you that she just wanted to be friends? She was going to marry this guy, huh?" asked Tasha.

"Of course, it bothered me. I wanted her to be mine after our very first blind date, but I knew if I made an issue of it, she'd stop seeing me, and I wasn't willing to take that chance. So, during college, we were just best friends—no sex involved."

"Wow!" said Tasha. "She must really be special."

"She is," answered Jake. "So what's up with your going to Berkeley," said Jake, changing the subject.

"Oh, I don't know. Yes, I know it's a real honor to be accepted there—it's a hard school to get into, but I think I'm going to feel like a fish out of water. There are so many students, and most of professors are either former hippies or wish they had been. I just don't know if I'll enjoy it as much as everyone thinks I will," said Tasha sadly.

Jake told her she'd have a ball in college. In fact, it had been the best time of his life. Getting to be on his own, playing football, parties—he'd loved everything about it. He suggested she go through Rush Week and join a sorority that best suited her. He knew she'd have no trouble being asked to join several. She could even try out for cheerleader if she wanted to. He told her that, of course, her studies had to come first, but part of the college experience was the growing up she would do. In the end, he reassured her that she would do fine.

"Would it be all right if I called you again, Mr. Kelly? Just to help me keep things in perspective."

"Of course," answered Jake.

With that Tasha hugged Jake tightly and kissed him on the cheek.

In the fall, Tasha started her classes at Berkeley. She thrived on the attention she was getting from the opposite sex. She was cute and she knew it. However, on Friday nights, during football season, Tasha would always go back to her high school alma mater for the home games, sit alone on the opposing side stands, and train her father's binoculars on Jake. In fact, she never took her eyes off him during the entire game, except to see if his girlfriend was there. He was going to be hers, one way or another. She'd decided that long ago. She was prepared to do whatever it took to get him.

Finally, one Friday night, Tasha finally saw her. She was dying to get a close up look at her competition, so when Maddie stood up and went to the restroom,

Tasha followed her. When Tasha saw Maddie, she couldn't believe it! Just looking at Maddie's teal eyes kept her spellbound. Words couldn't describe the instant hatred she felt that flowed throughout her entire body. She vowed to herself then and there to get rid of her. She didn't know how; she just knew she was going to do it.

Maddie, on the other hand, had no clue who Tasha was, let alone that she wanted Jake for herself.

For the rest of the game, Tasha alternated her binoculars to focus between Jake and Maddie. After the game was over, Tasha watched Maddie go down on the field to speak to Jake. She was surprised that she didn't kiss him; she would have. Then after speaking to each other for a few minutes, Maddie went to her car and left.

When Tasha arrived home that night, she lay in bed wide awake, thinking about how she could get Maddie out of the picture. She decided to wait until Christmas vacation to put her plan into motion. Tasha had become so obsessed with Jake and getting rid of her competition that she became not only a silent stalker, but also continued on a downward spiral into insanity. Nothing mattered to her except Jake. He was hers.

Their first confrontation occurred outside Macmillan's Department Store in Napa. Tasha boldly approached Maddie while she was with her children. She went right up to her and said, "I think you need to know that Jake belongs to me. We're going to get married soon. I want you to leave him alone. If you don't, I'll get rid of you and your kids myself." With that Tasha calmly turned around and walked away.

At first, Maddie was utterly shocked and then terrified. She went back into the store, phoned Jake, and explained to him what had just happened. He told her to stay in the store. He'd be there as soon as possible.

When Jake found Maddie and the twins sitting in the shoe department, he saw that Maddie was still shaking because she was so terrified.

"Maddie, honey, what happened?" he asked while he held her in his arms.

"I don't know. The twins and I were leaving the store, and this girl came up to me and threatened the children and me. She said you belonged to her, and you were going to get married," replied Maddie, still shaking uncontrollably.

"What was her name?" asked Jake quietly.

Maddie told him she didn't know, but Jake was pretty sure he knew exactly who she was—Tasha Thompson. Jake was furious. How dare she accost his family? He knew he'd have to take matters into his own hands.

"Who was she?" Maddie finally asked after she started to calm down.

"Honey, I don't want you to worry about it. What did she look like?" asked Jake, already knowing what her answer would be.

"Short, blonde hair, cute," answered Maddie.

"I'm pretty sure she's one of my former students named Tasha Thompson. She graduated last June. For some crazy reason, she must think I belong to her. I'll set her straight, believe me. Now, let's get you and the kids home. I'll follow you."

As soon as Maddie walked into the house, she went straight to the bar, poured herself a strong vodka tonic, and then plopped down on the sofa. Meanwhile, Rory and Rob went into Rob's room to discuss what had just happened. Since they were still fairly young at the time, they couldn't figure out who would want to hurt their mother or say such nasty things to her.

When Jake got home, he told Maddie about Tasha and what had happened last June.

All Madison asked was, "Did anything happen between you two?"

"Absolutely, positively not! Do you honestly think I would jeopardize what we have after what it took for me to get you?"

"No, Jake, I know you wouldn't. I believe you. She probably just has a school girl crush on you. I know I would," replied Maddie smiling.

"Really, honey, believe me; I'll take care of this. I'll get a restraining order against her tomorrow. I simply won't allow you or our kids to be harassed by a girl who evidently has some serious mental problems." With that Jake put his arm around Maddie and took her upstairs to make love to the only woman he'd ever wanted.

The next morning, Jake went to the police station at the courthouse in downtown Napa to take out a restraining order against Tasha Thompson of Vallejo, California. Of course, the Napa police didn't want to issue the warrant at first, not until Jake described the entire situation, including the fact that his young children also witnessed the confrontation. With that knowledge, the police instantly issued an order requiring her to stay at least 100 yards away from him and his entire family.

The Napa police served the warrant on Tasha on Sunday evening while she was in her dorm room at college. Tasha was stunned when she opened the door and saw the police standing there. Once they served the warrant, and she had locked the door behind her, Tasha started throwing everything in sight. She went berserk, screaming hysterically. How could he do this to her? He knew they were destined to be together. It was that bitch! She was the one who made him do it. Her Jake would never have done it unless that bitch had made him. Well, by God, nothing would keep them apart. She was going to make sure of that.

Tasha started openly stalking Madison, making sure to keep the required 100 yards away, so she wasn't violating the restraining order. She also made sure that Madison saw her each and every time. She did.

When Madison told Jake about her still watching her all the time, he'd had enough. He was going to end this. He would try talking some sense into Tasha first, and if that didn't work, he'd go to her parents. But before he was able to take matters into his own hands, Tasha accosted Madison again in a dressing room at Macmillan's. This time she had a butcher knife in her hand and was going to use it.

"How dare you keep Jake and me apart?" Tasha whispered hoarsely as she came up behind Madison.

Madison felt the tip of the knife on her and turned just before Tasha tried to plunge it into her back. But, during the struggle, Tasha was able to make a deep gash on Maddie's upper right chest, just above her breast. Realizing she'd missed her target, Tasha ran out of the dressing room screaming, "He's mine you bitch! Next time I'll kill you."

Seriously injured, Maddie stumbled out of the dressing room, holding her shirt against her bloody chest, trying to stop the bleeding. Macmillan's security immediately called the police and paramedics. Maddie then had them call Jake, who was at home. The police told him to meet Madison at the Queen of the Valley Hospital.

Jake ran to his car and sped to the hospital in record time. When the police told him what had happened, he immediately said, "I want to press charges for assault and the intent to do bodily harm, so arrest her now— Tasha Thompson!" he yelled as he ran to see Maddie in the emergency room.

Maddie was lying quietly in a hospital bed, with her right chest and arm bandaged from her shoulder to her elbow, when Jake entered the room.

"Hi, honey," said Jake tenderly as he went over and gave her a kiss.

"When can I go home, Jake?"

"Probably in around thirty minutes. You have to wait until the IV is finished. Do you want to tell me what happened?"

"Didn't the police tell you?" asked Maddie weakly.

"Yes, and I told them to have Tasha arrested immediately. She's probably at the police station right now being booked."

"Jake, are you sure you never gave her any reason to believe that the two of you had a future together?"

"Madison, Tasha is nuts. And, no, I sure as hell never gave her a reason to think we had a future. She needs psychological help—professional help in order for her to accept that she's got a problem."

"Jake, just take me home."

"You've got it," and he went to sign her release papers.

In lieu of a jury trial, which Madison wanted to avoid, Tasha Thompson was sentenced to a state psychological institution for at least three years. Madison and Jake really felt that Tasha needed help, but she also needed to be held accountable for her actions.

Tasha was sent to Napa State Mental Hospital, where she was given both group and individual counseling. While she was there, she took extension classes, so she wouldn't lose her college education. Tasha was also smart enough to know that in order to get out of this nut house, she was going to have to appear to be cured. She needed to make the doctors believe that she had overcome her obsession with Jake. And she did just that. Tasha was released after only eighteen months, with the understanding that the restraining order was still in force. If she violated the order, she would go straight to jail.

But, Tasha was far from cured and she was hell bent on revenge. Her first order of business was to legally change her name. She became Stacy Alexander. She also changed herself physically. She had her hair dyed dark brown and cut short into a new bob style. She started wearing hard dark brown contact lenses; that was the hardest thing for her to get used to. She also bought herself an entirely new wardrobe.

The new Stacy went back to UC Berkeley. Ironically, she majored in psychology, and received her degree in only two years, because of the classes she had taken while incarcerated. Instead of immediately getting a job, she decided to continue her education and received her master's degree in psychology.

Stacy graduated with Honors and soon became a member at a counseling center in San Francisco. Her major focus was on child and teenage issues. She became a highly regarded professional and was asked to speak at several conventions. At the same time she enrolled in a doctorate program.

Did she stop seeing Jake? Of course not.

She went to every Vallejo High game for years and sat on the opposing side, with her trusty binoculars trained on the love of her life. However, after going to the games for several years, the first thing she noticed was that he was wearing a wedding band. She was crushed—hurt just as much as the first time. But she wasn't going to give up that easily. Through her binoculars, she also saw Madison, the twins, and a very handsome man sitting beside her in the stands. *Who was he?* she wondered. She decided to make it her mission to find out.

44

While, Tasha was locked up, Maddie, Jake, and the twins were finally were able to get back to a normal life. The twins breezed through second, third, and fourth grade. They always had perfect grades and were polite, friendly, and well-liked by the other children. But just before fifth grade, the principal asked Jake and Maddie to come in for a conference. He told them the twins weren't in trouble. He just wanted to talk to them.

Jake and Maddie were still apprehensive about being summoned to the principal's office, wondering what the principal had to say. Of course, they worried that one of them had started acting up. They were wrong. Instead, he asked if he could give them the fifth grade exit exam and see how they would do. He was afraid that they weren't going to be challenged in the fifth grade. Perhaps they should skip to the sixth grade instead. After Jake and Maddie talked it over, they agreed to the test, but they insisted that Doctor Carter give it to them.

The twins skipped the fifth grade.

During these formative years, Maddie and Jake made sure to keep them involved in all sorts of activities. Both Rob and Rory loved sports. In fact, they were becoming excellent swimmers. Rob was already on a swimming team, while Rory enjoyed her diving team. Since they had a pool at home, Jake and Maddie gave them private lessons during the spring and summer.

Rob enjoyed T ball when he was very little. Jake spent hours working patiently with him. At the same time, Rory enjoyed dancing, so Maddie would sit at each of her lessons like her own mother had done. Both Maddie and Jake were hands-on parents. They really were a team, just as Jake had said so many years before.

The twins still saw Doctor Carter during these years, just to see if their IQs were increasing. They loved to see her. It was like a special play day for them, and the doctor was always astounded at how bright they were. They were the most intelligent children she had ever observed during her long career.

As they became older, Jake and Maddie attended every one of Rob's and Rory's activities. They sat together in the stands during Rob's Little League games, Pop Warner football games, and swim meets. Rob was an exceptional athlete, and Jake knew about athletes. They watched all of Rory's dance recitals and diving competitions together. The twins also watched each other as often as they could, too. Rob and Rory were truly best friends and always would be. They even had that special intuition that some twins possessed.

Rory had become such a good dancer that Maddie and Jake had even converted one of the many bedrooms in their house into a practice room for her. They had installed mirrors, a bar, and a stereo for her to practice. In years to come, Rory would also use this room to practice her tumbling when she became a cheerleader.

The years seemed to fly by. In fact, sometimes Maddie and Jake couldn't believe that the twins were already in high school, because they had skipped two grades. They had turned fifteen on January 20, 1984, and would be seniors next year. It seemed so strange to them that the twins would graduate at sixteen. They both already knew where they'd be going to college, too. They had both been offered full academic scholarships to Stanford. All of them were over the moon when they found out.

The twins had always been popular kids. Neither of them had had a serious romance yet, though, and that suited their parents just fine. They were too young to date. Besides that, they were also too busy. Their parents didn't know it, but the twins had made a pact when they were younger that each of them had to approve of the friends they chose. This promise really helped to keep them grounded and out of trouble.

As the years passed, the twins were still very involved in sports. Rob was going to be the youngest quarterback ever for the Napa High School Indians in the fall, played first base on the baseball team, and was on the swim team. Rory, on the other hand, was a cheerleader, dancer, and diver. It seemed that Maddie and Jake were always carting them to their practices or watching their games.

The one thing that Jake couldn't do was tell Rob anything about Vallejo's football team, since they played Napa High. He would help him with his passing and would hike the ball to him, but telling him their plays was out of the question. It was always a little tense around the house the week before Napa and Vallejo played. Rory would practice her cheers with her mother's guidance. The principal had discovered that Maddie had been a cheerleader for eight years, so he had asked her to be the cheerleading sponsor. Maddie said she would as long as she had an assistant, because she wouldn't be able to attend all of the games. Sometimes she would need to attend Vallejo's games where her husband worked. Even though Napa was a much smaller school than Vallejo, Jake secretly hoped that Napa might win this year. After all, his son was the quarterback, and a very good one at that.

Even though both Jake and Maddie were busy all the time with the twins, it didn't mean that they weren't still close. In fact, just the opposite was true. Ever since the twins were around seven, Jake told the twins he had a secret to tell them, but they had to crossed their hearts and promise not to tell Mommy. He would then tell them that he was going to take Mommy on a short trip somewhere. Sometimes it was Los Angeles, San Diego, San Francisco, Aspen, or even Las Vegas. It would be their little secret. The twins loved playing this game. Daddy would tell Mommy what kind of bag to pack and off they went. It was always a surprise for Maddie, which delighted her. She loved surprises.

It was on these getaways, which occurred about once a month, that Maddie and Jake would really reconnect. Their love life had always been very active, but when they were away and alone, it just cemented their relationship even more. They'd known each other for twenty years now and had been together for fifteen.

Jake's lovemaking skills never ceased to amaze Maddie. He had taught her so much throughout the years. They both knew exactly what buttons to push to get the desired response. Of course, to Jake, making love to Maddie was always a new high for him. Just seeing her naked would arouse him. She was still as pretty to him as the first time he had seen her in the college cafeteria all those years ago. Her body was still as taut as it had always been. She had become a relentless swimmer as she became older. Jake had always continued to work out and run, so he, too, was probably in the best shape of his life. But it wasn't just the physical attraction that kept them close. It was the emotional connection they both felt when they made love.

They often made love in different places, as well as different times of the day. They had decided early on that they were going to "christen" every room in their huge house, even the barn, and they had done just that. Sometimes, they would make love in the morning, sometimes in the afternoons when the twins were younger and napping, sometimes in the evening, and sometimes more than once a day.

One favorite getaway was to the Del Coronado, on Coronado Island, in San Diego, California. Maddie had always loved watching the ocean and walking on the beach. Their rooms always overlooked the water whenever he took her to a beach town. They had a wonderful dinner in the Crown Room at the hotel and had walked on the beach afterwards before returning to their room. Their room had a hot tub, so they decided to fill it up with bubble bath and have some fun. They laughed as they realized they had put in too much bubble bath, and before they knew it, it was spilling over the edges. They didn't care. They made love in the hot tub, slowly and tenderly. Afterwards, they cleaned up the wet floor and made love again in the bed.

As had become their custom, they talked before going to sleep. Jake wanted to remind Maddie of something she had once told him a long time ago while they were finishing off a bottle of wine.

"Maddie, do you remember telling me of the 'pact' that you and your high school friends made so long ago?" asked Jake.

"Honestly, Jake, I don't. I'd probably had too much wine as usual. But I do remember the 'pact,' why?"

"Well, it's 1984—your twentieth-year reunion will be this June. I hope you're planning to attend. Why don't you take the twins with you? I bet they'd love to see where Mom went to high school. You've never talked to them about that time in your life very much. Of course, they've been to Oklahoma many times to see their grandparents, but you've never suggested going to Avalon so they could see where you grew up. I think they'd really get a kick out of meeting your old friends. Besides, you haven't seen them in twenty years either," said Jake.

"I'll think about it," was all Maddie would say.

Since Jake didn't want to push her, all he said was, "Okay." He didn't want to tell her that he wanted her to go and try to put the past behind her. Maybe if she did, she'd be ready to get married. He would ask her again, though, next month. He really felt that until Maddie made peace with the past, their future would be forever up in the air. He was almost forty and Maddie almost thirty-eight. As he'd told Maddie many years ago, she'd be the one to decide when they would marry. He was pretty sure she was waiting until the twins had graduated. She'd always felt that the twins were her responsibility—no one's but hers.

They had a wonderful time in San Diego, and when they arrived home, both Rob and Rory could tell that they had needed this getaway.

"How was Coronado, Mom?" asked Rob.

"How did you know we went to Coronado, young man?"

"Mom, we've known for years where Dad takes you on your trips. It's always been our little secret with Dad," declared Rory proudly.

"I don't believe it. And you never told me?"

"Then it wouldn't have been a surprise, Mom," replied Rory laughing.

Jake had never ceased to amaze Maddie. True to his word, Jake brought up the "pact" and reunion again in late spring. He told Maddie that he really thought she and the twins should go. Besides, she had made a promise to her high school friends, and she needed to honor that.

Maddie wanted Jake to go with her, but he declined. He said he would be bored to tears. He wouldn't know any of the people there, and he'd feel like an outcast. He felt that they should go without him. After much haggling back and forth, she finally agreed to go, but only if the twins wanted to go with her. She would not go alone.

Much to Maddie's surprise, the twins were delighted at the prospect of meeting her former high school friends. They both agreed to go on the spot. Maddie was surprised because she felt that since they were going to be seniors next year, they wouldn't want to leave their friends even for a week. But since they did agree, she had to agree, too, even though she was dreading it like the plague. She just didn't want to dredge up old and painful memories.

Maddie didn't want to take the chance that Ryan might be there. If he were, he'd be able to tell immediately that the twins were his. Maybe he did die in Vietnam like she had told the twins whenever they had asked her while they were growing up. She hoped not, though. At this point in her life, she didn't wish him any ill will, but she still hated him for what he'd done to her. Even though she had tried her best to forgive him, she just couldn't. He had literally broken her heart, and she'd never really ever recovered from it. But it had been sixteen years since she'd last seen him. If he'd been going to find her, it would've been before now. In the end, she decided she had no choice but to take a chance and hope he didn't attend.

When the end of June came around that year, Jake drove Maddie and the twins to San Francisco to catch their flight for Oklahoma.

BOOK VI:
REUNION

45

"**H**urry up, Mom, or we'll miss the plane!" Rob shouted as he ran to Gate 8 in the San Francisco Airport.

"I'm coming," panted Madison Conrad.

"What's the rush?" asked Rory, Rob's twin sister, who was walking with her mother.

"You know your brother; he's always been the impatient one," declared Maddie.

Soon after checking in at the gate, American Airlines Flight 1898 boarded for the nearly three-hour trip to Oklahoma City, Oklahoma. Once the threesome found their seats, Madison Conrad sat between her two children. Since it was going to be a long flight, Maddie decided this would be a good time to tell them about some of her friends they might meet.

"Do you two remember when you were little and we'd play the 'I Remember' games?"

"Of course, but we aren't a little old for that now?" replied Rory, who thought she was fifteen going on thirty.

Undeterred by her daughter's sarcasm, Maddie said, "Well, I'm going to tell you a little about a few of my friends, not all of them, mind you, just a special few. And then when we get to Avalon, I'm going to see if you can recognize them from what I've told you.

"First of all, you already know that our group made a pact. That's the only reason we're going. There were eleven of us in all.

"Let's see. How can I describe Garrett? Well, he was our class president, and he'll probably be there because his family owned a lot of farmland. He was a big guy, even in high school, like a big farm boy. He was cute with black hair, a booming voice, and a great personality. He was easy going, outgoing, and always seemed to be in trouble for one thing or another. In fact, one time, Garrett and his buddies managed to put Limburger cheese in Shelly's locker our senior year. Obviously, the locker was unusable for the rest of the year, and Garrett, being the leader of the pack, was suspended for three days."

Both Rob and Rory laughed hysterically when they heard of the prank. They thought they'd be able to recognize him instantly.

Next, Maddie explained to them that her best friends in high school were identical twins. Unless you knew them really well, no one could tell them apart. Their hairstyles were the same; they dressed the same. But somewhere on their outfits would be a K or an S. Maddie said that they looked so much alike that they could even fool their boyfriends when they first met them. They'd actually done it before. And, of course, if they wanted to fool their teachers, all they had to do was change their blouses.

"You're kidding, right?" asked Rory.

"Nope. They really did. The boys were never really sure whom they were out with after the first time," replied Maddie, laughing at the prank, feeling like it had happened only yesterday, not twenty years ago.

Maddie said that Jennifer and Bethany rounded out her small group of girlfriends. Jennifer and Bethany were actually cousins, too, but didn't look at all like each other.

Next, she also told her twins about Stan and Jeff, Garrett's best friends and partners in crime. They had been friends since grade school, and they were always together. Dan and Bob, both tall basketball players, rounded out the list of five.

Maddie explained to Rob and Rory that all of them palled around together but didn't date each other. They'd go to parties and dances together as a group, take Garrett's truck to the drive-in on $1.00 a carload night, or go on hayrides together. They were all just good friends, not boyfriends and girlfriends.

"But didn't you say there were six boys, Mom?" questioned Rob.

"You're right," answered Maddie very matter-of-factly. "The other boy, Ryan, came right before his junior year. He played football, so he knew Garrett and the guys before school started. Then he started palling around with us." Maddie had no intention of telling them anything else about this sixth boy. Hell would freeze over first.

"So, when we get to the hotel, you two brainiacs get to see if you can pick out my friends from the descriptions I gave you. Okay?"

"You're on, Mom," said Rob. "I'll bet you a sundae that we'll be able to figure out who is who?"

"Okay," answered Maddie, just hoping that the sixth boy didn't show up.

Maddie told them what she remembered about the town of Avalon. When she arrived in the eighth grade, the population, including the air base, was around 25,000—about the same size as Napa but nothing like Napa. Avalon was built around the large courthouse. Stores were all around the main square: dress shops, shoe stores, Woolworth's, furniture stores, etc. Everything was pretty much centered in this one area. There were no strip malls back then. The last piece of information she gave them was to be prepared for a very different kind of landscape than Napa; whereas Napa was in a valley, surrounded by hills and grape vineyards, Avalon was surrounded by farmland. The land was flat as a pancake. In fact, most of Oklahoma was, except the Northeast.

"So, there you have it. Now, you won't be totally shocked or uninformed when we reach the reunion," said Maddie with finality.

After that the twins became engrossed in their books. Rather than read the *House Beautiful* magazine she'd brought with her, she closed her eyes and began to think. She really hadn't wanted to come to her twentieth-year high school reunion, but Jake, her fiancé, had told her she needed to keep her promise. She didn't know it, but Jake had an ulterior motive for insisting that she go. He was actually hoping that her first love, Ryan Richardson, would show up. Jake felt that this was the only way that Maddie would be able to let go of the past. She had to face him—and, hopefully, let her hate, and yes, love, for him go.

She was happy that she was going to get to see "the group" that she had avoided for twenty years. She wondered how much they'd changed. The one thing she was certain of was that the bonds they'd formed in high school would never be broken. Maddie was pretty sure she'd still be able to recognize "the group" even after all these years.

Maddie also thought how strange it seemed that her children were going to be seniors at Napa High School next year even though they were only fifteen years old. They had both skipped the same two grade levels and currently were planning to attend Stanford after graduation. In fact, Stanford had already offered both of them full scholarships. Madison was so proud of them. Rob, the more sensitive of the two, wanted to be a writer or correspondent. Rory, the perfectionist, wanted to be a pediatric surgeon, at least this month. There was never any question in Maddie's mind that they would both be successful. They were both highly intelligent—like their father, and yes, like her.

When Maddie had asked the twins if they wanted to see where she'd gone to high school, surprisingly, they had both jumped at the chance. Most teenagers didn't want to hang out with their mothers, even for a few days. Perhaps it was because she had very seldom, if ever, talked openly about those years. She had forced herself to forget her life before the twins were born. Now, it was all going to come flooding back to her, and she didn't know if she was ready for it, even now. Ryan had been the love of her life and soul mate, and when he broke her heart, a part of her had never recovered. She had lost some of her joie de vivre when it happened, and, even after several years of therapy, she was still stuck in the anger stage. She'd never been able to forgive him and didn't know if she ever could. Maddie was quickly brought back to the present, however, when the pilot announced that Flight 1898 would be landing in the next few minutes at Will Rogers World Airport.

Once they had landed and collected their luggage, the threesome headed for the Hertz Counter to pick up their rental for the next five days. Maddie had requested a convertible, preferably a Mustang. The kids loved the car that sat in their garage at home and couldn't wait to be able to drive it. In her junior year in college, Maddie's father had given her an early graduation present. It was 1966 dark green Mustang, with a very cool parchment top. Maddie just loved it and still drove it everywhere she went at home.

Since Maddie had to drive, Rob was relegated to being the navigator. He used their map and directed his mom to a toll road, which she had never her of, that would take them south to Livingston and then west to Avalon.

As they drove south, Madison was able to point out places of interest that she still recalled from all those years ago. They even stopped once so Maddie could take a picture of her teens by a herd of buffaloes.

Rory, who wasn't paying any attention to the conversation in the front seat, had been gazing at the miles and miles of flat farmland. The wind was hot and humid, nothing like Napa, her hometown. *Who would ever want to live here?* she wondered to herself. She did have to admit that she enjoyed the wind blowing through her long, dark auburn, naturally curly hair. What she didn't like, though, was the thought that she'd look like little Orphan Annie by the time they finally arrived in Avalon.

It only took around two hours for Maddie to start seeing billboards for Livingston and Fort Sutton. Once again, she began to question her decision to return. She instantly thought of Ryan and the time spent there with him during the summer of 1967. In fact, she deliberately looked straight ahead when they passed Fort Sutton and the motel where they had stayed. Both were still there after all these years.

In order to forget the painful memory, Maddie started looking intently for the exit for Avalon and for a particular place to eat that she wanted the children to experience. It didn't take long for Maddie to find the Sonic Drive-in, and she pulled into one of the parking spaces.

"What are we doing here?" asked Rory.

"Well, I want to give you guys a taste of Oklahoma, and besides, I thought you might want some lunch. This is the most popular drive-in restaurant in the state. We even had one in Avalon our senior year in high school. I'll order for us, okay?" asked their mother.

"Go for it," said Rob.

After Maddie had ordered, it didn't take long for the food to be delivered. This is the part that Maddie was waiting for her children to see.

"Mom, they're bringing our food on roller skates!" yelled Rob as both of her twins started to laugh hysterically.

"I know"—laughed Maddie—"that's what I wanted you to see. There are Sonics throughout all of Oklahoma. Besides, the food is pretty good here, too, especially the tater tots."

When they finished their lunch, they continued on the same two-lane road toward Avalon that Maddie had traveled so many times before. *Some things never change,* thought Maddie. The twins were still talking about the Sonic, with Rory complaining that she'd probably get a zit for eating the greasy food. They once again marveled about the flat-as-a-pancake land around them as they rode the last fifty miles toward their destination.

When she was within five miles of Avalon, Maddie started seeing billboards which advertised places that were still in business twenty years later. Not any major stores like Sears; this town wasn't that big even now, but a few of the family-owned stores named after sons and daughters, as is so often the case in small towns, were still there. *As much as things change, they remain the same,* thought Maddie. She did see signs that showed a few new motels had come to town. That was progress.

As they entered the immediate outskirts of the town, Maddie felt that she was entering a time warp. She recognized the old drive-in, still there, but much the worse for wear. She saw the country club—so many dances, so many years ago. When they hit the city limits, she noticed two new motels. One, the Ramada Inn, was where they would meet the rest of "the group." Shelly, the organized one, had made the reservations for everyone she thought would come. However, since no one knew where Maddie was living, Maddie had called around town and found where "the group" would be staying and made her own reservations for two rooms.

"Mom, we're supposed to be registered at the Ramada Inn. Turn in here," said Rob.

As Rob and Rory unpacked the Mustang, Maddie went inside to register. She had asked for adjoining rooms, so that she and the twins could visit back and forth. While she was checking in, she discovered that everyone else had already arrived.

Maddie and the twins quickly found their rooms, dumped their suitcases and garment bags on the floor, and went in search of their mother's friends whom she hadn't seen in twenty years. She found them in the bar, drinking wine and beer. She could hear Bethany making a toast. As Maddie walked toward them, the years seemed to vanish, and she was sixteen years old again. When the group noticed her approaching with two gorgeous-looking young adults in tow, they all stood up, cheered, and ran to greet her.

"Maddie," said Garrett, "it's not fair. You haven't changed a bit—still as tall and slender as ever."

Maddie's immediate answer was, "Put some glasses on. You never could see past your nose!"

Maddie then introduced her children, Rob and Rory, to her friends. Even though all of them immediately noticed the twins' uncanny resemblance to her and Ryan, they were all smart enough not to say anything. Maddie would tell them her story in her own way and in her own time, if at all.

Maddie told her friends not to mention their names, because Rob and Rory were going to see if they could figure out who was who through the descriptions she had given them on the plane. She should've known that they would have no trouble picking out most of her friends by name very quickly. Only their mother's friends, who were also twins, gave them a bit of trouble. They didn't dress the same anymore or wear the same hairstyle. Rob and Rory conferred for a couple of minutes before they made their decision. They were right on. What did she expect? Her children were certifiable geniuses, for God's sake.

After drinks in the tiny, dark, and crowded bar at the motel, everyone went to Bethany's and Jennifer's room to decide what time to go to the Class of 1964 mixer.

The group decided they should arrive fashionably late, so Maddie and the twins returned to their rooms to shower, change, and get ready. Like all women, Maddie didn't know what to bring to wear, so she had brought several possibilities. She finally decided on a teal backless sundress, the color of her eyes. The dress made her feel good and looked great with her natural tan. No one knew who would show up for this reunion, and since Maddie had not seen any of them since high school graduation, she had to admit she was curious to see who would be there and how much they had all changed.

Meanwhile, the twins were both ready to go early— it never took them long. Rob wore his usual khaki slacks and polo with its collar up, and his usual no socks loafers. Rory, who always looked fabulous no matter what she wore, was dressed in an adorable black sundress. She'd even had time to shower and get her Orphan Annie curls under control once again. Her makeup had always consisted of just blush, lipstick, and mascara, like her mother.

Maddie looked at herself in the full-length mirror on the closet door, and then realized she'd forgotten to put on her jewelry. Jake had given her incredible diamonds throughout the years. They were never gaudy, though. He always picked classic pieces. Maddie had taken them off when she took her shower. She now put on her spectacular engagement ring, the one-carat each diamond stud earrings he'd given her one Christmas, a two-carat solitaire necklace she'd received for her birthday, and, as always, her special gold bracelet that she always wore. She checked herself one last time in the mirror. *There,* she thought, *now I'm ready.* She threw a shawl around her shoulders, and then she and the twins headed for the lobby to meet at 7:30 PM as planned.

Everyone met in front of the motel, and they immediately determined that they were going to need at least three cars to haul everyone to the mixer. But Maddie suggested she and the twins take their car, too. Maddie wanted an escape route if she needed it. She had no idea how she was going to react once she saw everyone, especially if Ryan happened to show up, which she doubted. He would already be here if he were coming. *Just as well,* Maddie thought to herself.

While everyone was piling into their cars, they decided they'd all drag Main Street the way they used to on Saturday nights all those years ago. In those days, that had been the way everyone used to find out who was dating whom. Then they decided that they would drive by the old high school. As they did so, everyone in the other cars was talking excitedly about the good old days and memories, except Maddie. She kept quiet. She was lost in her own thoughts, especially as they passed the football stadium. *How many hours did I spend on that field practicing cheers, doing flips, and watching practice?* she wondered. Suddenly, she felt very uncomfortable and wanted to run back to the motel, grab her things, and get the hell out of town. Her previous resolve to face her demons, even with the twins with her, had all but disappeared. It was Kelly, the one riding with her and the twins, who suddenly brought her back to the present.

"Earth calling Maddie! What're you thinking about? You seem a million miles away," said Kelly.

"Oh, nothing—just how many hours I spent on that field falling on my butt trying to do back flips," laughed Maddie.

A few minutes later, they all arrived at the hotel where the mixer was being held. Before anyone went inside, however, they decided that since they'd all come together, they would all leave together, no matter what. Maddie agreed, but she was not so sure that she'd want to stay as long as the rest of the group. They had all been back to previous reunions; she hadn't. What if she became bored or if she was cornered by someone she didn't even remember? *Too late to turn back now*, she told herself and proceeded to walk through the front door with the twins.

As the group entered the room, everyone who was already there started screaming with delight. This graduation class had been small, approximately 180. Everyone knew everyone else. After greeting people she hadn't seen for twenty years, many she didn't recognize, Maddie headed for the bar in search of some liquid courage.

After getting a glass of wine, Maddie sought out a table where one of her best friends who still lived in Avalon was talking to a former boyfriend. Maddie listened while Debbie and the former love of her life talked about long lost love. *This is a mistake,* Maddie thought to herself when she heard the conversation. *It's hitting too close to home. I don't want to remember. I need to get out of here.*

Maddie went to the bar again and picked up a second glass of white wine, and then she headed to the corner table that the group was occupying and sat by herself, her back to the door, and just watched everyone talk at once about the events of the last twenty years. Many of her classmates had changed so much that she had a difficult time recognizing some of them. She would even have to look at their senior yearbook on the table in order to recognize people she hadn't seen for so many years.

Madison decided that after she finished this glass of wine, she'd tell the others that she wasn't feeling well and would take the Mustang back to the motel. This was all becoming too overwhelming for her. She didn't want to remember; she needed to get out of here. She wanted and needed some time alone. She knew the twins were having too much fun meeting all of her old friends and wouldn't want to leave so soon, so she decided she'd ask Bethany if they could catch a ride back to the motel with her.

Maddie had almost finished her wine and was getting ready to go tell the twins she was leaving when the impossible happened. Someone came quietly up behind her. While reaching for her purse, she felt a body lean over her, and a deep voice whispered in her ear, "YKTA." There was only one other person in the entire world who know what those letters meant, and it had been sixteen years since Maddie had heard them.

Oh my God, thought Maddie. She froze; her stomach was in a knot, and she was afraid to sit up and face the demon of her constant nightmares. She didn't move a muscle, not at first anyway. She immediately started trying to think of how she could escape this beginning nightmare. When the man behind her lifted her very gently from her chair and turned her to face him, she felt as if she were moving in slow motion, like a mime on a street corner in Paris. It was if the last twenty-two years of her life were flashing before her.

She found herself staring into the face of her very first love and soul mate.

"Hello, Maddie," whispered Ryan Richardson in the same deep voice she'd never forgotten.

"Hello," replied Maddie. She saw the man she had loved her entire life standing before her. He looked like the same Ryan she had known all those years ago. He was wearing navy slacks, a pale blue polo, and black loafers. She also immediately noticed that he was still tall and slender and stood ramrod straight from his days at West Point. His hair was still dark, but now there was just a touch of silver around his temples. His brown eyes were the only thing that seemed different to her. Instead of the softness and love she had always seen in them before, she saw a pain and hardness that had not been there when she had last seen him in 1968.

"You look incredible, Maddie," Ryan said softly, and he meant it. If anything, Ryan thought to himself, she looked even more beautiful than she had at twenty-one. She was more statuesque and more mature, of course, but time had been good to her. She was still tall and even thinner than he remembered. Her face was not wrinkled, except for the slight smile lines at the corners of her eyes. Now, her face was more angular, which made her high cheekbones even more pronounced. Her eyes were still that wondrous teal color like the deep waters of the Caribbean, and her hair was still long, with ringlets flowing down her back; that remarkable dark auburn color and shine were still the same. She had never worn much makeup, and this was still true. She looked magnificent to Ryan.

While Ryan was gazing in awe at Maddie, her first thought was of the twins. *Where were they?* She was worried. Thank God they had not been sitting with her when he arrived. They were off talking to her girlfriends, their backs to Ryan at the moment. However, she knew it would only be a matter of time before they turned around and returned to their table. She was right.

As Rob and Rory started back to their mother, they noticed she was talking to someone they hadn't met yet, someone who must have just arrived. His back was to them as they walked up to their mother to meet the newcomer.

"Mom, is this another old friend that we haven't met yet?" asked Rory.

"Uh, as a matter of fact, it is," said Maddie, trying desperately to keep her composure. "Ryan, I'd like you to meet my children, Rob and Rory Conrad," whispered Maddie.

Ryan turned around and found himself looking straight at younger versions of Maddie and himself. He was so caught off guard that he stared at them wide-eyed in total disbelief, and for a brief moment, he was speechless.

Maddie tried to break the most awful moment of her life by saying, "Rob, Rory, I'd like you to meet one of my oldest and dearest friends, Ryan Richardson."

As soon as Rob and Rory saw Mom's friend, Maddie noticed, just for an instant, a look of surprise on both of their faces. They knew immediately who he was. Who was she kidding? The resemblance was just too great.

Ryan had been so surprised and caught off guard that all he could muster was, "I'm pleased to meet you both."

Rob, the older by ninety seconds, was the first to regain his composure and introduce himself. "Hi, Mr. Richardson, it's good to meet you," he said and held out his hand to greet him.

Rory followed closely behind even though the look of surprise was still on her face. "Hi, I'm Rory. It's Mom's first time back to Avalon in twenty years. What about you?"

"Uh" said Ryan, trying also to regain some of his composure, "it's my first time back, too."

Maddie could tell that both of her children immediately recognized the similarities between themselves and Ryan. Any idiot would have. All Maddie could hope for right now was that one of her children wouldn't blurt out a rude, blunt, or sarcastic remark. But even though she could see the uncertainty and questioning look in their eyes, they remained polite and engaging.

"So, you know our mom from high school?" questioned Rob.

"Yes, in fact your mother and I lived across the street from each other at the air base," replied Ryan.

"Have you taken them out to the base yet, Maddie?" asked Ryan.

"No," replied Maddie bluntly.

"Well, if it's okay with you, perhaps tomorrow we could all go out and visit our old haunts together?"

Before Maddie could think of a good excuse to say no, Rory piped in. "Why don't we, Mom? The whole point of this trip is to see where you grew up, isn't it?"

"Maybe," was all Maddie could muster.

"Rob, why don't you and Rory go and get us small plates of snacks? And, please, ask the bartender to bring us two glasses of chardonnay."

As soon as the twins were off on their errand, Ryan looked at Maddie and said immediately, "We need to talk."

"Why, Ryan?" answered Maddie with a hardness in her voice that Ryan had never heard before. "You made a decision for us many years ago. Why not just leave it at that?"

"Madison, we need to talk. In fact, I insist on it," said Ryan as gently as he could.

Maddie could see that even though they tried not to show it, everyone was watching the exchange between the two of them. But no one was about to interfere with this moment. They all new better. They were just waiting for an eruption to occur any minute. The twins returned with the snacks, then took off to visit with some of Mom's other friends once again.

"Why don't we finish our drinks, say our good-byes to the group until tomorrow, and go tell your children we're going someplace to talk?"

"What in the hell do we have to talk about?" Maddie blurted out, louder than she should have.

"Madison, not here," said Ryan as he saw everyone looking at them.

"Why not here? This is as good a place as any," Maddie answered too loudly once again.

"Mom, it's okay," said Rob. "Give me the keys, and Kelly will drive us home after the mixer is over."

"Thanks," said Ryan. "Come on, Madison; let's go talk."

Maddie grabbed her purse and said, "Fine. This shouldn't take too long. I'll see you two back at the motel," before she stormed out of the mixer.

As soon as Maddie climbed into Ryan's rental car, she proceeded to cross her legs and arms and stare out the window. She was ready for this. He wasn't going to be able to intimidate her, but she was thinking about her children. What must they be thinking and saying to each other right now? She had lied to them for fifteen years—well, not totally lied. She'd only really lied about one thing, but that one was a doozie! Would she now have to tell them the entire truth? Of course she would. They had a right to know. Could she do it? How would they react? Would they both hate her and never want to speak to her again? All of these questions kept running through her head as Ryan was driving the car.

Ryan, too, was lost in thought as he drove. Empty silence surrounded them like a dense fog. Ryan adjusted the radio, hoping to find something to relax Maddie. The minute he saw the twins, he knew they were his children; hell, everyone knew they were his. They looked just like Maddie and him. Ryan couldn't believe that Maddie hadn't told him about their children. Did she hate him that much? Well, he was angry, too. Damn it, he had a right to know. He'd never had the chance to be a father to his own children. That wasn't fair. This must have been her way of getting back at him for calling off their West Point wedding two days before it was to take place.

When Ryan finally stopped the car, he realized that he had automatically driven them to their once favorite parking spot at the reservoir. Ryan unbuckled his seat belt and turned to face Maddie, who had continued to stare out the window the entire trip and had not uttered one word. Ryan knew he would have to initiate the conversation and not appear to be angry. He knew that if he raised his voice, Maddie would clam up and not say a word—he'd learned this lesson many years ago at this very spot. He would have to be patient if he expected Maddie to tell him anything.

"Maddie, I never realized you hated me so much that you wouldn't tell me that we have children together," said Ryan quietly.

Maddie just kept staring out the window.

"Maddie?" repeated Ryan again.

"I heard you, Ryan," said Maddie as she turned to face him with sixteen years' worth of anger filling her eyes. "Hate you? I despise you for what you did! Did you honestly think I would let you bounce back into my life just because I became pregnant? You know me better than that. You didn't want me, fine. Hell would have frozen over before I told you I was pregnant. These are my children, Ryan, mine alone. As far as I'm concerned, all you did was contribute some sperm. I don't feel the least bit sorry for you and never will!" screamed Maddie at the top of her lungs, as if letting sixteen years of anguish out of her soul for the first time.

"Maddie, I had a right to know," replied Ryan quietly.

"No, no, NO, you didn't!" shouted Maddie angrily.

"Yes, I did, Maddie," said Ryan calmly. "Whose name did you put on their birth certificates as their father, or did you leave it blank?"

That question really set Maddie off. "I knew who the father of my children was, Ryan!" screamed Maddie indignantly. "I used your name, of course. I wasn't about to let my children grow up thinking that I didn't know who their father was. It wasn't as if I just slept around with anyone!" shouted Maddie.

"Calm down, Maddie. I just asked because you introduced them as Rob and Rory Conrad. Why not Richardson?"

"Oh my God, I guess you must have forgotten—we never married. So, legally, I couldn't use your name! I wouldn't have anyway even if I could. Why would I want to use your name after what you did?" replied Maddie, sarcasm dripping from her voice.

To this remark, Ryan had no answer.

"Did you ever marry?" Ryan finally asked, trying to piece together the last sixteen years of her life.

"Are you kidding? Who in their right mind would want to marry a woman with two extremely precocious and exceedingly bright twins?" Maddie laughed.

"Well, I see you have a huge rock on your left hand. That must mean that you're engaged. Who's the lucky guy?" asked Ryan curiously.

"I'm engaged to Jake Kelly."

"Oh, you two finally met up again, huh?" asked Ryan jealously.

"Yes" was all Maddie would say.

"When's the big day?"

"We haven't set a date yet." At least she didn't lie to him; no way was she going to tell him how long they'd been engaged.

"What about you, Ryan? Ever marry? Ever find the 'perfect' soldier's wife?"

"Once—a nurse. It was a mistake and only lasted eighteen months. Every time she did something, I would think to myself, *'That's not the way Maddie would do it,'* so the marriage was doomed from the start. We had no children. After that, I decided I probably wasn't the marrying kind.

"I wish I'd known I had children, Maddie, especially with you. I've never stopped loving you—never," said Ryan. "I don't think a day ever went by that I didn't wonder what you were doing, if you had married, if you were happy. I tried several times to find you; I even called Terri once to see if she knew where you were."

"Ryan, you can talk until you're blue in the face, and I won't believe a damn thing that you say. I learned that lesson the hard way a long time ago. And while I'm at it, don't think for one minute I'm going to let you into our lives now. I simply won't allow it. We don't need you, Ryan," said Maddie, her voice still seething in anger.

"How were you able to rear our children by yourself?" asked Ryan patiently.

Maddie refused to answer. It was none of his business.

"At least tell me this, Maddie. Did you ever tell the twins about their father, about me? Did they ever ask about me?"

"They're not idiots, Ryan. Of course they did. Even when they were very little, they knew their friends had daddies and they didn't. Whenever it came up, and it did, often, I told them the truth, up to a point. Their daddy and I met and fell in love in high school, and he went to West Point. The last time I saw him was at his West Point graduation. After that, he went off to war but never came back. He was a war hero—he died in Vietnam. When they were older and more mature, I told them that they'd been conceived out of love, and since I didn't have Daddy anymore, God gave me the next best thing—two of his children to love. Obviously, I didn't tell them the truth about what you'd done—it wasn't their fault, and besides, for all I knew, you did die in Vietnam," said Maddie. Then, still seething from years of anger and hurt, she hissed, "For me you died the night you graduated from West Point."

Ryan sat with his hands gripping the steering wheel, his head bowed, and tears silently streaming down his face. He couldn't believe he'd never even known he had children, much less not being able to watch them grow up. He'd always known that not marrying Madison had been the biggest mistake of his life. But this made it so much worse. His life could have been so different had he known.

Madison was not moved in the least by his despair. She didn't know if she could ever forgive him for breaking his promise to her so long ago. It wasn't as if she hadn't tried to forgive him—she had. She'd been in therapy for the first couple of years after he'd dumped her to try to get over her anger and let it go, but no matter how hard she tried, she just couldn't do it. He was the only man she'd ever loved—they had been soul mates for six years. He'd always been her officer and gentleman. And then suddenly, on one night, in an instant, everything had changed forever.

Ryan finally composed himself to speak once more. "Please tell me about our children. I want to know everything."

"I don't have to tell you anything about them. You're not a part of our lives—never have been and never will be. What I will tell you is that they were born six weeks premature on January 20, 1969. Rob is ninety seconds older than Rory."

"Well, at least tell me where you've been living all this time," said Ryan.

"I moved to California after I found out I was pregnant with twins. Since my sister lives there, I decided that this was where I wanted to live and rear my children," replied Maddie in a calmer voice.

Before Ryan had a chance to ask her any other questions about the twins, Maddie demanded "Ryan, just take me back to the motel. I knew I shouldn't have come back here. We've nothing else to discuss. I'm done talking."

"You really hate me so much that you won't tell me about my own children?"

"You got it! Now let's get the hell out of here or I'll walk—your choice."

Ryan knew that Maddie would open the car door in a minute, so he started the car. Neither of them spoke during the ride back to the Ramada Inn.

When they reached the motel and before Maddie could get out of the car, Ryan decided to ask her about going to the base the next morning.

"Maddie, you've made it perfectly clear how you feel about me, but I think I deserve to spend at least one day with the children I've never known. Would you at least agree for us to go to breakfast, the air base, and let me spend a day with them?" begged Ryan.

"I don't think that would be a very good idea," replied Maddie immediately.

"Madison, all I'm asking for is one day, please."

"Oh, all right—one day. Be here at 9:00 AM." With that Maddie slammed the door and went inside.

46

E ven though Madison had agreed to spend the next day with Ryan and their teenagers, she was lying. The minute the twins returned from the mixer, they were all leaving.

As soon as she reached their rooms, she started tossing clothes into all of their suitcases so that they'd be ready to go. Once Rob and Rory returned and realized immediately that they were leaving, Rob was the first to ask his mother what was going on.

"What does it look like? We're leaving. Come on, pick up your suitcases. We're already checked out," said their mother.

"Why?" exclaimed Rory.

"Because I said so. I knew it was a mistake to come back here in the first place. Let's go."

Even though the twins wanted to stay, they knew by the sound of their mother's voice, it was a done deal. They reluctantly followed her to the car. The moment they were on the road, Rob decided it was time to ask the question that Maddie knew would be coming.

"Ryan Richardson is our real father, isn't he?" asked Rob.

All Maddie could do was bite her tongue and say "We'll talk about it when we get home and not a minute before,"

While Madison and the twins were on their way back to Oklahoma City, Ryan was lying in bed, unable to sleep. He was not only excited but also a little apprehensive about the upcoming day. He was anxious to get to know his children—the ones he ever knew existed until last night.

Ryan arrived at the Ramada Inn exactly at 9:00 AM the next morning, went up to the receptionist, and asked her to call Madison Conrad's room to let her know he was in the lobby. The answer that came out of her mouth stunned him.

"I'm sorry, sir, but Ms. Conrad and her children left last night.

At this moment, Maddie and her kids were at the airport in Oklahoma City. They had first-class tickets on the 11:00 AM flight to San Francisco, but Maddie didn't want to wait that long. She knew it might give Ryan time to find them, so she headed for a pay phone and called Jake.

Sobbing, she told Jake briefly what had happened, and that she'd refused to discuss it with the kids until they could talk to them together. She also told him that the next flight wasn't until 11:00 AM.

"Maddie, take a cab to Wiley Post Airport. I'll make arrangements, and there will be a plane waiting to bring you home. Don't worry about it, just go," said Jake gently.

"Okay," was all she could muster.

As soon as Jake hung up the phone, he arranged for a private plane to meet her at Wiley Post air field. He knew that his plan had exploded in his face.

Jake arrived early at the Vallejo airport to meet Maddie and the kids. Ever since she'd called him, all he could think of was the mess he'd created. He should have just kept his mouth shut about the "pact." He couldn't blame Maddie for what had happened. It was his fault entirely. Now, they were going to have to tell their teenagers the truth. Jake decided that since he was the one who had caused the mess, he'd be the one to fix it.

When Jake finally saw Maddie walking towards him, his heart was breaking. He could only imagine what she'd been through. As soon as Maddie reached him, he put his arms around her and hugged and kissed her. She immediately started to sob.

"Honey, everything will be okay. I promise," Jake said softly in her ear. Then he hugged Rob and Rory. "Come on; let's get out of here." They grabbed their baggage and headed for the car.

The ride home was very quiet; no one spoke. It was as if each of them was in his own world. Maddie wept softly during the entire trip. Once they arrived home, the twins went directly to their rooms, and Maddie picked up her aging Peke-A-Poo, Tinker, and held her close to her chest. Meanwhile, Jake poured Maddie a glass of wine, and they went to their bedroom.

"Honey, I'm so sorry about what happened. Are you up to talking about it now, or do you want to rest for a while and just wait until tomorrow?" asked Jake tenderly.

Maddie blurted out, "Oh my God, Jake, it was absolutely the worst day of my life. I didn't think he was coming since he didn't arrive until the mixer was almost over. As soon as he saw the twins, he knew they were his—hell, everyone knew. They look so much like both of us. I don't know who I thought I'd be kidding.

"As soon as Ryan got over the shock of meeting the twins, he insisted that the two of us go talk," continued Maddie.

"What did he say, honey?"

"Well, of course, he wanted to know all about his children, but I just couldn't make myself tell him. I was still angry after all these years, and he knew it. We were all supposed to go out to breakfast, then out to the air base and spend the day together. But I couldn't do it—I just couldn't! So, when the kids arrived back from the mixer, I insisted we leave and told them we'd talk things over when we got home. Oh, Jake, it's all my fault, and I don't know if Rob and Rory will ever forgive me. I know Ryan won't. You were right all those years ago when you told me I should tell him, but after what he did to me, I couldn't do it—not after what he'd done to us and our future. I wanted him to hurt as much as he'd hurt me," said Maddie tearfully.

"Well, all we can do now is tell them the truth," replied Jake, holding Maddie in his arms.

"When do you think we should talk to them?" asked Maddie.

"The sooner, the better. Let's do it now and get it over with if you're up to it," answered Jake.

"All right. Let's all meet in the den, and I'll talk to them," said Maddie.

Jake went and asked his teenagers to come to the den immediately. Their mother and he wanted to talk to them. As soon as everyone was together, Jake was the first to speak.

"Your mother wants to explain everything to you. Please have the courtesy to let her tell you her story in her own way before you make any judgments or ask questions."

While Maddie was busy trying to explain what she had done to the twins, Ryan was on a plane headed for DC. He was furious over what Maddie had done. He'd already decided that when he got back, he was going to ask the general to pull some strings and get him stationed in California, perhaps the Presidio since it was sort of in the middle of the state. He was going to do some investigating and find out where Maddie and his children were living. He planned to get to know his children one way or another. He hoped Maddie would come to her senses and say okay, but if she didn't, he knew he could legally get permission to see them. That would be a hassle, though, and would make Maddie even angrier, so he'd talk to Jake Kelly first, if needed.

When Ryan arrived home that evening, he unpacked, showered, and went to bed, but he couldn't sleep. He kept thinking about how beautiful Maddie was and about his children. It amazed him how much they looked just like Maddie and him at that age. He thought Maddie—and yes, Jake—had done a great job of parenting. His children seemed extremely intelligent, athletic, and personable. He knew Maddie was afraid they'd be rude or angry when they met, but she had taught them well. *God knows what's going on at their house right now,* thought Ryan. He knew that Maddie would have to tell them the secret she'd kept from them for so long.

In the meantime, after Maddie, Jake, Rob, and Rory settled in the den, Maddie took a large gulp of wine before she began to speak. For her, this was going to be the hardest thing she ever had to do.

Maddie sat on the arm of the overstuffed couch and looked and slowly looked in to the eyes of each twin. Her eyes blurred with tears and her words were soft, loving and halting. Madie spoke quietly, because she wished this day had never had to come. "I've dreaded this moment since the day you were born— never have known how I'd tell you the truth about your father—always told you what I thought you could understand as kids—."

She, took another sip, and then continued, "It all began in high school. This handsome boy moved in across the street—he was a football player and I was a cheerleader. On our first date, I *knew* he was the one," she smiled. "We went steady our junior and senior years and planned to get married right after college."

The twins didn't say a word, but their eyes said, *Tell us more.*

"You know I went to a small college in Wilmington, Oklahoma, but Ryan was accepted to West Point—that's in New York…" she rambled.

"Yeah, Mom," said Rob, "not too far from New York City."

"…and I only saw him a few times during those years. But, every time we were together, it was like we'd never been apart. We loved each other and made plans to get married at the West Point chapel after he graduated in June of 1968."

Maddie told them, "It was horrific when Ryan's father died in combat, but right before his funeral, he proposed and gave me an engagement ring. My mother had passed away about three months earlier. I guess we just weakened from the stress. We had waited so long and, up to that point, we'd never really made love—but, that night, it just seemed—right. We thought we were going to be together forever."

Oh, God, she thought. *I can't believe I'm talking about sex with my babies.*

Changing the subject, she said, "We were so excited about getting married. All the arrangements were made; the flowers, the cake, my beautiful dress, the Old Chapel at West Point—our friends and family members had made the long trip for the occasion."

"We were so in love. We'd waited six years, for this. We'd put it off to go to college, endured many family hardships, and now it was just hours away. Your father and I went to my motel room and made passionate love—it seemed, for hours. We lay there, exhausted and very happy. Then, he told me he didn't feel right about getting married before he went to Vietnam. He was worried that he would be killed or wounded and wouldn't be able to be the husband I expected... or something like that. I didn't understand. I went crazy. I screamed at him and said I'd waited long enough. If he wasn't willing to marry me now, he never would. And—oh, I can't believe I'm saying this, I was so hurt and so angry that I put all of my things back into my car and drove back to Oklahoma."

As Maddie took another drink, she felt the weight of years of lies and deception lifting off her shoulders.

Tears flew from her eyes and she burst out, "A few months later, I discovered I was pregnant with you two. Of course, Ryan was your father—he was the only man I ever made love with. You truly were 'love children,' but, I was terrified. In those days, unmarried women just didn't have babies. Even though Ryan didn't want me, I wanted you. I loved you. Abortion was never a real option."

"Mom, ..." said Rory.

"I'm not done," Maddie interrupted. She took another sip and glance at Jake. He just smiled and gave a reassuring nod.

"I was afraid that Ryan would find out and try to make me marry him. I wasn't going to marry a man who simply felt sorry for me, so I decided to move to Napa to be near your Aunt Mimi. I didn't tell anyone except my best friend Terri, and I swore her to secrecy. I didn't even tell my dearest friend, Jake."

She looked Jake in the eyes and said, "Oh, God, Jake. I'm so sorry I did that. So sorry I couldn't tell you."

"I know, sweetheart," he replied softly.

"This man is so wonderful," she said sincerely. "I was probably in love with him for years, but I was still so angry with your father, and so afraid, that I just couldn't see it."

She took another sip and laughed, "You know, it took Jake about six months to pry the secret from Terri. Then he moved out here, got a job at Vallejo High and bought this wonderful house. On Christmas Day of 1969, it became our home and Jake really became your Dad."

Maddie was emotionally exhausted, but the twins were exhilarated by finally knowing what they had suspected was true.

They turned to Jake and said, "We love you, Dad."

Now it was Jake's turn to get misty-eyed.

Maddie stood up and stepped a little closer to the twins. "The reunion was the first time I'd seen Ryan since you were conceived. It was the first time he knew we had children. It was solely my choice not to tell him, but now he knows and wants to get to know you. That's your choice, and I won't interfere or be upset if you do."

She sighed and took a last gulp of her wine. "Do you have any questions?"

Of course they did. Rob asked, "Whose name did you put down on our birth certificates as our father?"

"Ryan's, of course," answered Maddie.

"What was he doing in the Army?" asked Rory.

"Well, Ryan chose to go into the Infantry. That meant that he would be a soldier on the ground during the Vietnam War. I wanted him to choose Armor, because I didn't want him to be in the jungle all the time, but ultimately it was his decision, and it scared me to death," replied Maddie.

"So, he went to Vietnam?" asked Rob.

"I assume he did. Basically, all Infantry from West Point went there," said his mother.

"Is he married?" asked Rory.

"No, he isn't."

"Where does he live now?" she continued.

"Well, right now, he's stationed at the Pentagon in Washington, DC."

Jake interrupted and said as far as he was concerned, he was their father and had been for the last fifteen years. He and Maddie had tried to give them all the opportunities and advantages they could. He also told them that he had been in love with their mother for twenty years, and they might finally be getting married in the near future.

"It's about time, Dad," said Rob with a smile on his face.

Rory chimed in. "We know you're our dad and how much you love Mom, so I agree: it's about time."

"Well, the last twenty-four hours have been a tremendous strain on all of us," said Jake as he kissed Maddie.

"I don't know about you guys, but I'm tired and going to bed. We'll talk more in the morning. All you two need to know is that your mother did what she thought was best for you. Your happiness has always been her main concern, and I have, and always will, support her decisions," said Jake as he kissed Maddie.

About the same time that Maddie had finished her story, Ryan was getting ready for bed in DC and thinking to himself that everything that had happened had really been his fault. *Why in the hell did I have the audacity to ask Maddie to wait two more years just two days before our wedding? What in the hell was I thinking? No wonder she hates him so much,* Ryan thought before finally drifting off to sleep for a couple of hours.

The next morning, he went to his friend and boss, General Perry, the man who had helped him so much during his recuperation after he'd been injured. He asked him to get him stationed at the Presidio as soon as possible. The general asked why it was so urgent, and Ryan told him that he just found out he had a set of twins and went on to tell his friend the entire story. The general was dumbfounded. He'd always thought that Ryan was married to the Army and asked him what had happened.

"Son, how in the world could you have done that to this woman and let her get away? Of all the West Point men I've known you're the last one I would have ever expected to do something like this. Two days before the wedding? I don't believe it. That young lady would have stood by you through anything. How could you ever let her get away?"

"I know I was an arrogant fool" replied Ryan, choking back tears. "Believe me, I've regretted it all my life. But now, I need to be near my children."

General Perry told his friend he'd get his aide on it right away, and he'd probably know if they had a spot for him there by the next day. Ryan shook his hand and thanked him before he left.

Ryan went back to his office, shut the door, and started thinking about how he could find out where Maddie was living in California. He decided that the easiest way would be to hire a private investigator. The man he chose was well worth the $750 he'd paid him. She lived in Napa, California, and he'd even obtained their unlisted phone number. The Presidio was just across the bay from her.

Two weeks after that fateful day in June, Ryan called Madison. She'd been expecting—and yes, dreading—the call.

"Hello," said Maddie.

"Hi, Madison, it's Ryan. I want to let you know that I'm being transferred to the Presidio and should be settled in by the end of July. I'd like to see my children. I'm hoping you'll agree, but if you don't, I'll have no other choice but to go to court and get my visitation rights."

"That won't be necessary, Ryan. I've told our twins the entire story, and I'm sure they'd enjoy getting to know you. Call as soon as you get settled and we'll make arrangements, all right?" Maddie replied.

"That'll be great. I'll call you soon...and Maddie, thank you for not making this difficult for any of us. I really appreciate it. See you soon."

47

Once Ryan started to see his children on a regular basis, Maddie's initial indifference to him started to change. She finally apologized to Ryan for not telling him about his children. It had been her way of getting revenge for what he'd done to her. A part of her died on June 5, 1968, a part of her that she could never regain no matter how hard she'd tried. He had truly broken her heart. But after Maddie finally admitted her mistake, her old feelings for Ryan started to resurface. She didn't want them to, but she couldn't help it.

One afternoon, when they were alone, Ryan took her on a picnic. He took her to his favorite spot at the Presidio. It was exquisite. It overlooked the bay, and they could see for miles.

All of a sudden Ryan blurted out, "You know, I still love you, Maddie. I broke my own heart and have suffered for it for sixteen years, but I've never stopped loving you. How do you feel?" asked Ryan.

"I honestly don't know. I'm torn. You were my first love but Jake has been my second, and he's stood by me through every single event in my life, even when you were at West Point. And before you ask, no, Jake and I didn't make love until the twins were almost a year old. I was never unfaithful to you—never. What about you?"

"Maddie, the first time I had sex with someone other than you was right before my second tour in Vietnam. I've had sex with only a few women in my life, but I always compared them to you, even when I was married to my ex-wife," answered Ryan honestly.

He then rolled over on top of Maddie and kissed her passionately like he used to. It seemed as if sixteen years of both passion and regret were wound together in that kiss. Even though she knew she shouldn't, Maddie kissed him back just as passionately. Then they just held each other, both of them knowing where this could lead, and both of them knowing it couldn't.

"Oh God, Maddie, I'm so sorry. I made such a huge mistake. Please forgive me, please," cried Ryan.

Maddie wiped away his tears, which were mingled with her own. "Ryan, I loved you so much for so long. Even when I hated you, I still loved you. That's the only reason I didn't have an abortion. I wanted those babies because at least then I'd always have a part of you," cried Maddie. "A day didn't go by that I didn't think of you. How could it? I've seen you in our children ever since the day they were born."

"So, what's the answer for us? What can be done to undo all the years of heartache," asked Ryan desperately.

"I'm not sure anything can be done. Jake's been a part of my life for twenty-one years. I can't hurt him. I won't hurt him. He's always been there for me, for us," replied Maddie earnestly.

"I know he's been the husband and father I wasn't. I don't want you to hurt him either. That's not fair to him. But what about us? Doesn't our happiness count for something, too?"

"Ryan, I love you both. I always will no matter what happens. But I won't walk away from Jake on a whim. He's too good a man, and I owe him too much. I just won't do it until I've had time to think things through and find out if the 'real' Ryan, my Ryan, even exists anymore. I've always been a one-man woman, and that will never change," replied Maddie emphatically.

"I understand," said Ryan.

"No, I don't think you do. When I saw you for the first time at the reunion after all those years, the first thing I noticed were your beautiful dark brown eyes. I saw a hardness in them I'd never seen before. Everything else about you was the same, but not your eyes," replied Maddie.

"War and pain take their toll on people, Maddie. Sometimes it never goes away. I've never spoken to anyone about those years in Vietnam even though sometimes I still have nightmares and wake up in the middle of the night with sweats. I'll tell you about it if you really want to know, though," said Ryan.

"I don't, at least not yet." Maddie continued, "Ryan, I've had years to come to terms with the fact that for the last twenty-one years, you've been married to the Army. I guess I knew that was the way it would always be with us...the Army first, me second. I won't play second fiddle to anyone, not even the Army. That's why I need time to find out if the 'real' Ryan still exists in you."

During their talks, Ryan began to open up and tell Maddie of his life in the Army. After Vietnam, he went to Harvard on the Army's dime and then taught at his old alma mater, West Point, for four years. He was a captain when he began and a major by the time he decided to leave. He also spent time in Brussels at NATO headquarters. He was an aide de camp to a four-star general who represented the U.S. Joint Chiefs of Staff on the NATO Military Committee. While stationed there, he wrote speeches for the general and helped arrange his daily schedule, social activities, dinner parties, and travel schedules. In other words, he was the general's "numero uno" go-to guy. His verbal background had seemed to pay off far more than all the math he was forced to take in college. While in Europe, he traveled to many countries, such as Italy, Germany, Norway, and France, but it was Turkey that he'd found the most interesting. When Ryan told her about all the traveling he did in Europe, Maddie became wistful— she and Jake had offered to take the twins to Europe last summer, but they had turned them down. Maybe someday she'd get back to Cambridge, England, where she had lived as a child.

Ryan's service in Vietnam did eventually come up one day while they were at their special spot. He explained to Maddie about all the schools he attended before ever going to Vietnam. In fact, he didn't leave for Vietnam until June of 1969. He finally opened up for the first time to anyone in his life about his time there and when his unit was hit. He described to her how he was injured. He even told her how hard it was to overcome his injuries, both physically and psychologically. He left nothing out. Maddie was horrified. What he told her actually made her sick to her stomach. For weeks after this conversation, Maddie couldn't sleep. It was as if she was in that terrible place with Ryan, or at least that she should've been there to be a part of his recovery. He'd been alone when he needed her the most.

"Why did you volunteer to go back? I want to know your reasoning," said Maddie.

"Honey, I had no one waiting for me. I was single and needed to go back to prove to myself that I was a good soldier." He then explained to her why he felt it was his fault that his men and he were hurt.

Each time Maddie and Ryan met, she would find herself drawing closer to Ryan, understanding where he'd been and where he was going. She felt that much of his personal pain and anguish had ultimately been her fault. If she had agreed to wait, both of their lives would have been so different. Maddie became increasingly haunted by the idea that all of this was her fault even though Ryan always told her it wasn't. But she just couldn't shake the feeling. In fact, she started having nightmares about his being in Vietnam.

"I understand what you're saying, Maddie; I really do. The same thing occurred when some of my soldiers were injured with me. The nightmares really took their toll on me."

He also told Maddie that he understood how torn she must be between Jake and him. He wasn't in any hurry. He'd waited this long to be close to her again; he told her she could take as long as she needed.

At the beginning of May, the twins were told that they would be co-valedictorians of their graduating class. They couldn't wait to get home and tell their parents, and then they called Ryan. Ryan was over the moon. He asked to speak to their mother, so they readily handed the phone to her.

"Maddie, can you believe it? I'm almost speechless at this point. Is there any way I can be part of their celebration?" asked Ryan carefully.

"Of course you can. I've always said they got your brains and my looks."

"Uh, we both know that's not true, about the brain part I mean. You've always been just as smart as I, only in different areas."

"Yes. Me—language, you—math," replied Maddie, sounding like an Indian chief.

"You and Jake have done such a marvelous job with our children. I'll never be able to thank you enough."

"Well, you had a part in it, too."

"I love you, Madison," whispered Ryan.

"I know," replied Maddie. "I'll let you know about the celebration. We'll probably take the twins into the city for dinner on Saturday night. Of course, we'll want you to come."

"Let me make the arrangements, okay?" asked Ryan. "My treat."

"That's a great idea. Just let us know when, where, and what time, okay?"

"I'll call back with the info in the middle of the week. Will Jake be upset?"

"I don't think so, but even if he is, I don't care. They are your children, too," replied Maddie seriously.

After Maddie hung up the phone, she told Jake about Ryan wanting to take them all out to celebrate Rory's and Rob's accomplishments. He would make all the arrangements. If it was all right with Jake, they'd be going into the city on Saturday night.

Jake said it would be fine, but Maddie instantly sensed something was bothering him. She poured the two of them some wine and suggested they go outside and talk. Once there, they settled into their comfy wicker rocking chairs, Maddie asked Jake what was bothering him.

His answer didn't surprise her. She'd been expecting it. "I guess I just feel like I'm being replaced. I know I'm not, but I do," said Jake sadly.

"Honey, nobody in this world can replace you. You are the twins' father. You're the one who taught them to swim, throw a ball, ride their bikes; you wiped their tears when they fell. You have been the one constant in their lives. The twins just want to get to know their biological father. That's normal, too. In fact, we're very lucky, because they could've become very angry with us for not telling them about Ryan, but they didn't. We should be grateful that the situation has turned out so well. It easily could have gone the other way. We should be happy, joyous even. I am," said Maddie gently as she rose from her chair and sat on Jake's lap.

"I know, honey. It's just hard for me having to share you and the twins with Ryan."

"You're not sharing me with Ryan, Jake. Whatever gave you that idea?" asked a surprised Maddie.

"I just remember how much you were in love with him, and I guess I feel that you still are."

"Jake, I will always love Ryan on some level. He gave me the twins. But I don't love him the way I love you. You are my rock, my man. I love you," said Maddie as she put her arms around his neck and kissed him.

"Let's go to bed," Maddie whispered in his ear while at the same time taking his hand.

Upstairs behind closed doors, Maddie lit the fireplace and some candles. Then she and Jake showered together, throwing soap at each other, laughing the entire time. He then was able to do one of his favorite things in the shower with Maddie—wash her wonderfully curly hair.

After they had showered and dried each other off, they threw all the bed pillows onto the floor in front of the fireplace. Then they lay down together. They were both very comfortable being nude in front of each other. Maddie rolled over on top of Jake and kissed him deeply.

"You have no idea how much I love you, Jake. I know I take you for granted, and I'm sorry. I know I count on you too much, too," said Maddie lovingly.

"I know you love me, honey. I'm just afraid I'm going to lose you. I couldn't stand that. We've been together for so long. I know I told you I'd never ask you, but I have to. Why won't you marry me?" replied Jake softly.

"Jake, not marrying you has nothing to do with not loving you. You know my goal has always been to see the twins graduate from high school. They have been my responsibility since the day they were conceived," replied Maddie.

"They're going to graduate in a few weeks, Maddie. Will you be ready then?"

"Probably."

With that Maddie and Jake made love the slow and tender way they always had. They knew each other so well—what each of them liked and how to arouse each other to the greatest heights of human pleasure. Some women let their husbands have sex with them out of habit, not necessarily because they wanted to, but Maddie had never been that way with Jake. In fact, she probably initiated sex with him as much, if not more, than he did. Maddie could never get enough of feeling one with him. And, tonight, she made it a point to tell him so.

After they made love, Jake told Maddie to tell Ryan they'd be happy to attend the celebration of their twins' achievements.

"Are you sure?" asked Maddie. "We won't do it if you don't want to."

"I'm sure, my love."

After the twins graduated from Napa High School as co-valedictorians, they had the entire summer to relax before leaving for Stanford in the fall. Maddie and Jake had offered to take them to Europe for a month again, but the twins decided that perhaps they'd go next summer instead. Jake and Maddie completely understood the fact that they just wanted to relax and hang out at home with their friends before they all went their separate ways.

Rory and Rob enjoyed spending time with their real father and getting to know him, but they asked their parents if it bothered them too much. Of course, Maddie and Jake couldn't say yes.

Sometimes the twins would drive to the Presidio and visit their father. Ryan tried to explain his relationship with their mother to them. He took full responsibility for what had happened to them. However, he did explain he had tried to find her.

Whenever the twins asked him about Vietnam, they always noticed that their father seemed as though he was in another world. He didn't tell them about the horrors of this senseless war that killed over 58,000 men, including their grandfather. He did offer to take them to Washington, DC, and give them a tour of the city and show them their grandfather's name on The Wall. The two of them really wanted to go, so they said they'd ask their parents.

It was obvious to Rory and Rob that their father was still in love with their mother. Surely, she had to sense it, too. How did she feel about their real father after all of these years? They decided they were going to ask her when the time was right. They needed to know how she felt.

Maddie and Jake were shocked when the twins told their parents that they wanted to go back to Washington, DC, with Ryan. They'd offered Europe and they'd said no. Now, they wanted to spend two weeks in DC with Ryan. Their parents asked them why. Their answer was simple. They wanted to learn more about their father. They felt a "need" to get to know him. Maddie and Jake told them they'd talk it over and let them know.

When Maddie Jake talked it over, they weren't at all happy about the idea; however, they could understand why. Maddie told Jake that she knew it was all her fault. She'd made a huge mistake by not telling Ryan about the twins and running away. Maddie was taking this "trip" idea much harder than Jake. Jake was always the steady one. He wasn't happy either, but there was nothing he could do about it. And he knew it. He didn't blame his children; they were just curious. What worried him the most was losing Maddie. He never asked her, though, because he was afraid of what her answer might be.

Maddie, on the other hand, didn't know how she felt about Ryan, even now. She just tried to avoid thinking about him. But, yes, she had to admit to herself it was difficult. She could also tell that the twins wanted to ask her about Ryan. She was waiting for them to approach her about their father and how she felt. She didn't know when the conversation would take place; she just knew that it would, and Maddie had absolutely no idea how she was going to respond when the time came.

In the end, Maddie and Jake allowed the twins to go to Washington, DC, with their father for two weeks. What were they going to do alone for two weeks? They'd never had two weeks alone together in fifteen years.

The night before the twins were scheduled to leave for DC with Ryan, Jake went into their rooms to see them while they were packing.

"Do you remember the game we've always played ever since both of you were little—whenever I was going to surprise your mother and take her away for a long weekend, just the two of us?" asked Jake brightly.

"Of course we do. It has always been our 'little secret,'" exclaimed Rory.

"Where are you taking Mom?" asked Rob happily.

"Well, I'm going to take her to Hawaii while you two are gone. Do you think she'll like it?"

"What? Are you kidding, Dad? She'll be blown away! What a great idea. We know Mom isn't too keen on our going to DC with Ryan, so this will be a welcome treat for her," answered Rory excitedly.

Jake gave them a piece of paper of where they'd be staying, phone numbers—everything they'd need if they needed to contact them for any reason. He also reminded them that it was still their "little secret." Maddie knew nothing about it yet.

"Don't be surprised if your mother calls you while you're gone. I know she has misgivings about this trip of yours. She'll want to check in on you both. You know your mother," Jake told them.

"Yep, we know Mom, and no, we won't even ask where you guys are unless she says something. Okay, Dad?" replied Rob. "Besides, you both need a break, too."

"I won't disagree with that," said Jake. "Okay, well, you know where we'll be if you need us. You two have a great time."

As he was turning to leave, Rory came up to him, kissed him on the cheek, and said, "Dad, we love you. You know that, don't you? This has nothing to do with that. You always have been and always will be our dad."

"I know, but I'd be lying if I didn't say this is bothering me." With that he left the room and went to see Maddie.

Upon returning to the master suite, Jake shouted, "Pack a swimsuit, Maddie. We're going on a trip!"

The twins had a wonderful time in Washington, DC. Since Ryan had been stationed at the Pentagon for several years, he knew every inch of the city. He was even able to get them into the Pentagon for a visit. He went to see his old friend and mentor, General Perry. He was extremely proud to introduce his children to him.

The twins spent hours in the Smithsonian once again, and the monuments were more impressive the second time around, because their father could give them all of the details about them.

The day the twins visited The Wall was a very somber and emotional one for all three of them. Ryan had been there many times before, recognizing the names of fellow graduates and soldiers who had died before their time. Today, Ryan brought paper and pencils with him so that the twins could each make a rubbing of their grandfather's name. Both of the twins took the task very seriously and wanted to make sure that their rubbings were perfect. Ryan couldn't help it; his eyes filled with tears while they were so intently engaged in their task. These rubbings would become one of their prized possessions in the years to come. Ryan had already told them about their grandfather's plane crash in Laos, so they knew they wouldn't find his grave at Arlington when they visited. That really disappointed them—not as much as it did Ryan, though.

One their way back to California, Ryan and the twins made a stop for a couple of days in Ohio. They met their real grandmother and other relatives for the first time. Their time there, while enjoyable, seemed surreal. They were being introduced to the family they had never known existed until now. Ryan, on the other hand, was so proud of his children. Of course, it was Maddie who was their mother. One only had to look at Rory to see that. He told his mother once again that she'd been right that morning at breakfast so many years ago. She'd never agreed with his last-minute decision, but she was totally enthralled with the grandchildren she had never met until now. They were truly gifted, and both of them were delightful young people. *Maddie has done a good job,* she thought to herself. In the fall, they were both headed to Stanford on full scholarships. She was one proud grandmother!

The two weeks seemed to go by too quickly for the three of them. They had seen and done so much that it would take each of them time to digest what had happened on the trip. The one decision the three of them made, however, was that there would be more trips for them in the future.

48

While the twins were gone, Jake and Maddie were island-hopping in Hawaii, having the time of their lives. Jake had never seen Maddie happier. It was the first time that she had actually allowed herself to relax in a long time. During the day, they sometimes lay on the beach, drinking tropical fruit drinks. Maddie was getting a fantastic tan already. When she put on her white bikini, Jake felt he'd died and gone to Heaven, and this gorgeous woman belonged to him. He was so proud of her.

At night, the two of them would go out for a nice dinner, perhaps a little dancing, or a little shopping. Every night, though, ended with a walk on the beach together hand in hand. Then they'd would go back to their suite overlooking the water and make love with the windows open in the moonlight. It was like the honeymoon they'd never had.

Maddie and Jake had needed this vacation. They rode bikes and even took surfboarding lessons. They rode Jet Skis and even rented a sailboat. They were like kids in a candy store. They wanted to try it all. Anyone who saw them could tell how much in love they were.

One night, early during their visit, Jake surprised Maddie while at dinner. He handed her a small black box. Before she opened it, however, he said, "Madison, I know we don't have that piece of paper, but I've been holding onto this piece of jewelry for far too long. I wish you'd agree to wear it. It'd make me very happy."

When Maddie opened the box, she saw the wedding bands that completed her magnificent engagement ring. The rings were two pieces. Each piece surrounded her engagement ring. Each piece had been made especially for Maddie's ring, and each piece was a circle of diamonds and sapphires that fit around her engagement ring perfectly. Maddie couldn't believe what she was seeing.

"How long have you had this, Jake?"

"Ever since we became engaged, about thirteen years ago."

"Honey, of course, I'll wear them. We've been husband and wife for many years now, right?"

"Right," answered Jake, as he helped Maddie put the rings together. When her engagement ring was surrounded by the wedding bands, the look was breathtaking. Both Jake and Maddie started to cry.

All of a sudden, Madison looked at Jake and said, "Honey, let's get married here on the beach in Hawaii. What do you think?"

"Are you sure you're ready, Maddie? If so, we'll do it while we're here. But I don't want you to feel pressured and regret it later," replied Jake in total shock. He'd been waiting to hear those words for so many years now that it almost seemed unbelievable it was really going to happen.

"I'm positive, Jake. I've loved you for many years, you know that. But for some stupid reason, I felt that the twins were my responsibility—mine alone—and it was up to me to get them to college. Well, they're there, so I feel free. Yes, I want to be your wife more than you'll ever know," said Maddie.

"Okay, honey, we'll do it and get our license tomorrow."

That night, when they made love, Jake called her Mrs. Jake Kelly for the very first time. Maddie told him how much she liked that sound—Mrs. Jake Kelly.

The next morning, they went and obtained the license. Then they picked out a wedding band for Jake. He wanted a simple gold one, but it had to be sturdy. They finally ended up with one that had a deep herring bone design engraved in it. A plain gold one would have scratched too easily when Jake taught weight training.

Next, Maddie quickly found a strapless wedding dress with a full skirt and a bustle all the way down the back; attached to that was a huge bow. She looked stunning in it. Of course, she wouldn't let Jake see it until the next day. Meanwhile, Jake found a pastor to bless their union the next evening at sunset.

Maddie put on her dress and her headdress, which was a circle of plumeria flowers with ribbon flowing down her hair. Her only jewelry was what Jake had given her over the years. When she finally came out, Jake just stared at her. She was the most beautiful woman he'd ever seen. Jake came up to her in his rented tuxedo and kissed his wife-to-be while handing her a bouquet of plumerias, blush roses, and lilacs.

"Are you ready to become Mrs. Jake Kelly?"

"Absolutely!" declared Maddie happily. She took Jake's hand, and they left the hotel and went to the beach where the pastor and two witnesses they didn't even know were waiting.

The ceremony itself took about twenty minutes, but it was the most wonderful twenty minutes of Jake's life. Maddie, too, was happy, but the ghost of Ryan still seemed to haunt her a little. Afterwards, they immediately returned to their hotel where Jake had ordered a special room-service dinner for them.

"I can't believe I'm a married woman," announced Maddie as Jake was lifting her up and twirling her around.

"I've been waiting a long time to call you my wife, Mrs. Jake Kelly," said Jake happily. "You will never know how much I love you, Madison."

That night when they made love, the fact that they were truly a married couple, made it even more special. Jake took a great deal of time getting Maddie ready to legally consummate their marriage.

After they finished making love, Jake asked Maddie if she wanted to call the twins and tell them the good news. But Maddie said no. She wanted the two of them to tell them together when they got home. Maddie also told him that she was the one who had to tell Ryan about her decision.

After Maddie and Jake made love, she had a difficult time trying to sleep. No, she wasn't thinking about Ryan— she was thinking about Jake. Jake truly was her soul mate. They'd been together for so many years and he'd taught her what real love was all about. Jake had made her a woman.

Before that, she really was just a child trying, but failing, to be an adult. He'd always been so steadfast in his love—never wavering, even when Ryan had re-entered their lives. He'd always been her best friend and confidante. She knew her decision to marry him today had been the right one. In fact, she'd been stupid to wait so long—but it had been worth it. She didn't know what she'd do if she ever lost him. He was her rock. After thinking about how lucky she was a while longer, and thanking God for giving Jake to her, she finally slept.

Rob and Rory were already home when Jake and Maddie arrived from Hawaii. The twins could tell that their parents had enjoyed their much-needed vacation. They both looked happy, relaxed, and rested. They both had great tans, and their mother's hair had lighter streaks in it from the sun.

Maddie asked Rob and Rory to meet them in the living room where she and Jake were holding a bottle of champagne.

"What are we celebrating?" asked Rory as soon as she saw the bottle.

"Well, your dad and I have something special to tell you and wanted you two to be the first to know. We got married in Hawaii!" exclaimed Maddie happily. Then she and Jake held out their left hands and showed them their rings.

"Oh my God, you guys finally did the deed! It's about time; I didn't think I'd ever live to see this day," said Rob as he kissed both his mother and father.

Rory seemed equally as happy for them, but the truth be told, she was a little disappointed that her mom and Ryan hadn't gotten back together.

Once they drank their champagne, Maddie explained to the twins that she didn't want them to say anything to Ryan. It was her place to tell him—in her own way and in her own time.

That day came sooner rather than later. Unknown to Jake, Maddie and Ryan had continued seeing each other even after the twins had graduated and were off at Stanford. They would only meet on Saturday afternoons during football season. Jake was now the head football coach, as well as the athlete director, so he was busier than ever. Besides, his team was headed for the playoffs again this year.

On this particular Saturday, Ryan knew immediately that something had changed. He saw the ring on Maddie's finger and knew. He lifted her hand and said, "I see you married Jake."

"Yes, in Hawaii," was all Maddie said. "Ryan, I wanted to be the one to tell you myself. I love you both. I always have and always will, but Jake has always been there for me. Even when we were in college, when my mother and your father died, he was my go-to guy. You weren't around. I had no way to reach you, except through letters, a few phone calls, and a few visits. You were always too busy playing soldier. You bought into the West Point propaganda machine hook, line, and sinker. I guess I knew that I'd never be number one in your life. You'd be married to the Army. Every time we met, you were a little more gung ho soldier and a little less the Ryan I'd known and loved. But I'd decided that I loved you enough to play second fiddle. Then, in an instant, you changed my entire world. That was unfair and you know it. We probably would've made it Ryan, but you decided that I should wait some more. I had absolutely no input in the decision. When you said that, I was done. It was over."

At that moment, all Ryan could think of was that the only woman he'd ever loved was now legally married to someone else. Maddie had always made it clear to Ryan that she wouldn't have an affair with him. She'd actually considered it, but ultimately she wouldn't do it because of Jake. Ryan knew Maddie well enough to know that she wouldn't be able to. That's why he'd never suggested it. Maddie really was a one-man woman and always would be.

Ryan told her that he was happy for her, but he'd be lying if he said he didn't wish he'd been the one she had chosen. But he'd had his chance and had blown it. That was something he'd never forgive himself for.

"Of course, you're still the twins' father and will always be a part of their lives. I wouldn't have it any other way," said Maddie seriously. "You are the one who gave me the greatest joys of my life, and I will be forever grateful," continued Maddie.

She and Ryan talked a few minutes longer before Maddie told him that she needed to get home. She said she'd still enjoy meeting him for lunch occasionally if it wouldn't bother him. Ryan agreed. He wouldn't pass up any time he could spend with Maddie, married or not.

49

Even though Rob and Rory were now entrenched at Stanford, the two of them would always make it a point to come home on Friday nights whenever Vallejo High School played a home game during football season. They'd always sit in the stands with their mom, and many times Ryan would join them, too. In fact, the four of them decided that it needed to become a tradition for them. At least it would give them some family time away from their studies.

This year, the Apaches were still undefeated and on their way to perhaps another state championship. Jake was a superb head coach, and all of them were really proud of all his hard work. Of course, Maddie was the one who took it in the shorts for his success. In August of each year, Jake would kiss her good-bye on the first day of two-a-day practices and tell her he'd see her in December. It became a standing joke between them. But Maddie wouldn't have had it any other way. Jake was doing what he'd always loved and what made him happy. That was more important than anything else to Maddie.

Unknown to Maddie, however, another young woman was always in the stands at home games, but sitting on the opposing side. It was Tasha, the stalker who now called herself Stacy Alexander. Maddie would never have recognized the new Stacy; she looked nothing like the girl who had attacked her years ago. Stacy had always gone to Vallejo's games ever since she'd been released from the psychiatric hospital, and even after she'd finished at UC Berkeley with a master's in psychology. No, Stacy had never forgotten Jake; she never would. If anything, Stacy was more obsessed than ever. She brought her binoculars to every game to spy on Jake and Maddie. Sometimes she'd just focus on their wedding rings. Stacy really believed that she was in love with Jake, and she was consumed with the idea that somehow he still belonged to her. So, no matter what the law said or what Jake wanted, she was determined to have him. Of course, that was crazy. Even crazier, Stacy was well aware that she was a sociopath, and she blamed Maddie for her problem.

One evening, when Stacy zeroed in on Maddie, she saw her sitting between a very handsome man on one side and her children on the other. The twins now looked to be high school age, and it was obvious to her that the man was their real father! There was absolutely no mistaking it. The two teenagers looked like carbon copies of their father and mother. She reset her binoculars back to the man. *Ah,* she thought, *he's not wearing a ring.* And she began scheming ways to "accidentally" meet him.

As Ryan was busy ordering Cokes and popcorn, Stacy maneuvered through the crowd to be directly behind him. The clerk had put everything into two carriers. Ryan picked them up, turned, and bumped right into Stacy, spilling the drinks all over him.

"Oh my God," said Stacy, appearing surprised. "I'm sooo sorry." She lied, "I didn't see you. Please let me help you," she said as she grabbed a handful of napkins and started to wipe off his shirt.

"No problem," said Ryan in the lowest voice Stacy had ever heard.

"Oh, please, I insist on replacing them for you. I've always been clumsy," she replied as she abruptly ordered five Cokes.

As the clerk was getting the new order together, Stacy introduced herself. "Hi. I'm Stacy Alexander." Then she handed him one of her business cards.

"Hi. I'm Colonel Ryan Richardson," he replied as he kept trying to dry himself off.

"Oh, you must work at the Presidio," said Stacy with a big smile.

"That's right. Nice to meet you, Stacy."

"Likewise. I'm really sorry about the mess I've caused. Let me make it up to you. How about we meet in the city for a drink—my treat for increasing your laundry bill?"

"That's not necessary," Ryan answered, wanting to get back to Maddie and the kids.

"Oh, I know"—she persisted—"but I feel I owe you something. Do you have a card?"

"Sure." Ryan smiled, pulling a card from his wallet.

"Thanks. I'll give you a call," said Stacy. Then she took her Coke and headed back to the opposing side bleachers.

When Ryan finally returned to the stands drenched in Coke, Maddie knew immediately what had taken him so long.

"Wow! You really got it. What happened?" asked Maddie.

"Nothing really," said Ryan. "Some woman bumped into me as I was turning around to leave."

"Well, was she cute at least?"

Ryan thought for a minute before answering. "Hmmm," grunted Ryan. "I guess she was—that's some consolation."

Back in the stands, Stacy trained her binoculars back on the foursome across from her. Her little deception had worked. Now, she knew for sure this Ryan Richardson was the real father of the twins—it was just too obvious. The young man was the spitting image of his father, and the young lady looked like him, too, except for the auburn hair and Maddie's teal eyes.

Stacy left the game early. Driving home, she started to formulate a plan in her mind. If she couldn't have Jake, why not the second best thing? She thought Ryan may have been Maddie's first love, so her revenge might even be sweeter. She would wait a couple of days, and then she'd call him to meet her for a drink. He would believe it was her way of repaying him for ruining his clothes, but she was really setting the hook.

Two days later, Stacy did just that. She waited until the evening when she figured Ryan would be home from work. She wasn't the least bit nervous about making the call; sociopaths have no conscience or remorse, because everything centers around them and their needs.

Ryan answered his phone on the second ring with, "Hello, this is Colonel Richardson."

"Hi Colonel Richardson." She cooed. "Wow, that sounds official! I don't know if you remember me, but this is Stacy Alexander—aka the klutz who spilled Coke all over you at the football game."

"Oh, I remember you, Stacy." Ryan laughed. "How could I forget?"

"Well, I wanted to ask you to meet me for a drink as my mea culpa for the drenching," said Stacy pleasantly.

"Oh, you don't have to do that," said Ryan. "No harm, no foul."

"No, I insist. It's the least I can do. How about meeting me at the top of the Mark this Saturday night? And before you say a word, 'no' is not an option."

Ryan thought for a moment. It had been a long time he'd been with a woman who showed this kind of confidence. And she was very attractive. "I'd be happy to, Stacy."

"Great! Let's meet around 8:00 PM. See you then," answered Stacy.

As soon as Stacy hung up the phone, she was grinning from ear to ear. It was so easy to manipulate people. It hadn't taken much prodding on her part either, so maybe he was interested in her, too. Of course, that didn't matter. Ryan was just a pawn in her game.

Ryan had surprised himself by accepting so quickly. He wasn't used to dating all that much, and for him to agree so readily wasn't like him at all. But he thought that she was really cute and well educated, so it might be an interesting evening. Besides, Maddie was now married, and it was time to get on with his life.

Both Stacy and Ryan were nervous as they dressed for their date Saturday night. Stacy took extra time with her hair and makeup and had decided to wear a seductive silk blouse, tight black skirt, and sky-high heels. She kept her jewelry simple, too, just diamond studs and a one-carat diamond necklace. She figured that Ryan wouldn't like the flamboyant type. She was right.

Ryan took more time than usual getting ready for the evening, too. He decided to wear grey slacks and a grey shirt and purple tie under his black sport jacket. He even put on cologne for the occasion, something he almost never did in the Army.

Ryan was already seated at a small table by the window when Stacy arrived. The moment he saw her, he stood to greet her and help her with her chair.

Stacy had figured that they might have been nervous at first, but that fortunately wasn't the case. Like old friends, they talked for hours and polished off a bottle of wine in the process. Ryan was pleased that he felt so comfortable talking to a relative stranger; he concluded it was because Stacy was a psychologist and a very good listener. It seemed that she let Ryan do most of the talking. Actually, she was guiding the conversation to pry out personal information. Ryan had no inkling that Stacy had an ulterior motive for their getting together. She wondered if he'd mention Maddie and the twins—he didn't. But she figured he'd get to that when he felt more comfortable with her.

As the evening drew to a close, and they were waiting for the valet to deliver their cars, Ryan boldly asked if it would be all right if he called her and asked her out on a real date.

"Absolutely, I'd love that," declared Stacy happily. Her plan was working. Soon he would be like putty in her hands.

"Good," replied Ryan. "I'll call you next week."

"Great. This time I'll let you pick the place," said Stacy.

Ryan politely kissed Stacy on the cheek before opening the car door for her. "See you next week," said Ryan. He wanted to feel her full lips, but—after all—he was an officer and a gentleman.

50

Ryan and Stacy started dating about twice a week. As Stacy had planned, Ryan's initial interest in her was becoming infatuation. On each date, she did something new to loosen his ties to Maddie and to increase his infatuation with her. Ryan thought their age difference might be a problem. He was several years older than she even though she acted much more mature. He thought, *What the hell? I deserve a "trophy" girlfriend.* When she discovered that Ryan had graduated from West point, she knew why he was always the perfect gentleman. She also understood what she had to do to make him hers.

Eventually, Stacy invited him over to her place for dinner. She had waited a long time before asking, because she wanted him to think stepping up their relationship was his idea, not hers. *Poor Ryan,* Stacy smiled to herself. *This big boy doesn't have a clue what kind of game I'm playing with him.* Ryan really was naïve for a grown military man, and Stacy knew, by the way he talked, that he hadn't been with very many women.

When she thought he was vulnerable enough, Stacy approached the subject of Maddie. They were having a candlelight dinner, and she casually asked Ryan if he'd ever been married. He answered without any hesitation, telling her that he had been married once to a nurse for eighteen months, but it hadn't worked out. She skillfully got him to talk about "the one who got away." Ryan wasn't ready to go into details about his relationship with Madison Conrad Kelly, but he did admit she was his first love, and he'd never really gotten over her. Using her professional skills, she got him to tell her that he hadn't known that they had children together until the twins were fifteen. Now, he was trying to make up for lost time and adored them. He also told her that they were both attending Stanford and were barely sixteen.

Stacy listened intently as Ryan talked. It was obvious that he was still in love with Maddie; it didn't take a psychologist to figure that one out. Stacy rose from the sofa, went to where he was sitting, put her arms around his neck, and whispered in his ear how sorry she was for his lost years with his children. Then she proceeded to kiss him passionately for the first time and was pleased that Ryan responded so well. Her snare was closing.

Ryan spent the night with Stacy, and she discovered he really hadn't had many sexual relationships. She didn't want to scare him off by being too aggressive, so she acted like a demure, naïve woman. Inside, she was really a barracuda toying with its prey, and she was pleased to see that it didn't take much to excite him.

From a personal standpoint, she was pleased to learn he had the largest "member" she'd ever seen, and that made their first sexual encounter all that much more pleasurable for her.

It had been quite a while since Ryan had been this close to a woman, but it didn't take him long to get back in the saddle. Stacy had a gorgeous body, not as great as Maddie's, perhaps, but without clothes, Stacy looked like a Playboy bunny. She had big brown eyes, sinuous lips, and dark brown hair cut into a short bob. In Ryan's mind, no woman would ever match Maddie— but Stacy was beautiful.

It didn't take him long to become hard. He was nervous, though. Overall, Ryan enjoyed having sex with Stacy. Their first lovemaking session was a true work of art. She had entered their sexual encounter like a virginal school girl, and, four hours later, finished like a well-experienced "lady of the night." Ryan was exhausted but very pleased with himself. She had pushed all of his masculine buttons and left him believing that he was the teacher. She was brilliant— and wicked.

They showered together. Then she took his hand, led him back to her living room couch, handed him a glass of wine, and snuggled up next to his hard body. Ryan was mellow and very defenseless. Talk now came easily. He told Stacy how much he enjoyed being with her and wanted to keep dating her, but he was a one-woman kind of man. Stacy manufactured crocodile tears, kissed him passionately, and promised she would date him exclusively. He was hooked, and they dated as often as Ryan's schedule allowed. On weekends, they stayed at each other's apartments. Soon, he no longer thought of Maddie as his destiny.

Stacy had Ryan right where she wanted him. She was, or would become, the love of his life, and eventually she'd get him to marry her. Her goal was to ruin Maddie's life, and, even if it took a long time, she would succeed. Meanwhile, compared to most men, Ryan was a good catch, and she kind of liked being with him.

Truth be told, she could never love Ryan like she did Jake; there would never be another Jake in her life. She did like Ryan, but he was just a means to a greater end. What a surprise she had in store for Jake and Maddie! She could hardly wait to see their faces when they finally figured out who she really was.

However, sometimes the best-laid plans can change in an instant. She and Ryan had been dating for seven months, and her duplicitous plan was reaching its a totally unexpected climax. The phone call came when Stacy was at work. Ryan left a message on her home answering machine. That evening, she played his message over and over and over....

BOOK VII:
ENGLAND

51

During the spring of 1985, Maddie was giddy with excitement ever since Jake told her to pack an umbrella and raincoat; they were going to England for their long-overdue honeymoon. She kept packing and unpacking. She decided to use the colors red, white, and black so she could mix and match. Jake just laughed watching her bouncing around their bedroom with her clothes all over the floor.

Packing was easy for Jake. He would pack a suit, sport coat, shirts, ties, polos, shoes, and a raincoat. He could be ready to go in an hour. But it took Maddie a week to finally figure out what she would take.

Jake hadn't told Maddie, but he had an ulterior motive for their trip. He knew that Maddie had loved England since she had grown up there. He also knew that she had always wanted to have an English cottage in a small village, preferably in the beautiful Lake District. After they'd returned from Hawaii, Jake was downtown updating his will, leaving everything to his legal wife, Madison Conrad Kelly. While there, he stopped at Campbell Realty and talked to Meredith. He asked Meredith to look into properties for sale in the

Lake District in England for him. And, no, Maddie was not to be told. A few days later, Meredith gave him a list of places for them to see while on their trip. Jake's wedding gift to Maddie was to give her that English cottage. He figured the entire family could summer there and use it as a home base when the four of them traveled throughout Europe.

Maddie met with Ryan the Saturday before she and Jake were set to leave for England. She asked him to take charge of the twins while they were gone and gave him a list of their itineraries in case he needed to reach them. Ryan was welcome to stay at their house if he wanted, but he declined. He told her not to worry, that he'd already made plans for the three of them to do things on the weekends, and that he'd take them out for dinner several times. He was anxious to get to know all about his children, their personalities, goals, aspirations. He'd missed sixteen years of their lives and wanted to make up for it in the worst way. He wanted to see if any part of him was in his children besides their looks. Anyway, their longtime nanny/housekeeper would keep them in line when they came home from Stanford on the weekends. Ryan also gave Maddie a card with all the numbers where she could reach him if needed. Never again would she have no way of getting in touch with him. West Point had taught him that lesson—one he would never forget. Maddie thanked him, put the card in her wallet, and said she might call him from time to time to see how their teenagers were doing.

Ryan had been devastated when Maddie so impulsively married Jake in Hawaii. They hadn't even told Rob or Rory until they returned home. In fact, everyone was shocked by their sudden marriage. Ryan had a difficult time accepting Maddie's decision even though he tried not to show it. Truth be known, he still hadn't fully accepted it even now. He'd lost her a second time. *I guess it was just a pipe dream,* thought Ryan, *to think I still might have that second chance with her.* He knew that in her heart, Maddie would always love him, she told him as much, but he also knew that she didn't trust him anymore. That was solely his fault. Once a trust is broken, it seems everything can fall apart. Maybe he was a fool to think that he could win her back. He couldn't fault Jake for what had happened. He was a good man, and he'd reared his children as his own. He would be forever grateful to him for that. But his heart just ached when Maddie married Jake. He knew he would love Madison forever, and, because of the twins, the five of them would always be connected.

The twins, on the other hand, each reacted differently to the news of the marriage. Of course, they had watched their mother agonize over what to do. She loved both men. They also knew it was the most difficult decision their mom had ever made. Rob was delighted about the marriage; Jake was the only father he'd ever known. He'd taught him how to ride his bike, throw a football, hit a baseball—all the things a father does. On the other hand, Rory was a little disappointed. She loved Jake; he was her dad. But so was Ryan. Ever since she'd found out that Ryan was her real father, she'd been curious to know all about him. She was more anxious than Rob to get to know him. Maybe now that her parents were going to be gone for a few weeks, she'd get a chance to know him a little better—at least that was what she was hoping.

When Maddie and Jake were ready to go to the airport, and the limousine was waiting for them, they kissed their kids good-bye and told them that Louise was in charge when they were at home. But if they needed anything, they could call Ryan. Jake and Maddie didn't know it then, but it might be the last time they would ever see their children.

Maddie finally started to relax on the plane. They were sitting in first class, so they toasted their marriage and upcoming honeymoon with cheesy airline champagne. It didn't take Maddie long to fall asleep, but sleep didn't come easily for Jake. He looked at the woman he'd loved for over twenty years and still couldn't believe she was finally his wife. But Maddie had been worth the wait. He couldn't imagine his world without her in it. Of course, they'd had their ups and downs, but the ups had mightily outweighed the downs.

Jake was anxious to see how his wife was going to react to her "English" wedding present. He knew she'd say she didn't need a wedding present, but he also knew it was the most special gift he could give her. Just thinking about seeing her surprise made him grin to himself. Finally, sleep came. His world was now going to be complete.

Jake and Maddie spent a week in London seeing all the sights in this ancient city. She proudly made him go to the ballet to see where her life could have ended up.

They saw *Romeo and Juliet,* performed by the Royal Ballet of England. And, of course, Maddie was totally enthralled with the lead female ballerina. Jake, on the other hand, was watching his wife. When tears glistened in her eyes, he wished she'd had her chance on the big stage, but then he would never have met her. Perhaps his wedding gift to her would help make up for her lifelong disappointment.

Jake and Maddie devoured London for a week, then rented a Jaguar and drove on the M1 motorway north towards the Lake District. It took Jake a while to figure out driving on the left side of the road and to realize that no one paid attention to the speed limit on the M1. Jake saw what a beautiful country England really was, with its rolling green hills and lots of tiny villages. They spent the first two nights in Cambridge. Maddie showed him where she grew up and went to school. Cambridge Common had been right outside her front door, and Jake pictured Maddie doing cartwheels on it or riding her bike with a white wicker basket on one of its many bike paths.

They even visited the university. In all, there were over thirty colleges that made up the university, believed to have been started by Henry VIII. Maddie explained how different this university was compared to Oxford. For example, if you were accepted at Cambridge, you had to commit to all four years, because their teaching methods were different from most colleges. The student classes contained about ten students at most, and they had one professor. Whenever a professor thought you were ready to test out of his class, he would give you the test. If you passed, you went on to another professor. If you didn't, your original professor would tutor you some more until he felt you were ready to take the test again. So, the students had very individualized instruction. At least that's the way the university used to be run.

Before leaving Cambridge for the Lake District, Maddie insisted that they go bunting down the River Cam. It reminded Jake of what the Venice gondola rides must be like. Jake could see why Maddie was still an English girl at heart.

When they entered the Lake District, Maddie started to cry. She'd wanted to come back here for thirty years. This area was one of the most beautiful places Jake had ever seen. No wonder Maddie loved it here so much. There were misty lakes surrounded by three laden hills and fields covered with heather.

They spent their first night in the district in a fully stocked little cottage on the outskirts of Keswick that Jake had rented for the week, and it was equipped just the way Maddie had described to him all those years ago. She plopped down on the floral sofa, grabbed Jake to her, and kissed him deeply, thanking him for bringing her back home.

While Maddie put their clothes away, Jake started stoking the fireplace. Although it was summer, the nights were still very cool in England. Jake heard a soft rain start to fall on the thatched roof of the cottage. When he looked up, he saw Maddie standing before him dressed in a gorgeous off-white revealing negligee with a matching robe. Jake grabbed her to him and led her to the sofa. They made love on the sofa in front of the fire. Afterwards, they held each other quietly and watched the flickering fire together. They had always enjoyed making love to each other, but the emotional connection that they both craved was just as important to them as the physical aspect—maybe even more. Jake decided this would be the perfect time to tell her about the special surprise he had in store for her. When Jake told her he needed to tell her something, of course Maddie worried right away that something was wrong.

"Honey, nothing is wrong. In fact, I'm hoping you'll be happy with what I have to say."

"Okay, sweetheart. What is it? I'm all ears."

"Well, I haven't given you a wedding present yet."

"Jake, I don't need a wedding present. I've got you. That's all I need," declared Maddie.

"Maddie, hush, let me finish, please. I haven't given you your wedding present yet. So here's what it's going to be. Meredith found a few cottages available for sale here in the district. Tomorrow, we're going to start looking at them. This is going to be my wedding gift to you. I want you to have your own English cottage," Jake said softly.

"Oh my God, you must be kidding!" exclaimed a stunned Maddie. "I don't believe it."

"Well, my love, believe it; it's true. You'll be the one to pick out our cottage. We'll come here whenever we want and explore the villages all the way to Scotland, and maybe even Ireland. It will be our get-away-from-the-world place. Of course, the twins will come with us whenever they want."

Maddie threw her arms around her husband's neck and said, "Honey, you don't need to buy me an English cottage to make me happy," and once again, she reiterated that she didn't need anything in her life, except him and their children.

"I know," said Jake gently. "Money has never been important to you. You've never really asked me for anything, Maddie. This is something I want to give you—something you've always dreamed about having. So, tomorrow, dear wife, like it or not, we are going cottage-hunting, and I won't take 'no' for an answer."

True to his word, the next morning, after an early English breakfast, the couple started their quest of finding the perfect English cottage.

Most of the roads in the Lake District—actually everywhere in England where there were only small villages—there were only one-lane roads. Whenever another car approached from the opposite direction, Jake and Maddie would pull off to the side to allow the other vehicle to pass. In several hamlets or villages that made up the vast area of the Lake District, six houses were available for sale. They decided to view two or three each day before making a final decision. Once again, Maddie tried to tell her husband that she didn't expect a wedding gift, but Jake would merely answer, "Well, you're getting one."

The first day, they visited two of the cottages on Meredith's list. Although Maddie liked them both, neither was exactly what she was looking for. What she wanted was an English cottage with at least two— preferably three—bedrooms, along with some of the modern conveniences she'd become accustomed to, like a washer, dryer, dishwasher, and, if they were really lucky, two bathrooms. Yes, Maddie was well aware how spoiled she was. Jake had done that to her.

The second day of their search, after having a ploughman's lunch at a local village tavern, Jake and Maddie found the perfect house. It was down a tree-laden road and looked to be an almost-new build, which hardly ever occurred in this area. The owners had owned the land for many years but lived and worked in London. They were both solicitors, the English term for lawyers, and barely had any free time. When the time finally came, and they were able to build their summer cottage, the wife had been diagnosed with terminal pancreatic cancer. Government health insurance often didn't cover full treatment for older people, so they now needed to sell the property quickly to help pay for the costs.

Maddie loved the house before she ever walked inside. Instead of a thatched roof, which had been outlawed years ago, the roof was slate shingles. It was a one-story stucco with about 2,500 square feet: three bedrooms, two baths, two fireplaces, and an up-to-date kitchen, and yes, even a washer and dryer. What really sold Maddie on the house, however, was the huge backyard, which had a running brook and a view of one of the lakes. She could just picture their family spending leisurely afternoons out back, maybe even playing a game of croquet or badminton.

Jake loved the house because Maddie loved it. He was happy it was a new build, even though it was made to look ancient. He didn't want to have to worry about wiring, plumbing, and all the other things that can go wrong with a really old house.

As soon as they decided that "this was the one," the two of them made their way back into the small quaint village of Grasmere to see the banker. Maddie couldn't believe that the bank was still the old-fashioned kind, with bars on the teller's windows and typical old-banker hours. It closed every day at 3:00 PM and wasn't open on weekends. They beat the clock by forty-five minutes.

Jake didn't quibble about the asking price; that had never been his style. Besides, in this case, he felt that the money was going to a good cause. Always efficient, Meredith had asked every banker in every village they would visit to have complete property ownership papers ready. Jake handed over a huge cashier's check in pounds sterling that he had picked up in San Francisco before they left on their trip. Jake and Maddie walked out of the bank with the deed, the blueprints, and the keys to their new second home.

That night, they went to the local pub for beer and bangers and mash to celebrate and meet a few of their new neighbors.

When they returned to their rented cottage, Maddie started pouring over the blueprints of their house. She spent hours figuring out what she wanted to put where because she wanted to be ready to pick out furniture once they returned to London. Of course, Jake laughed at her with her reading glasses halfway down her nose and asking him what he thought about a sofa here or a table there.

"Honey, decorating this place is all up to you. I did that once, remember?"

"But, Jake, it's ours and I want you to be a part of it," answered Maddie.

"Okay, let's just say I'll tell you what I do or don't like what you're looking at. How about that?"

"Great!" replied Maddie.

The rest of the week, they would visit their new home every day and explore their new countryside. They went to the Beatrice Potter Museum, rented bikes with wicker baskets, and marveled as they rode around the countryside. They were amazed by old, tired, worn rock walls that separated the owners' lands. One day, Maddie and Jake even discovered a large group of rocks in the form of a circle, like the megaliths in southern England made by the Druids.

Before the week ended, Maddie had compiled a list of furniture to buy in London. They left their rented cottage early and headed back on the M1. By lunchtime, they were nearing the crowded portion of their trip. Naturally, it was raining off and on, and the roads were slick. Jake felt uncomfortable being boxed in by eighteen-wheelers; actually, their small Jaguar was totally surrounded by them, at least three or four trucks deep.

Jake was a great driver, but being on the "wrong side" of the highway, he found it almost impossible to feel safe amidst the sea of trucks. Liverpool is one of the largest manufacturing cities in England. In the rain, the traffic entering and leaving the M1 had Jake worried. They were approaching the exit for Liverpool when, suddenly, an eighteen-wheeler several rigs ahead of them started to slide on the slick pavement. The driver couldn't pull it out of its skid, and his truck jackknifed across the three lanes. So did the next truck, and the next, which was directly in front of them. He knew they were boxed in, and there was no way to avoid a collision. In a desperate move to spare Maddie, Jake turned the wheel so that his side of the car would take the brunt of the crash. Days later, all that Maddie could remember was glancing over at Jake and seeing his side of the car begin to slide under the semi. She never heard the metal ripping or the glass shattering. Never felt her bones breaking or her flesh tearing. Never heard Jake's warning. There wasn't even time to scream before she lost consciousness.

52

J ake and Maddie were unconscious and covered with blood when they were pulled from the wreckage. It took six minutes for the emergency truck to get to the mangled vehicle and another nineteen minutes for the firefighters to lift the trailer and pull the wreck from under the jack-knifed semi. The jaws-of-life took another eight minutes to cut apart the squashed car and five minutes for paramedics to lift Maddie's lifeless body onto the gurney. Her vital signs were weak but hopefully could be stabilized in the ambulance. With lights flashing and sirens wailing, EMS sped their delicate cargo to the trauma center at Liverpool's Mercy Hospital. It had taken less than thirty-five minutes from the time Jake said, "OH, SHIT!" and made his selfless decision to save the love of his life.

Maddie's body was severely broken, but Jake's heroic maneuver had made him the buffer between the truck and his beloved wife. The ER doctors stabilized Maddie and found she had suffered a broken left ankle and a broken right forearm, probably from hitting the steering wheel on impact. Much more worrisome were the internal injuries, and the nurses prepared her for emergency surgery.

When Maddie arrived at Mercy, the rescuers were still trying to get Jake's mangled body out of the wreck. Unaccustomed to driving on the left-hand side of the road, he had over-compensated his turn, and the car skidded sideways on the wet pavement. The maneuver clearly saved Maddie's life, but it caused the car to careen underneath the huge truck, squashing the driver's compartment like an empty can. EMS had to lift the trailer off the car before they could cut the twisted metal away from Jake's body. He was so bloody they couldn't see his injuries, but his vital signs were almost nil. Carefully, they put him on a backboard and into the ambulance and applied temporary life support. It seemed unlikely he would even survive the trip to the hospital.

Maddie needed surgery; she needed it right away. But, being an American citizen, the British National Health Care system required that they get permission to operate from a member of her family—first! That rule must have seemed like a brilliant cost saver to some politician, but the doctors knew the protocol could cost the American woman her life. Every second of delay could be fatal. The chief surgeon yelled for the paramedics who brought Maddie in. One of the attendants had recovered a purse from the wreckage, and she gave it to the chief surgeon. He dumped it out on a gurney so they could all look for contact information. They found Maddie's passport, driver's license, and a business card with the name "Lt. Col. Ryan Richardson." It had two USA phone numbers.

The doctor noted the time difference between England and California and dialed the colonel's office number first. He figured that whoever this Ryan fellow was, he would probably be at work. "Colonel Richardson's office," a female voice answered. "May I help you?"

The secretary ran into Ryan's office, yelling that he had an emergency call from England on line two. Ryan lifted the phone, said his name, and listened. The doctor said Maddie was bleeding internally, and they had to stop it or she wouldn't survive. But he needed permission from a member of Madison's family to operate immediately.

"I'm family," Ryan instantly replied. "You have my permission to treat Madison Conrad Kelly in any manner you feel necessary to keep her alive. I'll be on the next flight to Liverpool," stated Ryan in a voice as authoritative as he could muster. "Just keep her alive."

Ryan closed the door to his office, put his head on his desk, and started to cry. He just couldn't believe it—not Madison. Not now! He and Stacy had just returned from a wedding week in Las Vegas. When Maddie married Jake, Ryan realized he would never have her, and Stacy seemed to be a good alternative. So, when the seductress said, "Let's go to Vegas and get married," Ryan agreed. In his mind, it was the best of all worlds; he was married to a hot younger woman, and he had full access to his children and childhood sweetheart. At the time he thought, *I couldn't have planned this better.*

Ryan chose not to tell the twins about the accident until he had all the details. He called his base commander and directed his aide to make flight arrangements. Then, he went straight to his apartment. On the way, Colonel Richardson made one other call. He knew his bride would be at work, but he'd rather leave her a message than try to explain on the phone. When the machine picked up, he just said, "Stacy, this is Ryan. Sorry, honey, but an emergency's come up, and I'll be out of town for a while. I'll call you as soon as I can." The message was terse, concise, and unfeeling. Ryan was back in military mode.

About the time Ryan's plane was lifting off the runway, Stacy was walking into her apartment. She noticed the message light blinking and listened to the recording—once, twice, three times. *What the hell is going on?* she thought. *Where's he going? What just happened?*

The next day, Stacy called Ryan's office, but the only answer his secretary would give her was that he was out of town until further notice. She didn't know when he would return.

Stacy didn't know it at that time, but all her scheming and maneuvering to hurt Maddie would now have to wait—perhaps forever.

53

R yan's aide had discovered that the direct flights to England were booked solid for several weeks, but one seat was left on the red-eye flight to London that night. Ryan stopped at his apartment just long enough to throw his Dopp kit into his pre-packed carry-on bag and headed for the San Francisco airport. It was during emergencies like this that military aides really earn their stripes. Ryan was so upset by the news of Maddie's accident that he might have become a road hazard. But Specialist 7 Billy Woods calmly made sure Ryan's paperwork, passport, and reservations were in proper order. Then he drove his boss to the San Francisco airport, and delivered the colonel to the gate with plenty of time to make his plane.

After the call from Mercy Hospital, Maddie was the only thing on Ryan's mind. She had been seriously injured in a wreck on the M1 by Liverpool and might die. Nothing was going to keep him from her— absolutely nothing. He'd been in love with Maddie his entire life. Now, even though she'd married Jake Kelly and he'd married Stacy—the old feelings returned. He finally admitted to himself that it had been his fault; he had quashed their West Point wedding just two days before it was to take place. Maddie had never forgiven him. He had never forgiven himself for that either. Now, Ryan was feeling guilty and a huge sense of loss once again.

Ryan tried to sleep on the flight, but it was useless; his mind would not shut off. He kept wondering what condition Maddie would be in when he arrived in Liverpool. *Please, God,* he said over and over to himself, *help Maddie survive.* Heathrow, England, is about 5,348 miles from San Francisco, and it took the Boeing 707 nearly eleven hours to make the great circle flight. When his plane finally landed, he all but ran through customs. (Once again, his faithful aide had done well preparing his papers.) Billy had a rental car waiting for him, too. It had been years since he'd driven in Europe, especially England, so he took it very slowly at first. Thank God, the M1 was easy to reach.

Once he was on the M1 heading north, he picked up his speed to keep up with the other traffic. He needed to concentrate on his driving, so he soon focused on the "wrong-way" traffic and stopped thinking only of Maddie temporarily. It took a couple of hours to reach the exit for Liverpool. When he saw it, memories of Maddie came flooding back again.

Liverpool was only thirty minutes off the M1, but it seemed he would never get there. When he finally saw the signs for Mercy Hospital, he became obsessed about Maddie's condition. He parked the car and ran into the emergency entrance. By the time he reached the nurses station, he was out of breath.

He told the nurse who he was, and she immediately showed him to Maddie's room. She told him that he was welcome to stay with Madison, and then she ran to page the doctor.

"Hi, Maddie. It's me, Ryan. I'm here now, honey, and everything's going to be all right," he said to the love of his life.

Ryan was sitting by Maddie's side when the doctor came in. He snapped to attention and introduced himself.

"Hello. I'm Colonel Ryan Richardson. How is Maddie?"

"Oh, good to meet you, old chap," smiled the old doctor. "I was a major with the 4th Fusiliers, during the In-jah Campaign of—oh, terribly sorry—I'm Doctor Heiland. We have a very sick woman here. She was in a rather messy highway crash. Her companion is in a coma—might not make it, you know. Must have been quite a pretty girl. Quite frankly—it is a bloody miracle she survived at all. We've had her in for two nasty surgeries already, repaired compound fractures of her arm, leg, and ankle. But of course we were much more concerned about her internal injuries. She was bleeding quite badly, so we had to take her spleen. One of her lungs had collapsed, and we pumped that back up. We think the spleen's where much of the bleeding was coming from, but we're watching her intensely.

"As you can tell," he continued, "she's unconscious, probably from hitting her head when her car slammed sideways into the truck at such a high rate of speed. Hard to tell what she hit—could have bounced off the driver's head, hitting sideways like that—there's not much protection. Sounds a bit morbid, I suppose, but that man's body may have saved her life. He's a bit of a hero, you know. If he hadn't turned the motor car like that, they both would have died instantly.

"What are her chances?" asked Ryan directly. "Tell me the truth."

"Hard to say, chap," the doctor mused. "If she comes out of her coma and her brain has reprogrammed itself, and if there are no further complications, she could make it."

"So all we can do right now is wait?" asked Ryan.

"Righto," said the doctor. "But I'm sure that your being here will help her more than anything else."

"What about Jake Kelly? How is he doing?"

"Oh," said the doctor in lowered tones. "Well, I'm afraid we don't have much hope for that chap. Looks like when he realized the crash was going to be unavoidable, he turned their car so his side would take the impact. Bloody brave thing to do, you know. He's in a deep coma and on total life support. He did have a pulse and some brain activity, so we're obligated to keep him alive for a few weeks, anyway. Was the bloke a friend of yours?"

"Does Maddie know about Jake yet?" asked Ryan.

"No. She's been unconscious since the crash. When she awakens, it would probably be best if you tell her," replied the doctor.

"Oh God," cried Ryan. "I don't know if I can do that."

"Believe me, Colonel. I've learned from experience that it will be better coming from a relative than a doctor." As the doctor turned to leave, he paused, saying, "We have all the contents from their car: suitcases and papers.

If that might be of some help to you, I can have the nurse bring them to you. She also can make accommodations for you at the hotel across the road."

"Yes, thank you. That would be a relief," replied Ryan. "I don't know that I'm thinking straight right now, and I won't leave Maddie's side until she wakes up."

"I'll take care of it right now," said Doctor Heiland. "You know perhaps if you just talk to her—even read a book or the papers—it will help both of you. I'll be back to check on her in two hours." With that he was gone.

Once again, Ryan was alone with Maddie. Tears streaming down his face, he took her hand and tried to talk to her. He told her that their children were doing well at Stanford. So far, they both had a 4.0. They had taken advance placement exams and entered Stanford as second semester freshmen at the age of sixteen. He told her he'd had dinner with them several times while she was here in England, just to make sure they were not overwhelmed or intimidated by being at such a prestigious school at such a young age. But they were studying hard and loving every minute of college life.

Ryan told Maddie how proud he was of her for rearing such wonderful children. He wished he could have been there for her. But he was here now and would absolutely positively never leave her again. Ryan had broken other promises to Maddie, but this was one promise he told her he wouldn't break. During this moment of unimaginable distress, Ryan had totally forgotten he'd married Stacy. Of course, that little fact would come back to haunt him. Totally exhausted, he just laid his head on her bed and cried. Finally, he slept.

It took three days for Maddie to begin coming out of her coma. True to his word, Ryan hadn't left her side. He slept in a chair the staff had provided and had used his Dopp kit to freshen up in the tiny bathroom in her room.

As soon as Maddie started moving and moaning, Ryan ran to get the nurse, and she paged Doctor Heiland. He was doing rounds, so it didn't take him long to get to Maddie's room.

Ryan watched the doctor talk to Madison. He told her to open her eyes if she could hear him. She did. He asked her to move the different parts of her body. She did. He checked her pupils and had her follow his finger. She did. Then he asked her if she could tell them her name. She answered, "Madison." But when asked her last name, she said, "Richardson." The doctor said she was suffering from what he hoped would only be temporary amnesia. The doctor suggested that Ryan talk to her and see if she recognized him.

"Hi, Maddie, do you know who I am?" asked Ryan.

"Of course I do. You're Ryan. We've been together for years, ever since they were sixteen. We have twins, Rob and Rory," replied Maddie.

Ryan didn't know how to respond, so he just said, "That's right, honey. I'm Ryan. What's my last name?"

"Richardson," replied Maddie, seemingly becoming confused.

"That's enough for now, Maddie," interrupted the doctor. "We're glad to have you back with us again, madam." Then he led Ryan out of the room.

Ryan told the doctor that her name was Madison Kelly, and that she was married to Jake Kelly. He didn't

538

bother to tell the doctor the entire story. That could come later. What mattered to him now was that Maddie was awake, but she didn't exactly know who he was. Everything else would sort itself out in time. All he could do was pray that this was temporary, and she'd remember the truth soon.

When Maddie was fully awake, he planned to call their children, but he had absolutely no idea what to say to them. He didn't want to explain everything over the phone, so he called and told them that Jake and Maddie had been in a traffic accident in England, and he was arranging for them to fly to London as soon as his aide could get tickets. He assured them that he'd be there to pick them up. Of course, they wanted to know all the details immediately, but he told them he'd tell them the entire story when they arrived. Ryan honestly had no idea how he was going to break the news about Jake to Maddie and their children. He did know that the time had come for him to tell them the truth about everything. All the years of deception and lying were finally over.

However, for Ryan, Maddie, and Jake, the pain was just beginning. (To be continued.)

"For of all sad words of tongue or pen,
The saddest are these...it might have been."
John Greenleaf Whittier

ACKNOWLEDGEMENTS

Several people deserve to be recognized for their help in the completion of this novel.

First of all, I want to thank Tom Bird and his writing retreats for making me believe that I really could write and for standing by me even when I faltered. This novel would never have been completed without his help, guidance, and belief in me. I would also like to thank all of Tom's associates, especially RAMA, who helped me at every stage of production.

Kudos must also go to my formatting team. They did everything I asked of them and in the process made my novel that much better. Thank you all!

Next, I want to thank my best friend Carol Perry, who conducted "Camp Perry" at her home for a week. Carol not only read the novel but also made suggestions for improvement. You are "just" such a good friend!

I would also like to thank Frank Ayala, my hairdresser and friend of many years. Frank, also an established photographer, kindly offered to take my pictures for both my novel and website. Thanks, Frank, for your friendship and support throughout the years.

Another thank you goes to Howard B. Carron, PhD. Thank you for reading the novel and your constructive criticism.

The biggest THANK YOU of all must go to "Ryan Richardson." This novel would NEVER have been written at all without his outstanding input and help. In fact, he was the impetus for my writing this novel in the first place. His patience—and yes, even impatience—in answering all of my questions gave me a personal insight into the world of West Point and the war in Vietnam. I know that some of the information he provided to me probably brought back painful memories, and I appreciate his sharing them with me more than he'll ever know. Thank you from the bottom of my heart, "Ryan". As always promised, the first copy of the novel is yours.

I must also thank Steve Shannon for all the hard work he did for me. He helped me edit the entire book and read it from a man's perspective. He spent hours and hours reading and making suggestions in order to make the novel better. Thank you, Steve, from the bottom of my heart! Without your help and support, I would never have finished this novel! If at all possible, I will deliver your copy of the novel to you personally in Houston. Hugs!!

Most of all, I would like to thank my husband Bob. He kept encouraging me to meet my goal even when I was faced with adversity, illness, and wanted to give up. Thank you for keeping the home fires burning during my absences, taking care of "the girls," and giving me the privacy I needed to finally finish this novel. Thank you for your unconditional love and support: I love you.

***CHEERS, MY LOVE,
AND THANKS TO ALL OF YOU!***

AUTOBIOGRAPHY

Toy Easley Keller attended high school, college, and graduate school in Oklahoma. She taught Honors English in Oklahoma and Arizona for thirty-three years before retiring in 2003. *Ultimate Love and Betrayal* is her first novel, part one of two she hopes to complete. She currently resides in Arizona with her husband Bob and their two adorable lap dogs.